ISBN 978-1-304-60770-6
First Edition, March 2014
Cover design by Alexxander Dovelin
Crest design by Jisuk Cho, Remy Fransen, Kim Cassin
Editing by Lauren Mori, Minah Kim
Cover summary by Claire Gillam

Special Thanks
Yuki Salinas
Yapi Santiago
Ariel Lacsamana
Jessica Swanson

FISHBONES
Jisuk Cho

01

Ferris was running.

He didn't run very often and wasn't what one would call 'good at it.' He had only been running for a few blocks and could already feel his legs protesting. Of course, he wasn't dressed for the occasion, nor had he woken up with a fist in his palm and the firm intent to go for a few laps around his neighborhood. In fact, the only reason that his shoes were pounding so hard against the wet pavement, that his sweater was starting to make him sweat, and that his scarf had fluttered off into a gutter ten yards back, was that he was being chased.

His chasers were a trio of teenage boys – his classmates. As wealthy, popular teens, they were simply fulfilling their role at the top of the social food chain by regularly preying on the weak to assert their superiority. Ferris was one of their favorites, but this was because he usually never ran. All three boys, especially the heaviest one, found this new development very annoying.

The chasee, Ferris Levinstein, was a quiet, lanky know-it-all. He clearly deserved to be beaten up. For some reason, Ferris had gotten it into his head that on this particular day he would rather not get repeatedly punched in the face. He stumbled over a crack in the sidewalk, then regained his footing. If he truly deserved anything, it was a scratch-n-sniff sticker for the valiant effort he was putting into this whole running thing. It was unfortunate that, as mentioned before, he wasn't very good at it.

The boys caught him easily. One grabbed his arm as another took a handful of his short hair. Ferris' glasses went flying as a fist hit his cheek. Something trickled down his chin – he hoped it was blood and not spit. This was already embarrassing enough. When he looked up, he could see a fist aimed between his eyes, hungry for the crunching sound noses made when they broke.

A screeching of car tires halted the fist in mid-air and all four boys turned towards the street. A black Lincoln Town Car had skidded to a stop next to the curb. In the driver's seat sat a dignified looking Italian with silver streaks at his temples and a pair of thick spectacles. Next to him was a skinny, pale teenager with sleek black hair and a cigarette dangling from the corner of his mouth. The older one stepped out of the car, his eyes burning.

"What did I tell you, you fucking faggots?" he shouted, pushing fat shells into a shotgun and running the action forward.

"Fuck," said one of the three boys. "Go! Go go go!"

They pushed past one another, tripping over their own feet as they rounded the corner and dashed out of sight. Ferris knelt down to pat the sidewalk for his glasses, paying no mind to the man with the gun. His fingertips brushed over the frames and he hastily replaced them on his face. Once he could see, his eyes shot daggers at the boy in the car.

"Demos, you idiot," Ferris snapped. "You were supposed to meet me in the library."

"Ah, shit, I knew I forgot something," Demos said, slapping his forehead while ashing his cigarette out the window.

"You didn't forget, you just wanted to go home and look at yourself in the fucking mirror!"

"Oh, come on," Demos protested.

Demos Giorgetti was Ferris' closest friend, not that there was much competition for the spot. He liked things that would normally interest fifty-year-old men, such as fine suits and wine. Demos also enjoyed things that fifty-year-old men would have no interest in, like stupid pop songs and looking at himself in the mirror. The driver of the Lincoln, Victor Giorgetti, was the boy's uncle and foster parent. Victor loved his car, his family, and not much else.

"You had study plans today?" Victor asked. "Jesus Christ, Demos, what did I tell you about—"

"God, fine! I'll do it tomorrow!"

"Tomorrow!" Ferris emphasized.

"*Tomorrow!*" Demos repeated.

The two boys glared at each other for a minute before Demos spoke up.

"You're bleeding," he said, gesturing to his own chin as he tossed his cigarette butt out the window.

Ferris wiped the corner of his mouth with his hand, pulling it back to examine the red liquid on his fingers. So it *was* blood.

Thank God.

Ferris first met Demos when they were both twelve years old.

He knew that guests were coming over that afternoon because his mother had spent the entire day cooking and had asked him to tidy up the living room. Despite his contribution, he had been banished to the top floor of their brownstone apartment because 'Your father needs to talk to the grown-ups and shouldn't be bothered.' The television was downstairs, which meant he couldn't get through the game he was playing. Because of this injustice, Ferris felt he was perfectly validated in spying on his father's meeting. He'd wondered for a long time what his father spoke about with his frequent guests and what conversation could possibly be so 'grown-up' that he wasn't even allowed on the same floor. Ferris' method of spying was not very sophisticated. He simply sat near the top of the stairs, out of sight, and listened.

The doorbell rang and Ferris quickly recognized the voices of the two men who came in. The older, more dignified voice belonged to Gino Giorgetti, a close friend of his father. Though the man had lived in the States for many years, he still carried hints of an Italian accent. The other voice had clearly been locally grown. Victor was Gino's eldest son. He ran the family restaurant, *Ristorante Giorgetti*, and was also a regular at the Levinstein household.

"Harold," Gino said. "We brought wine."

"I can see that," Ferris' father replied good-naturedly. "You also brought a new face."

"This is Demos, my grandson. Just flew over from VRN on Thursday — transferred at Fiumicino. He's still a little jet-lagged."

"Hello, Mr. Levinstein," the unfamiliar voice answered. It was that of a young boy and curiosity drew Ferris to peek around the stair wall to get a look. The child was well-dressed for a twelve-year-old, wearing a white Oxford shirt and pressed slacks. A shock of black hair nearly covered his left eye. He looked thin and tired. Ferris would later learn that he always looked this way.

"He's about the same age as your son, isn't he?" Gino said as Harold took their coats. "I believe they're only a few months apart."

"You look half-starved, let's find you something to eat," Ferris' mother said, taking the boy by the shoulder and leading him towards the kitchen. In truth, Ruth said this to everybody, all the time, and would continue saying this to Demos each time he crossed the threshold of their front door. Once Demos was out of earshot, the men began talking.

"I sent the documentation over last night. Don't worry about the deadline," Harold said, pouring a glass of scotch and handing it to Victor. Harold had quite a different physique from his son. Where he had a round, bearded face and friendly eyes, Ferris was spindly and his eyes were much too world-weary for a boy his age. They did, however, wear the same style of glasses, and both had a head of dark, curly hair. Sadly, Harold had lost most of his to the consequences of age. A few years down the road, Ferris would have a barber cut off his as well, but only out of sheer embarrassment.

"Good. And the delivery?" Victor asked, taking a sip.

"Signature confirmation."

"No problems?"

"No. Well, actually... about Alonzo," Harold said. "There was a, ah, repeat of last month's little issue."

Ferris leaned against the wall and listened more carefully. He wished they would stop being so vague. His father's job was relatively simple. Harold was an accountant; he took care of other people's money. He would dress in a suit and tie, have coffee, and drive to work every morning in an office building downtown. There were many clients that depended on him and he was very good at his job. The Giorgettis, however, weren't normal clients. Ferris wasn't an accountant, but he knew the difference between regular taxes and suspicious taxes. He wanted to understand what they did and why they came to his father, but whenever he asked there was never a clear answer.

"You're kidding me," Victor groaned, setting his glass down with a dramatic clink. "How many times have I—"

"He needs to be dealt with," Harold said simply.

"Every fucking time he does this, it costs me money. What was it last time — eight, nine grand?" Victor continued. "If he weren't my cousin I'd say take him under the Midtown Bridge and clip him. He's a waste of life."

Clip. To cut, or cut off or out, as with shears: to clip a rose from a bush. To trim by cutting: to clip a hedge. None of these definitions really applied to this situation, seeing as Alonzo was a man and not a shrub. As a metaphor, the assumption would be...

Ferris swallowed, unconsciously clenching his fingers in anticipation of what he was learning. He was still young, but understood more about how the world worked than his father

10

assumed. He'd seen newspapers, television dramas, and classic films. He knew what the mafia was.

"Victor," Gino said firmly. "You may want to watch your language in front of your nephew."

"Oh," Victor said, looking sideways. He hadn't noticed Demos reenter the living room. Ruth wasn't far behind, embarrassed at having let the child escape.

"Why don't you go upstairs and say hello to Ferris?" Harold suggested to the boy. "He can take a break from his studies for a bit."

Ferris panicked, nearly hitting his head on the wall. He scrambled to his feet and rushed down the hall into his bedroom. That was right — he was supposed to be studying. He barely had the time to grab a book before Demos appeared in his doorway. Ferris stared up at him, a proverbial deer in headlights.

"Hello," the boy said.

"Hi," Ferris replied. The word had struggled somewhat in his throat before escaping his lips. "Uh, what's your name?"

"You know my name," he answered. "You were listening to them talk."

"What?" Ferris blurted, snapping his book closed. "What do you mean?"

"I saw you on the stairs. It's okay, I won't tell anyone."

"Oh. Right. Thanks," Ferris said. Demos entered the room, walking past him to browse his bookshelf. Every so often he would place a slender finger on the top of a book's spine, tilt it out halfway to examine the cover, then carefully press it back into place.

"So... you're from Italy, right? How long are you visiting for?" Ferris asked, tapping his fingers on the textbook in his lap.

"I'm not visiting," Demos replied, pulling a book out to flip through the pages. "I'm going to live with my uncle Victor."

"Oh. For school?"

"My mother died," Demos said, his eyes half-lidded. He put the book back in its place. "Did you arrange these by color?"

"Ah! Oh, I'm so sorry. I didn't—... wait, what?"

"These aren't sorted by title or author. You placed them on the shelves in color order."

"Well, yeah, but—" Ferris stammered. "But what about your dad?"

"I'm not sure where he is," Demos said. Ferris was mentally screaming at himself. Nearly every question he asked turned out to expose a touchy subject. He wanted to take the book in his hands and smack his forehead into it. Ferris didn't know what to say. He had no experience in consoling or comforting others.

"I'm sorry," Ferris repeated.

"It's okay."

"Aren't you sad?"

Demos didn't answer immediately. He thought for a while, then sat down on Ferris' bed with folded hands.

"I'm not sad when I don't think about it. So I try to think about other things. Uncle Victor said I'm too old to cry now," Demos said. His voice then grew very quiet, almost as low as a whisper. "But I saw him cry, too."

Once again, Ferris had no idea what to say. He immediately felt childish for being upset about video games. This boy had lost his parents and had been thrust into a strange, new country with no friends and a not-quite-sensitive uncle.

"Ferris... that's your name, right?" Demos asked after a moment.

"Yeah."

"Do I have an accent?" Demos asked, finally making eye contact. He looked worried.

"An accent?" Ferris said, blinking. "Well, no, not really. Did you take a class?"

"No. My dad spoke English." Despite having brought up the touchy topic of his father again, Demos only looked relieved. It seemed as if he was self-conscious about his speech. Though his English carried hints of British influence, he would later develop an entirely American accent from his time in Southport.

Ferris scratched his collarbone, now coming up with an idea. He approached his bookshelf with purpose, skimming the titles before pulling out two pieces of literature. He handed them to Demos and sat down next to him.

"What are these?" Demos asked.

"That one is *Moby-Dick*. It's really good. And that one is *TMNT*... it's also really good. They'll help you think about other things, so you won't be sad."

Being twelve years old, Ferris didn't understand the concept of a proper mourning process. Luckily for him, neither did Demos, who accepted the books quite happily.

12

"Thanks," Demos said, smiling for the first time since he'd arrived.

"Be careful with *TMNT*, though. That's a first printing."

As Demos lowered his head to peruse the pages of *Moby-Dick*, Ferris noticed that the hair covering the boy's eye had actually been concealing a thick, white scar above his eyebrow. He decided against asking about it. Ferris had clearly passed his quota of awkward questions per day — he would save this one for some other time.

02

Science was one of Ferris' favorite subjects, though the class itself was not one of his favorite places. An analog clock above the blackboard ticked laboriously as the instructor wrote the day's assignment with determined clicks of chalk. The teacher was an older man with stark white hair and intelligent eyes. His voice was patient — likeable, even. The boys sitting to the right of Ferris' desk were a bit less intelligent and much more unlikeable. Despite their run in with an angry man wielding a shot gun a few days before, they continued to eye him like a piece of meat. Ferris was focusing so intensely on his notes that he couldn't read them. It took considerable effort to ignore their stares and snickers.

Less than a week ago, the boys had approached him after class. They had politely requested that he throw the upcoming exam in order to give the class a lower grading curve. To this, Ferris had simply insisted they study as much as he did. This was his first mistake.

His second mistake was turning his head when one of them whispered his name. He'd barely looked at the boy before a folded paper football made a field goal between his eyes.

"*Ow,*" Ferris hissed, putting his hand to his face as the trio exchanged high-fives. He peeked up at the teacher through his fingers. The man was still writing away, his back turned to the class. Ferris could feel his ears growing hot and was so taken with his own embarrassment that the sound of the school bell startled him. Books shuffled into bags as his classmates stood to leave.

"Pussy," one of the boys said as he walked past, sliding Ferris' notebook, along with all of his fantastic notes, to the floor. By the time the room cleared out and he was able to pick up his notebook, there was a lovely black shoe-print over his scrawls about Punnett squares. He sighed wearily, looked up at the ceiling, and snapped it shut.

The boys' bathroom was his last stop before leaving school for the day. Ferris slouched in front of a mirror. He pushed up his glasses with one hand, rubbing the red spot the paper football had left with the other. Could paper even leave a mark like that? Next to him, a younger student was loosening the tie of his school uniform while checking his teeth in his reflection. Satisfied with his smile, he turned to leave Ferris alone with the urinals and sinks. The door, however, didn't close behind him. A hand caught the edge, holding it open as three new bodies entered the stage. In the mirror, Ferris could see his dear friends from science class coming up behind him. They all either had uncannily synced bladders, or had followed him in. Being rather logical, Ferris quickly assumed the latter.

The members of Ferris' fan club were Rudy, Zach, and Paul. Each of them belonged to relatively distinguished families, giving them the impression that they could get away with pretty much anything. In this assumption, they were correct. They were especially correct if there was no one around. Ferris' only witness, his last hope with the dazzling smile and loose tie, was already long gone.

"What's up, faggot? Where's your boyfriend?"

"Oh, we're sorry, did he break up with you?"

Ferris did not have the time for this. He had no intention of repeating the fact that he wasn't (not that it should matter) gay, nor did he have a romantic relationship with Demos. Avoiding eye contact, he turned to leave the bathroom. His body stopped — someone was grabbing his sleeve.

He turned sharply to look, noticing that Zach had gripped onto the bottom of his cuff.

"Let go."

"Don't be so rude, Ferris. We don't leave when *you* walk into a room."

"Let go!" He twisted his arm, forcing his wrist free and stumbling backwards a step. After glaring at them one last time, he hurried through the door.

"Fine, you fucking kike!"

Ferris' heart was pounding by the time he was down the hallway, once again having the sound of their laughter stuck in his head. His hands were clenched and he realized that he wanted nothing more than to hit that boy. He wanted to shut him up — to hurt him. He closed his eyes tightly, telling himself to stop. That wasn't how he was raised. What would his parents think if he hurt a classmate? On top of that, the boys were much stronger than he was and would surely beat the tar out of him.

Ferris walked home alone. It wasn't until he was going down into the subway station and pulling out his fare card that he sensed he was being followed.

"You have got to be kidding me," he said under his breath. He avoided turning around – he didn't want to discover that he was right. He held onto a subway pole, letting his fingers close tensely around the cold metal. The doors closed and he glanced to the side. There wasn't anyone familiar in the car. He lifted his chin to look past the window, noticing movement in the train car behind his. His skin started to prickle.

'*People move around on trains all the time,*' he thought to himself. '*It's nothing. Stop being stupid.*'

A few stops later, the train braked at his station. He disembarked, glancing both ways before heading up the stairs to the exit. He could hear the sound of six feet. There were three people behind him. He started to feel sick, having the sudden urge to just stop walking. It would be easy to find out; all he had to do was look over his shoulder. What if he turned around and they were there? What could he do? Running wouldn't really accomplish anything — he had already tested that option and it had ended in utter failure. Ferris' pace quickened. He made a turn but the long shadows didn't fall back.

He was almost home. Did he even want to go home? Did he want those boys to know where he lived? There was a bodega on the corner; maybe he could just duck inside. The sound of laughter made him choke on his next breath. He knew that laughter – he would know it anywhere. It was definitely them. With a shaking palm he pushed the store's door open and slipped inside, setting off a bell. He stood next to the front counter and stared hard at a wall of magazines. The interior of the bodega was dim, smelling of newspapers and cat litter. There was a thudding in Ferris' chest as he glanced to the door from the corner of his eye. Between the plastered stickers and cigarette ads, Ferris could see Rudy's familiar grin. There was brief eye contact, then the three boys went away.

Ferris gripped his own elbows, wishing that he could calm down. They were gone. They'd left — he was safe.

No – he couldn't calm down. They'd followed him again, even after Demos' uncle had waved a shotgun in their faces. They were never going to stop.

"You need help? Looking for something?"

When Ferris glanced up he realized that the clerk, a graying Bengali man, was speaking to him. Ferris' eyes flashed before he looked down again.

"No. I... I was just—" He couldn't even make up a name for a magazine that he could pretend to want. He couldn't think at all. "Sorry."

Ferris swallowed, letting go of his arms and taking in a slow breath. Avoiding the clerk's eyes, he ducked his head and stepped back outside. He stared up and down the street, listening to make sure they were really gone. A minute passed, then five. The only sound he could hear was that of the occasional passing car and his own hurried breath. Satisfied that they had truly left, he turned the corner to head home.

Ferris went upstairs without speaking to his parents. He spread a stack of notes over his desk, attempting to distract himself with his studies. Vague sounds drifted up to his window from the street, drawing him to the blinds for a quick peek. A knock on the door made his spine go straight.

"Ah... yeah?" he stammered.

The door cracked open, revealing his father's nonplussed expression.

"Ferris, when did you get home?" Harold asked, adjusting his glasses. "You didn't say hello."

"Sorry Dad, I... I have a lot of homework."

"Well, dinner's ready. You should come down, okay?"

"Sure. I'll be right there," Ferris answered. His voice cracked and Harold, simply attributing it to puberty, cleared his throat to keep from laughing. Once the door was closed Ferris sighed deeply, closing his notebook. He didn't think he'd be able to get much studying done that night.

Ferris was thankful when the weekend finally came and he didn't have to worry about school for a couple of days. He was sitting on the edge of his bed, wiping a cloth over the body of his violin. Carefully, he cleaned away fingerprints and bits of rosin dust. Though it had been half a week since he'd been followed home, the stone in his gut had signed a long-term lease.

Stanley was sitting on the floor, watching intently and waiting for some possible attention. Stanley was a pug — a fat one — that was barely a year old. The dog had been a gift from his mother in an attempt to make him smile more often. It hadn't really worked.

Stanley put his wrinkled face down onto his paws, whining softly.

"What do you want?"

The pug responded by bowing, wagging his tail, rolling over, and other sorts of shameless grasps for attention. When Ferris didn't respond, he hopped up onto four legs, rushing in a circle before lowering his front into a playful bow.

"I can't play right now."

Stanley whimpered. The sound became more high-pitched until he made a sharp bark, backing up awkwardly and bowing again.

"Oh God, fine. Just a short walk."

Stanley had been with him long enough to know what the word 'walk' meant and grew more excited. Ferris put away his violin, pulling on a coat and tossing a scarf around his neck. Stanley was impatiently rushing back and forth, making it harder for Ferris to clip the leash onto his collar.

"Hold still, seriously. Just a second. There."

If the pug was any bigger he'd have been excited enough to pull Ferris headfirst down the stairs. Instead, he tugged in vain until they were out the door, quickly rushing to the nearest tree to smell for other dogs. Ferris shuffled behind, unable to comprehend getting this excited over, well, anything.

"Are you almost done?"

Stanley wasn't anywhere near being done, still tugging down the sidewalk until they were several blocks from home. The sight of the same corner store he'd ducked into the other night gave Ferris a nervous chill. He looked up and down the street. Now seemed like a good time to go back. To the dog, however, it seemed like a good time to squat in the middle of the sidewalk. Ferris readied a plastic bag.

"Yeah, sure. Shit in the middle of the sidewalk. You're too good for the curb."

As he tied the bag shut and tossed it in the trash, something down the street caught his eye. Ferris stared, slowly stepping backwards as he saw three familiar faces looking around on the corner. They hadn't seen him yet.

They must have come looking for his house this time. He'd never seen them out of uniform, but they'd retained their general aura of unpleasantness. It was Zach who spotted Ferris first, motioning to his friends. They approached quickly and Ferris' nervous backpedaling accomplished little in term of escape. His eyes darted back and forth; there weren't any other people out on the street. His pulse was jumping under his skin.

"Hey, Ferris," Paul leered as they formed a human wall around him.

"What do you want?" Ferris swallowed, feeling a lump in his throat.

"What's your problem? I just said 'hey.'"

"You followed me home."

"Yeah, you dropped a penny." Rudy grinned. He dug around in his coat pocket and pulled out a copper coin, offering it to Ferris. "We thought you'd freak out or something if you lost it."

"That's not funny," Ferris said, avoiding the penny with his eyes.

"What, you don't want it? Go on, take it. It's yours," Rudy pressed.

"I don't want it."

"Come on, take it."

The boys were starting to laugh. The sound was like the screeching of steel, of nails on a blackboard. Ferris had heard it nearly every day for years; he'd heard it in the halls and in his dreams. His ears felt hot; they could probably see him turning red. Ferris' eyes narrowed, flickering up towards Rudy. His classmate was tall and towheaded with a military-styled buzz cut. Paul had longer, darker hair. It hung loosely around his face as if he were a celebrity rather than an awkwardly proportioned high school boy. Zach was the most average looking of the three, standing at about the same height as Ferris. He enjoyed making stereotypical jokes about Ferris' nose. This was only to cover for his insecurities about his own nose, which had been broken in a fight when he was ten.

"Just leave me alone," Ferris said, turning away after rediscovering his ability to move. Paul's hand clamped onto his shoulder.

"But we came all this way just to see you," Paul said, feigning hurt feelings. "Don't be like that."

"Oh, nice. Is that your dog?" Rudy said, crouching. "Ugly little guy."

Ferris had almost forgotten about Stanley. He had no idea what Rudy would do to the dog and didn't want to find out. Tugging the leash, he urged Stanley back towards his heels. Stanley wasn't sure what to do, torn between Ferris' wishes and the attention of the newcomers. Before Ferris could rectify the situation, Paul grabbed his wrists, allowing Rudy to take the leash.

"Stop! Give it back!" Ferris snapped, fumbling against Paul as he reached for the leash. Paul twisted Ferris' arm behind his back, keeping him bent forward in a half nelson.

"What's wrong? Is this your little brother? He looks just like you," Rudy said, picking the dog up by his scruff. "See?"

"Rudy, I'm serious. Put him down!" Ferris said, still attempting to pull away.

"What? What's wrong? He likes it!"

"Put my fucking dog down!"

Stanley squirmed uncomfortably and the boys laughed once more. As Paul snickered, Ferris felt a slack in his grip. He jerked his wrist free, elbowing the other boy hard in the ribs. While Paul was doubled over, Ferris rushed Rudy and pushed him back against a tree. Stanley dropped to the sidewalk. He shook his head, rattling the tags on his collar.

Ferris couldn't remember ever being angrier. He lost all restraint, throwing Rudy down to the pavement. Ferris was quickly on top of him, punching him once, twice — completely ignoring the sound of skull on pavement.

"G-get him off!" Rudy spat as he tried to shield his face with his arms. There was a spray of blood and saliva as he spoke. "Fucking get… him off!"

Rudy's voice snapped the other boys back into reality and they immediately grabbed Ferris by the arms. They threw him down, kicking him over while Rudy pulled himself up against the tree.

"What the fuck was that?!" Rudy snarled, wiping his chin with his sleeve. "Crazy asshole."

The impact had skinned Ferris' cheek and he'd lost his glasses somewhere in the fall. Everything was blurry. His head was pounding; it felt as if his brain had swollen and was trying to ooze out of his ears. Ferris gripped his temple with one hand, trying to push himself up on one elbow. He barely had time to inhale before he was picked up and shoved up against a tree. Zach kneed him hard in the stomach. The sensation to retch instantly rushed up from his gut. When he tried to breathe, he could only gag. Paul held him against the tree by his neck, letting go only to punch Ferris across the cheek.

Ferris wondered if he should regret hitting Rudy. He also wondered why he'd cared so much about his stupid dog. As he was dropped to the ground once again and kicked in the abdomen, he could only wonder if Stanley had gotten away or not. The dog was probably so stupid that he'd hung around to watch. A sharp bark confirmed this; Stanley was still bristling at the strangers instead of running away. In a way, it was flattering that his dog would stay at his side. Ferris tried to focus his eyes — the sidewalk was fuzzy and gray. Small red spots began to appear on the cement and Ferris realized that his nose was bleeding. A brief lick confirmed that his lip was also bleeding. Something pushed him onto his back and he felt a weight on his hips. Paul was sitting on him, growling something as he grabbed the collar of Ferris' shirt.

"You ever hit one of us again and we'll—"

"Paul, someone's coming," Rudy hissed, gesturing for them to leave. "Forget him."

20

Paul looked up to see a woman with a stroller crossing at the intersection. He dropped Ferris, whose head hit the sidewalk with a dull thump. Ferris could hear them curse and scuffle. Their footsteps faded as they rushed down the street – out of sight of the approaching woman. For a while, everything was quiet. He closed his eyes and listened to the traffic a block away. Stanley was licking his hand. There was a soft rolling noise, like a cart of some kind. The wheels stopped and he could hear the voice of a middle-aged woman.

"Are you okay? Can you hear me?"

The voice faded into the traffic – then there was no sound at all.

On Monday Ferris hadn't shown up at school. He'd refused to talk about what had happened, only quietly claiming it had been "some guys on the street." His mother had paced outside of his room in worry, wishing he would tell them more about it.

He'd been taken to the hospital when he passed out, treated for sprains, mild cuts to his face, and several broken ribs. His face had become frightfully bruised and his left eye had swollen dramatically. He was using a spare pair of glasses, ones he hadn't used since fifth grade. They felt tight on his head and the old prescription was giving him a headache. His new pair wouldn't arrive for another week.

Ferris was lying on his side, staring blankly at the wall. He wasn't in the mood to do anything; not even reading seemed appealing. All he could manage to do was stare. Stanley was sleeping on his bed, curled up next to him and snoring as he had the annoying tendency to do. Shifting, Ferris rolled onto his back, changing his gaze from the wall to the ceiling. There was still a sick feeling in his stomach which hadn't left since the day before.

Ferris shut his eyes as he touched the side of his face, wincing as he felt over a bruise. He'd been lying undisrupted for hours. When there was a knock on the door he considered ignoring it.

"Yeah?" he answered with little enthusiasm.

"Demos is here. He has your homework," came his mother's voice.

"Okay," Ferris answered, burying his face in a wide pillow. He didn't want Demos to see him in such a sorry state. The door cracked open. Ferris glanced over from the corner of his eye; he could see Demos slip inside and shut the door behind him. Demos rolled the desk chair over, sitting down next to Ferris' bed. He was holding a small stack of folders.

"Ferris," Demos said, his voice eerily commanding. "Look at me."

Ferris mumbled something against the pillow. Not content with his response, Demos quickly jerked the pillow away.

"Who did this to you?"

Ferris avoided eye contact, not sure if he wanted to explain. He definitely didn't plan on ever telling his parents. They would throw a fit and blame themselves for putting him in that school and have guilt issues for the rest of their lives. He decided to just change the subject.

"Is that my homework?"

Demos scowled.

"Yeah. Biology and World History. There's an essay you have to do."

"Fine, give me the assignments," Ferris said, sitting up and holding out a hand for the folders.

"Tell me what happened."

"I got mugged."

"Mugged?" Demos asked, clearly not convinced.

"Yeah. Mugged."

Demos sat closer, his voice coming through his teeth.

"Who was it? Tell me the truth."

"Some guys," Ferris said with a hand gesture.

"Do you think I'm stupid, Ferris? I know when you're lying. You suck at it."

"I do not."

"So you *are* lying?" Demos asked.

"No."

Ferris furrowed his brow, wishing Demos would stop interrogating him. He looked away, refusing to make eye contact and knowing full well that he was being immature about it.

"Tell me or you're not getting these assignments," Demos demanded.

"You can't blackmail me."

"Yes I can."

"This is stupid, Demos. Just drop it," Ferris said. Demos was being just about as stubborn as his mother.

"No. You're my friend," Demos insisted. "I care about you. I want to know."

Ferris looked down at his hands, flattening his lips together. He looked uncomfortable, as if he were wearing an itchy sweater. Demos waited, not speaking as Ferris considered it.

"Rudy Sauber."

"And?"

Ferris exhaled, exasperated. Demos asked again.

"Who else?"

"Why do you think there was someone else?"

"Because Rudy Sauber is pathetic and you could take him any day. Why are you trying to protect these guys?"

"I'm not protecting anyone," he sighed. "I just..."

"What?"

"I don't want it to be a big deal."

Demos considered him for a while, finally understanding. Ferris didn't want this to get out, to become a court case, or to involve his family in a hassle.

"It won't be. I promise."

Ferris finally made eye contact with him again, trying to decide if he was telling the truth or not. He was quiet for a minute before finally speaking.

"Paul Bennett. And Zach Straight."

Demos finally relaxed, sitting back in his chair. He'd figured it had been that group of boys. He wouldn't tell any authorities. It wasn't what Ferris wanted, especially when there were better ways to deal with the situation.

"Demos, why do you want to know so badly?"

"No reason. Here's your homework." He set the folder down on the nightstand, getting up out of his chair. "Get some rest, okay? I'll see you soon."

"Right. See you," Ferris said. "Oh, um…"

Demos paused, looking back at him.

"Thanks for stopping by," Ferris finished. Demos smiled and wordlessly opened the door. Ferris slid back down in his bed, folding his arms over his chest as Demos left. He could have sworn he'd seen an unsettling glint in the boy's eye right before the door shut.

When Ferris finally went back to school, he had a hard time stepping into his afternoon science class. He was standing outside of the classroom door, already a few minutes late. Going in and seeing the three boys was not something he was anticipating. He swallowed, looking down before opening the door. Silently, he made his way to the back of the class, taking a breath before looking up to see them. He blinked.

They were gone.

Not saying anything, he sat down in his seat. The other students seemed to notice that he'd been absent a couple of days and had now come into class looking like he'd been mauled by a bear. Ferris' mind started to run over different possibilities. Maybe they had all just skipped class together — they did that sometimes. He started to unconsciously bite his lower lip, feeling light in the stomach for a reason he couldn't explain to himself.

"Hey."

Ferris came back to reality, slowly turning his head to look at the boy who was whispering to him.

"…Yeah?"

"Were you in the same car accident as them?"

"Car accident?"

"Yeah. They were all hit by a car? Some crazy guy, I think."

Ferris only stared at him, eyes widening behind his glasses. Another classmate leaned over to join the conversation. She whispered as well, asking if the rumor was true that the car had struck Rudy, then backed up to chase down Paul and Zach as they were running away. It seemed that they were alive but in bad condition at the Southport General Hospital.

Ferris quieted, knowing that this could be the result of only two things. Either karma was incredibly effective in this day and age, or this had something to do with Demos Giorgetti.

That evening, Ferris was over at Demos' home to study for a midterm. Ferris excelled at math, where Demos failed utterly. They had a symbiotic relationship in which one would help the other in their weak spots, as if putting two minds together to create a flawless super-mind — in theory.

"Multiply 1/2 to row three and add it to row two." Ferris was sitting on the floor with an open book in his lap. A calculator rested on top of the pages as he followed the problem Demos was attempting.

"Is this right?" Demos asked, showing the other boy his calculator. He was sitting next to Ferris with similar books and papers.

"Yes," Ferris replied. "For once."

The room was silent for a minute; only the sound of pencils scratching on paper could be heard. Though they were working, the air was terribly awkward. Ferris took in a breath as if to say something but decided against it. His mouth closed and he continued working, going over the same problem for the fifth time.

Finally, his curiosity got the better of him and he straightened himself, adjusting his glasses on his nose.

"Is there something you want to tell me?"

Demos picked up his head, blinking at Ferris.

"Tell you?"

"We're not kids anymore. We need to talk about this."

"Ah," Demos cooed, tapping his pen against his smirking lips. "Are you confessing your love for me?"

"I'm serious!" he said, snatching the pen from his friend's hand. "You know exactly what I'm talking about."

At this, Demos' mood soured and he averted his eyes.

"I really don't," he muttered.

"So you're telling me that Paul and his friends are in the hospital because of karma?"

"I didn't hear about that," Demos replied, his voice growing softer with every word.

"Demos, what's wrong with you?" Ferris asked, his eyes narrowing impatiently. "I thought we were friends. Why are you lying to me?"

"Just drop it. It's not what you think."

24

Ferris took in a sharp breath, no longer able to keep his frustration buried.

"How fucking stupid do you think I am?" he hissed. "You'd have to be blind not to realize that your family is *in the mafia!*"

Something snapped behind Demos' eyes. He stared back with an unreadable expression, his body eerily still. A moment later, he shifted to stand, but Ferris caught his wrist before he could leave.

"Why can't you just tell me the truth?" Ferris demanded, his grip tight on the other boy's sleeve.

"Because," Demos murmured, his expression softening, "...you're my only friend."

Puzzled, Ferris blinked. His fingers opened, freeing his friend's wrist. Demos kept his eyes turned away, swallowing before reseating himself on the floor.

"What do you mean?" Ferris finally asked.

Demos took a breath, then began to speak.

"I didn't have many friends in Italy. They all knew," he began. "But here, nobody really knows. They think it, but they don't know."

Ferris said nothing, only listening as Demos began to open himself.

"I didn't want you to get scared," Demos continued. "I didn't want you to leave."

Ferris chewed his lower lip before replying.

"But," he said, "...you're *my* only friend, too."

The room fell silent. Both boys dared a glance at one another, making the same realization as their eyes met.

"Oh my God," Demos blurted. "We're pathetic."

Ferris clamped his fist over his mouth, fighting the tremble in his shoulders. He and Demos only lasted a moment before bursting into laughter. The sound carried through the room and into the hall, inciting an angry call from Victor.

"I don't hear studying!"

"Sorry!" Demos called back, finally regaining control of himself. The room was silent once more and both he and Ferris glanced at one another. Though the tense moment had been eased, there was still a rather large elephant in the room.

"I promise I won't be scared," Ferris said, "if you promise to tell me the truth."

Demos looked down at his hands. He thought for a moment, his eyes still as he willed himself to reply. Finally, he picked up his head.

"Okay."

Demos explained everything. He outlined the Giorgettis' long history in organized crime, up to Gino's expansion to the United States – how a crew of soldiers reported to Victor, who in turn followed Gino's every order. There were many men in many ranks, all tasked with different assignments and territories. Their money came from countless sources — from extortion, loansharking, and gambling. The Giorgetti empire had been built on a foundation of blood and exploitation, leaving Gino with a world of power in his fist.

"...And it was Nicky," Demós continued. "He ran them over with his car. He works for Uncle Victor."

"Oh," Ferris replied, his eyes cast down.

"*Oh?*" Demos repeated, knitting his brow. "You promised you wouldn't be scared."

"I'm not scared," he insisted, shaking his head. "You just know a lot more than I thought."

Truly, the boy had a rather clear grasp of his family's line of work. It would seem natural to keep children in the dark – then again, Demos had not been a child for quite some time.

"Do you... do you know how to use a gun?" Ferris asked.

"Yes," Demos mumbled, his face heating as he spoke.

Ferris gave a faint smile, unable to help but see his friend in a new light. That light, however, was not the horror Demos had been expecting.

"That's so cool."

03

Ferris had his first experience with death when he was still thirteen years old. It was winter and Southport was heavy with snow. The city lights reflected neatly off of the ice that formed along the curbs. His family had gone to Ristorante Giorgetti for dinner that evening, but at the end of the meal Gino had come to talk to his father. Their conversation had taken a serious turn and they'd gone into a back room, leaving his mother to gossip with Victor's wife and Ferris dying of boredom. Victor's son Sergio was tending the bar for the evening. He leaned over the counter, noticing the blasé looking boy.

"Hey Ferris, you want a cocoa or something?"

"Could I have coffee?"

Ferris had taken to occasionally drinking coffee with his father in the morning. His parents thought it was fairly amusing at first and let it go, realizing he was probably old enough to handle it.

"Sure thing."

Sergio was wearing a black vest and a bowtie, looking dignified as he poured coffee from a carafe into a ceramic mug. Smiling, he passed it over to the teen. Ferris glanced down to see that there was no cream or sugar in the cup. He paused. Somehow, he couldn't bring himself to ask for either in front of Sergio. Mature men drank it black, didn't they? Attempting to look collected, he took a sip.

It tasted like the bottom of a burnt shoe. His face contorted into a forced smile and he ignored the sweat that had formed on his forehead.

"It's… great," Ferris said with clenched teeth. "Thanks."

Sparing Ferris the embarrassment, Sergio only bit back a smile and focused his attention on cleaning the bar.

"You know, I think I saw Rocco wander into the kitchen," Sergio said thoughtfully. "I hope he doesn't get fur on anything."

Rocco, a fussy white Persian, was Gino's cat. He was only allowed in the restaurant when no customers were present and was most certainly not allowed in the kitchen. Desperate for something to do, Ferris picked up his head eagerly.

"Want me to go get him?" the boy offered.

"Sure, if you don't mind."

Zeroed in on his quest, Ferris abandoned his cup of bitter regret and headed towards the swinging kitchen doors.

Ristorante Giorgetti's kitchen was empty for the night. He crept through, passing spotless steel counters and a row of gas ranges. A flicker of white was the only sign of life, drawing him to peer below a prep table. Sure enough, the cat was settled beneath it. Rocco glanced back at Ferris, unimpressed.

"Come on, boy. You don't belong in—"

Before Ferris could finish, the Persian darted out into the aisle between stoves. It was only when he reached the doors leading into the alley that the cat stopped. Ferris froze – the doors were wide open.

"N-no, wait!" he blurted, arm outstretched as he hurried forward. He was too late. Rocco slipped outside, a pale flash through the threshold. Heart pounding, Ferris rushed out into the alley. The last thing he wanted to do was tell Gino Giorgetti that he'd lost his beloved cat.

It was getting dark earlier now that it was December. Though the streetlights had come on, the driveway was angled, blocking any view of the main road. It was dark, forcing the boy to strain his eyes in search of the cursed cat.

Finally, he saw it – a stroke of white against the dark of the alley. There was a car parked in front of the service entrance, its trunk cracked just enough to reveal the cat's tail. Unable to help but feel smug, Ferris slowly approached. The hems of his pants grew damp as he stepped through the snow, steadying both hands on the trunk before pulling it open. It was only when his eyes focused that he realized it hadn't been a cat's tail at all.

The slip of white was a piece of cloth – cloth that was part of a man's shirt.

Ferris inhaled sharply. The cold air seared his throat as he staggered backwards. His eyes locked on the pair that were staring back at him, pale and unmoving.

The body in the trunk was bloated and pale gray. Dried, reddish-brown blood was caked on the man's matted hair and throat. He was still and cold, staring back as if caught in the moment he'd been killed. It smelled terrible, like rotting meat and feces, blood and bacteria. Ferris swallowed, desperately fighting the bile that wanted to come up the back of his throat. He could feel his heart thumping, preparing him for the run of his life. He took one more step backwards before a gloved hand clamped hard over his mouth.

He'd been grabbed from behind, his mouth smothered by the leather of the glove that was flattened over it.

"Don't scream," came a stern, calm voice.

Ferris quickly nodded in response.

"Good."

The hand hesitated, then let go. A figure stepped around him and slammed the trunk shut. The white, gazing eyes were gone, though Ferris could still see them clearly in his head. What had once been a living person was now decomposing in the trunk of that car. The corpse had locked its gaze on him, eyes glazed and accusing. Ferris clenched his fists to keep his hands from shaking. The man finally turned around, staring down at Ferris with an unreadable expression.

"M-Mr. Giorgetti..." Ferris stammered when he finally found his voice. He instantly recognized him as the man Demos called Uncle Victor. Victor was in his late 40's, already sporting white streaks past the temples of his dark brown hair. He wore thick Italian frames which were starting to fog. Victor folded his arms, leaning back onto the trunk of the car as he tried to figure out what he was going to do.

"Ferris." He adjusted his glasses. "You don't like upsetting others, do you?"

Ferris was silent, only shaking his head slightly.

"You wouldn't want to frighten your mom or dad, right?" He shook his head again.

"So you understand exactly what you saw in that trunk, correct?"

"Nothing," Ferris replied, his tone flat.

"You're quick."

Ferris didn't respond. His heart was still pounding in his ears. Victor could sense his discomfort and he reached forward to put a hand on his shoulder. Ferris almost flinched, but stopped himself.

"You have to promise me that you'll never tell anyone. Not Demos, not even your dog. You got me?"

"Yes." Ferris was still quiet, his expression empty. Victor sighed, then lowered his voice.

"If it makes you feel any better, he was a very bad man."

Ferris nodded in response, not really listening. If he hadn't been a friend of the family, if his father wasn't close to them, what would Victor have done? Would he have killed him to keep him quiet? Would he have ended up just like that body – pale and rotting in the trunk of a car?

"Get back inside, you'll catch a cold," Victor said, gesturing towards the entrance.

"Okay." Ferris stepped away slowly, taking a moment before actually walking properly. He avoided any second glances at the car, keeping his eyes straight ahead as he walked. Victor watched until he was out of sight, then patted his coat pocket for a pack of cigarettes. Tugging one out with his teeth, he cupped his hand to light it. Behind him, smugly perched on the car trunk, Rocco began to clean his ears.

Everything was dark. It took Ferris a moment to realize that a simple solution would be to open his eyes. He squinted; the sun was bright on the snow, burning his eyes as if he were staring into a light bulb. His pupils adjusted, shrinking back within his irises. When he looked around, all he could see was a massive field of snow and a grouping of trees on the horizon. They were white birch – crooked, skeletal hands reaching up out of the earth.

It was cold. As he trudged through the snow, his long, red scarf trailed along behind him. The crunching of his footsteps was the only thing he could hear.

As he walked, he noticed a part of the snow that seemed to be breathing. The white pile shifted, then sat up straight. It was an ivory cat. Its ears twitched and it sniffed the air before pouncing off through the snow.

Curious, he followed, jogging after it at a flimsy pace. He stumbled a little, not used to running through thick snow. His breath came up short, puffing into the air as the cat ran faster. Suddenly, it disappeared.

He stopped, panting and staring down at the empty patch of snow. Before he could stop to think, dark red liquid started to bubble up from the same spot. He narrowed his eyes at the growing pool, taking a step closer to see better.

It was blood. Something appeared to be surfacing. Red trails seeped away from its features until he saw two white eyes and a swollen, pale face. Ferris' breath caught and he staggered back. The corpse pulled itself out, clawing the surrounding snow in a stiff, exaggerated effort. Blood stained the white as it dragged itself closer. Ferris froze at the sight of it. His pulse began to echo in the back of his head.

Ferris opened his mouth, but the corpse's hands reached for him before he could make a sound. Tight, dead fingers grasped his legs and he slipped backwards into the snow with a shout.

His eyes immediately opened. His entire body tensed before he realized he was in his bed. Taking in sharp breaths of air, he paused to notice that he'd been gripping the sheets. His knuckles were white from holding too hard and his skin was burning.

For a long time he couldn't move. He could feel the fear holding him down, sitting on his chest and paralyzing him to the tips of his fingers. Finally, he managed to put his hand over his mouth. It was only a dream – one he'd had many times before. Stanley was still sleeping on the end of his bed, curled up and unaware of the nightmare.

He couldn't get those eyes out of his head. They had been so glazed and piercing that even then, a year later, he still had a vivid memory of them. His stomach tightened. Clumsily reaching over to the nightstand, he grabbed the frames of his glasses and slid them on. He made his way to the bathroom, turning on the light and shutting the door.

Ferris looked at himself in the mirror; anxiety reflected back in his own eyes. He twisted the faucet handle, cupping his hand underneath the running water and touching it to his jaw and neck. His skin still felt too hot and he was nauseated. There wasn't anything he could do or anyone he could tell. He could only hope the memory would someday fade – he never wanted to see those eyes again.

04

Demos stood with Ferris outside of St. Basil's Private Academy, both boys looking up at the building with blank expressions. Demos was holding a school bag at his side and a notebook to his chest. Ferris had all of his books and supplies, but neither of them were ready to return to school.

"Well, back to this shit, I guess," Demos mumbled.

"Winter break was too short," Ferris replied. He'd been too busy working on extra credit assignments to get much rest.

The high school was in an elegant old building that consisted of two stories and deep, red brick. It was aged, but well maintained. Dark ivy crawled up the sides and the grounds were sculpted with oak and birch. Other students walked up to the front doors around them, all wearing the same dark gray uniform and burgundy ties.

"See you in fifth period," Demos said, giving a small wave. Ferris gave his friend a slight smile. Demos was one of the few people on Earth who ever saw the boy do anything but frown.

"Yeah, see you."

That particular Thursday afternoon, Ferris had stayed late at school to use the library, having spent a couple of hours at a table with half a dozen books. Though Demos was perfectly happy doing his papers thoughtlessly and at the last minute, Ferris felt the need to overachieve on nearly everything. He had almost gathered enough notes to write his paper when the librarian started to close up, shooing him out with a bony hand. He frowned before putting his paperwork together, shoving it into his schoolbag before leaving.

He went down the stairs of St. Basil's Academy one at a time, staring down at them and pulling his scarf in more tightly. He was about to turn onto the sidewalk when a voice interrupted his movement. It belonged to a girl.

"Hey, you got any smokes?"

He slowly looked up to see a girl his age blocking his path. She very clearly did not go to his school, as she was not in any kind of uniform and was dressed much like a public school student – a poor one. What she was doing in this neighborhood at this time of day was beyond him.

"I don't smoke." He knit his eyebrows at her, a little annoyed that she was in his way.

"Well then, you got some money?"

He stared at her, wondering what was going on in her mind that gave her this kind of nerve. She seemed rather confident, having no apprehension in her voice despite her small stature. Though she was wearing a heavy black coat, he could still tell that she was quite thin. It was almost enough to make him guess she was homeless.

"No," he answered incredulously, emphasizing the annoyance in his voice.

She quirked her lips, stepping into an uncomfortable proximity. One of her hands stroked his collar while the other went directly into his pants pocket. He tensed and stammered as she pulled out his wallet, flipping through it to find a ten dollar bill.

"Don't be so cheap," she said.

"Hey, you can't just—"

"Thanks." She smiled. "See you around."

She tossed his wallet back, leaving him fumbling to catch it as she walked off. He couldn't do anything but gawk, still unable to believe what had just happened. Did she just mug him? Had he been robbed? He'd been robbed.

He didn't see her again for several days, feeling relief each time he came outside to find no one there. Then, four days later, she was there again. His eyes pinched at the sight of her. Ferris started to wish that his mother hadn't given him a standing deference of women, or he'd have definitely given her the lecture of a lifetime.

"What do you want?" he asked skeptically.

"To pay you back."

This was the last thing he had expected to hear from her and he found himself staring again.

"… What?"

"Remember? The ten dollars I borrowed," she explained.

"Yeah. Borrowed."

She took out a package of cigarettes and pulled one out with her teeth, lighting it with a cupped hand. Shrugging, she pocketed the pack and smiled at him. Demos had recently started to smoke as well. Ferris didn't really see the appeal and vaguely started to wonder what store on Earth would sell a fourteen-year-old girl a pack of cigarettes. She probably stole those, too.

"Do I look like a thief to you?" she asked, still grinning.

"Yes."

"Come on, I'll make it up to you."

"Come on? Where exactly are we 'coming on' to? I don't even know you."

"Are all rich boys this uptight?" She tapped some ashes onto the cold sidewalk. He narrowed his eyes at her again, trying to figure out what her motive was. Maybe she was going to lure him into an alley where a bunch of guys would jump him and take everything of value that he owned.

"I'm not rich."

"Sure you're not," she mused, reaching for the collar of his neatly pressed school uniform. He stepped back, cutting her arm away with his wrist.

"Don't."

"What, afraid I'll get 'poor' on it?"

"I'm going home." He shifted the strap of his schoolbag. "Don't follow me."

"Do you really never want to see your money again?"

He stopped in his tracks, his back facing her. He frowned and tried to think, wondering if the effort was even worth it. Why did he have to follow her somewhere, why wouldn't she just give him some cash? This had to be some kind of trick, but really, what was the worst that could happen?

Exhaling heavily, he ignored the puff of breath that came out into the cold, slowly turning to face her again.

"Fine. This better be quick."

"Great. This way."

She led him down the street, still nursing her cigarette. He watched her as they walked, trying to figure her out. The girl's hair was black and styled into a bob – if 'styled' was the correct word. It looked as if she'd cut it herself. Her sneakers were long past their glory days and she wore a lot of eyeliner for a girl her age.

"Where is it?"

"Just a couple more blocks."

They passed by a bank, an OTB, several bodegas, and a few street vendors that were grilling kebabs for four dollars. The smell of charred meat grew overwhelming as they walked through the smoke. He was about to open his mouth to ask exactly how much further it was, when she stopped walking.

"Here we go."

He looked up curiously at their destination. The sign read *Westway Diner* in red, blocked neon.

"It's… a diner."

"No wonder you go to private school!" She smiled again, opening the door and motioning for him to follow. Rolling his eyes, he went in after her. At least he couldn't get jumped and robbed in a diner.

A man at the counter motioned for them to sit wherever they liked and she pulled him into a booth with red vinyl seats. Lacing her fingers together, she leaned her elbows on the tabletop and rested her chin on her hands.

"So, what do you want to get?"

He glanced down at the laminated menu briefly.

"The uh, ten dollars looks pretty good."

"Food, stupid," she said, frowning.

"I'm not hungry. What's the point of this? You're wasting my time."

The girl didn't respond, looking up at the waitress that had approached their table. The woman looked kind, but tired.

"Julie honey, who's your friend?"

"Hi Mom, this is uh—"

She made a face at Ferris, emphasizing for him to introduce himself.

"Ferris." He replied bluntly, but with forced politeness. It suddenly made sense. The girl didn't have any money, so she was going to pay him back with food – food that was free to her, since her mother worked here. He couldn't say he needed food, or wanted food, but he had to give her a little credit for even trying.

"Yeah. He's going to have a soda and—"

"Water," he corrected.

"And a... cheeseburger—"

"Tuna sandwich," he corrected again.

"Okay, I'll have the burger, then." The next line, she sneaked in. "And a milkshake."

"You'll get a milk."

"...Shake."

Her mother smiled as she scribbled down "milk" onto her notepad, turning to go put in the order.

The girl picked up a sugar packet, playing with it idly as she spoke to him.

"So. Is your name really Ferris?"

"Yeah. And I guess you're Julie."

"You just get smarter and smarter."

"Look. You can keep the money. I have other things I need to be doing."

Her expression changed as he started to get up and she quickly reached forward to grab his sleeve.

"Wait. Please?"

He sighed again, looking up at the ceiling before sitting back down. Resting his jaw on his fist, he mirrored her fidgeting by fiddling with a coffee creamer.

"So..." He paused, trying to think of what to say. "Which school do you go to?"

She looked as if the question caught her by surprise, glancing to the left and mumbling her answer.

"Uh, I.S. 154. It's just a public school."

"Nothing wrong with that." He still wasn't making eye contact with her, looking down at the creamer container as his fingertip spun it in a circle on the tabletop. "Uh..."

The awkward air reminded him of the times that his mother had tried to match him up with girls from synagogue. Other than that, he didn't have much experience talking with girls. Maybe it would be best to just pretend he was talking to a boy. The kitchen door opened and shut, exposing the sound of sizzling and cooking from the back.

He found himself wanting to know about her. It wasn't out of any kind of fondness, but rather, she was different. Ferris had never met anyone like her before.

"Thanks. For coming back," he managed to say.

She picked up her head to make eye contact, looking as if she hadn't expected his words. Quite briefly, her eyes softened.

"Sure."

Their afternoon went considerably better from that point on and she seemed to slow down on the snappy remarks. The food wasn't half bad, and neither was her conversation. Though she didn't seem big on education, arts, or politics, she was bright. He started to feel self-conscious, hoping that he wasn't boring her. It was a strange feeling; normally he didn't care what anyone thought of him.

The sky grew dark, though neither of the teens took notice.

"So what did you say to him?" Ferris asked with a quirked brow.

"I told him to suck it! Who talks like that, anyway?" Julie replied, smirking self-confidently.

"Douchebags, I guess."

Interrupting their conversation, Julie's mother came up to take away their plates.

"You should go home before it gets too late."

"'Kay, Mom."

It was that moment that it hit him — he was getting a free meal from a woman who was supporting her family on tips. He cut in, fishing out his wallet.

"That was $7.50, right?"

"Oh, no honey, it's all right. It's on me." The woman smiled again, looking sincere. Ferris looked away, somehow embarrassed as he nodded. When she left, Julie leaned forward to whisper, her voice seething.

"Why are you trying to pay? Do you feel sorry for me or something?"

"No, it's not that," he said. "I just—"

"Put your wallet away." She folded her arms and leaned back, still irritated.

He sighed, sliding it back into his coat pocket and feeling uncomfortable again. She got up out of her seat, straightening out her jacket before looking out the window and frowning at the dark sky.

"Hey," he started.

"Yeah?"

"Want me to walk you home?"

She knit her eyebrows at him, studying him for a moment. "You'd really do that?"

Ferris didn't seem to think it was a big deal, but apparently it was.

"Uh, yeah. Sure."

After momentarily fighting with her pride, she gave in with a smile.

"Thanks."

As they left the diner he started to wonder if his parents would be worried. He had a tendency to stay at school for a while studying, but he would normally let them know ahead of time. He'd have to go straight home afterwards and pray she didn't live on the other side of town.

Their walk was longer than he'd hoped and her neighborhood was different, to say the least. The apartment buildings were stained and clustered. More used to finely trimmed brownstones, he started to wonder if she would be more useful in a bad situation than he would. Bits of litter blew down the street, getting caught in the gutter. He scratched the back of his neck, trying not to show that he was nervous.

"Is your dad at home?" Ferris asked, trying to make conversation.

"He left a while ago. It's just us and Mom."

"Us?"

"I have two sisters. I hate my older one, she treats me like shit."

"So, your mom pays for everything."

"Yeah. She has two jobs."

Ferris couldn't possibly relate. He was an only child whose parents both loved him, whose father had a comfortable and lucrative career, and whose mother was a whimsical housewife who spent her time playing cards with the neighbors. He'd never met someone from such a different walk of life. He knew she didn't want pity, but couldn't help but feel it for her. She wasn't a bad person. She'd paid him back — sort of.

"Dad comes around once in a while, but he's usually just drunk and wants something."

"Oh. I'm sorry."

She caught on to his uneasiness, giving him a snide smile.

"Maybe I should be walking you home. You look a little pale."

"It's just cold," he muttered, stuffing his hands into his pockets as if proving his point.

"Well, this is me."

He looked over at the building. It was made of beige brick, lined with rusty fire escapes and peeling paint. A dog was barking from one of the apartments, momentarily distracting him from his thoughts.

"Julie."

"Mhm?"

He pulled a twenty from his pocket, taking her by the hand and pushing it into her palm.

"I don't need your charity." She looked upset again, trying to pull her hand away.

"It's not for you, it's for the meal. You can pay me back some other time." He closed her fingers around it. Slowly, she looked down at her own hand, struggling with her thoughts.

"Ferris…"

"Take it."

Julie was quiet, looking angry, but humbled. Finally she exhaled, catching his eyes.

"Okay."

He let go, putting his hands back into his coat pockets. The bill was just snack money his mother had given him in an attempt to make him fatter. Pushing his glasses up on his nose, he stepped back to leave.

"Goodnight, then."

"Hey, wait," she stammered quickly.

"Hm?"

Her hand held onto his arm as she leaned in, kissing his cheek.

"Thanks."

He stared as the door shut behind her. No woman under the age of forty had ever kissed his cheek. His face reddened. It was clearly not from the cold outside, but from the prickling feeling she'd left and the anxious pounding of his heart. When he belatedly started to walk home, he was too delirious to even care if he was mugged.

The following week he checked the front stairs of the school every day to see if she had returned. It had been eight days and the only person waiting outside for him was Demos.

"Gee, you look thrilled to see me."

"Sorry, I'm kind of out of it."

"I can tell. Hey, can we study at your house? Emily is going to have her friends over and they're probably just going to talk about *Harry Potter* all night."

"Yeah, sure. Want to stay the night?"

"That'd be great." Demos fell into step alongside Ferris, happy to be studying if it meant being away from a pack of girls. "Hey, you think your mom will make those macaroons again? Those were fucking good."

They took the subway together, walking through Ferris' snow covered neighborhood to his home. Demos was a familiar face in their house and Ferris' mother was always happy to see him.

38

"Demos, come here, let me look at you. Oh, you haven't gained a pound, what are they feeding you? I thought you were Italian, this is horrible!" Ruth lamented. She was already prepared with a plate of assorted cookies, one of which Stanley was eating near the entrance.

"Hey, don't give that to Stan, it's bad for him!" Ferris said. At least the cookie wasn't chocolate.

"He appreciates my cooking much more than you do."

Stanley loved to beg for human food and Ruth loved to give it to him. As much as Ferris protested her bad habit, she only continued to feed him biscuits, pastrami, and matzoh balls. The dog had grown up with a roly-poly figure which his mother adored and Ferris simply found embarrassing.

"Come, come," Ruth continued, offering the plate to Demos. "I made these."

"Mom, we need to go study."

"Quiet! Your friend is dying and you want to keep him from eating?"

"He's not *dyi—*"

"Yes, I am," Demos interrupted, taking the entire plate. "Thanks, Mrs. Levinstein!"

Somehow, they escaped to the second floor. Demos spread out on the floor, sifting through a stack of papers to find his assignment. He was holding a cookie in his mouth as he found the right paper, reading over the terms without much enthusiasm.

They were halfway through their work when Ferris found his mind wandering. Without thinking, he began to twirl his pen around his thumb; it was one of his more common fidgets. He wasn't sure why, but he couldn't stop thinking about Julie. He wondered what she was doing and if she was okay. They hadn't made any plans to meet up and he started to worry that he'd never see her again.

"Hhy," Demos mumbled, breaking his line of thought.

"Huh?"

Demos took the cookie out of his mouth, holding it with two fingers.

"I said 'hey.' We should just forget this and sneak out. Seriously."

"Come on, Demos. Do you really want to—"

"What, get a B? Oh, the horror," Demos said, clutching his imaginary pearls.

"It would be stupid for someone as smart as you to get any less."

"Thanks, Dad."

"Shut up, maybe you really *are* an idiot."

"If I agree, can we go out?"

"No."

Demos frowned, mimicking his friend's grouchy expression. "Fine."

Ferris smirked at Demos' display, already used to it. It was strange when he thought about it, that Demos would rather put in an hour of effort figuring out a way to cheat on a test than to put in an hour of studying to just pass it the normal way. He was brilliant, but he only applied it to being conniving. The boy was a conundrum, though in the end it was quite appropriate considering his family's line of business.

"I... uh, wanted to talk to you about something, too," Ferris added quietly.

"I thought we already had this discussion," Demos said, his tone dry.

"No, not that," Ferris said. "Something different."

Curiosity piqued, Demos leaned in closer.

"Oh? Different how?"

"Um, well..." Ferris began, unsure of how to word it. "Have you ever liked a girl?"

"*W-what?*" Demos blurted, his spine stiffening in panic.

"I met one," the other boy mumbled.

"Oh. Oh, right," Demos replied, exhaling in relief. "Of course you did. Where?"

"On the street."

The room was silent for a moment. Demos said nothing, only staring at his friend.

"No! Not like that!" Ferris quickly insisted, waving his hands in protest. "Just a regular girl!"

With that out of the way, Ferris began to explain what had happened with Julie. Demos listened with interest, completely forgetting about his homework assignment.

Ferris' mind worked in a different way than Demos'. He had the social graces of a deciduous tree, probably because of the fact that he knew what one was. Demos didn't really care much for such things — he liked to read and had a quiet love for classic novels, but his intelligence stemmed mostly from common sense. It was because of this that Demos started to feel uneasy at what he was hearing, finally opening his mouth to speak when the story was over.

"You shouldn't give strangers money."

"I know. I just—"

"You don't know anything about her. Don't get soft just because a girl is cute."

"I never said she was cute."

"You think she is, I can tell."

"Yeah, sure. You should add psychic to your resume, along with busybody," Ferris muttered.

"I'm just trying to help, Ferris."

"It's really that hard to believe a girl would spend time with me?" Ferris was tense, his tone uncharacteristically defensive.

"That's not what I meant," Demos replied softly.

"Yeah. Okay."

Their evening was silent from that point on. Ferris had immersed himself in his textbook and Demos didn't feel bold enough to venture further. Something didn't feel right, though it was possible that he was merely afraid of losing his best friend to some girl.

From that day on, Ferris' mood hadn't improved. The next few days went by slowly and he didn't notice much around him aside from the dirty, melting snow and bare trees. He had been nearly ready to forget everything, stop worrying about it, and get on with his life, when he saw her again.

He stopped in his tracks at the top of the stairs, looking down at her on the sidewalk. She gave him a small wave and a smile and his entire week of self-pity instantly fell away.

When he came down to meet her, she shifted her weight to her heels, looking apologetic with her hands in her pockets.

"Hey," she finally said.

"Hi."

"How you been?"

"Okay," he lied. "You?"

"Okay," she repeated.

Before their greetings could become clumsier, she grabbed him by the elbow and started to lead him down the street.

"Come on, I want to show you something."

"Another sandwich?"

"No. It's my favorite place."

"Oh, okay." This seemed more acceptable, though in her case it was still quite vague. Her favorite place could have been anything from an carnival to a car lot. In this case, however, it was a park. More specifically, a playground.

It was too cold for any children to be out and they were a few years too old to be using the equipment. Even so, she sat on a swing, letting it sway as she looked up at him thoughtfully.

"I came here when I was little," she said.

"I know this park, my house isn't very far from here."

"Really? I'd like to see your house sometime."

"Yeah, sure."

He gave in, sitting on the swing next to her and holding the base of the chains. They were cold on his fingers, still wet from melting ice.

"So…" He started, unsure of exactly how to ask his question. "It's kind of been a while."

"Oh. Yeah, I…" She averted her eyes. "Sorry. Dad came home."

Ferris picked up his head, knitting his eyebrows.

"What happened?"

Julie was quiet for a while, working her mouth and trying to decide on what to say to him. She seemed hesitant to tell the truth.

"Mom wouldn't give him any money, so he got really mad. He sprained her arm so I stayed home to do chores and cook." She started to fiddle with the edge of her coat sleeve, mumbling. "He took the money you gave me."

Ferris' mouth parted, though he wasn't clear on exactly what he wanted to say.

"I—"

"It's okay," she cut in, waving her hand. "Don't worry about it."

As if to emphasize her point, she gave him a soft smile once again. He couldn't take it; her forgiving expression only made him feel more frustrated.

"Julie, that's fucked up. He can't get away with that."

"It's not as bad as it sounds."

"I can't fathom that."

"You're a nice guy, Ferris. I think maybe you're too nice."

"I'm not nice at all," he mumbled. "I hate everyone."

She laughed, shaking her head at him. He'd heard her laugh before, in the diner when they spoke. It was light and honest. He liked the way it sounded, especially because it didn't seem as if she did it very often. He didn't notice, but it brought the corners of his mouth to a slight smile.

"Hey, you have a nice smile," she said, leaning over to poke him in the face.

"I-I do not," he protested, swatting her away.

"You should do it more often."

"Yeah, sure."

He gave a slight laugh, not even realizing that it had started to snow. They spent an hour in the park, talking until their hands were frozen and their ears had reddened with the cold. Noticing that it was getting late, she stood up and threw the tail end of her scarf over her shoulder.

"Ferris, let me walk you home."

He'd been rubbing his hands together, breathing some warm air onto his palms when she asked. Curious, he looked up at her from his seat.

"Shouldn't I be walking you home?"

"Are you kidding me? I'm way tougher than you. Plus, I want to see your house."

"Ah, all right."

As he took her offered hand, she startled him by pulling him close. Though he'd stiffened, she didn't let go, taking advantage of his proximity to ask him a question.

"Do you have a girlfriend?"

Ferris swallowed and his face grew unbearably hot. He wasn't sure what was more embarrassing, the fact that she was asking, or that he didn't have a girlfriend of any sort.

"N-no." He made a slight face. "Why?"

"Just curious."

She held onto his arm as they walked, claiming it was to keep them both warmer. He didn't particularly mind and was happy to blame the cold for his reddened expression. He had to stop halfway through to wipe the fog off of his glasses. She didn't let go until they got to his home, looking up at it almost sadly.

"Hey, you want to come in for a minute?"

"Maybe next time," she mumbled, hoping he would understand what she meant. He gave her a faint nod, not pushing her further. She would probably feel out of place in his house, though he knew his mother would probably just try to feed her like any of his other friends.

"Look," he trailed, rubbing the back of his jaw. "If you ever need to get away from your house or… if things are bad, you can always come here."

Ferris motioned up to a window on the second story.

"That's my room."

She smiled in appreciation, nodding. Julie had underestimated his guile, not noticing that he'd put more money into her pocket when they were walking. It had made him even more irritated to hear her father had taken the twenty, but he knew she would just refuse any more handouts. Hopefully she wouldn't notice until she got home.

"Thanks. I'll remember."

"Night, Julie."

She put her arms around his neck, hugging him. Her cheek brushed his as she replied.

"Night, Ferris."

With that, she was gone, taking her warmth with her as he watched from the front steps of his home. He started to regret not setting up another time to meet, but he had a feeling he would still see her again.

From that night on, Julie came to see Ferris much more often. How he'd managed to get all of his studying done, he wasn't quite sure. He began to look forward to school, as each day brought another chance to see her. Demos had even noticed that his friend wasn't quite as grumpy as he normally was. They were both in the study hall together, doing work for separate classes. Ferris had started taking French as well as Italian, having written a letter to allow dual language study.

"Quelle heure est-il?" He had a pencil behind his ear as he mouthed what he was writing. "Il est trois heures et demie."

"Sorry Ferris, can't help you there." Demos was accustomed to correcting his Italian but French went over his head completely.

"It's all right, I got it."

Demos went back to his English paper, glancing occasionally at Ferris over his laptop. He'd been assured that Julie was honest and there was no reason to suspect her of wrongdoing. Even so, he continued to see Ferris around less and less. He hadn't really been himself lately. When he thought about it, was that really so, bad? Ferris was normally distant, lackluster, and cynical. Lately he'd been talking with emotion in his voice and even smiled once in a while.

"So…" Demos cleared his throat. "Ferris."

"Yeah?" He looked up from his book, adjusting the edge of his frames as his head lifted.

"Is Julie… your girlfriend now?"

"Uh—" Ferris seemed caught by the question, but not upset. "No. We're just friends."

"You spend a lot of time with her lately."

"I guess so." Ferris looked back down at his papers, finishing up his writing.

Demos had hit another dead end. He went back to typing his essay, still unable to help but watch Ferris work from the corner of his eye. If he didn't know any better, he might have guessed that there was a fondness in his eyes. Really, who could possibly enjoy French that much?

Later that night Ferris was sitting on his bed, setting his alarm for the next morning. The room went blurry as he set his glasses on the nightstand, pressing his face into the pillow. He felt sore from the day and the cool bedcovers felt good against the ache. The walls snapped into darkness as he turned off the bedside lamp, shutting his eyes to sleep.

Recently, he hadn't been thinking about the corpse, or the mob, or being a social disaster. Though he had a tendency to experience insomnia, that night he quickly fell into a deep, comfortable sleep.

Stanley was the first to notice the noises at the window. He stood at the foot of the bed, bristling and stamping his paws. After about a minute of this, Ferris cracked an eye open. He didn't look pleased to be woken up, groggily mumbling at the pug.

"What is it?"

There was another noise outside and he sat up. It sounded like hail. Either the weather had turned bad, or someone was playing golf in his yard. Crawling over the edge of his bed, he peered out the window to see what it was.

44

It seemed that Demos had come up to his house and was throwing small pebbles at his room. That was right – they'd gone through this routine before. He grabbed the fire escape ladder under his bed to drag it over to the window. The glass slid open as Ferris dropped the ladder down, motioning for him to come up. He was still only half awake, squinting and hoping his friend hadn't come over for a casual two a.m. visit.

It was only when the figure had completely come up and over the window ledge that Ferris realized it wasn't really Demos at all.

"Julie?"

It was dark and they had similar physiques – in addition, Ferris lacked both his glasses and proper consciousness.

"H-hey," she said, her voice shaking.

He offered his hand, supporting her as she stepped down.

"What happened?" he whispered, keeping his voice low. It was terribly cold out and he quickly shut the window behind her.

"I'm sorry, I know it's late."

"It's fine. Jesus, you're cold," he muttered. Her fingers felt like ice in his palms. He sat her on the edge of his bed, pulling the blanket up around her shoulders. It was still warm and she clutched it around her arms. Ferris sat next to her, his expression concerned.

"Where's your coat?"

"I ran out too fast."

He was quiet, waiting for her to continue. When she noticed, she turned her head away anxiously. After what seemed like ages, she murmured.

"Dad came home when I was asleep. Mom's still at work..." Julie trailed, leaning on his shoulder and turning to face him more, as if silently asking to be held. Hesitantly, he put a hand on her back, easing her into finishing.

"He was drunk," she stammered. "He tried to grab me. So I just ran away."

"Julie..."

"I'm sorry, I know you were sleeping and—"

"It's okay. I'm glad you came. Ah, just whisper. Mom and Dad are sleeping down the hall."

She nodded, burying her face in his chest. It didn't seem that she had gotten over the incident; she was still nearly shaking in his arms. Stanley was excited by the new visitor, smelling her elbow curiously.

"It's okay," he repeated.

"Let me sleep in your bed." Her whispering was muffled by Ferris' shirt and he wasn't quite sure if he heard her correctly.

"What?"

"Let me sleep here. With you."

45

He watched her uncertainly, not knowing how to answer. It wasn't as if he could just say "no." Why would he say no anyway – what was he afraid of? He didn't think he'd ever been in the same bed as another person, not to mention a girl. Taking in a breath, he relaxed.

"Okay."

They lay down in the bed, facing each other. She curled her head in, closing her eyes and mumbling.

"I'm so tired."

"Julie... you'll have to leave before six. My mom comes and checks on me, and—"

"I understand," she whispered sleepily. Before he could get another word in, she had already passed out. The extent of her exhaustion was evident as he watched her, realizing he'd never seen her sleep before. She seemed peaceful, an expression that was rare for her face. His dog gave up trying to get attention from her, finally realizing that she was much more interested in sleeping than in him. The pug curled back up on the edge of the bed and was soon snoring again. It wasn't long after that Ferris fell back asleep as well, not noticing when she curled up against him for warmth.

It was six a.m. on the dot when he was stirred by a knock on the door.

"Ferris? You awake?"

His mother liked to make sure he was conscious before his alarm even went off and this morning was no exception. He felt a quick panic as he looked to the side, wondering what the hell he was going to do with Julie.

He stared, blinking at the empty spot on the bed. She was already gone.

"Yeah, Mom."

"Good, don't fall back asleep!"

"Uh huh."

Ferris would have wondered if the entire thing had been a dream, but a flat palm on the mattress answered his question. It was still warm. His legs slid out from under the covers and he stepped over to the window, tugging it open. The fire escape ladder was still dangling in place. He held the edge of the frame as he gazed down at the street. The morning looked rather cold and he frowned at the thought of her going through the frost in her pajamas again. It took him a while to double take at the hook on his wall, smirking a little. She'd taken his coat.

05

Ferris pushed his dinner in a tedious circle around his plate, not feeling very hungry that particular evening. His mother's cooking was always good, but there was a knot in his stomach. It was a result of piling several days of anxiety into a final climactic night, leading to one question whose answer would change the rest of his high school experience. He took a sharp breath, cutting into his parents' small talk at the most opportune moment.

"Dad, can I have a computer?"

Harold took a sip of his water, raising his eyebrows at his son.

"What do you need a computer for?"

"Schoolwork." He already had this thought out. "Research, programming, and uh—"

He mumbled the next part.

"Gaming."

"Well, what's wrong with our computer?"

"I need my own. You're using it half the time, for your work. If I got my own, then it would just be your personal computer instead of ours."

"What about me?" Ruth chimed in.

"You never use it, honey."

"What's that supposed to mean? I use internets all the time!"

"*The* internet, Mom."

"Whatever." She looked away, unconsciously turning her nose up at the conversation.

"Quit your kvetching, Ruth, he's trying to make a point."

"Yeah, yeah." She waved her hand in irritation, as if shooing him away.

"So I think it would be a good investment, Dad."

"I completely agree," Harold replied easily, rubbing his beard.

"Really? You do?"

"Of course. I fully support you. So, how are you going to pay for it?"

Ferris glared at his father, not appreciating his sense of humor at the moment.

"Dad, that's why I was asking you."

"Well really, if it's your computer, you should pay for it."

"I don't have any money."

"That's what jobs are for," his father replied cheerfully.

"Oh Harold, just buy him one. Quit being so cheap," Ruth chided, hitting her husband's arm with a napkin.

"He needs to learn the value of a dollar."

"Bist meshugeh? He's fourteen years old!"

Ferris buried his face in his hands. His parents continued to bicker for the next 45 minutes as their food got cold. He should have known better than to bring it up at dinner; a long informative letter might have been a better plan. The argument had gotten nowhere as a result of Harold's determination to make Ferris get a job and Ruth's general stubbornness about anything and everything.

"Can I be excused, please?" Ferris finally interrupted, looking weary.

"You get a job if you want that computer, and that's final."

"All right, Dad."

"Don't listen to your father, bubele, he's just like your zayde."

"Hey, you leave him out of this," Harold protested.

Before the sound of their back-and-forthing could be permanently embedded in his head, he left the table, taking his plate to the kitchen and putting it in the sink. The hot water ran over his hands as he grew lost in thought. He was certain that one had to be at least sixteen to hold a normal job, so he would have to do something menial like raking leaves or dog walking.

When he started to feel bitter about it, he was unexpectedly reminded of Julie. Her family didn't even own a computer, not to mention one for each of them. Ferris also thought of her mother, who worked two jobs to feed three children in a cramped apartment. She never complained, did she?

After wiping his hands dry with a dish towel, he replaced it on the hook and went upstairs to start a list of possible job opportunities. Hopefully being under the legal age limit to work wouldn't put too much of a damper on his search.

The question came up once again during lunch at school. Demos was nearing the age where girls were starting to notice how attractive he was and he enjoyed spending lunchtime as far away from them as possible. Ferris had no qualms with being away from gaggles of other high schoolers. They happily spent their lunch period in an empty classroom, sitting on the desks in privacy. The room was massive and open, with a freestanding chalkboard near one end and wooden desks lined in rows facing it. Several shelves of books created a makeshift wall along the other side.

"A job, really?"

Ferris looked over his unimpressive cheese sandwich with disdain.

"Yeah. Or I can't get a computer."

"Hey, we could just rob a bank."

Ferris looked over at Demos, unimpressed.

"I'm just joking, come on."

"With you, I never really know."

"Well, I can help you get a job."

"I'm not going to kill anyone for you, Demos."

"No really, maybe in our restaurant? I mean, with all the shady crap they do, I'm sure that hiring a minor won't really be a big issue. We can just pay you cash."

"You know, that's actually not that bad of an idea."

"You sound surprised," Demos muttered.

"Hey, you work there sometimes too, don't you?"

"When they need help. Grandpa is teaching me how to cook." Demos finished his leftover manicotti with a plastic fork, closing the Tupperware his aunt had given him that morning. "Come with me to the restaurant after school, we can talk to him."

"Sure, thanks."

The night was busy for a Wednesday. They had received many reservations and the kitchen was noisy with the sounds of cooking and talking. Gino was standing by the bar, engaged in a hearty conversation with Victor and a customer. He had founded and owned the restaurant, but knew he was getting too old to control both a crime syndicate and a dining establishment. His son Roberto would be coming to the States in a few years to help him run things. Until then, Gino was aided by Victor and some trusted associates.

Demos and Ferris weaved through the many people and wait staff, approaching the older men respectfully. Gino was, as always, quite pleased to see his grandson. He put an arm around the teen's shoulder, introducing him to the guest they were speaking to. Demos nodded and shook the man's hand politely, giving the good impression he was trained to.

"If you'll excuse us, I need to catch up with my grandson."

"Of course, Mr. Giorgetti. It was a pleasure."

They shook hands again and the man moved to a table, leaving the four of them alone. Gino turned his attention to Ferris, smiling at him in a way that only an old Italian gentleman could. His face was aged with crow's feet and ashy eyebrows, but his eyes were bright blue and expressive.

"Ferris, good to see you here. You'll have dinner, yes?"

"Actually, Mr. Giorgetti, I wanted to ask you if you had any openings in your staff."

"Ferris needs a job," Demos cut in, putting his hand on Gino's shoulder. "There's plenty he could do, right?"

Gino considered Demos' friend for a moment as his eyes went into a state of thought. Victor was leaning on the bar with a hand in his pocket, the other straightening the rims of his glasses.

"He's a good kid, Dad." The man gave Ferris a knowing look and the teen knew exactly what had made Victor think he was trustworthy. As much as it bothered him, he had never said a word about the body in the trunk.

"Yes, yes, of course. As long as you stay and eat something."

"R-right." Ferris couldn't have protested if he wanted to, immediately being led away by the wrist. "Thank you, Sir."

Victor led the two boys to the back room, leaving Gino to finish his work. Ferris hypothesized that that was probably the easiest job interview he would ever have in his life. It had been so simple that he wondered what the catch was going to be.

"You two sit here, I'll bring you some manicotti."

"Aunt Vanni packed me some for lunch," Demos protested.

"Oh, right, of course. I'll get you some chicken marsala." He held up one finger, motioning for them to stay put. "Hold on a second."

Demos leaned forward on the table casually as Ferris looked towards the door.

"I wonder what they're going to have me do. Dishes, I guess?"

"Maybe. I do prep work, like weighing out the pasta and everything. Oh, you'd make a slick waiter."

"Yeah, a fourteen-year-old waiter. I hope the Department of Labor head comes in for a bite. It'll be real good times."

Demos laughed, folding his arms across his chest with a shrug.

"Grandpa's got every cop and judge from here to Jersey bribed somehow or another."

Victor came back in, pushing the door open with his hip as both of his hands were occupied with plates.

"Mangia, have some wine too."

"Thanks, Uncle Vic."

"No problem, boys." He turned his attention to the left. "Ferris."

"Yes, Sir?"

"You start next Monday. And no need to call me 'Sir.' I like that, you're a mannered kid, but we're family, okay?"

"All right, thanks."

Once the man was gone, Demos raised his glass to toast.

"Well, here's to your new career."

Ferris smirked, not sure which was more disturbing — a career as a dishwasher, or a career with the mob.

06

Julie Ward lived north of what used to be the meat packing district in Southport. The building her family lived in was a five-story walkup, with their apartment on the fourth floor. The evening had been loud and unpleasant in their home. Julie's older sister had lost an earring, blaming Julie for it, who insisted there was no fathomable reason she would steal one single earring. The youngest sister, a toddler, had responded to the situation by crying. Rather than deal with the embarrassment of showing Ferris even more of her dysfunctional family, she'd dragged him out into the stairway and up to the roof. Most buildings in Southport had locked rooftop access, but their superintendent hadn't given a damn for at least a decade.

Winter was giving way to spring, making the temperature outside still cold, but bearable. Breathing out a puff of air in frustration, Julie started to fish through her pockets for a cigarette.

"I hate that bitch," she mumbled, cupping her hand around the cigarette and lighting it against the wind.

Ferris looked out over the city, though a five-story height didn't provide that impressive of a view. He paused before speaking, clearly hesitant about what he was going to say.

"Have you considered quitting?"

"Smoking?"

"No, water polo."

"Shut up, smart ass," she said, shoving his arm.

"I'm serious."

"I know," she replied, tipping some ashes onto the street below. "I'll try later."

He made a face and shrugged, giving up for the time being. Grinning, she reached over to his face, trying to grab his frames.

"Let me try on your glasses."

"Hey, come on. Don't—" he stammered as she slid the plastic frames off of his ears. "Give them back, I can't see a damn thing."

She held them out of reach, looking up through the glass like a telescope before trying them on.

"Jesus, ow. You're so blind."

"Thanks, I know. Now you see why I need them back."

"So, if I ran away from you right now," she mused, "you couldn't catch me?"

"I'd fall down a stairwell and die, yes. Can I have them now?"

She took them off, folding the frames in her hands and putting her face up close to his.

"So, can you see my face?"

He forgot to be irked for a second, distracted by her proximity.

"A little."

She pushed up against him, keeping her nose inches from his.

"What color are my eyes?"

"I think you'd have been able to figure that out by now, Julie."

"No, really."

He looked at her carefully. It was dark, but the city was lit well enough to highlight her features.

"They're green. I think." He squinted. "Are they?"

"That's right."

He forgot to ask for his glasses back, momentarily content to just watch her. He didn't protest when she pocketed them, putting her hands on his face. Her fingers touched over his cheek and before he realized what was happening, she was kissing him.

It didn't register at first. He was very fond of Julie and thought of her as a good friend. He did not, however, ever assume he had a chance with her beyond friendship. Any flirting she might have done went over his head into what he assumed was a joke. So this, what she was doing with her mouth, had taken him by surprise. His eyes opened quickly and he tensed; his pupils shrank and locked on her.

After a second he relaxed, allowing his eyes to close. He could feel her breath on his face when she pulled back – it only lasted a moment and she moved in once again. Her arms had wrapped around his neck and he was lost on what to do. Trying his best, he put his hands around her, carefully returning the kiss. A very unromantic car alarm went off several blocks away, but he didn't notice.

She kept her mouth close to his as she whispered, keeping her eyelids half open.

"Ferris."

"Mhm?"

"I want to be your girlfriend."

To her surprise, he laughed.

"No, you don't."

"Yes I do," she insisted.

"I'm a nerd."

"I like nerds."

"Sure."

"Ferris," she said firmly, grabbing him by the face and making her look at him. Her eyes were intense and she knit her brow at him. "Take me seriously."

52

"I am." His voice calmed, growing quieter.

"Then tell me yes or no."

He was about to make another dry remark when he remembered he was taking her seriously. He couldn't imagine anyone saying 'no' to her and certainly wasn't about to now.

"Yes."

"Good." She smiled, touching the back of his neck.

"Can I have my glasses back, now?"

"No."

He reached for her pockets as she squirmed away, laughing as he pulled them out and slipped them back over his nose. Narrowing his eyes at her, he blinked as if making a realization.

"Oh shit, you're Julie. I thought it was someone else."

"Shut up."

"I take it back, I can't go out with *you*."

"You really are a nerd," she smirked, flattening her palm on his face as he backpedaled to get away.

He stayed with her on the roof for another half hour, but it quickly grew too dark and too cold. She'd kissed him goodbye when he left. Ferris had a feeling in his chest that was so warm and so tight that he could have happily fallen through a frozen lake and felt right as rain about it. His hands went into his pockets as he walked home, feeling light in his breath and in his steps. Even speckling, cold rain on the sidewalk didn't ruin his mood. When it started to come down harder, he took shelter underneath a bodega awning, looking down the street for a cab to take home.

His heartbeat was weightless and fast; he could still feel her and hear her. Something that seemed impossible had really happened and it was still slowly clicking in his mind that he had a girlfriend. The only thing that could have distracted him from his thoughts as he patted his own pockets was the fact that he had no wallet for cab fare.

Confused, he checked his pants pockets as well as his coat's, trying to think of the last time he'd seen it. Maybe it had fallen out on the roof when they were playing around. Though this was a setback, it was a small one, and he backtracked towards her building in the same warm mood.

Climbing the five sets of stairs was never very easy for him and he was out of breath by the time he was at the roof. The access door had been left open.

Ferris was about to step out to the roof when he heard voices. Unsure of what he was hearing, he stepped back into the stairwell before he was seen. His eyes glanced around the edge, trying to figure out who the figures were. After a bit of squinting he could see Julie's silhouette. Next to her was a boy holding an umbrella. He might not have even called the figure a boy, as he was at least a few years older than she was.

"When did he leave?" The male voice sounded irritated.

"I don't know, I guess ten minutes ago."

She started to touch the stranger's face with a fondness that made Ferris' heart stop. His breath caught when he saw her lean closer, wrapping her arms around the boy's neck for a slow, deep kiss. Ferris' throat started to feel raw. The kiss lasted for a minute; he could hear the wet sound their lips made together and suddenly felt nauseated. Finally they separated and the boy grumbled against the wet air.

"Did he give you anything this time?"

"Yes, and no." She sounded pleased with herself.

"What's that supposed to mean?"

"I stole his wallet."

Ferris froze against the wall, staring ahead blankly as he listened.

"Let me see." There was a pause. "Holy shit, there's like sixty bucks in here."

"I know, he always has money. He won't even notice until he gets home."

"God, I hate these spoiled kids. We have to work so fucking hard for shit and they just lay around and do nothing."

"I know," she responded calmly.

"How much is that now?"

"Well, he's given me like 120 so far, so this makes it 180, right?"

"This is the best idea you ever had. Just forty-six dollars and fifty cents and we can get those tickets. We'll be in California, Julie. No more of this family bullshit."

"I know. I can't wait. Maybe I'll just tell him my dad took my money again."

"He falls for that?"

"Yeah. Seriously, fuck this place, Brandon. I need to be out of here so bad."

Ferris stopped hearing what they were saying. His brain couldn't put words together and understand them as sentences anymore. His heart had dropped into his stomach and he felt like he could throw it up if given the word.

He hadn't blinked for a whole minute, still staring at the peeling paint on the opposite wall. His hands were shaking as he gripped his coat sleeves, unsure of whether he could continue standing or not. He wanted to die. He wanted to go down the stairs, miss a step, and crack his head open.

Somehow, his eyes were dry. They were as dry as his hands — as the inside of his mouth and throat. He managed to grip the railing, making it down the stairs without falling to his death.

It was still raining when he went outside. He still couldn't call a cab, as his wallet had remained in her possession. Without

54

an umbrella, he let his eyeglasses dot with droplets as he headed home.

When he came home he didn't greet his parents, only going up to his room and shutting the door. The only hint he left of his presence in their house was a wet trail of rainwater up the stairs. It dripped off of the wood, threatening to warp the finish if not wiped up relatively soon.

The chefs had gone home for the evening, leaving Demos to prep for the next day and Ferris to do the dishes. They had been working quietly in the empty kitchen, not speaking for the last half hour or so.

The silence was making Demos uncomfortable as he sliced bell peppers on a cutting board, listening to the hollow sound of the blade nicking the wood. From the side came the only other sound in the kitchen – the rattling of dishes and the hard spray of water. Ferris had been working robotically, rinsing dishes, setting them onto the plastic rack, and shutting the industrial washer firmly. The machine churned as he went to the next stack of dishes, his expression stoic as he rinsed them one by one. He was either very firmly concentrating on his work, or wasn't thinking about it at all. The machine blinked green and he opened the door, releasing a wall of hot steam and a rack of sterile dishes. His glasses fogged but he didn't make a move to wipe them.

"Ferris, are you okay?"

There was no answer.

"Ferris?"

"Hm?"

"You all right?"

"Yeah," came a flat reply.

Demos looked back down at his vegetables, separating the row of cut pieces apart with a push of his hand. He was quiet for another minute before attempting conversation once again.

"How much do you have saved for your computer now?"

"Nothing," came another dull reply.

"But..." Demos picked up his head, confused. "You've already worked three days. That should be like fifty dollars or so."

"Sixty one dollars," Ferris said in monotone. He still hadn't looked up from his dishes.

"You didn't save it?"

"I bought a Coke." He paused. "Julie has the rest."

"Ferris..." Demos groaned. "I told you not to give her any more money."

"I didn't."

Demos slowly picked up his head, watching his friend carefully as he started to put things together. Ferris hadn't stopped working, moving as if their conversation hadn't happened. He picked up a wine glass, sprayed it clean, and set it on the rack.

"She stole from you?"

"It's not important."

Ferris' hands were red from the scalding water and his fingertips were already starting to get damaged from handling hot plates. His left hand, however, was already so calloused from violin strings that it remained free of any pain or impairment. At the moment he was wrist deep in dishwater, but didn't seem to care. The only thing he could accomplish, other than dishes, was the act of staring down blankly.

Demos kept his eyes on him, knowing it would be pointless to keep asking him questions. It was something Ferris was going to have to tell him on his own. Setting down his knife, he walked up behind his friend and turned off the water. Suddenly cut off, Ferris finally made eye contact with the young Italian.

"Ferris, why don't we take a break? I'll go with you."

"I'm fine."

"Just take ten minutes. I need a smoke anyway."

Ferris looked from Demos to the sink, realizing that his friend wasn't going to take 'no' for an answer. With a heavy breath, he wiped his hands dry on the apron around his waist, untying it and tossing it over to the countertop.

"Okay."

Demos led him out the side door and into the alley. Ferris usually remembered it as the place where he'd seen the dead body in the car trunk. Tonight, however, it didn't cross his mind. All he could see was dark brick and pavement that needed a good sweeping. He leaned against the wall as Demos sat down on the stair, pulling out a cigarette and lighting it with a match. He shook the match out with a couple flicks of his wrist, tossing it down to the ground as he inhaled. Looking over his shoulder, he offered it to Ferris, who declined with a slow shake of his head. They both shared a mutual silence for a while, listening to the cars drive by outside of the alley and a garbage truck two blocks away. Subtly, Demos glanced at his watch.

After exactly six minutes and forty seconds, his patience paid off. Ferris started to speak.

"You were right."

Demos put out his cigarette with the bottom of his shoe, watching it smolder.

"No I wasn't. I only said that because I was jealous."

"I should have listened to you." Ferris' arms were folded across his chest.

"There's no point in regretting it."

"There's no point in a lot of stuff." Ferris sounded distant. "My hands smell like onions. I'm going back inside."

Demos looked up as Ferris pushed open the door, returning to the kitchen. With a sigh, he followed suit, getting up and dusting the side of his pants. He realized that for the time being, it was unlikely he'd be able to coax out any more of what had happened from his friend.

It was two days later that Julie returned to the high school steps to meet Ferris after school. He stood blankly as she approached; his mind battled over whether to be disgusted or simply in agony at the sight of her. He didn't respond to her greeting of a small kiss. She noticed his discomfort and pulled back, speaking with concern in her voice.

"Ferris? What's wrong?"

Eyes half-lidded, he let his gaze go from her eyes down to her palm. He took her by the hand and forced a wad of crumpled bills into it, inside of which were folded two quarters. She furrowed her brow at him, unsure of what to think.

"What is this?"

"It's forty-six dollars and fifty cents. Go to California." He couldn't help but glare as he spoke. "And stay there."

Her eyes widened, exposing the whites in shock.

"I never want to see you again," he snapped, pulling away from her and turning down the street. His heart was pounding in anger and shame and he didn't think he could say any more without breaking down in front of her.

"Wait!" She grabbed his sleeve, which he forced out of her fingers. He continued walking away, and she snatched his wrist in desperation.

"Let me explain, please!"

Finally at his limit, he quickly faced her, jerking his hand away.

"Fuck you, Julie!"

Her grip went limp as she stared at his reaction. She'd never seen him angry before. When she didn't answer, he turned back around, leaving her standing in the middle of the sidewalk. Any explanation she might have given him would only have been another lie.

Julie stared down at the wrinkled money in her hand, unable to explain the ache in her chest. By the time she picked up her head, he was gone.

The next day Ferris was sitting in the living room to study, though it was a futile effort. He still could not concentrate on even the simplest tasks and his handwriting had deteriorated into illegible scrawl. His palm supported his chin as he stopped reading, taking in a short breath. Stanley was sleeping next to him, making his usual distorted snoring noises and squirming a bit in his sleep. It seemed as if nothing could wake the dog until the doorbell rang, sending a pleasant chime through the house. Stanley was roused from his dream, huffing and making a few tired barks towards the door.

"Shut up Stan," Ferris mumbled, pushing himself up by the coffee table and making his way to the front. The bolt unlocked and he cracked the door open, looking through to see who it was. To his surprise, it was nobody.

Knitting his eyebrows, he opened the door all the way, looking up and down the street. There wasn't anyone around. He started to think it was a stupid neighborhood kid playing a prank when his eyes caught something sitting on the stoop.

It was his wallet.

He'd been trying his best not to think about her, but she was once again being shoved into his face. His eyes softened as he crouched down, picking it up and looking it over in his hands. He stood, staying in the doorway for a while before getting the nerve to open it up. His school ID was still inside, along with a frequent coffee house card and a pass for an arcade. There was no money in it, but in its place was a yellow sticky note.

He unfolded it with two fingers, frowning as he read over the two words written with blue pen.

I'm sorry.

"So am I," he mumbled, crumpling it up in his hand and tossing it into the bushes. He normally wasn't one to litter, but in this case he made an exception. Not caring if she was watching somewhere, he shut the door, going back inside to finish his attempt at studying.

Julie had a lot to think about as she boarded the 4:50 bus to San Diego. The sky was overcast and gray, not giving her very much to miss for her last look at Southport. Brandon snapped at her, reminding her to hurry up and stop standing around. She adjusted the strap of her bag, going down the narrow aisle and taking her seat next to him. An elderly man was seated across the aisle with a clarinet case, but the bus was mostly empty. Her forehead pressed up against the glass and her breath fogged the window. Julie didn't speak as the bus pulled out of the station, leaving behind the city, her past, and her regrets.

07

The first year of high school had come and gone. Ferris eventually stopped feeling sorry for himself, continuing to make perfect scores in class and working at the restaurant twice a week. He had finished his freshman year with straight A's and Demos came in after with a basic B average. Demos was still the target of attention for the girls in the school, but in a matter of delicious misfortune, he had no interest in any of them. Ferris had calculated that Demos was more than likely going to end up interested in boys, mostly because fate had a cruel and ironic sense of humor.

It was summer now and the days were long and humid. Ferris was growing closer to his goal, having about half of the money required to buy a computer. His job wasn't very fulfilling but it wasn't difficult either. He estimated that they gave him twice his salary in free food each night, especially considering that it was a five-star restaurant with an exclusive set of patrons. Once in a while Victor would slip him a few extra twenties, just to be nice. The summer was slower than the other seasons. Many restaurants received more business from the tourists, but Giorgetti's regular customers were at their summer homes elsewhere or vacationing thousands of miles away. It was during these dawdling hours that Victor would sometimes send Ferris on errands, delivering cash or messages to nearby locations. Little Italy was sweltering hot and the air was sweet with the scent of gelato and ice. He didn't mind getting out of the kitchen, even if it meant going into the heat.

That evening had been especially slow and he was sitting on a barstool near the back counter. His elbow was resting on the steel surface, idly reading a book to pass the time. Demos wasn't working that night and the kitchen was nearly empty. Victor was standing next to him, murmuring over some papers on a clipboard as he tapped his pen on the edge.

"Hey Victor, Sal's here!" called a voice from the dining area as the door cracked open. Victor sighed, rolling his eyes.

"The fuck does he want."

Ferris tried to hide his smirk as the older man begrudgingly set down his clipboard, pushing through the swinging kitchen doors to go see what Sal was going to complain about this time.

A minute or so passed before Ferris' curiosity started to poke at him. He glanced at the papers Victor had left from the corner of his eye, then looked over to the kitchen entrance. His attempts to stay focused on his book were proving useless and he eventually gave in to hover over the clipboard with interest.

It seemed to be a record of numbers. The restaurant's costs, outside income, and everything else was written down. His eyes flickered over each figure and his mind started to calculate unconsciously. Forgetting his place, he picked up the pen and started to write.

He scratched things out, doing multiplication in his head and division in the margins. After about fifteen minutes of this, he had crossed out the final total, $29,986, and replaced it with a new one, $41,550.

It was just then that Victor returned, raising his eyebrows at the teenaged boy who was writing on his very important documents.

"Whoa, hey, what're you doing?" He snatched the clipboard back, looking irritated as he read over what had been scribbled. Ferris didn't have very good handwriting.

"Oh, sorry," he apologized, suddenly realizing what he'd done and feeling embarrassed.

"How do you figure this? That's impossible," Victor questioned, circling Ferris' new number with the pen inquisitively.

"You forgot to add in the bar revenue. The liquor was all through the backdoor, so you don't need to figure in the tax. But you're right, that's incorrect," he admitted. "You would really have to emphasize the desserts. It says here only eight percent of customers order any, but desserts have a really high profit margin."

Victor stared as Ferris continued, explaining with more handwriting on the paper.

"I think if you added a few new options and put them on display, they could go up to maybe thirty or forty percent. The new total I figured out is with a thirty percent dessert rate, which I really think you guys could accomplish with no problems."

He clicked the end of the pen, snapping the tip back up into the body.

"Plus, dessert always adds to customer satisfaction, which is good for everyone, right?"

When all Victor did was stare at him some more, Ferris cleared his throat.

"I'm not just saying this to get some pastries. I don't even really like dessert..."

He trailed off, making an awkward face and looking away.

"Sorry I wrote on your paperwork," he mumbled.

Victor blinked, as if shaking himself from a daze. He quickly put his hand on Ferris' shoulder, getting the boy's attention once again.

"No, no. Va bene! No wonder they say you're a genius, this is perfect."

"Who says I'm a genius?" Ferris looked at him incredulously. "My mother?"

"Ridiculous, a boy like you, washing dishes." Victor pinched Ferris' cheek firmly, apparently very pleased. "I'll get you a big tip this week."

"Uh, yeah. Sure," Ferris answered with disbelief. At the time he wasn't quite aware exactly how big of a tip Victor was describing, and if he did, he'd probably have fallen off of his barstool.

The next evening Harold Levinstein was sitting at the dinner table, reading a newspaper with a cup of coffee. Ferris had been standing in front of him, unnoticed until he cleared his throat. His father looked up, and Ferris motioned down to the table. Curious, Harold lowered his newspaper.

The last thing he expected to find sitting on his dining table was a row of neatly stacked twenty dollar bills. He glanced up at his son, who looked determined.

"What is all this, for my birthday?"

"I saved up enough to buy my computer."

Harold raised his eyebrows, lowering his glasses and looking carefully at the money. He made a couple thoughtful sounds, touching his beard in speculation.

"I see."

"So I'd like you to take this and let me use your credit card."

"Ferris." It seemed almost as if Harold had ignored the last thing his son had said. "You did a good job. I'm proud of you."

Ferris looked worried – something felt as if it wasn't going to go to plan.

"What I want you to do," he started, "is take this money and open up a bank account. Save it."

"But—"

"And I'll buy you a new computer."

Ferris took a second to realize what his father had said and he blinked in brief shock. The worried, frustrated look he had changed quickly to a smile, and he forced a short laugh.

"Thanks, Dad."

"And in twenty years, when it's built up, you're going to buy me a Lexus."

"Yeah, sure, whatever you want."

Ferris hugged him around the neck, seeing as his father was too comfortable to get out of his seat. Ferris looked back at his piles of cash, starting to wonder if he was going to end up keeping his job or not. Though it was menial and paid very little, he did know that he would definitely miss the free Linguine al Salmone.

08

The boy's bathroom on the second floor of St. Basil's Private Academy was empty but for one person. While the other students were in class, Ferris had excused himself on account of a terrible headache. He stood in front of the sink, leaning on it with one hand. The other hand held his temple in discomfort as the tight, grinding feeling didn't seem to be going away.

"Damn it," he muttered, shutting his eyes and wishing he hadn't run out of aspirin. He'd been prone to headaches for most of his life, but recently they had become more frequent and painful. Normally he had a bottle of aspirin in his bag but he had used the last of it the day before. As if his day could not get any worse, someone was about to track him into the bathroom.

Seamus Aston had been attending the school for a little over a month. His mother had moved to Southport from London to attend an alcoholic rehabilitation center, one which she had already abandoned in favor of lying around the house in a drunken stupor. She was rolling in alimony and perfectly happy accomplishing nothing at all.

Seamus, though given an Irish name, was English. His father's favorite poet, by the name of Seamus Heaney, was his namesake. Mr. Aston no longer lived with them, but did provide enough money for Seamus to attend a first-rate private school. Because the teen was well off but neglected, he had several mild emotional issues, one of which occasionally led him to bullying.

Ferris discovered this mental issue firsthand as he was pushed up against a bathroom stall, his shoulder blades knocking hard into the painted metal. His suit collar had been snagged with two fists, their grip nearly lifting him from the floor.

"You look like a smart one." Seamus' English accent was glaringly evident.

"Um, thanks," Ferris mumbled, glaring at his attacker.

"Happen to be any good at maths?"

"Look, if you want my lunch money or something, all I have is kugel, which you probably won't even like—"

The taller boy interrupted him, shoving him harder against the stall.

"I didn't ask for money, I'm asking for answers," Seamus snapped.

"That's very deep, but I really should be getting back to—"

'To' was the last word he managed to say as the Brit's fist found its way into his abdomen. Ferris wheezed, groaning in pain and subsequently shutting up.

"Test answers. Sources say you're the smartest little shit in this school, so I figure you can provide me with some numbers to work with."

"Take your fucking hands off of me," Ferris replied with gritted teeth. His dentist had told him many times to stop grinding his teeth, but it was usually an unconscious effort that he didn't notice himself doing.

"What was that?"

"I thought they spoke English in England."

"And I thought this was the land of the free."

Ferris narrowed his eyes, taking a good look at his assailant. Other than being tall, he didn't have any of the traits of a regular bully. Rather than looking awkward or too big for his clothes, the boy was actually fairly handsome. His face appeared to be the type that, when not shoving other students up against bathroom stalls, could charm young and old alike. His bleached hair was naturally dark, evident from his black sideburns and eyebrows. Ferris, however, did not give a damn how charming or attractive this particular individual was. All he really wanted was to be let go and to maybe hit the guy back a little. That punch to his stomach had really hurt.

"I'm not giving you test answers."

"Then I'm going to have to rough you up. I apologize in advance," Seamus said with a hint of mockery in his tone.

Ferris was thrown to the opposite bathroom wall, his face hitting the tile with a crunch. As his attacker came at him, Ferris finally pulled back and punched him hard across the jaw. They grabbed each other, each trying to get the upper hand before the boy grabbed him again. He was forced up against a sink, arm twisted behind his back as the Brit muttered into his ear from behind.

"You're just making this harder than it needs to be."

"What are you going to do with them, anyway? Sell them?" Ferris gasped, struggling back against him. "Demos already has that market covered."

His nose was bleeding and it dripped red circles onto the white porcelain sink.

"Jokes on you, mate. I'm working with Demos."

"No you're not," Ferris mumbled, unimpressed.

"How would you know?"

"He's my best friend and he wouldn't deal with a stupid ape like you."

The English boy stopped, not answering for a few seconds. Then, suddenly, he let go. Ferris turned to look at him dubiously. The boy was scratching the side of his ear, considering Ferris thoughtfully.

"You really do know him?"

"Yes, I know him," Ferris snapped impatiently.

"Well then, sorry about all that." The boy dusted his hands, suddenly laughing. "He'll be pretty mad when he finds out, won't he?"

Ferris gawked at him, bruised and still bleeding from his nose.

"Well, anyway, I go by Seamus." He wet a paper towel in the sink, leaning in to wipe the blood off of Ferris' upper lip. Ferris only turned away, not accepting the gesture and looking very annoyed.

"Oh come on. I apologized, didn't I?" Seamus insisted.

"Yeah," he muttered, snatching the paper towel from him and wiping the blood off himself. "I don't think 'sorry' cuts it, you probably broke one of my ribs."

Seamus looked at Ferris' reflection in the mirror, standing behind him almost cheerfully.

"Well, let me make it up to you."

"Okay. You can start by staying 200 feet away from me at all times."

"Moody little bugger, aren't you?"

Ferris frowned, glaring at Seamus' reflection with little amusement in his eyes.

"You wouldn't happen to have any aspirin on you?"

"Sorry. Got a flask, though." Seamus pulled it out from the inside of his blazer, shaking it a little to see how much was inside.

"No thanks." Ferris leaned in to the mirror, wiping off the last bit of blood from his chin. "How do you know Demos, anyway?"

"Helped him out of a little tough spot. He's clever but bloody useless in a fight." Seamus unscrewed the cap of his flask, taking a swig of the liquor inside.

"That about sums him up."

Ferris tossed the bloody paper towel into the trash can, unbuttoning his suit to straighten his tie. Well, at least his headache wasn't the least of his problems anymore, if that could be considered a good thing.

"I'm going back to class," Ferris said bluntly. "You should too."

"In a bit. I'll see you 'round lunch then?"

"Not if I can help it."

"Great, catch you then," Seamus replied cheerfully, ignoring Ferris' cynicism. He was taking another drink from his flask when Ferris left, not giving him another reply. As Ferris walked down the empty hall he touched his sore jaw, narrowing his eyes at the nerve of that guy. He was definitely going to have to talk to Demos about this.

It was at lunch the same day that Demos asked what the hell had happened to Ferris' face, something his friend was glad to reply to.

"Seamus happened to my face."

"You know Seamus?"

"Unfortunately. He tried to get test answers out of me."

"What?"

"He cornered me in the bathroom until I told him I knew you. Is he in on your little scheme now?"

"Well, yeah, but when he said he'd take care of the answers I didn't know he'd—"

"It's fine," Ferris muttered.

"God, what an idiot." He glanced at Ferris suddenly, having an idea. "Hey, you want in on it too? I'll cut you a third."

"You want me to provide you with test answers that other students can buy?"

"Pretty much."

"I have no interest in helping these idiots cheat their way into Ivy League."

"If it's not like this, they'll find another way. Anyway, I made $400 last month."

Ferris picked up his head, his interest piqued.

"And," Demos continued, "if you're in on it we can sell twice as many."

Ferris looked thoughtful, sucking on his bottle of water in consideration.

"I'll try it once. If I hate it, I'm out."

"Great," Demos said with a smile, shaking Ferris' hand to seal the deal. "No problem."

Finishing his water, Ferris wondered if he'd made a mistake, or if he could possibly predict what he was getting himself into.

09

Partita No. 2 by Bach swelled through the second bedroom of the Levinstein house. Ferris had now been playing violin for over nine years and had been practicing between thirty minutes to an hour nearly every day of those nine years. The violin that was tucked below his chin was made of dark, stained Yugoslavian maple. He had finally grown enough to warrant the need for an adult sized instrument and his parents had made a substantial investment in the violin.

His normally stoic eyes would soften when he played. Any emotion that he may have bottled up over time occasionally found a way out through the bow, giving his instructor the impression that he was expressive. At the moment he was going over a song he particularly liked, not really in the mood to practice the pieces he'd been assigned. He was a member of the Southport Youth Symphony Orchestra, now given a chance to once again work with a group. He was one of the top three violin students, along with two girls of exceptional talent. His third finger pressed down smoothly, using vibrato to add a slow warmth to the note.

Though he liked to play with his eyes closed, he opened them to watch the rain outside. It was coming down hard enough to spatter across the glass, leaving long, wet trails down the length of the window. He had decided to play without his mute, enjoying the full sound of the song. It continued to haunt the corners of his room and down the hall of their home, unnoticed by his napping father and absent mother.

Though in many ways he was wholly unremarkable, Ferris had several distinct skills. He could multiply three digit numbers in his head, mark any country on a blank map of the world along with its capital, and had been tuning his own instrument before his peers had even finished learning the different strings. Despite all of this, he was still lacking in social graces and had not yet discovered the proper way to smile.

There was a low rumble outside as a sharp snap of lightning reflected across the opposite wall. He waited a few moments, counting the seconds before a peal of thunder followed suit. He stopped at six seconds; it was 1.2 miles away.

It was just as well that a storm was coming; he had finished his song. He held the bow in his lap, loosening the screw and sliding it back in place. The hard case was black and lined with blue velvet. It comfortably held the instrument, two bows, his rosin, and a soft cloth.

It was at that moment that the telephone rang, as if it had been waiting for him to end his playing. It rang down the hall in the study and he tentatively willed himself up and out of his room to go answer it. The plastic of the receiver felt cool in his palm as he picked it up.

"Hello?"

"Ferris?"

"Hey Demos," he replied, tucking the phone between his shoulder and ear.

"Hey. You doing anything right now?"

Ferris glanced out of the study window, watching the rain come down harder.

"Not... really. Why?"

"Eric didn't come in today and we need some help in the kitchen. Do you want to come down?"

"No, but I will," he replied bluntly. He needed the money.

"Great, thanks! See you soon."

Ferris said goodbye and hung up the phone, making a face at the weather and wondering if Eric had just decided it was too disgusting of a day to get out of bed. Going back into his room, he picked through his closet to find something that he wouldn't mind getting wet. The best he could manage was a hooded sweatshirt.

He led his bike onto the sidewalk, pulling the hood up over his head and stuffing a plastic bag into his pocket for the seat. Already noticing specks of rain forming dots on his sleeves, he threw a leg over the bar and started to ride.

Riding in the rain was something he understood to be relatively stupid and uncomfortable, but his father did not like to be roused from naps and stealing one of his parents' cars was obviously not an option.

Water spotted over his glasses, obscuring his vision as cars rushed past him. By the time he arrived in Little Italy, he was cold and soaked. He came in through the service door, immediately grabbing the base of his sweatshirt to tug it off over his head.

"Ferris, you're dripping wet," Demos observed as he took the hoodie from Ferris, putting it up on a hook.

"Gosh, am I?" he replied with a subtle sting in his voice.

"Let me get you a coffee before you start."

Ferris dropped the sarcasm – a hot drink sounded ideal. He leaned on a kitchen counter as Demos poured it for him, wiping the water off of his glasses with the dry shirt he had on underneath.

"All we have to do is prep for tomorrow. I'll cut the steaks for Eric, you can chop my salad," Demos explained. He handed the cup to his friend, getting one for himself as well.

"Sure," Ferris answered easily, letting his coffee mug heat his cold hands. His mouth hovered over the rim, waiting for it to be cool enough to drink. He was starting to finally relax when the kitchen door was abruptly pushed open.

"Hey, Demos."

It was a young man with a smart profile and dark brown hair. Ferris had seen him a few times around the restaurant but had never really spoken to him. He didn't look old enough to warrant the need for suspenders but wore a pair of black ones anyhow.

"Yeah, Pi?"

'Pi' was short for Pietro, which was the man's full name. More accurately, his full name was Pietro Giorgetti, the eldest son of Alonzo Giorgetti and the oldest of Demos' cousins. He loved European history and hated being called 'Pi.'

"Have you seen Nick? He was supposed to be here an hour ago."

"Mh, no. Sorry."

"Damn," Pietro muttered, leaving the kitchen and letting the door swing shut. Demos shrugged as he stirred his coffee and Ferris took a slow sip to test the temperature.

They started to talk about school, loitering until Ferris had dried off a bit. He washed his hands, tied an apron around his waist, and slid a long knife out of a drawer. Demos was cutting up a side of beef on the opposite counter, explaining how much he hated one of his teachers. Ferris firmly held a head of lettuce, chopping it with quick, even strokes. It was then that the side door slammed open so quickly that he nearly cut off one of his fingers.

They both looked up instantly to see three men stagger inside, one of them being dragged between the others. Wind and rain rushed in after them as they lay him down onto the tile floor.

"Nicky!"

Demos' eyes widened at the sight of the bleeding man. He stumbled over, going down to his knees to see if Nicky was all right. Ferris could only gape, still holding the knife in one hand and the lettuce in the other.

"What happened?" Demos asked firmly.

Nicky Morello was in bad shape. Dark red blood stained his shirt and poorly shaven face; he'd been shot in the side and there was a shard of glass behind his ear.

"Meeting went to hell," answered Sergio, who was holding up Nicky's head. "Nick started running his mouth and they got tired of his voice."

"Fuckin' pricks deserved every word," muttered Salvatore, the third man who had come in with them.

68

"Damn it, Nick," Demos whispered under his breath. "Sal, you've been shot, right? Can you pick the bullet out?"

"Are you fuckin' kidding me?" Sal blurted. "Since when does being shot make me a doctor?"

"Fine, I'll do it," Demos muttered. Grabbing a thin knife, he asked Sergio to grab a cloth and water. Nicky was wheezing uncomfortably, looking pale as his hands started to tremble.

"Nick, you hear me? Answer me," Demos demanded firmly.

"'Fanculo," Nicky answered in a low groan. A curse word was a satisfactory answer for Demos. At least Nicky was still himself.

"Ferris, get me the wrap in the first aid kit," Demos said, his voice sounding older than it normally did.

Ferris snapped out of his daze, quickly nodding and pulling the kit off of the wall. By the time he'd dug through it and found the gauze, Demos had already cleaned the wound and picked the bullet out. The shard of glass came next. Nicky bit hard on a rag, groaning at the pain of the process. Sergio had been holding him down, keeping him from shifting with firm hands.

Blood seeped along the spaces between the floor tiles, creating a speckled red grid beneath his body. Demos took the cloth wrap from Ferris, working efficiently to close the wound. A couple minutes later he was wiping Nicky's face dry with a clean, hot rag.

"Did someone call Will?" Demos asked, referring to the family physician.

"He's on his way," Sergio replied as he helped to hoist Nicky off of the floor. Together, and with some effort, he and Sal hefted the man out of the room. Pietro had apparently been in the hall, as his panicked voice was clearly heard the moment he saw them.

Demos sighed heavily, eyes locked on the door that Nicky had just gone through. His arms were wet with blood up to his elbows and his apron had been stained as well. Ferris couldn't think of anything to say.

"Demos..." Ferris trailed off.

"Hm?" he answered almost sleepily, looking over his shoulder.

"Where did you learn to—"

"Dad," the Italian replied, letting his eyes fall to the floor. "Oh, Jesus, I better mop this up."

Demos grabbed a bucket from the closet, filling it with cleaner and hot water. He was quiet as he splashed the solution down onto the reddened tiles, mopping it up as if it had been spilled marinara.

"Guess we have to throw this mop out now, huh?" he laughed.

"Uh huh." Ferris rubbed the side of his neck, giving up and sitting down on a stool.

"We should take a break," Demos said as he dumped the water down the drain. "I'm not really in the mood to cut up meat after that."

"Yeah." Ferris took in a deep breath, letting it out slowly. "Seriously."

10

School had been out for two hours, but three sophomores remained on the front steps. Demos and Ferris sat on the stairs, while Seamus was lounging along the concrete banister. The Brit was flipping a cigarette between his fingers, pondering lighting it up. He could only use the excuse that he was foreign so many times before he was expelled for smoking, but he decided that he didn't really care. Snapping open his metal lighter, he let the tip redden and exhaled a puff of soft smoke.

"Sure I can't tempt you, Fer?" Seamus had taken to calling Ferris a nickname that the boy wasn't really fond of, which only encouraged him to use it even more.

"I told you, I don't smoke," Ferris replied bitterly, turning a page in his notebook.

"Your loss," Seamus shrugged, breathing out another plume. He passed it to Demos, who happily accepted the offer. "So how're those problems going?"

"I'm almost done. I haven't taken this class yet, give me a break."

Ferris had been working on the Calculus II midterm. Seamus had managed to steal the original copy; he had a talent for determining exactly when teachers left their classrooms unattended and was able to easily slip in to rifle through their paperwork. He'd taken a high resolution photograph, then placed the paper back in its original spot, completely unscathed. The teacher would be none the wiser, unless perhaps a higher percentage of the class passed than was normal.

Ferris took a second from his work to calculate that they were breaking at least four school rules and they were doing it directly in front of the school. Sometimes he couldn't tell if his friends had a lot of gall or a lot of stupidity.

Seamus had continued attempting to befriend Ferris, but each attempt had been shot down disastrously. His personality led to hair ruffling, teasing, and public spectacle, each of which Ferris had no patience for. Seamus was flirtatious, tactless, and had barely a care in the world. In other words, he was Ferris' complete opposite. If he was summer, Ferris was winter. And if he was smoking and drinking in front of school, Ferris was doing math problems. He considered the last question as he helicoptered a pen between his fingers.

"There, it's finished," he said indignantly, tossing the notebook at Seamus before he could properly catch it. The Brit fumbled with it for a moment before getting a proper hold, glancing over the writing with raised eyebrows.

"Well, great. This means bugger all to me, so I hope it's right."

"It's right."

"I'm trusting you on this one," he deliberated, sounding almost wary.

"It's *right*, so shut up or give it back."

"Seamus is just giving you a hard time," Demos said, leaning back on the stairs.

"When is he *not* giving me a hard time?"

"You're just so easy to tease, Fer," Seamus goaded good-naturedly.

"I'll type these up," Demos cut in, stealing the notebook from Seamus. "I already have a waiting list for this one. I heard the teacher is a real hard ass."

"By the look of those questions, he is," Ferris muttered between his teeth. "Can't wait to take that class."

Before Seamus could answer, the school doors opened. He quickly tossed the cigarette to a step, crushing it with his foot and leaning back casually. A teacher walked out, glancing at them and noticing the smell of smoke, but saying nothing as she made her way to the parking lot. Ferris, an Ivy League hopeful, found himself embarrassed to be associated with Seamus. He'd covered his eyes with a hand, looking down at his calculator as if it were suddenly very fascinating.

When she was out of earshot, Seamus spoke up again.

"Wasted half a fag. Bloody shame." He picked up his foot, looking at the crushed tobacco sadly.

"Maybe it's a sign," said Ferris disdainfully.

"That I should quit smoking?"

"No, that you're half a fag," snapped Ferris, pulling the pencil from behind his ear and starting his own homework. Demos snorted.

"Oh, but I am," quipped Seamus, much to Ferris' astonishment. "In fact, I think I've got a thing for you. It's the real reason I tease you so often."

"Go jump in traffic, Seamus."

Demos laughed, followed by Seamus. Ferris rolled his eyes, putting his attention back to his work. If they were a trio now, he was going to have to get used to Seamus.

That night, Ferris stopped by the restaurant. His intention had only been to drop off some documents from his father, but he had of course been conned into staying for dinner. After several months of testing Ferris' suggested dessert strategy, Ristorante Giorgetti had experienced a hearty increase in profit. On top of this, their customers always left a little fatter and more satisfied. Victor was more than happy to give Ferris another large bonus for his work. Having saved up a significant amount

72

of money, Ferris had eventually given up his job as dishwasher to put more focus on his studies.

He ordered what he usually had — fish. Ristorante Giorgetti carried many different dishes featuring fish, varying from snapper to sea bass, but his favorite was always the salmon. Though Gino had founded the establishment, he no longer had the time to come in and actually cook. The chefs remained true to his recipes, but nothing was quite like receiving a meal prepared by Gino himself. That evening, however, Gino had come in to flex his sautéing muscles and had been happily working for several hours. According to kitchen gossip, only his grandson Demos had come close to matching the ability shown in his dishes.

"You kids want anything else?" asked Sergio, dressed smartly in a waiter's tuxedo.

"Do we have any sfogliatelle left? The one with chestnut mousse," Demos replied between sips of his wine.

"Yeah, sure. What about you, Fish?"

Ferris hesitated at answering to the nickname.

"Me? No, I'm fu—"

"Mangia e stà zitto," Demos interrupted, snapping his fingers at Ferris to shut him up. "He'll have some spumoni."

"Right, be back in a minute," Sergio said with a smirk.

As the young man left their table, Ferris turned his attention to his friend with a squint in his eyes.

"*Fish?* What was that supposed to mean?"

"It's what they call you in the back," Demos said, his attention elsewhere. "It's short for 'Fishbones.'"

"Why the hell would they call me that?"

Demos stopped drinking, setting down his glass and finally turning his gaze over to Ferris. He smiled, as if the answer were obvious.

"It's all you ever leave on your plate."

Ferris observed him for a moment before glancing down at what was left of his meal. True to the tale, all that remained was the white skeleton of a Dover sole.

"Can't they call me something else?" Ferris muttered, reaching for a glass of water.

"How about Jew-fro? I think Sally called you that once. Oh, I know. Heeb. How's Heeb?"

"Okay, fine, I'll stick with 'Fishbones.'"

"It could be worse. They call Nicky 'St. Nick' because he's so fat," Demos mused.

"I don't even have a fro. My hair is like half an inch long," Ferris said, feeling over the back of his head carefully.

"Sal's just jealous because he's going bald and he's not even forty yet."

Before Ferris could complain any more, Sergio returned with a tray and two plates. The sfogliatelle was presented with a vanilla sauce on a white dish and Ferris' spumoni was large enough to feed a couple.

"Jesus Christ, Demos. I can't eat this."

"You have to. Your mother said she'd give me fifty dollars if I fattened you up a bit."

"You conniving little—"

"Cin cin!" Demos interrupted, lifting his wine glass to offer a toast. "To your new nickname, and the promise of a healthy fro in the years to come."

"I hate you sometimes, I really do," Ferris answered, clinking his glass against the young Italian's. His words were overshadowed by the smile on his face.

"L'chaim," Ferris finished, going along with the toast.

They both took a drink, swallowing wine that had been bottled six years ago in a villa across the Atlantic. A nickname really did mean more to him than it seemed. It was a sign of acceptance, however irrelevant or unflattering it was. He didn't have a drop of Italian blood in his body, but somehow they had made him feel like family.

Ferris would later learn of the other nicknames scattered throughout the Giorgettis. Victor was occasionally called 'Ash.' He used his habitual smoking as a front for the term, but anyone worth their salt was aware that he liked to burn down businesses and homes to get his point across. Salvatore was sometimes called the 'Red Hook,' simply taken from the Brooklyn neighborhood of his birth. He didn't mind the nickname, seeing as it was sinister sounding and he was more than proud of being a New Yorker at heart. When Ferris thought about it, his nickname could have been worse. He would much rather be known for eating fish than, of course, sleeping with them.

Having stayed up too late, Ferris was not in a good mood the next day. The trio had given in to conformity for the afternoon and were eating lunch in the dining hall with the other students. The chatter did nothing to help his slowly growing headache. He was examining a potato chip, not really in the mood to eat it.

"You gonna eat that?" Seamus piped up, looking hopeful. Though he came from a disgustingly wealthy family, his mother didn't usually give him any lunch money as a result of being too drunk to remember. What Seamus ate was mostly stolen or scrounged from other students, though once in a while Demos would buy him something. Ferris suspected Seamus would continue this behavior even if he did have sufficient funding, as it appeared to simply be part of his nature.

"Here, take them." Ferris slid the chip bag across the table to Seamus. "I'm not hungry."

"Aw, what's the matter?" Seamus asked, more than happily accepting the bag of chips and eating them with very little delicacy. Ferris raised his eyebrows at him, deciding to pretend that the Brit was sincere in his asking.

"I have a headache."

"You should get that checked out sometime." Demos looked a little worried. "It might be migraines. And if you take too much aspirin it can make your stomach bleed."

"Oh come on, Demos, I'm tryin' to eat here," whined Seamus. He then proceeded to suck a bit of salt off of his thumb.

"I'm fine, I just stayed up too late," Ferris insisted.

"If you say so. You have a lot of stress for a fifteen year old."

"Me? Look at you." Ferris' voice dropped to a mumble. "You picked a bullet out of a guy with a kitchen knife."

"You did what?" Seamus looked intrigued. By now he'd caught on to Demos' lifestyle and what his family did for a living and, like Ferris, it didn't seem to phase him.

"It wasn't a big deal," Demos muttered under his breath.

"Yeah, right." Ferris humored him, taking a drink of his water. It was a few minutes later that his head was starting to feel better, but the atmosphere had turned decidedly sour.

"Hey, Levinstein."

Only students who didn't know him would call him that. He didn't look up at the boys that were behind him, only taking in a breath through his nose and staring forward with half-lidded eyes.

"Yeah?"

"I got a deal for you."

Slowly, he turned around. His elbow rested on the lunchroom table, eyeing the boys with no hint of trust in his expression. Demos and Seamus were both paying attention, not looking any more trusting than Ferris did. He didn't answer, only giving them his vague attention.

The boy grinned, offering him a burger wrapped in foil.

"If you eat this, I'll give you twenty bucks."

Ferris didn't look at it, not in the mood for a stupid game.

"No thanks." He moved to turn back around, but found his shoulder being grabbed. Demos narrowed his eyes.

"I said 'no thanks.'"

"Oh come on. Have you ever even had a bacon cheddar burger before? Do you seriously follow that kosher shit? It's delicious, I swear."

"Fuck off, okay?"

Ferris did, in fact, follow a basically kosher diet. The rules of this lifestyle were fairly complicated, but it did not take a scholar to know that a bacon cheeseburger was definitely not on the list of acceptable foods. Determined to get under his skin, the other student pressed further.

75

"Tell you what, I'll give you *fifty* bucks," he goaded, waving a handful of bills.

Ferris was about to deny him once more when there was a sharp sound of scuffling. The boy had been pinned down to the table behind them, his body knocking a couple of drinks over. The sticky soda dripped down the side, forming a small brown puddle on the floor.

It was Seamus.

Ferris stared in disbelief as the Brit pinned his classmate down by his collar, looking livid.

"Tell you what. You can give *me* fifty dollars to not crack open your fuckin' head."

The boy looked panicked as the surrounding students gawked at them.

"I-it was just a dare, okay?" he stammered, not liking the feral look in Seamus' dark brown eyes.

"Just a 'dare,' huh? Go on, dare me not to hit you."

"W-what? I—"

Seamus punched him hard, sending a blood coated tooth flying across the table. It clattered to the floor, spinning before coming to a brusque stop. The victim's friend only watched uselessly, not having any interest in becoming part of the fight.

"You're not very good at this game, are you?" Seamus pinned him back down to the table by his throat. Inappropriately, he gave a small grin.

By now their one-sided fight had gotten the attention of the staff, who were pushing their way through the crowd of students to bring the fight to a halt. Looking up briefly, Seamus glared back down before snatching the dollar bills out of the boy's hand and stuffing them into his own pocket. His target made no protest, only clutching his swollen jaw in anguish and groaning dramatically.

The instructors were infuriated, unable to believe that students of such a reputable academy would resort to fisticuffs. It hadn't been the only fight that week, but the headmaster enjoyed ignoring that. They were both reprimanded on the spot before being led off for further punishment in the school's office. Seamus looked over his shoulder at Demos and Ferris, giving them both a helpless smile as he was carried off.

The two of them were left wordless as they stared at the empty spot where Seamus had just been. They both knew that he would not only take full blame for the fight, but would charm his way out of expulsion and suffer nothing more than a firm chiding.

"I—" Ferris realized suddenly that speaking was harder work than it seemed. "I can't believe he did that."

Ferris knew Seamus was prone to fighting, but had never expected him to come to his aid so intrepidly.

76

"I can," said Demos softly. His eyes caught the lost tooth underneath one of the tables.

"What do you mean?"

"I know he gives you a hard time, but he cares about you." Demos crumpled up an empty plastic wrapper, cleaning up the table. "He doesn't have that many friends, so he'll do anything for the ones he has."

Ferris went quiet. He didn't realize before, but it was another way they both were similar. They only really had each other.

"You sure he doesn't just like fighting?"

Demos smirked, tossing his trash into the can near the cafeteria exit as they walked out.

An hour later Ferris was still waiting outside of the office, having skipped his next class to go see Seamus. The principal had made several attempts to call his mother, but she had been much too hungover to even bother picking up the receiver. Finally settling on writing a firm letter, they released him from the office. The other student received a long lecture on racial tolerance, spending the rest of his day in the nurse's office.

The office door was made of dark oak and frosted glass and it swung open slowly as Seamus made his way out. He was rubbing the back of his neck indolently when Ferris spoke up.

"Hey."

Turning to see who was speaking, Seamus smiled at the sight of him.

"Oi, you're not in class. I'm stunned."

"Yeah." Ferris looked uncomfortable, trying to put his words together. "I just—"

Slowly, he took in a deep breath.

"Thanks. For sticking up for me."

"Forget it, it was no big deal," Seamus answered, still smiling. "Oh, I wanted to ask you something."

"Hm?"

"Doing anything after school? Besides studying, I mean."

"Not really."

"Want to catch the new Bond film? Demos isn't a fan."

Demos truly wasn't a fan, as James Bond reminded him quite unnervingly of his own father. Though many would thrill at the idea of having a Bond-like parent, Demos found no pleasure in having an English hitman as a dad. Incidentally, like the secret agent, Mr. Belmont had a habit of leaving behind a trail of women.

Ferris considered the offer, his expression softening. He was going to say yes, but not because he felt that he owed Seamus a favor. He was going because he could honestly, and willingly, call him a friend.

"Sounds great."

11

As promised, his father had bought him the laptop he'd been eyeing. It was silver and lightweight, carrying more processing power than many desktops and more drive space than comparable models. Taking advantage of the wireless card, he'd started carrying it to a coffee shop downtown to work on essays. The café was warm and comfortable; it did well but was never crowded or noisy. Ferris was happy to simply sit in the back in an armchair with the computer in his lap. He never spoke to anyone and normally, no one spoke to him. It was an ideal situation.

It was a cold Tuesday evening and he'd opted for the café instead of the school's library. Somehow having coffee with his work made it go more smoothly.

Ferris was growing quickly, having entered the time when boys had the habit of gaining several inches in height. He'd started to shave, as minor an effort it was. Though he kept his lip and jaw clean, he had decided to leave the sideburns in front of his ears. His face, he decided, was rather plain, and there was a chance that they would add something to his features. Idly, he scratched one of them as he went over his English paper for the third time.

He slouched a little, sliding down in the comfortable armchair as he slowly finished his coffee. A pair of headphones fit comfortably over his ears, effectively blocking out the noise of the public around him. This was one of his favorite ways to pass the time. In fact, the moment would have been perfect if one of his peers hadn't decided to sit down in the seat across from him.

It wasn't that she was sitting there, but it was more of the fact that she was looking at him. It made him uneasy and he furrowed his brow, ignoring her and reading further into his paper.

"Hey."

Shutting his eyes bitterly, Ferris pulled at the sides of his headphones, letting them rest around the base of his neck. He exhaled before answering.

"Yeah?"

"Hey, you got any smokes?"

Ferris swallowed hard, slowly looking up at her. He'd heard those words before.

The girl was a year or so older than he was, having red hair to her shoulders and a frank smile. He tried to answer her, but his mind was stumbling over itself. Why was she bothering him?

Why couldn't she just go away and ask someone else? His chest started to feel tight.

"I—" Ferris' words caught in his throat. "I don't smoke."

Bitterly, he put his attention back to his laptop screen, hoping that was all she wanted.

"Oh, me neither." She laughed nervously. "I just wanted an excuse to talk to you."

"Why?" he snapped.

"Well, I—" She seemed caught off guard by his question, not expecting such a harsh response. "I guess, I just thought…"

She'd trailed off, dropping her voice to a mumble.

"I just thought you were cute," she admitted, now reddened from embarrassment. "I'm sorry."

His eyes narrowed. What did she want from him?

His blood was moving through his body at a faster rate. He didn't know why, but he was angry. It must have been his computer; maybe she assumed he was rich. It could have been that he was doing homework — she might have needed an essay done. Whatever it was that she wanted, it annoyed him. His hands clenched on top of his keys, putting his attention back to the screen.

"Sorry. I'm busy," he responded, his voice flat.

She picked up her head, mouth parted slightly. Her expression was different from the friendly, amiable one she had earlier; her eyes were distant.

"Jeez, asshole," she muttered, getting up out of the seat and clutching her coat to her chest. "Fine."

He didn't answer her, keeping his eyes on the typed text as he put his headphones back over his ears.

Without looking back, she left. He was glad that she was gone; he liked having the back corner to himself. Even so, he couldn't help but lose concentration. Knowing she'd only been an irritation, he had no way of explaining the empty ache in his chest when she was gone.

The more he thought about it, the stupider he felt. Was he really such a wreck that he couldn't even be polite to a girl? If his mother were there she'd probably have smacked him upside the back of his head. He couldn't just let Julie fester in his mind like a sore. Almost an entire year had passed. Didn't time heal all wounds? Was there some kind of mental Neosporin for this kind of thing?

Ferris shook his thoughts, turning his attention back to the essay. Cracking the joints in his hand, he started typing the conclusion to his paper. He was nearly finished when a new figure sat down across from him, once again staring in Ferris' direction.

"Look, I—" Ferris started, removing the headphones and looking up. He stopped when he saw who it was.

"I figured you'd be here," Demos said with a smile. "You weren't answering your cell."

"Demos."

"Hi," his friend replied, still smiling. "Grandpa and Uncle Vic are waiting in the car. You're still coming to the show tonight, right?"

"Fuck, I forgot," Ferris sighed, dragging his palm down his face. "Sorry, just let me save this."

"It's all right. Hey."

"Yeah?" Ferris asked, not looking up as he packed his laptop into its bag.

"You okay?"

"I'm fine. Why?"

"You just—" Demos looked out the windows at where the car was waiting. Victor was parked in front of a hydrant, looking particularly impatient. "Never mind, let's go."

They both piled into the back, quickly shutting the door as Victor pulled out into the street. The traffic that evening was particularly heavy, something Victor was quick to stress over.

"Fucking parade, why can't they do this shit when every asshole in the city isn't trying to get somewhere?"

"It's fine, Victor. There's no hurry," Gino said calmly. Ferris wished that the man's attitude was contagious, as the traffic was getting on his nerves as well.

"Oh yeah, cut off by a cop, too. That's just great," Victor griped as a police car crept into their lane. He tapped his brakes, coming to a complete stop to avoid hitting the bumper. A few minutes later the traffic seemed to ease, allowing them to drive at a decent pace down the expressway. Victor's mood improved only mildly and it didn't last long.

For a reason that wasn't quite clear to the Giorgettis, the police car slammed on its brakes. It had in fact missed its exit and was making a desperate attempt to catch the ramp, but the ensuing collision made the exit the least of their problems. There was a shriek of scraping metal as the headlights of Victor's Lincoln Town Car violently met the other vehicle, sending shattered glass tumbling down the paved stretch of road. Ferris cringed at the sound as a long, gray scar raked down the door of the police car. Victor slammed on the brakes, sending his Lincoln in a sharp curve before halting. Black rubber streaks trailed his tires, sending an unpleasant odor into the air.

The police car stopped several yards away. A moment later, a pair of red and blue lights popped on, accompanied by a few wails of the vehicle's siren. As he threw the door open to look at the damage, Victor's immediate response was less than apologetic.

"*Testa di cazzo!* My car!"

The policemen, both rather young, approached carefully.

80

"Sir, we need you to step away from the vehicle and calm down."

"Protect and serve *my dick*! Look at this!" Victor gestured wildly at the busted headlight. Though he had a foul mouth, he never lost his temper unless it was over something very serious – or his car.

"I can see the damage, Sir. If you could just provide your license and registration, we can—"

"Excuse me, gentlemen," Gino interrupted, getting out of the passenger seat. His tone was civil, showing no stress over the accident that had just occurred. The old Italian pulled a leather wallet from his suit, readily handing over his license.

"I don't think this needs to be reported. It seems quite unnecessary."

The younger of the two officers examined the license, squinting with disapproval.

"Sir, we need to report every incident with the—"

"You must be new," Gino interrupted. His voice had become remarkably stern. There was a silent moment between the men before the older policeman murmured something to his partner about the name being familiar. He took the license and walked hastily back to the police car, leaning in the front seat to make a radio call.

Ferris and Demos watched with interest as the red and blue lights reflected off of the windows, which they had cracked open to eavesdrop. The remaining officer exchanged a glance with Victor, then Gino. His brow made an attempt to be rigid, but his eyes gave away a nervous tick. A minute later, the man returned.

"Mr. Giorgetti," he started, handing back the license. "We're very sorry, we weren't aware. Please disregard this. Chief Blakely sends his deepest apologies."

The man wasn't making eye contact as he spoke, staring nervously at the ground. There was a soft shudder in his voice.

"No harm done," Gino said, his voice frighteningly airy. "Well except of course, my son's Lincoln."

"The department will send you a check for the damage immediately, Sir."

"Very good. Give the Chief my warmest regards."

"Yes, Sir."

Gino returned to the passenger seat as the officers retreated to their vehicle. The police car pulled back into the road much like a dog with its tail between its legs, hastily and awkwardly.

"We better not be late," Victor said between gritted teeth, restarting the car.

"We'll be all right, Victor," Gino reassured him. The window cracked and he lit a cigarette, leaning back in his seat. Ferris knit his brow, looking from the back of Gino's head over to Demos' face. He was aware of the influence that the man carried, but hadn't realized just how far it went until that moment. Though he wanted to ask about it, now wasn't the time. Demos looked back at him with a helpless smile.

The car turned back onto the road, leaving behind a few bits of broken glass and steel. Though Victor was still in a bad mood because of the damage to his vehicle, they managed to make it to the show with a few minutes to spare.

12

One of the things that Demos and Ferris had in common was a love for foreign food, especially sushi. Seamus would sooner play with it than eat it and had declined their invitation, knowing that that particular restaurant had a strict carding policy when it came to alcohol. Without liquor, he had no real reason to force down raw fish.

The two boys sat across from each other, drinking hot tea in an attempt to counter the cold weather outside. The restaurant was small, but good — *Umemura Sushi* took pride in being both local and authentic.

Demos snapped apart a pair of wooden chopsticks, quite ready to eat. His lunch had been half scavenged by Seamus and his stomach had been tight for the remainder of the day. Ferris watched him with amusement, slowly sipping at his tea. His throat was sore and the hot liquid was soothing.

"Relax, we just ordered."

"I know," Demos admitted, setting the chopsticks down on a napkin. "But I'm hungry."

Demos started to suck the salt off of a hot soybean, not giving any thought to his composure for once. Ferris was distracted as well, but with other things. He hadn't been alone with Demos for a while and it reminded him of the last time they were together. The image of Gino sending the cops off like spanked children was still very clear in his mind. It had gotten him thinking.

"So, what does Gino have on Chief Blakely, anyway?"

Demos' eyes slowly went up from his drink to Ferris' face, raising a brow at the question.

"What makes you think I know?"

"You know," Ferris said bluntly.

Demos smirked briefly, swirling the tea in his cup.

"It's not a pretty story."

"Tell me."

Demos glanced to the side, making sure no one was in earshot of their conversation. His voice dropped and he locked eyes with Ferris.

"One of the guys in our territory owns a motel. Usually pays on time. Big perv. He videotapes a few of the rooms so he can jerk off to it later."

Ferris was starting to understand how this story wasn't 'pretty.'

"Anyway," Demos continued. "Sometimes the Chief brings in women. That motel is his favorite place. But this one time—"

Demos held up his hand, emphasizing his tone.

"The girl was underage. Couldn't have been older than fourteen. He raped her."

Ferris stared at him, narrowing his eyes in indignation.

"The manager got it on tape. Offered it to Gino in exchange for a year of protection fees. It was worth it. Now that Blakely knows we have the tape, he'd lick dog shit off of Gino's shoe to keep it from getting out."

"What the fuck, Demos? He *raped* her. He should be in *jail*," Ferris snapped, looking livid.

"Hey, come on." Demos shrugged. "As long as he stays in that position, we're set for life. We've got his entire force at our feet."

Ferris went silent, looking away uncomfortably. Demos could tell that Ferris was torn and softened his voice as he continued.

"Ferris... this is one of the only things keeping Grandpa out of jail. Blakely knows we've got an eye on him – he's not going to do anything like that again. Living as a mob puppet is punishment enough for that guy."

"Yeah," Ferris said quietly, still not fully swayed.

"And now—"

Demos' response was interrupted as the waiter placed their food down. Trying to lighten the mood, he gave his friend a quick smile.

"Now that you know, I'm going to have to kill you."

Ferris smirked, but then his face contorted with a sharp inhalation of air. Squinting, he sneezed into his sleeve, releasing the rest of the breath with a shudder.

"Drink some more tea." Demos frowned, pushing the ceramic kettle across to him. Steam curled up from the cup as Ferris obediently poured it, noticing that his sinuses were starting to feel stuffy as well. He'd gone the last couple years without getting the flu and now it might have caught up with him. If he was lucky, it would only be a cold. The ivory white teacup warmed his fingers as he sipped it, appreciating the clean, dry taste.

"Is Blakely the only one?"

"No," Demos answered softy. "There are a few."

Ferris started to wonder just how many men Gino had in his pocket and if all of their stories were as bad as the police chief's.

"So, is it a cold or a fever that you starve?" Demos asked, thoughtfully changing the subject as he eyed Ferris' meal.

"A fever. It's an old wives' tale, so... no, I'm not going to hand over my yellowtail. Nice try though." Ferris sniffed again, finishing his tea.

"Oh well," shrugged Demos. Though he normally ate small portions at a finicky pace, tonight his entree was already gone.

84

Another thing he was quick at that day was grabbing the check, which he snatched up the moment the waiter placed it down.

"I got it."

"Demos, it's okay. I brought cash."

"I have to kill you, remember? I at least owe you a last dinner."

Ferris raised his eyebrows, unamused.

"And if I don't get you, that flu will," Demos finished.

"It's good to know I have such caring, sensitive friends."

Ferris gave up as Demos handed the check back to the waiter with cash, asking him to keep the change. Ferris put his newsboy cap back on as they left the restaurant, noticing small, white flecks drifting down along the street.

"Hey, look," Demos smiled, holding out his hand to catch some. "First snow."

"You sure they aren't just burning trash somewhere?" Ferris lowered an eyebrow, looking over to the horizon for a sign of smoke.

"You're such a charmer," Demos said, rolling his eyes.

Ferris shrugged as Demos stopped in front of him, readjusting his friend's scarf so that it crossed more tightly over his chest.

"You can't even dress yourself, it's why you're sick."

Ferris, despite his imminent flu and the odd story he'd just heard, was in a rare good mood. The snowflakes were coming down more thickly, looking like potato chips as they collected on the cars and bushes. It dusted over his coat, melting on his cheek from the heat of his approaching fever. He knew that within the next day or so he'd be bedridden, so he thoroughly enjoyed the walk home while he could.

The original entry in Ferris' planner for the date of December 8th was to meet Demos at the art museum downtown. In the calendar box was written, in very bad handwriting, "Demos, museum, 3pm." This proposal, however, along with several others in the corresponding dates, had been scratched out with a black pen. Ferris had done this between two sneezes while curled up in a blanket on the sofa, waiting for the space heater to kick in. Hopefully he would live past Tuesday, or the rest of his planner was going to look very messy as well.

"Put that book away, bubele. And lay down, I'll make you something to eat."

Ruth was standing in the kitchen entrance with a mug of hot tea, stirring it before setting it on the coffee table next to her son.

"I'm not hungry," he mumbled weakly, burying his face in the fleece throw he'd taken from the couch. "And it's not a book, it's my planner."

"Planner? Why are you worrying about planning? You're sick!" She headed back to the kitchen, mumbling to herself dubiously. "Oy, my son."

Ferris huffed uncomfortably against the soft blanket, feeling another chill coming on. His face was flushed from the fever and his glasses had been left folded on the coffee table.

"No, no." Ruth was back in the living room, snapping her fingers at him. "I said lie down, this isn't lying down. You shouldn't even be in here, go up to your room."

"But Mom..." he groaned, not wanting to get up. He hadn't even started drinking his tea yet.

"But nothing! Go upstairs. And you get in bed and go to sleep."

"Fine."

Ferris grabbed his glasses, stealing the throw and trudging up the stairs. He buried himself under the covers of his bed, trying to ignore the chill in his limbs and the sweat on his forehead. His body was starting to grow sore, but his raw throat was painful enough to keep him from noticing.

It was the first day of school he'd missed in his sophomore year. As annoying as some of his classes could be, nothing compared to the nagging of his mother. Turning over in bed, he started to long for school. It might have just been the fever, but he found that as well as the learning, he actually missed his friends.

His friends, coincidentally, were thinking about him as well. Because of his perfect attendance, Ferris' absence was a remarkable disturbance in the daily scheme of things. Seamus, on the other hand, came to school on random whims and seemed to skip classes just as often as he attended them. He augmented his deviant record by leaving school an hour early, perusing a grocery store for something to bring his ailing friend. He couldn't make chicken soup from scratch. Seamus' mother could barely microwave leftovers and had obviously never taught him the finer points of soup preparation. Buying it in a can felt cheap. Ferris seemed like the type to be fussy about food and it was possible that he hated processed junk. It took Seamus another half hour of intense scrutinizing before finding something he deemed suitable.

Ferris' mother was very good at looking out for him and she normally would have avoided letting guests disturb his rest. Unfortunately, her joy at seeing he actually had friends overcame her logic and Seamus was quickly ushered upstairs. His concerned tone and charming smile hadn't hurt, either. Seamus cracked the bedroom door, slowly putting his head into the room and squinting at the lump of blankets on Ferris' bed.

"Oi, Fer?" he whispered sharply.

There was no response.

86

"Oh don't tell me you're dead, after I went through all this trouble."

"I think—" came a slow, muffled reply. "I think that I hear Seamus' voice. But I already had this nightmare."

"Oh good, you're all right."

Seamus flopped himself onto his friend's desk chair, spinning backwards and wheeling over to the bedside. Tentatively, he reached over to pull back the edge of the blanket, revealing the back of Ferris' head.

"What are you doing here?" Ferris groaned.

"Just checkin' up on you, mate." Seamus felt the side of Ferris' temple with the back of his hand. "You feel awful."

"Thanks, doc."

"No, honestly. All sweaty and clammy. It's really rather disgusting."

"Then stop touching me." Ferris swatted him away with his wrist, curling to his side to cough a few times.

"But I can't, I love you ever so much. I waited all day just to touch you," he teased, continuing to poke Ferris in the temple. "The fever's makin' you ornery."

"No, you are."

"Don't be that way, especially when I brought you a present and all," Seamus said, presenting a large bunch of grapes. He didn't mention that he'd already eaten a few.

"The hell are these for?" Ferris asked, eyeing them suspiciously.

"What, you don't do grapes in the States?"

"So this is some weird British ritual," Ferris said plainly, staring at the fruit in his lap.

"I can see you're not impressed. But wait, there's more! I saved the best gift for last."

"Oh God, what is it? It's not porn, right? You didn't bring porn into my house."

"Oh give me a little credit, Fer. I brought you a cure," Seamus smiled, pulling a silver flask from the inside of his jacket.

"That's a flask."

"It's a cure."

"Flask."

"No, look. Whiskey and lemon. With a bit of hot water. My grandad swore by it, works like a charm. Just try it."

Ferris gave Seamus a long, uneasy look. Hesitantly, he took the flask, holding it under his nose in an attempt to sniff it. His eyes trailed sideways in contemplation, considering the idea of drinking it just to humor him. Giving in, Ferris sat up. His head tilted back to take a quick drink. The flask left his lips and he shook his head, looking like he was trying to shake off a feeling.

"Good, eh?" Seamus pressed.

Ferris took in a breath, clearing his throat and feeling his chest. He inhaled again, looking mildly impressed.

"It's a little better."

"Right, that's all you need to fix you up. That old git was a genius."

"I suspect he was also a bit of a drunk."

Seamus teetered his hand in a gesture that meant 'possibly,' giving a helpless shrug.

"You haven't mentioned him before," Ferris continued. "Actually, you never talk about your family."

"Oh, well uh—"

Ferris waited patiently for Seamus to speak, not caring that he was stalling.

"Well I told you before about, you know, my dad and all. My grandad's his father, you know how it works. Family tree?" Seamus made crude gestures that Ferris guessed were symbolic of a family tree.

"No, actually. I don't even know where your dad is."

"He's dead," Seamus said with a heavy stare.

Ferris went silent, looking back at Seamus with an awkward blink and a stammer.

"Ah, I-I'm sorry, I didn't—"

"Just jesting, mate. He's in London."

"You asshole, get the fuck out," Ferris snapped, relieved that he hadn't actually caused an awkward moment.

"You're breaking my heart," Seamus lamented, though his grin didn't make a very convincing act. Ferris lay back down in the bed. His friend was distracting him from his miserable illness, but he was still exhausted and cold. His eyes were barely open as he went back to his side, wondering if he should have another drink of that whiskey.

"Go on, then," Ferris said.

"Dad runs a few companies. Pharmaceuticals and all that. Never really understood the whole lot, nor do I care to."

"When did they split up?"

"Mum and Dad? Oh, early on. Can't say I was older than ten. It was because of me, too."

"I doubt that, Seamus."

"I'm sort of a living, breathing symbol of their hatred for each other. An' as I grew, so did their desire to strangle one another," Seamus narrated dramatically.

"You were just a kid, it couldn't have been your fault."

"Doesn't matter. Why we goin' on about this anyway? I came to visit my sick friend and end up in the psychiatrist's couch. Go on, Freud. Ask another question."

"Forget it."

"No really, ask me. Go on, anything you want."

There was a pause.

"They didn't pay much attention to you, did they?"

Seamus laughed. He held out his index finger, shaking it as if he heard a very good joke.

"Well, aren't we clever? Think you got me all figured out."

Ferris only shrugged. Seamus took the flask, having a drink before remembering it was mixed with lemon and water. He made an uncomfortable face, setting it back on the nightstand in disappointment.

"Bloody lemons," Seamus mumbled.

"Great. Perfect, you idiot. Now you're going to get sick, too."

"Ah well. Bound to happen sooner or later, what with us kissing so much."

"Hah," Ferris said bluntly. "A real comedian."

Seamus didn't respond – Ferris could tell that he was thinking. Had his assumption been correct? It would make sense that Seamus didn't receive much attention as a child, seeing how intensely he craved it as a teen. He wondered if Seamus would be any different if he had been raised by normal parents without an endless, unguarded supply of alcohol. It seemed Seamus would rather put on an act than complain about anything, no matter how intensely it bothered him. His demeanor was casual and assured, but how often was it a facade? A sharp knocking at the door interrupted Ferris' thoughts.

"Sweetie, you need to get back to sleep."

"Ah, best get going then," Seamus said, getting up from the chair and stretching his back. Ferris handed the flask over, but Seamus held up a hand to deny it.

"No, you keep it for now. There's still some left."

Ferris looked down at it, then back up at Seamus.

"...Thanks."

"Your mum really loves you, yeah?"

"Yeah. Um—"

"Hm?"

"Thanks for coming." When Ferris looked up, he was smiling. Seamus was quiet for a moment before returning the smile.

"My pleasure. Finish that whiskey up and call me in the morning."

Seamus shut the door behind him and went down the stairs, sucking the taste of whiskey off of his lower lip. Although he'd given up his flask and had to revisit suppressed childhood memories, the expression on his friend's face had made it worth it by far.

13

December was nearly over now; Christmas had come and gone. Chanukah had been early this year. Ferris had spent a good hour or two explaining it to Seamus, trying to clarify that it was one of the least important Jewish holidays and was only famous because of its proximity to Christmas. Ferris' cynicism had a tendency to intensify during the holiday season, especially when he had to wait in line for 45 minutes just to buy a package of AA batteries.

Tonight was the new year and they'd spent the last minutes until midnight at Demos' house. His aunt and uncle had gone to an adult gathering, giving them the run of the house. They kept it small, content just being a trio in their celebration. Demos had wanted to play a duet while they had the chance, so Ferris had brought over his violin case to rehearse Dvorak's *Romance*. Not surprisingly, Seamus had taken full advantage of the holiday and used it as an excuse to drink enough to float a yacht. He was now leaning on Demos, barely able to keep his eyes open or his hands off.

"Come on, Seamus, sit up," Demos grumbled, leaning away from his friend and letting him slip down onto the piano bench. Ferris laughed, leaning back into the armchair and folding a leg over his knee. He'd had a few drinks, but couldn't compete with the Brit's love for alcohol.

It was around one a.m. when Ferris rubbed a hand over his face, checking his watch with disappointment.

"I better get back, we have a concert rehearsal in the morning."

One might have expected a conductor to give a week off around Christmas, but Mr. Rensch made absolutely no exceptions for rehearsals. It was expected that many students probably wouldn't show up, but Ferris, the wretched perfectionist, didn't have that privilege.

"Me too," mumbled Seamus, forcing himself upright. "Promised Mum I'd be home."

He knew that his mother would probably have forgotten and wouldn't come home until the next afternoon, but suffered his usual denial at the suspicion. Cumbersomely, he started to dig into his coat pocket for his car keys.

"Yeah, how about no," said Demos, seizing the key ring and putting it into his own pocket. "Idiot."

Seamus was a year older than his two friends and had gotten a car from his father as a Christmas gift in an attempt to win his love without actually having to interact with him. This was incongruous, as his father essentially did not care if his son loved him or not. The presentation of capital or gifts was the man's usual way of one upping his ex-wife, who had given Seamus a half empty bottle of gin.

"Whad'dya expect me to do, walk home? It's bloody freezing," Seamus slurred, speaking more slowly than he usually would.

"I'll take him," grumbled Ferris, getting out of his seat and helping Seamus up by the arm. "Come on, champ. If I can walk, you can walk."

He pulled his friend's arm around his shoulder, supporting him as they stood together. Demos held open the door, recognizing that it was going to take a lot of work to get Seamus home.

"All right, good luck. If he gets too heavy just call a cab I guess."

"You callin' me fat?" Seamus squinted, looking indignant.

"Yeah, sure," Demos said, leading them outside. He wished them luck, looking a little bleak at their situation but giving a warm goodbye nonetheless.

Ferris put an arm around Seamus' back, keeping him upright as they walked down the sidewalk. His other hand was holding the violin case, making it even more difficult to support Seamus. What would normally be a twenty minute walk seemed like it was going to be at least twice as long. His drunken friend hung onto him shamelessly, panting alcohol-tainted breaths into the cold air. Ferris knew his friend could drink a dozen sailors under the table and started to regret letting Seamus have quite so much that night. It took a lot of alcohol to get him staggering and it didn't seem healthy. Then again, Seamus was never very concerned with his health.

They left a peculiar set of footprints, half dragged and uneven in the snow. Though Seamus was heavy and reeked of gin and wine, he was at least warm against Ferris. January was biting Ferris' skin, chilling the exposed parts of his face. As they dragged down the street Ferris noticed how quiet it was. Each step their feet made in the unsalted snow released a crisp sigh.

"You shouldn't drink this much," Ferris mumbled. Snow drifted down around his head, settling contentedly on their coats.

"And you should get your migraines checked by a bloody doctor," replied Seamus, still speaking groggily.

Caught in a stalemate, Ferris rolled his eyes, already having gone over this before.

"It's not a migraine, it's just a headache. Aspirin makes it go away."

"No one should be taking five aspirin a day," argued Seamus, his voice vinegary.

"No one should be drinking a bottle of gin a day," Ferris retorted.

"It's not always gin," grumbled the Brit, failing in his defense. He was slipping and Ferris adjusted his grip, holding tightly to him with a gloved hand.

"M'fine," insisted Seamus, pulling away. "I can walk."

He stood up straight, letting go of Ferris and taking a couple inept steps forward. Staggering, he lost his balance, catching his hand onto Ferris' shoulder once again. Ferris was nearly dragged down, but kept them both up, grasping Seamus' elbow and pulling him flush against his coat. He'd nearly dropped his violin, relieved that he'd kept his hold on it.

"No you can't."

"Eh," Seamus murmured, giving up and letting his friend bear his weight for a second time. They had almost started their ungainly walk again when a group's silhouette appeared in the gray, snowy air. Squinting his eyes, Ferris tried to see if they were familiar; perhaps they on their way home from a party as well.

Unfortunately, these individuals were quite familiar and did happen to be on their way home from a New Year's party.

It had been two years since Rudy, Paul, and Zach had been run over by Nicky's car, and they had been terrified enough to leave him alone since then. Though they were dense, they knew danger when they saw it. Or in their case, felt it. However, on that particular evening, logic gave way to an astounding amount of beer and blood alcohol content.

Ferris stared at them as they approached; he wondered if they were sober enough to recognize him. The only movement he made was a shaky breath, feeling unsteady somewhere in his chest.

They were talking loudly to each other, still carrying their bottles. Their staggering and shoving indicated that they were intoxicated. It only took a moment, but they were indeed sober enough to distinguish Ferris in their path.

"The fuck are you doin' out here, Levinstein?" Rudy spoke accusingly, as if the sidewalk was on his property.

Ferris didn't answer; he couldn't think of anything to say. Seamus blearily looked up at the three boys, not really grasping what was going on. They came closer and Ferris took a step back, pulling the drunken Brit with him.

"Answer me!" Rudy demanded.

Ferris' insides knotted. In his left hand was a violin case and in his right, Seamus. He couldn't run, he couldn't fight them, and his brain was starting to shut down. At a time when he could have used his ability to calculate bearings, his mind completely failed him, offering a blank to his quandary.

"Clear off, cunt," Seamus snarled between gritted teeth, apparently having more brainpower than Ferris. He once again tried to stand upright, only stumbling back. This threw the boys into fits of laughter as they decisively moved in. Zach gave Seamus a hard shove, sending him back against a lamp post. It shook, sending lumps of built up snow down onto his head. He slid down the length of it, stopping on the ground with a perturbed groan. He was too intoxicated to even pull himself up properly.

"Seamus..."

Ferris turned, taking a quick step towards his friend in order to help him up. The other two boys stepped in his way as Rudy got into his face, backing him away from the street light.

"What's wrong?" He shoved Ferris lightly. "Come on. Where's your mafia guy, huh?"

Rudy shoved him again, harder. The grip on his violin case tightened as he staggered backwards, glaring hard at the blond.

"You probably thought that was pretty fucking funny, huh? I was in the hospital for two weeks, you little *shit*," Rudy spat.

Ferris still hadn't responded to them, but it only seemed to make them angrier. Rushing him, Rudy heaved his palms against Ferris' chest, knocking him flat onto his back and kicking up gritty snow. The violin case tumbled to the sidewalk, making a thick cracking sound. Noticing it for the first time, Rudy turned to it furiously, pulling a leg back to kick it open. The case rolled three times and the clasps snapped off, spilling the polished wooden instrument onto the coarse pavement.

Ferris felt a frigid horror rising in his throat. The blood drained from his face as he reached forward, heart racing behind his ribs.

"No! *No!!*"

His fingers fell short as Rudy's black winter boot came down on the bridge of the violin, splintering the glossy, dark maple. The strings snapped off, sending a sharp trill through the frozen air.

Something else snapped inside of Ferris' body. It spread through him like cracks over glass, cinching his hands into tight, white fists. His breath clouded like the steam of an engine, rising from a bed of glowing coals. He locked on the splinters that were scattered across the icy sidewalk. The strings were curled and strewn, leaving thin impressions in the snow.

Ferris didn't think as he tore forward, shoving Rudy hard enough to knock out his breath. The boy fell hard onto his spine and there was a muffled cracking sound as a bone somewhere in his body splintered from the impact. Furious, Rudy shifted, pushing himself up on his hands just in time to see Ferris' heel meet his temple. Before he could land a second kick, Paul and Zach rushed to pull him back.

Half fuming and half terrified, they pinned him to a tree to knock the vigor out of him. After two punches his glasses had flown off to the side, lost under a bush somewhere. Blood was starting to stain the white, speckling the snow as well as their clothing. Ferris closed his eyes. He expected the beating to continue until he was unconscious, so he was quite surprised when they both suddenly stopped.

Somehow, Seamus had managed to stand up, stagger over to the tree, and grab both boys by the collars. He hurled them back, turning around to face Zach and Paul as they picked themselves up. His dark eyes narrowed as they came at him, watching their movements as best as he could.

With the help of some cold air, the passage of time, and the sound of splintering wood, Seamus had sobered enough to stand his ground. His arms were slender, but dense, and Zach felt it as four knuckles indented into the soft spot where his jaw met his throat.

Ferris stared, panting as he watched the fight. Paul had sunken his fist into Seamus' stomach, just after Seamus had knocked the spit from Zach's mouth. They both grabbed him, flinging him to the ground and landing a punch to his temple. Throwing them off, he pounded into Paul's face, hoping to mangle him beyond recognition.

This fight was different from the one Ferris had experienced two years ago. This wasn't a couple punches and some broken ribs. He could see bloody, matted hair and snapped limbs. He wasn't afraid for Seamus' pain tolerance or victory; he was afraid for his life. Ferris picked up his head to do something when suddenly, both Zach and Paul stopped moving.

Seamus appeared to be gagging on his own blood, hunched over and coughing. The other boys were worse off, lying unconscious at his feet at awkward angles. Moving quickly, Ferris hurried forward to catch Seamus before he fell, holding him against his chest with what little strength he had.

"Fer," Seamus groaned, breathing hard for air. "Think... m' gonna be sick."

"Seamus, hold on."

He helped him to the side, supporting him as he retched behind a bush. Seamus coughed once more, shutting his already swollen eyes. Giving up on the idea of standing, he fell limp against Ferris' body. Ferris moved down to the ground, no longer able to hold up both himself and his friend.

Seamus' face was mottled with dark bruises and his lip was inflamed. Blood stained his hair and temple, running down from both his nose and mouth. He was silent for a minute, only his panting gave testimony that he was conscious.

"You all right, mate?" he whispered, voice hoarse from the cold and muffled from pressing into Ferris' coat.

94

"I'm fine. I have to call you an ambu—"

"S'alright. I'm tough."

This was the last thing Seamus said before he passed out, leaving Ferris the only conscious person on the Birch Street sidewalk.

The new year was already three hours old by the time they arrived at the hospital. The building's interior was still decorated for Christmas in an attempt to add warmth to the sterile, bleak environment. A nurse pushed a wheelchair past the emergency room doors, unnoticed by the fifteen year old waiting in the lobby.

Ferris was sitting hunched over, leaning his chin on his hands and staring at the floor. It was an off-white tile, flecked with gray and in need of a quick mopping. He'd been waiting for an hour, sick with apprehension and exhausted from the night's events. Seamus had been gurneyed in past the swinging double doors sixty-two minutes ago and he hadn't heard a word since.

He had managed to find his glasses in the bushes, though one lens had a thick crack down the middle. He wore them anyhow, deciding it was better than being completely blind. When the ambulance came, two policemen started to question him about what had happened in detail, making him uncomfortable and tense. He was relieved they didn't take him in to the station, only wanting to see if Seamus would be all right.

The emergency room had a very long waiting period and he had opted out of seeing a doctor for his mild bruises. A small portion of bloodied tissue was wedged in his left nostril, but he didn't pay it any mind. All he could think about was Seamus and his injuries. The hospital staff had tried calling Seamus' mother several times, but there was never an answer. He could remember them discussing something about blood alcohol content and then hearing the word 'minor' in the voicemails they left her.

The colorless, musty waiting area did nothing to ease his anxiety. The atmosphere felt stale and cold and the white fluorescent lighting did nothing to flatter the scrapes on his hands. He felt as if he'd been breathing in the same diseased air over and over. Behind him a man was coughing, vainly trying to clear dried mucous from the back of his throat. Ferris didn't like hospitals.

Running on his last vanishing fragments of energy, his eyelids started to feel heavy. He might have given in and closed them if a man in a white coat hadn't stopped directly in front of him.

"You brought in Mr. Aston, correct?" The man was flipping through a stack of papers on a clipboard.

Looking up in both fear and concern, Ferris quickly nodded.

"Yes," he answered, surprised at how dry his voice was.

"It looks like he has a mild concussion, but nothing permanent. We gave him some stitches and some acetaminophen. He'll be out in a minute."

Ferris exhaled the breath that had unconsciously welled up in his chest, nodding silently.

"Just make sure he gets some rest and keeps ice on his bump for the swelling. He might be a little confused from the hit to his head, so don't worry if he starts repeating things."

"Okay," answered Ferris, now feeling a warm relief replacing the nervousness. "Thank you."

"One more thing... your friend had a BAC of .09 percent, which is illegal and very dangerous. Because of what you two went through tonight, they're going to let it go. Don't let it happen again."

Ferris was pretty sure part of the reason they were 'letting it go' was because Seamus' mother was impossible to get a hold of.

"Okay. We're sorry."

The doctor left and Ferris rubbed his arms, not from the cold, but from anticipation. He was getting restless and the minutes started to drag on more slowly. Ignoring his headache, he tapped his fingers on his knee in a jittery, nervous pattern. Finally, the swinging doors opened.

A woman in a sea foam uniform was pushing Seamus' wheelchair, stopping when Ferris rushed up to them with what little energy he had left.

"Seamus..."

The English boy in question was grinning up at him, looking unsightly and tired. His arm was in a sling and there were bandages wrapped about his head. They had cleaned off the blood, revealing the discolored bruising along the side of his face and collar.

"Hey Fer," Seamus interrupted, appearing to be back to his usual self. Squinting up at Ferris, he lowered an eyebrow.

"What happened to your nose?"

"We got in a fight, remember?"

"Oh right," Seamus murmured, suddenly recalling. "I won, didn't I?"

"Yes, you won," Ferris smiled, drawing back his eyebrows. "How do you feel?"

"My head hurts." Seamus' accent appeared to be thicker when he was dazed. "And 'm tired."

Slowly, Seamus tilted his head, looking hopeful.

"Hey, ya got my flask on you?"

"No," mumbled Ferris, narrowing his eyes at his friend. "Not now."

"Well, you're no fun," griped Seamus, leaning back in his wheelchair. Catching Ferris' expression, he raised his eyebrows.

"What's with the look on your face?"

"Hm?" answered Ferris, caught off guard. "Oh, I just—"

He bit his lower lip, stuffing his hands into his pockets and glancing down.

"I'm just glad you're all right." He looked Seamus in the eyes again. "I thought you..."

"Thought what?"

"Nothing, I was just..." he murmured, "worried."

Surprisingly, Seamus laughed.

"What?" Ferris said with a scowl.

"Mr. Levinstein, I think you're fond of me," he answered, looking pleased with himself.

"No, I'm not. You're annoying," Ferris argued.

"You like me. You thought I was going to die! I bet you cried."

"I did not cry," muttered Ferris, glaring at him.

"Oh, my best friend Seamus got in a fight, what'm I gonna do, I can't live without 'im," teased Seamus, in falsetto for some reason.

"I'm going to push your wheelchair down a hill," Ferris retorted.

"I'd love that, but I think I can walk now, really."

"Last time you said that you almost fell on your ass," Ferris snorted, folding his arms.

"I mean it. Come on, Fer, help me up." Seamus reached for him, taking his hands and tensing himself to try and stand. Not feeling very confident about this endeavor, Ferris eased him up carefully. To his shock, Seamus managed to stand on his own.

"Told you, m' all right."

"Come on, let's go home." Ferris already planned on taking Seamus to his own place, not wanting to put him in an empty, cold house full of alcohol.

"Sounds good. Oh, hey Fer?"

"Yeah?"

"Happy New Year," Seamus finished, giving his friend a cocky smile.

"Yeah," said Ferris, weakly returning the expression. "You too."

14

A few weeks later Seamus had recovered completely, giving relief to those concerned about him. He quickly returned to being his tactless, blithe self, crawling back to his gin and cigarettes the moment he had access. For the time being, things had returned to normal.

When Demos found out the details of what had happened, he was unusually quiet. Ferris could tell he was thinking and didn't want to know what he was going to do to those boys. Demos would have to wait until they were released from juvenile hall, however, as they had all been arrested for intentional battery. Though two years ago he'd protested the violence, this time around Ferris didn't care what happened to them. They'd nearly killed Seamus and they had broken his violin.

Fortunately, the instrument had been insured. His mother had ordered another one, making sure it was just as good as his original. He wouldn't admit it, but he had been dotingly attached to his violin and would have to get used to the new one once it arrived.

For most families, mid-January was a quiet time of year. The Giorgettis, however, had Gino's birthday to celebrate. The occasion was his 71st year, and though it wasn't quite the landmark of his 70th, his family didn't hesitate in making it memorable. The restaurant was closed for the private function, now full of family members and close friends. Mr. and Mrs. Levinstein came with their son and were quick to get into deep-seated conversations with the other guests, passionately complaining about politics and the cost of real estate. Gino's cat, Rocco, had been allowed into the restaurant on the premise that there were no customers around to complain. The white feline was circling the table legs, rubbing underneath chairs and waiting for the occasional dropped bit of food.

Ferris, as expected, sat with Demos and several of the Italian's other cousins. Sergio had stepped outside for a cigarette and Pietro was busy trying to make his younger brother's hair presentable. Emily, Victor's only daughter, was helping her mother serve food. She was holding a tray in one hand, looking a bit like an underaged waitress.

"Hey, you guys want some bruschetta?"

Ferris picked his head up, noticing her for the first time that evening. She was wearing a cream dress with a black bow and there had been an attempt to pin back her bangs. Her brown hair was short and boyish in a way he wasn't sure was intentional or not.

"Sure," Demos said, taking a piece. "Thanks."

Ferris had met her many times before, seeing that she lived in the same house as Demos and was his younger cousin. She normally stayed out of their way, keeping to her room or her own friends. Though she was only two years younger, he always thought of her as a bit of a child. That evening, however, she seemed different.

His thoughts didn't last long as he remembered that she was Demos' cousin.

"I'm good," Ferris declined, averting his eyes.

"Your loss," Emily said, taking a piece off of the tray and eating it herself. She looked contemplative for a moment, tasting it. "This is good. It's almost like grandpa made it."

"I made it," Demos said, raising his eyebrows.

"Jeez, you're getting too good at this, Demos. They're going to pull you out of the business to work in the kitchen."

"Che posso dire?" he replied easily, forgetting his modesty for a moment.

"It's just bruschetta, it's kind of hard to screw up," Ferris said, eyeing his friend.

"Shut up, Fish."

It appeared that Emily knew about their line of work. On one hand, it seemed strange to be so careless about illegal activity in front of children. On the other, that sort of thing could be rather difficult to hide for so long.

"Hey Emmy, we got any more of those eggplant things?" Victor called over his shoulder, sitting at a table with his father and siblings.

"No, Dad. You ate them all."

"Well, excuse me if—"

"I'll make some more," Demos cut in. "They're easy."

"Bring out some more wine while you're at it. A couple glasses," Pietro added as he saw Demos get up.

"Yeah, yeah. Hey Ferris, want to help?"

"Uh, sure," Ferris lied, following his friend into the restaurant's massive kitchen.

Demos snagged an apron from a hook, quickly tying it on and grabbing a knife to start cutting a large, fresh eggplant.

"Grab me some ricotta, would you?" Demos asked, turning on the industrial stove to fry the slices. Ferris complied, getting the cheese out of the walk-in. The family made it themselves, as they did with most of their ingredients. Ferris was content to lean against the counter, watching Demos work with mild interest.

"So, what is he now, 71?" Ferris asked, making conversation.

"Yeah. You know, he was my age when he pinched his first business."

"That's... that's really touching."

"No, really," Demos insisted. "It's inspiring."

Ferris wasn't really sure how he felt about making businesses pay the Giorgettis a weekly fee in order to exist in their territory. It was bullying, plain and simple, and many of the establishments were family owned. They worked hard. On occasion, the protection fee actually did pay for protection. Whether some neighborhood punks were giving the shopkeeper a hard time, or a restaurant needed a good review to get itself off the ground, the Giorgettis were there. Still, not every business paid the fee willingly. Some were forced.

"I think they're going to have me start soon," Demos finished.

"Really, you? But you're—"

"What, too young?"

"Well, that and… you're not very intimidating."

Ferris stared at his friend, who was a meager 5'6" and was built more like a ballerina than a mobster.

"Sergio's going to help," Demos insisted, sounding a little annoyed. "I know what I'm doing."

"If you say so. I'm going to bring Pietro his wine, okay?"

Demos simply nodded as Ferris poured two fresh glasses, holding them by the stems as he pushed through the kitchen's swinging doors. When he came back into the room, the first thing he noticed was Emily. She was speaking to a young man, smiling and keeping her hand on his shoulder. Her smile was striking and Ferris found it difficult to look away. He was so distracted that he didn't notice Rocco slip past his ankles until it was too late. Staggering to avoid stepping on the cat, he stammered before tripping and descending awkwardly to the floor. The wine glasses tumbled across the ground as he fell, his palms feeling the burn of the carpet.

"Rocco, you stupid—" he grumbled from behind clenched teeth, feeling his face heat up in dramatic embarrassment.

"Ferris! Are you okay?"

His eyes left the scampering cat to glance up. Emily was kneeling in front of him, offering a hand to help him up. He forced a laugh, trying to act as if he weren't utterly humiliated.

"Yeah, I'm fine," Ferris said, taking her hand.

"You got wine on your shirt," she said, reaching for a cloth napkin. "Here."

He looked down as she reached forward in an attempt to blot the wine. Indeed, there was a long, plum colored stain down the front of his white shirt.

"Shit," he mumbled. Not only did he waste expensive wine and fall in front of a girl, but his shirt was ruined.

"It'll be ok, just mix some dish soap and hydrogen peroxide," Emily said, as if reading his mind.

"Oh," he said stupidly, unsure of what to say.

100

"We drink a lot of wine," she said, smiling at him. "You gotta know these things."

"Right."

The young man Emily had been speaking to earlier approached, looking curious.

"You done here?" he asked her, only half joking.

"Yeah. Hey Chris, this is Ferris. He's a friend of the family. And this is Chris, my boyfriend."

Ferris opened his mouth to speak, but hesitated. They shook hands, though he sensed it was purely a formality.

"Nice to meet you," Chris said.

"Same," Ferris replied, feigning interest before averting his eyes to the floor. "Ah, I'd better clean this up."

"It's okay, I'll get it," Emily said. "You should check on Demos."

"Sure," Ferris replied gratefully. "Thanks."

"Remember what I said about the dish soap and—"

"And hydrogen peroxide, yeah. I'll remember."

He pushed back through the doors to the kitchen, already having forgotten about Pietro's wine request.

"What the hell happened to you?" Demos asked, trying not to laugh at the wine stain.

"That stupid cat walked in front of me and I tripped."

"What were you doing, walking blindfolded?"

"Something like that," Ferris mumbled, pulling the bottom of his shirt out to get a better look at the damage.

"Well, these are finished," Demos said, putting the eggplant rolls onto a plate. "I'm done in here. Grab that wine bottle for Pietro. He can pour his own."

As they came out, the attention went directly back to Demos.

"Hey Demos, come play some piano for your grandpa," Nicky called out, waving the teen over with a hand.

"Oh I'd love to," Demos said, setting the plate of hors d'oeuvres down next to Victor. "But grandpa likes violin best, doesn't he?"

"Oh no, you don't," Ferris protested. He hated performing for people he knew. "My violin is busted – you know that."

"I brought your old one, bubele," Ruth said happily, having smuggled the instrument over in the car. Ferris put his face into his palm.

"Oh, great."

"Ferris," Gino spoke up, smiling. "Why don't you play something for us? I haven't heard your violin since you were a child."

Ferris didn't want to stand in front of thirty people with a wine stain down the front of his shirt and play an instrument for the crime lord of Southport, but it was impossible to deny Gino's request. It was the man's birthday, after all.

"Okay," he gave in, taking the violin case from his mother. "But only because it's you."

Gino laughed, unusually easygoing for a mob boss.

"What would you like to hear?" Ferris asked as he tuned the old violin.

"Oh, let's see... *Air on the G string*." Gino was a lover of classical music and knew his favorite pieces intimately.

"Sure." Ferris knew the song well and it wasn't very difficult. He finished tightening the screw on the bow, holding it out to examine the hairs. After taking in a quick breath, he started to play.

The first up bow was slow and long, playing out sweetly across the room. This sort of thing didn't usually make him nervous. When he performed for the Youth Symphony Orchestra, it was for a crowd of strangers that he wasn't likely to ever see again. Tonight, however, his heart beat unsteadily as he played. He wasn't sure if it was Gino's presence or the stain, but he found himself needing to concentrate harder. Playing an old instrument that had been hibernating in storage didn't help his anxiety.

The stain went unnoticed by the guests of the party. The normally talkative family was quiet as they listened, taken with the song. Gino had chosen a beautiful piece. It wasn't until the last note faded that his eyes caught Emily staring at him. He didn't look away from her as he finished, lowering the instrument in silence.

His thoughts were interrupted by applause and Nicky's demand of a duet while Emily's attention went back to the family and their chattering. Demos was happy to comply, coercing Ferris into another performance. More food and wine was brought out and more music was played. Despite the rising mood of the get-together, Ferris was quiet the rest of the night. He was distracted by uncomfortable thoughts, realizing that what made him nervous hadn't been Gino at all.

15

The rest of the school year had gone by uneventfully. Summer had come early to Southport, leaving its residents testily dragging through the heat.

Ferris was leaning against the window of Gino's Quattroporte, looking out at the expressway as the radio played a song by Ennio Morricone. Demos was sitting next to him, looking dignified but bored. Ferris was equally bored, pining for the novel in his backpack. Chronic motion sickness, however, ensured he would be unable to read during the long trip. At the opposite window sat Emily, wearing a pair of headphones and looking content with her music.

The car was only an hour from their destination, a summer home in Long Island owned by the Giorgetti family. They went every year for a week or two and this was the first time that Gino had allowed Demos to bring a guest. Ferris had readily accepted the invitation, looking forward to some time away from the city heat. His eyes went from the window to the front, where Victor was driving with Gino in the passenger seat. Behind them was another car, driven by Sergio and carrying the other family members (plus a carrier for Rocco). Talking casually with Demos wasn't as easy with two adults in the car and they had both settled with staring at the scenery with mild interest.

Finally giving in, Ferris grabbed his book and opened it to the marked page. He grew readily immersed in the spot he had left off, forgetting his weariness for a few minutes. The diversion didn't last long as a familiar ache built in the front of his head, paired with an unsettling feeling in his stomach. He snapped the novel shut, closing his eyes in discomfort. Hopefully the drive wouldn't last much longer.

When the car pulled into a gas station, Ferris awakened from a mundane dream. It seemed that he had fallen asleep. He removed his glasses, rubbing a palm over an eye as he groggily asked where they were.

"Pit stop," Demos answered, taking a cigarette from a pack with his teeth.

"No," came a firm command from Victor in the front seat.

"What? But you said—"

"*I* need a smoke. Not you," Victor interrupted.

"Yes I—"

"If your aunt sees you smoking, she'll kill me."

"What if I go around back and—"

"I said 'no.' Here," he said, plucking some bills from a gold clip. "Go buy yourself some candy or something."

"I'm not five," Demos mumbled begrudgingly as Victor left the car. He watched longingly as his uncle joined the other men and flicked open a Zippo.

"If you don't want candy, I'll take it. I need a Coke," Ferris offered, his voice lacking sympathy.

"Me too," Emily added.

"I hate you guys," Demos said, passing the money and stepping over Ferris to exit the car. Ferris watched him walk around the edge of the building, plainly disobeying his uncle.

"Guess I'll join him," Ferris said, handing Emily the folded bills. "Here."

"Thanks."

With his hands in his pockets, Ferris looked around the corner of the convenience store. As expected, Demos was cupping a hand to light a cigarette. Ferris approached, leaning against the wall next to his friend.

"This is so stupid," Demos muttered.

"You really need one that bad?"

"It's the principle. They let me shoot a gun, but I can't even smoke with them."

"I think it's more a fear of your aunt than anything else."

"I guess," Demos said, exhaling a plume. His pride was clearly shot. Ferris looked up at the sun over the trees. It was low in the western sky and it seemed to be getting late in the day.

"Well, we're almost there."

"Yeah. At least you're with me. You know... it's weird."

"What?"

"You're the first person outside of the family that's coming to this house with us."

"Are you serious?"

"You see Nicky or Sal?" Demos asked, flicking his cigarette.

"Couldn't you have brought Seamus?"

"No. They didn't ask me to invite a friend. They asked me to invite you."

"Oh," Ferris answered simply, looking away in thought.

"I think they really trust you."

Demos looked at his friend, his eyes markedly warm. Ferris wasn't sure what to say. It was a compliment that he didn't know how to handle.

"Why's that?" he finally said. "Is the house made of gold or something?"

"No one else really knows where it is. When someone gets in trouble, they hide out over there for a while. And uh..."

"What?"

"Grandpa keeps a safe there. Remember what I told you, about Blakely's tape? It's there, with everyone else's dirt. If anyone ever stole that stuff, we'd be fucked."

104

It was easy to believe. Without certain judges and politicians under his belt, Gino's authority would be quite lackluster. There would be nothing keeping him out of jail.

"Oh."

"Hey, don't tell anyone," Demos said, as if realizing what he had just revealed. "Not a soul, ever. Swear to me."

"I swear," he answered easily, unable to imagine why he ever would. The serious moment was interrupted by a girl's voice.

"Hey guys," Emily said, looking around the corner. "We're going."

"Okay," Demos said, putting out his cigarette on the ground with his foot.

"Here, I got you a Coke," she added, handing Ferris a cold can as they walked. He looked down at it, then back at her. He'd forgotten about it and was surprised that she had even thought to get him one.

"...Thanks."

"Wasn't my money," she said with a smile, getting back into the car.

It was nearing evening when the cars pulled up in front of the large beach house. Ferris pulled his suitcase from the trunk before slipping a bottle of aspirin from his pocket. The long ride hadn't agreed with his body. He palmed a couple of pills into his mouth, carefully lifting his head to look at the summer home. The house was large, easily holding at least eight bedrooms. Vintage iron gates enclosed the plot, pointed with barbs that threatened to pierce anyone who might attempt a climb. The exterior of the building was lain with strong, intricate stone and the beach was visible past a number of trees. If this was the Giorgetti hideout, a life on the lam didn't seem like such a terrible concept.

"This everyone?" Ferris asked as the second car pulled up along the stone driveway.

"No, there's another car coming. And my uncle Roberto is coming in from Italy with his family," Demos said anxiously, already itching for another cigarette.

Ferris didn't even want to think about what a disaster it would be if his entire family tried to get together in one place. Every Levinstein wedding, reunion, and Bar or Bat Mitzvah was an incredible ordeal brimming with bickering. Yet somehow, the Giorgettis did this every year. They seemed to put the 'organized' into organized crime.

"We're sharing a room," Demos continued. "Come on, it's upstairs."

Ferris wasn't surprised. It was doubtful that any person on the premises would have a bedroom to themselves and one didn't have to be a mathematician to figure out why. They were a large family, relatively speaking.

The bedroom was spacious enough for two full beds and had a pleasant view of the water. Ferris had barely set down his suitcase before Demos dragged him back outside so he could smoke again. They had gone around back on the sand, out of his watchful aunt's view. The wind came in over the water and the sky was overcast. Ferris caught himself staring at the ocean, also noticing that sand had gotten into his canvas shoe.

"It's nice," Ferris said distantly.

"That's *Allegra*," Demos said, gesturing to a docked twelve-meter cruising yacht. Unlike *La Veloce*, Gino's motor yacht back in the city, this one had a sail.

"He has two?"

"He likes boats," Demos answered simply. The man did indeed love boats. There were a few framed oil paintings of sailing ships in his office and he built models in his spare time. Demos' cigarette was almost out when Emily's voice came up from behind them.

"Hey, Grandpa's starting dinner. He wants you to help." Demos nodded, tossing his cigarette stub into a bucket on the deck.

"Don't bore Ferris to tears with girl talk, okay?" Demos said as he went up the wooden stairs to the house. If Emily were a few years younger she would have stuck her tongue out at him. Instead, she rolled her eyes, looking at Ferris testily.

"He's the one who can't stop talking about fashion and cooking."

Ferris smirked, only because it was true.

"How are your parents doing?" Emily asked, trying to make some kind of conversation. As she spoke, Ferris made himself look away from her face, gazing with feigned intensity at the sea.

"Alive and kicking, last time I checked. How's um—" Ferris realized he couldn't ask about her parents, seeing as they were twenty yards away. "How's your boyfriend?"

"He's... okay. He's good. If I saw him more often I could probably tell you more."

"What, really? What could possibly be better than spending time with you?"

"Ha ha," Emily said, deadpanned. Ferris stiffened, realizing she thought he was being sarcastic.

"No, I—... really! I'm serious!"

"Sure you are," she smiled. "You *love* spending time with me."

"Uh," Ferris said, scratching the back of his neck. "Yes."

"Do you remember when we first met?" Emily asked, her eyes inquisitive.

"Um," Ferris attempted to answer, but didn't want to admit that he couldn't remember at all. Why did Demos have to leave him alone with her? Ferris was being as articulate as a toddler.

106

He stuffed his hands into his pockets to keep from fidgeting any further.

"You made me cry," she said, smiling at him.

"I did?" he asked. He looked at her carefully, lowering an eyebrow.

"Yeah, I was five and you were seven. Dad was having your family over for dinner."

"I don't remember that. How did I...?"

"They let us play in the study while the adults talked, but you ignored me the entire time. You just kept reading some book."

"Oh," Ferris said, embarrassed, mostly because it sounded exactly like something he would have done. Why did his past self have to sabotage his future self?

"When I kept trying to get your attention, you called me annoying and told me to go away."

"Um, sorry," he said, feeling foolish about his poor social skills, even as a child.

"Oh, it's okay. It's pretty funny if you think about it. I mean, you turned out to be pretty nice."

"Seriously?" Ferris said, narrowing his eyes at her suspiciously.

"Well, you are to me."

"Maybe," he said, rubbing his chin. "It could just be an act."

"I'll let it slide if you help with my homework next year."

"Oh right," Ferris said, suddenly remembering that summer vacation didn't last forever. Outside of this trip, it wasn't much of a vacation. He was enrolled in multiple summer honors programs and had just as much homework to do now as he did the rest of the year. "What do you suck at? Math?"

"How did you guess?"

"Because you're an artist. And a Giorgetti."

"Oh, you help Demos with it too, don't you?"

"Yeah. What is it with your family and math?"

"That's why we pay your family to do it for us," Emily said with a smirk.

"Ah, yeah. Though you mostly pay us in food," Ferris said, then looked back towards the house. "I wonder what they're making tonight."

"Oh, the usual. Grandpa will form some kind of mountain of pasta covered in meat and cheese. It's a wonder I'm not some kind of land manatee."

"A cow."

"Did you just call me a cow?"

"No! I mean... a manatee is a sea cow, so a land manatee would be a land... a cow. I—" He ran a hand over his forehead. "Uh, never mind."

By now Ferris' face had heated up. He could easily have had this same conversation with a professor or even Seamus, but a girl? Oh no, not a girl. To his relief, however, she laughed.

"It's okay, Fish," she said. "I get it."

"Oh, now you're using it too?" he asked, not quite thrilled to hear his nickname again.

"Of course I'm using it."

"I'm going to start calling you 'Land Manatee.'"

"You do and they'll never find your body."

Somehow, Ferris didn't doubt it. At the same time, he was reminded of something.

"Why doesn't Demos have a nickname? I can think of plenty."

"He does," she smiled, as if excited to share what she knew. "He just failed to tell you what it was."

"What is it?"

"Spettro," she shrugged, crouching down to pick up a stone from the sand.

"...Ghost?"

"Yeah. Or 'Ghostie.'"

"Why's that?" The name didn't seem so bad. Okay, *Ghostie* was bad.

"He's paler than a corpse, that's why. Nicky calls him Casper sometimes."

"I thought he got his complexion from Gino."

"Yeah, but nobody makes fun of Grandpa," she grinned, tossing the rock out over the water. Gino's lineage consisted entirely of northern Italians, leaving him with a fair skin tone. Some of the other Giorgettis had married into other regions, giving them darker complexions and making Gino and Demos look even paler by comparison.

"Speaking of those two," she said quietly, looking back at the house, "we should go see if dinner is almost done. I can't wait to eat."

"I thought it was just a 'mountain of pasta,'" Ferris mused, pushing up his glasses.

"I never said it didn't taste *amazing*."

It wasn't long before the sun set and the men finished their cigars to retire for the night. The dinner had been magnificent, but it was no surprise from the combination of chefs that had made it possible. One of the only things that could make Demos enjoy cooking more was sharing the task with his grandfather. Ferris wasn't normally a ravenous eater, but it took all of his willpower not to eat every last bite of sea bass. He had been introduced to some new faces at the dinner table, but was sitting too far from the newcomers to make an impression.

108

Four hours later, the entire household had gone to sleep. Demos and Ferris lay in their respective beds with a table lamp giving some light to the room. Being teens, they had a tendency to stay up later than the appropriate time, passing the last few hours with reading and talking.

"This summer home," Ferris said, trying not to scoff, "is nicer than most regular homes."

"This line of work has its perks," Demos said, as if it was obvious.

"Yeah, not just money, either."

"What do you mean?" Demos asked, facing Ferris and leaning on an elbow.

"Oh, I don't know. Maybe how when we both had English, I did ten hours of homework a week and you didn't do any. Yet, somehow, we both got A's."

"Oh, that," Demos said quietly, looking to the side thoughtfully. "That didn't really have anything to do with—"

It was then he went silent, closing his mouth in regret of what he'd said.

"What?"

"Nothing."

"Demos," Ferris said sternly, closing the book he had been skimming. "How the hell did you get an A?"

Demos was shying away from the subject, turning onto his back to avoid eye contact.

"I don't know," he mumbled.

Ferris answered with a roll of his eyes, followed by a sigh. After a minute of silence, he pressed further.

"Come on."

"Come on what?"

"Tell me the truth."

The moment dragged on and neither boy spoke. Ferris only waited, giving Demos some time to think. Finally, his friend gave in.

"I kind of flirted with the teacher."

Ferris was about to shrug, say 'Oh,' and go back to his book, when he remembered something crucial.

The teacher had been a man.

He wasn't quite sure how to respond, or if he should mention it at all. The silence between them was awkward at best. Demos finally broke it by continuing.

"I'd been meaning to tell you. I mean, I-I don't like to keep things from you." Demos' voice was uncharacteristically nervous. "Because we're friends."

"What exactly did you want to tell me?" Ferris asked slowly. He wasn't stupid; it was pretty clear what Demos was trying to get across. He was only hoping Demos would have the courage to actually say it.

Demos was quiet again, looking away to think. Ferris didn't rush him, letting him get his words together for as long as he needed.

"I think… that sometimes, I don't know," Demos attempted, stalling before going on. "Sometimes I'm… attracted to guys."

Though it was striking to actually hear out loud, it wasn't anything that surprised Ferris. If he were a little more insensitive, he might have laughed at how Demos was simply stating the obvious.

"I see," Ferris said gently, trying not to put any conflicting emotion into his tone.

Demos swallowed his anxiety before turning to look at Ferris again.

"Does it bother you?"

"Why would that bother me?"

"Well, does it?"

"No," Ferris answered simply. "Of course not."

Demos sighed as if he'd just put down a heavy object.

"I was worried you'd be, I don't know, grossed out."

"Grossed out? What am I, five?" Ferris paused for a second, scratching behind his ear. "…Or Republican?"

Demos forced a quick laugh, clearly still nervous about his confession.

"Don't worry," Demos added. "I don't have a crush on you or anything."

"I assumed as much. I'm not really your type."

"Oh, yeah? What's my type?" Demos asked with a raised eyebrow.

"Handsome, sophisticated," Ferris started listing, counting off on his fingers, "and I guess… old."

"The professor wasn't my type. I did it for the grade."

"You know, if I didn't like you so much, I think I'd hate you."

"Just don't tell anyone, all right?" Demos said, holding his elbows uncomfortably.

"What, about the teacher, or about you being…?"

"All of it. I mean, my family… they'd be so—" Demos struggled to find the right description. "So disappointed. *Furious.* Uncle Victor would…"

Demos sighed, not wanting to think about it. His family meant everything to him and letting them down was the last thing he wanted. Their own flesh and blood, a fruit. It would bring shame to their entire syndicate. Demos knew that they loved him, but he also knew that they were traditional, conservative, and Roman-Catholic. If he wasn't disowned, they'd definitely send him away for a long time.

"I won't tell. I promise." Ferris didn't know what else to say. They were going to have to find out someday. Years in the future, when their attractive, rich, intelligent nephew was still

110

unmarried. Even now Demos was teased about needing a girlfriend and Ferris didn't see that letting up anytime soon. It wasn't an ideal situation. For now, however, things could stay quiet.

"Thanks, Ferris." Demos lay back down, looking up at the ceiling in relief. They both didn't speak for a few minutes, digesting what they had just discussed. After a while, Demos broke the silence in a tired voice.

"We should get to sleep. Grandpa's taking us out on the boat tomorrow and he likes to leave early."

"Yeah, good idea."

The light clicked off and they both turned over in their beds, making their own attempts at falling asleep. It didn't take long for Demos to drift off, breathing evenly on his side. Ferris, however, was having trouble losing consciousness. It was difficult to sleep in an unfamiliar place and his mind was crowded with worries and anticipation. Though he hadn't lied about not being bothered by his friend's confession, he couldn't get it off his mind. Did this change anything? More than that was different, though. The entire day was giving him too much to dwell on.

After an hour or so of turning around under the covers, he kicked them off and slid his glasses back on. Being careful not to wake Demos, he opened the bedroom door and slipped out into the hall. Once downstairs, the door to the deck caught his eye. Maybe some fresh air would help clear his head.

The moment the glass door opened, Ferris could hear low voices. He considered backpedaling into the house, but the figures on the deck took notice of him. There were two of them. Ferris recognized the pair from dinner – Gina and Benny. Gina was one of Demos' older cousins. She looked every bit like the female version of Demos – slender and pale with long black hair and a permanent look of boredom. Benny, born Beniamino, was her brother. In stark contrast to his sibling, he was large, muscular, and tanned. He had a head of dark, curly hair above a set of friendly blue eyes. Ferris hadn't had much of a chance to speak to either of them earlier and now felt as if he were intruding on something.

"Oh, sorry. I didn't know you were out here. I'll just go ba—" he started to say, but was interrupted by Benny.

"No, ah, nessun problema! It is okay," he said with a smile. His accent was thicker than any Giorgetti Ferris had ever heard. Gina didn't look too thrilled with her brother's invitation for this intruder to stay but didn't voice her opinion. She tapped some of the ashes of her cigarette on the deck and glanced away from them.

"Ah, all right," Ferris replied. He hadn't realized that Benny was so warm. When compared to the rest of his family, Benny was definitely the most intimidating in appearance.

"Are you not sleeping?" Benny asked after a moment of considering his English.

"No, I can't—... er, I'm not tired. Anche tu?" Ferris said, mustering up the courage to use what he'd learned in his Italian classes.

"Oh! Parli Italiano? E' fantastico! We has, eh, plane lag."

"Jet lag," Gina said, visibly trying not to roll her eyes.

Ferris ignored her tone and focused on Benny, who seemed much easier to talk to despite his weak grasp of the English language.

"So you flew over from Italy today?"

Benny considered the sentence for a few seconds, then nodded.

"Si, arriving at JFK... questa mattina?"

"In the morning?"

"È così! Yes."

Ferris smiled, despite himself. This man spoke very little English and Ferris spoke even less Italian, yet he found himself enjoying their conversation. He vaguely wondered why Gina was so blasé where her brother was so open, but similar upbringings didn't necessarily mean similar personalities.

"You are Demos, ah... migliore amico. He writes you in letters," Benny said, making the motion of writing an invisible letter.

"He does?" Ferris said, suddenly feeling embarrassed. Best friend — that was what that translated to, wasn't it? His face felt warm. "Er, yes. We spend a lot of time together."

"How nice for you," Gina scoffed, exhaling smoke. The mention of Demos seemed to shift her mood from 'uninterested' to 'irritated.' So irritated, in fact, that she'd decided to go back inside. She tossed her cigarette butt aside and gestured to her brother. "Sono stanca. Vado a dormire."

Benny gave Ferris an apologetic look. He was familiar with his sister's moods.

"Mi dispiace," he said, turning to follow Gina back into the house. "Dormi bene!"

"Goodnight," Ferris said with a weak smile. He looked out over the water as he heard the door click shut behind him. So Demos told other people about him? Part of him wondered if it was just complaining, but Ferris knew better. Demos trusted him enough to bring him to their summer home, and he trusted him with his deepest secret. After thinking for a moment, Ferris realized he didn't have anything interesting about himself that he could share in return. He would simply have to return the gesture by keeping his friend's secrets quiet – all of them.

16

Summer soon came to an end, giving way to autumn and a new school year. They were now in their Junior year, which wasn't quite young, but wasn't quite old. Ferris was looking forward to doing his best in every class and Demos was anticipating charming his way through the same tasks. Seamus, if he was thinking of anything, was most likely trying to figure out how many days he could skip without being expelled or deported.

This year, like each one before it, held various activities after school. They weren't always savory, and they weren't always legal, but they were certainly worth the time. This afternoon, Demos and Ferris accompanied Victor on a timeless family tradition.

The Giorgettis often went to the shooting range to fine-tune their marksmanship, but this was the first time that Ferris was joining them. Demos had asked for him to come, 'just in case,' whatever that meant. If Demos thought they would ever be in a situation where Ferris would actually shoot someone, he needed to take some time off to revise his tactics.

The shooting range was located downtown in the basement level of a large office building. The entrance was nondescript, visible only to those who were looking for it. Most of the Giorgetti men were well-known members. This was made clear by the familiar greeting Victor received upon their arrival.

"Vic, you brought the kids." The owner was a black man in his late fifties — he'd lived through Vietnam and had several memorial tattoos to prove it. He ran a hand over his bald head, taking a glance at the teenagers in Victor's wake.

"Hi, Ben," Demos said, picking up his head in greeting. Ben nodded in return. Demos was a familiar face. The young Italian had embarrassed many of his other customers by way of accuracy bets. Most had not considered the possibility that they would be defeated by a boy who didn't even own his own handgun. Demos was well respected, but his talent and age combined were terribly annoying. It didn't help that the kid was smug, either.

Ben laid a rifle and several handguns out on a wooden table, asking Demos which caliber he wanted to try that day.

"Actually, I have my own now."

This was received with a smile. Ben's eyes crinkled at the corners, not caring to mention that Demos was too young to legally own a gun. They already knew. He wouldn't have been surprised if the Giorgettis pulled more than a couple strings to get him a license. The wait was normally half a year.

"What'd they get you, kid? Not a pop-gun, I hope."

"No." Demos gave a slight smile, pulling a tiny silver and black revolver from its case. "A snub nose – it's a .357 Magnum. Birthday present."

A snub nose wasn't a hobbyist's hunting gun. It was made to be carried and concealed. If someone owned one, they were either a detective, or up to no good.

"That's a nice piece of work. Smith and Wesson, from stingy old Victor? I'm surprised." Ben grinned.

Victor was quick to give a patronizing laugh, folding his arms across his chest.

"*Stingy old Victor* got the kid some stock. The gun's from his grandfather," Victor added snidely.

"Hey, what about him?" Ben asked, jerking a thumb towards Ferris. He'd been silent the entire time.

"We're going to teach him the basics. Rifle for now," Victor said.

Ferris, clearly just going along with what was being said, nodded briefly. The hefty amount of firearms on the table and in everyone's hands made him a little anxious.

"All right," Ben said shifting the toothpick in his mouth to the other side. "Take this."

He passed an unloaded rifle into Ferris' hands, picking up one of the same model to explain.

"This is a standard .22 caliber. This button on the side, that's the safety. When it's red, safety's off. Always treat a gun as if it's loaded."

Ferris looked down at the weapon in his hands. It was lighter than he'd expected and the grip was made of cool, black plastic.

"Rule two," Ben continued. "Never point the muzzle at something you aren't willing to destroy."

"I don't have to fill out any forms?" Ferris asked, looking wary.

Ben laughed as if Ferris had been joking. Ferris supposed that the Giorgettis didn't *do* forms. It was plausible that they were above bureaucracy and the law in a place like this. He listened carefully as the man explained every aspect of the weapon, from how to load it to what to do if it was jammed. Demos sat by, unable to help but looked bored. He knew the workings of most guns better than many men knew their own wives.

"Yeah, so anyway, just watch where you're aiming it. Can't tell you how many times some asshole was standing around talking to his friends and then blows a hole in the wall. You don't want to shoot Demos or anything, do you?"

It was then that it hit Ferris that he was holding an object that was capable of killing someone. It wasn't the same type of

114

weapon as a knife or hammer. It held a power that nearly made his skin prickle. If he didn't pay precise attention to what he was doing, someone could very easily drop dead next to him. It was almost enough to make him want to just put it down.

Ben and Victor finally left the boys to themselves in the next room. They loaded ammo for Ferris' rifle, silently counting as they filled the magazines. Golden metal shone under fluorescent lighting as dozens of rimfire cartridges splayed over the dark table-top. The ammunition clicked as it went in, leaving their fingers stained with dark smudges.

"How long have you been doing this, anyway?" Ferris asked, setting a full magazine to the side.

"Legally?" Demos asked thoughtfully.

"At all."

"Dad showed me how a gun worked when I was five. I guess he didn't want me to find his stash and accidentally kill myself – or him."

"Charming."

"He was weird," Demos mumbled, going quiet. He didn't speak of his father often. The last bullet snapped into place and Ferris set the packed magazine at the end of his neat row.

"Ready?" Demos asked, handing him earmuffs and plastic eye protection.

"Honestly?" Ferris muttered, still feeling pale.

"You'll be fine," Demos said, giving his friend a smile as he slid the eyewear behind his ears. "Just remember what he told you."

Ferris nodded. The last few words out of Demos' mouth were muted from the ear coverings he'd put on, but he got the general idea. They went onto the shooting line, closing the door behind them. Victor was already going, holding an automatic pistol with both hands and quickly sending a half dozen holes into the paper target ahead of him. Even with the headset, it was loud.

Ferris' palms hadn't stopped prickling. He loaded the rifle, cocking it before pulling it up to aim. It was difficult to keep his hand steady and the small sight wouldn't sit perfectly still beneath the bull's-eye. When would he ever have to use this weapon? If the time came, would he actually have it in him to shoot a human being? He wasn't even sure if he'd be able to shoot a squirrel. On his left and right, the sound of heavy gunshots pierced the air, echoing despite the thick muffs covering his ears. He didn't want to imagine the noise without them.

Taking in a deep breath, he waited a moment. His finger tugged, and the rifle fired. The kickback was slight and the bullet punctured the target with a sharp snap. Squinting, he looked past his glasses to see where it had hit.

The hole was within the inner circle. It hadn't been a perfect bull's-eye by any means, but it was in the correct vicinity. He ignored the nervous sweat behind his ears. All he could think of, quite guiltily, was how good that had felt. The item in his hands personified power. The feeling was addictive and he didn't waste a moment bringing the rifle back up to fire once more.

When he had emptied the first magazine, he removed it, looking around the short wall to see how Demos was doing. The boy had already pulled in his target, having emptied over two dozen bullets into it. The result was rather strange. Instead of thirty little holes scattered about the paper, they were all neatly clustered together. It was dead-center. Demos held the target up, looking at Ferris through the golf ball sized opening. He winked.

"Are you winking?" Ferris asked. "I can only see one eye. Actually, I'm not even sure if you have two eyes," Ferris said, losing a little of his newfound pride. No wonder the older guys couldn't stand him. Of course, Demos hadn't heard his friend's muttering through the muffs and simply smiled before turning back to reload his gun.

Soon, they reconvened in the back room. Ferris removed his eye protection, letting his skin get some fresh air. He couldn't believe that he was tired; all he'd done was pull a trigger. His lungs were weary and his skin was damp. He exhaled heavily, tugging the headset down to rest around his neck.

"You're doing pretty well," Demos said, drinking from a bottle of water.

"Don't patronize me, Demos."

"I'm serious. A lot of guys go all crazy cop-movie mode and don't even bother aiming."

"I hadn't realized you were that good."

"You sound bothered."

"I guess I shouldn't be, as long as I'm on your side."

"There you go," Demos said with a smile.

"So, you ready to go home?" Ferris said, grabbing a broom for sweeping up discarded shells. Demos didn't answer. He was staring over Ferris' shoulder, his expression hard to read.

"Demos?" Ferris asked, hesitating before turning to see what his friend was staring at.

A young Irish man was at the counter, buying a few boxes of cartridges. A steaming paper cup was in his left hand, presumably coffee or tea. His skin was pale and worn and he seemed perpetually flushed over his cheekbones.

"Who is that?" Ferris asked quietly, wondering why Demos was so distracted by the man. Then, as if he could feel the teen's eyes, the man looked over. His hard features contorted to form something similar to a grin.

"Well," the stranger started, walking over through the doorway to the back room. He looked over the two, noticing that

116

Ferris had a broom. "If it isn't *Ghostie*. And his skivvy, I suppose."

"Hello Bob," Demos said bluntly, keeping his tone curt.

"I told you not to call me that," the man replied with a snap. His accent was thicker when he was angry. Ferris had heard of him before. His given name was, unfortunately, Brian O'Brien. Those that did not fear him tended to use 'Bob' for short. Ferris glanced quickly between the two. The tension was thick enough to cut with a machete.

"So, you done for the day? Shame," Brian said, smirking. "Guess I can't whip you in another bet."

It was no wonder Demos had been staring a hole in this man's head. Brian had bested him and Demos had a fragile ego. The banter seemed to get under his skin and Demos didn't have anything to respond with.

"And what's that?" Brian continued, slapping a hand to his own face in feigned surprise. "What a wee little gun! Suits you perfectly, boyo."

"I'm not going anywhere," Demos finally answered, gathering himself. He managed a snide smile. "And I'm not going to lose again."

"You're on, then. And what shall we bet?"

"Why don't we use testosterone, since you seem to have it in excess."

Brian snorted. In lieu of response, he took a sip of his hot tea. As he set the cup down onto the table, his eyes drew up to match Demos'.

"How about that little revolver of yours? It's so small, you wouldn't miss it anyway."

Ferris could see the gears in Demos' head turning. His grandfather had given him that gun. Demos didn't want to imagine having to say the words 'I lost it in a bet.' In that case, he simply would have to avoid losing at any cost.

"And if you lose," Demos said carefully, "I get your Beretta?"

Brian opened his mouth to answer, but hesitated. His gun was easily twice the value of Demos'. The semi-automatic had never failed him in the past. He didn't plan on failing today.

"That's right," Brian said, his green eyes narrow with anticipation.

"Fine," Demos said over a quick, firm handshake.

The patrons of the shooting range were familiar with the rivalry Brian and Demos had. When the two approached the line, the room quieted. Demos, though externally confident, had a nervous tick in his heart rate. Short barreled guns were more difficult to aim properly. The snub nose also kicked harder, making it trickier to achieve accuracy. Not only was Demos less experienced, but he was playing with a handicap. The thought of borrowing one of the range's other guns crossed his mind as he loaded the cartridges, but it was too late now. Brian was already aiming.

"Twenty-five yards. Five shots each. Best total wins," Brian said bluntly. The Italian only nodded, snapping the cylinder shut and holding it up to aim. He pulled back the hammer, swallowing testily.

The next ten shots that rang through the air melted into each other, filling the line with echoing noise. Ferris only stood behind the glass and watched, positive that this was a terrible idea. Sometimes Demos was too confident for his own good. If he lost his first gun, it wasn't likely that Gino would be hopping to buy him another one. This was a gamble that only an immensely swelled pride would be willing to take. Ferris sighed as they both put down their guns, anxious to see the results.

Brian wheeled his target in immediately, unclipping it to pass to one of the staff.

"Add that up. Not my best, but it should do for the likes of him," Brian said coolly, making a poor attempt at modesty. The bullet holes had sliced through compactly, leaving a neat cluster in the middle with a couple shots along the edge. It was impressive.

Demos had brought in his target as well, holding it in both hands wordlessly. Ferris craned his neck to see it. Demos wasn't speaking. It meant he had either done exceptionally well, or exceptionally terrible. Brian snatched it from his hands, holding it up to the light.

"Two hits? You only hit it twice? Tell me this is a joke," Brian laughed, putting a hand on his chest in disbelief. Demos didn't reply, only looking over to Ben for backup. The man took the target, examining it carefully.

"Actually, Bob, he hit it five times."

"What'd you call me?"

"Mr. O'Brien," Ben corrected himself nervously. "Look, four of them just went into the same hole is all."

"Give me that," Brian snapped, taking the paper back to stare intensely at the bullet holes. Indeed, the hole was a bit larger than it should have been. Four bullets had passed through the exact same spot.

"That last shot was a fluke," Demos said slowly, describing the small hole one centimeter away from the other. "Muzzle flash."

Demos held his hand out, motioning for Brian's Beretta. It was his now.

"You little cocksucker," Brian sneered. "You're lying, the both of you."

"You're not backing out now, are you Bob?" Demos smiled in a way that made the Irishman want to slap him. Brian's face had grown a deep shade of pink and his hands nearly shook with anger.

"You cheated, there's no way you could have done this. You're a teenager and a feckin' wop."

"There a problem here?" A steady voice came from over Brian's shoulder. Victor stood firmly behind him, looking ready to gut someone. Brian clenched his teeth to keep from lashing out. Any man who spoke back to Victor Giorgetti woke up with a burnt house and a dead family. Wordlessly, he slapped the gun into Demos' hands. He gave Demos a hard glare, then turned to leave. The door slammed shut behind him.

The moment they were alone, Victor smacked the backside of Demos' head.

"*Ow!* What was that for?"

"I ever hear of you betting a gift from your grandfather again and you won't be having another birthday."

"Yeah, okay," Demos mumbled, rubbing the spot he'd been hit. The scolding didn't end when he stepped out of the range.

"I can't believe you did that," Ferris blurted, exasperated.

"Yeah, I wasn't too bad, huh?"

"No, I mean, I can't believe you bet your gun against that guy. What would you have told Gino if you lost it?"

"I'm not really sure. I didn't plan on losing."

"You weren't even nervous," Ferris said incredulously.

"Are you kidding me? I nearly shit myself, I was so fucking scared. But I couldn't let him know that, could I?"

"I guess."

"And look," Demos continued with a smile, "two guns."

He held them both up, a little too proud. Ferris only sighed, shaking his head in a way that meant '*idiot.*'

"Admit it, Ferris. That was pretty cool. It was like Robin Hood."

"Robin Hood gave his loot to the poor."

"You want me to give a semi-automatic pistol to a homeless person?" Demos asked with a raised eyebrow.

"Shut up, Demos. That guy took it really hard. You're probably going to end up in his trunk," Ferris muttered. Demos only laughed. Regardless of what his uptight friend was saying, or what he'd risked, he came out on top. Today, he'd won.

17

A drop of red hit the bright ceramic of the toilet seat. In the third stall down, Ferris was attempting to stifle his bleeding nose with a wad of thin toilet paper. He leaned against the steel wall and it shifted back with his weight. The paper was dry and scratched the sensitive skin on the wings of his nose. Sniffing in once, he looked up to the ceiling in an attempt to coax gravity's help. The dusty tiles were speckled with spit wads and there was a single pencil lodged into its surface. Low thunder grumbled in the distance outside, sounding like an angry, empty stomach.

The cause of his bloody nose was nothing special. He'd replied to a lewd remark with a backhanded compliment and received a single punch to the face. There wasn't any distress or anger in his eyes; he knew that he'd deserved it. If anything, he felt foolish for not thinking quickly enough to hold his tongue.

Ferris pulled the wad back, examining the bright red stain that had soaked the center. A wet trail escaped down the corner of his mouth and he quickly pressed the tissues back to his nose. It would probably be another minute.

Another roll of thunder filled the air outside and there was a space of two seconds before the bathroom lights went out.

"Damn it."

The issue had already dropped from his mind when he met Demos at the bodega down the street after school. His friend had asked to meet him there with the promise of a discussion and Ferris had never denied him before. The location was on 21st and Bow and Demos had parked his uncle's car along the curbside. Ferris waited outside the tiny store with his hands in his pockets, idly looking over the beer ads in the window. Demos emerged with tired eyes and a package of cigarettes. He was by no means old enough to purchase them, but had by now established a relationship with the shop's purveyor. Being the nephew of made men didn't hurt, either.

"Hey," Demos said casually, packing the tobacco into the filters against his palm.

"Funny meeting spot," Ferris muttered in response.

"I ran out, I couldn't wait," his friend answered with a shrug, pulling a cigarette out and pocketing the rest. Opening the complimentary box of matches he'd received, he covered the end to light it. Ferris didn't reply, looking out over the street and waiting for the Italian to bring up whatever he'd been meaning to talk about. It was quiet for the moments it took Demos to exhale and he tossed the burnt match to the sidewalk.

"Looks like rain," Demos offered, looking up at the gray sky.

"Got a feeling in your bones, or did the power outage tip you off?"

The blackout had been unceremonious. The lights had returned to the building within seconds and classes had resumed normally. Demos' remark seemed to have been on cue, however, as the sidewalk began to speckle with dark spots. The bodega's awning was sufficient shelter for the time being.

Demos looked as if he was still considering his words. His pupils were staid and distant and it seemed as if he might change his mind and end up saying nothing at all.

Ferris noticed that Demos wasn't flicking his cigarette. The paper was slowly burning down to a long, fragile column of ash, one that would only fall when its own weight was too much to bear.

"I need to ask you something, Ferris."

"Go ahead."

Demos had inhaled and held it, stalling for time before he breathed out a long plume.

"Would you follow me to the ends of the earth?"

Ferris didn't look at him, thinking the question was a little silly.

"The earth is round, Demos."

Demos shot him a look. Ferris only glanced back, humoring him with a scarce smirk.

"Sure. Why not."

The cylinder of ash broke, sending flakes of burnt paper to the damp sidewalk below.

"Then get in the car."

Ferris' hand stopped short of the passenger side door as Demos spoke.

"No. I need you to drive."

Ferris hesitated, giving Demos a glance before complying. They both got into the vehicle and there were a few seconds of silence as Ferris waited for him to say more. The rain speckled on the windshield, making a soft pattering which only intensified the quiet.

"Head to 9th and Manning."

The car started smoothly as Ferris pulled into the street. It took a few blocks of driving before his curiosity got the best of him.

"So, where are we going?" he asked.

Demos took in a breath. It seemed he'd been trying to explain the entire time but was having difficulty doing so.

"O'Connell's Pub."

"You... need an emergency pint of Guinness?"

Demos shook his head. Ferris let him gather his thoughts. It was rare to see his friend without quick, articulate responses.

121

"Uncle Victor gave me... some territory. I get ten percent."

"O'Connell's is part of it?"

"Yeah. It was going well the first few weeks. They paid on time and there wasn't too much attitude about it. But—" Demos' mouth flattened and he stared harder out the window. "I screwed up."

"What happened?"

"They don't take me seriously because I'm so young."

'And tiny,' Ferris thought, but kept it to himself.

"They know I'm gay."

Ferris stared at him.

"They have photos of me with—" Demos stammered. "Uh, well, with a boy. If... if Uncle Vic—... if my family found out, I don't know what would happen to me. My life would be over."

Demos' tone made it sound as if he meant it literally. His hands started shaking.

"They make me pay them to keep quiet," he finally admitted. His voice cracked with shame. Here he was, trusted with collecting protection, and he'd ended up a puppet of some pub owners. For a moment Ferris wondered exactly who Demos had been caught with, but this wasn't the time to ask.

"Demos, it's not your fau—"

"I don't care, it doesn't matter."

Not only was this a hit to Demos' pride, but the situation could potentially ruin his entire life. He obviously couldn't go to his family for help. Outside of Ferris, he didn't have anyone he could tell. He was desperate. So desperate, in fact, that he'd opened the glove compartment to start loading a gun. Ferris saw it from the corner of his eye and felt his heart skip.

"Demos, what exactly are you planning on—"

"Just drive, okay?"

"Wait, you're not going to—"

"Here. Stop here."

Ferris had been so caught up in the intensity of the moment that he hadn't noticed their arrival at the pub. The car stopped at the curb and they both sat motionlessly.

"I'll be right back," Demos said, reaching to open the door. The lock made a hard click as the knob went down, stifling his effort. He looked over at Ferris, who was glaring back at him.

"Ferris, unlock the door," Demos demanded.

"No. We're going home."

"You said you'd—"

"I never said I'd drive you to your *grave*," Ferris hissed.

"I'm going to do this with or without you."

"Like hell you are," Ferris snapped.

"Ferris..." Demos' expression calmed. He looked back at his friend, speaking quietly against the rain. "I know what you're

122

thinking. But I have to do this. I could come back later and do it alone, but..."

He sighed, forgetting his pride for just a second.

"I need you here."

Ferris' glare slowly faded and his eyes went over Demos' features in calculation. His finger was still over the door's master lock. If he pressed the button, he could be sending his best friend to his death. He would have to live with that decision for the rest of his life. If he drove off right now, Demos would be stupid enough to do it anyway, but he'd be alone.

He couldn't abandon him.

Ferris exhaled, ignoring the sick feeling in his chest. For a moment there was only the sound of drops hitting glass. Seconds later, the lock clicked up.

The corners of Demos' eyes tightened gratefully as he said what might have been the last words Ferris would ever hear him say.

"If I'm not the first person out the door, drive away."

Before Ferris could reply or think, the passenger seat was empty.

The next few minutes dragged on as if they were centuries. Ferris' eyes were locked on the door and his hands were tight on the steering wheel. There was a dull thudding in his chest as he waited for something, anything, to happen. The prickling in his hands intensified. He couldn't see through the windows of the pub or hear anything from the inside. What if Demos had pulled out the gun and they knocked him out? What if they'd taken him to some back room and stabbed him and he was already dead, or—

Ferris shut his eyes tightly and shook his head, telling himself to stop thinking the worst. He swallowed despite his dry mouth. His pessimistic train of thought came to a harsh stop when a sound broke his thoughts. Three gunshots.

They were followed by two more, then silence. He sat up straight, staring a hole into the door. His pulse had invaded the inside of his head – pounding, deafening. Then, the door flung open. Ferris' lips parted, making out the silhouette.

It wasn't Demos.

The man rushed outside, looking around desperately. His skin was bloodied along the side of his face. He noticed the running car, then Ferris. As their eyes met, Ferris remembered what he was supposed to do.

He couldn't do it. His foot wouldn't push the pedal. It was impossible — Demos hadn't lost. Ferris trusted him. He trusted him to know what he was doing and to make it out okay. This wasn't happening.

The injured man quickly approached, but Ferris didn't move. As the man grasped the car's door handle, another shot rang out.

The body jerked, collapsing against the glass of the passenger door before sliding to the ground. Blood smeared down the window, but Ferris could still see past it. Demos stood in the doorway, still aiming his gun at the corpse. They looked at each other before Ferris blurted the first thing that came to his mind.

"Get in the fucking car!"

Demos complied hastily and the door slammed shut. They were both breathless as the vehicle pealed out of the spot by the curb, speeding down 9th Street and onto an infrequently used side street at the intersection.

"The warehouse," Demos said breathlessly. Ferris knew exactly what he meant. There was blood on the car and if the police stopped them, it would all be over. There was a warehouse only a few blocks away where the family stored stolen cars and contraband. Demos leaned over Ferris, shakily entering the pass code into the machine. They only managed to breathe when the gate closed behind them.

They parked inside the dark warehouse, taking time to gather themselves before speaking.

"What happened?" Ferris said, turning the car off. He noticed that Demos seemed as if he were trembling. His friend didn't answer at first, only holding up small manila envelope that had been stained with blood. When Ferris didn't answer, he elaborated.

"The negatives."

Ferris took the envelope from Demos' hand in disbelief, unable to think of anything to say.

"I—" Demos was having trouble speaking. He looked even paler than he normally did, making the blood on his face stand out against the white.

"They refused to give the... I... I shot them. Th-three of them."

Demos went quiet, clearly reliving the moment in his mind.

"I've never killed someone before," Demos said faintly.

Ferris' eyes widened as the Italian put a hand over his mouth, looking ill.

"I feel—" Demos' eyes shut tightly as he fumbled for the door's handle. "I need to—"

Ferris understood immediately, getting out of the car and helping the other out. He put a hand on Demos' back as the boy retched against the warehouse wall. When he was finished, Ferris helped him back to the passenger seat. He took a handkerchief from the glove compartment, wiping the blood from Demos' temple instinctively.

"Is this...?"

"It's not mine," Demos answered. "I'm fine."

He curled forward, holding his own body as he tried to keep from choking.

"Relax, breathe slowly."

Demos was on the brink of a panic attack. All that Ferris could think to do was rub his back and speak to him, attempting to ease his symptoms.

Once Demos had calmed, Ferris remembered that he was angry.

"I can't believe you just ran in there with a gun. Three guys? There were three guys and you still did it? I almost had a heart attack. You scared ten years off of my life! I hope you're happy with—"

"Ferris..."

"What?"

"Thanks. For staying."

Ferris stopped, looking down at the ground in thought.

"Well," he started, "someone had to."

Standing, Ferris unlocked the trunk to find something to clean the door with.

"But next time I'm leaving your ass on the curb, got it?"

"Got it," Demos replied, unable to help but smile.

18

Though the percent of cash Demos received from his 'work' was low, it was still an impressive amount of money for a sixteen year old. He made much more money from hassling businesses than he did doing a small-time test answer market at school. The boys' yearlong enterprise came to a close as they mutually decided to quit while they were ahead. Their customers complained, but the trio found very little sympathy in their hearts.

With his newfound wealth, Demos spent the last few weekends looking at car dealerships. He was searching for the perfect vehicle, one which his pickiness had kept him from finding just yet. Nicky, being particularly good with cars, had accompanied him each time. His presence kept the dealers from thinking they could rip the boy off and he also had a way with haggling. Victor had insisted it was a result of Nicky being a 'cheap bastard,' but Nicky preferred to call it a skill.

That particular evening Demos had asked Ferris to accompany them to give a second opinion on a model he had test driven.

"No, this car is totally gay." Ferris was sitting in the backseat of the Volkswagen with his arms folded impatiently across his chest.

"But look at the op—"

"No. I'm serious. If you drive this around, I'm walking."

"It comes in black, t—"

"I would rather die than be seen in this car."

"Yeah," Nicky cut in. "It *is* pretty gay, Demos."

"Doesn't that one chick drive one of these, the president of the Spirit Club?"

"At least she isn't in the *Mathletes*, Ferris."

"Hey, I only joined for one semester to keep your ass from failing. I can't believe I had to cut a deal with the teacher. You owe me. You also owe me for making me sit in this car."

"Fine, fine! I won't get it. Jesus. What do you want me to get, a Hummer?"

"Yeah, the one car that's gayer than this one. Nice."

"Well, Vic said to have you home in two hours," Nicky said, looking at his gold wristwatch.

"I'm never going to pick one at this rate," Demos complained. "Especially if I keep bringing Captain Homophobe to cry about every car I like."

"I'm not a homophobe. I hang out with you, don't I?"

Nicky laughed while Demos rolled his eyes, turning to the uncomfortable looking dealer in the seat next to him.

"I guess this isn't the one," Demos said slowly.

"That's all right, Sir. If you'd like to look at our—"

Nicky interrupted by clearing his throat and tapping his watch.

"Sorry," Demos apologized, "Have to run."

By the time they'd escaped the persistent dealer and made it back to Nicky's car, ten more minutes had passed. Ferris could tell that Demos was still sour about the car and put a hand on his shoulder from the backseat.

"Hey, sorry if I was a jerk. But it was for your own good."

"Yeah, yeah."

"I'm just jealous because I still ride a bike."

It wasn't long before the car pulled up in front of the Giorgetti home.

"Hey, stick around, Fish. I'll give you a ride home, too," Nicky said, readjusting the toothpick he'd been chewing.

"Thanks, Nicky."

Demos relinquished the passenger seat to Ferris as he said goodnight and went inside, already imagining the next car he would test drive.

"Hey uh, kid. You mind if we make a quick stop? Only be a minute, it's not far."

"Sure," Ferris answered slowly. His house wasn't very far from Demos'; he couldn't imagine what important thing could possibly be on the way over. He wasn't, however, in the mood to walk, so he kept his mouth shut.

"You two, you're pretty good friends, huh?" Nicky asked, driving with one hand.

"Yeah. It's been... four years, I guess."

"Heard they took you on their summer trip, too."

Ferris was quiet for a moment. He knew that only family members normally went on that trip and that Nicky had never been invited. He started to wonder how Nicky knew he'd gone at all.

"Yeah," he answered finally, his voice quiet.

"Hey come on, don't be shy or nothin'. Just making conversation."

Ferris forced a short laugh, starting to feel silly. Nicky was like family to him. He was starting to wonder why he felt anxious when the car came to a stop. It was a small warehouse surrounded by chain-link and empty parking spaces. It was deserted and seemed like an odd place to be stopping. Then again, Nicky was a gangster. It wasn't like he did his business at Toys-R-Us. The engine stopped as Nicky got out, pocketing his keys and lighting a cigarette.

"Come on, don't wanna leave you out here by yourself."

Ferris nodded, opening the door and stepping out as he stared up at the building. He usually felt at ease with Nicky, as if the man were simply his fat older brother. This, however, was strange — it didn't feel right.

A flickering light hung above a steel door with chipped paint, one with a lock that Nicky fumbled with for a few seconds before pushing open. The door's frame scraped the floor as it swung in, looking too heavy for the hinges. Ferris glanced behind them before going in, unable to shake the feeling that he was being watched.

They went down a dim hallway into a room. There was only one figure and a table, lit poorly by a single light bulb hanging from the ceiling.

"Hey Nick," the figure said, standing and moving into the light. Ferris felt relief at seeing a familiar face – it was Sal.

"Sal," Nicky said with a nod. His attention turned back to Ferris as he motioned to a flimsy chair.

"Why don't you have a seat?"

Ferris opened his mouth to say something along the lines of 'I thought this was just going to be a quick stop,' but thought better of it. Hesitantly, he sat down, keeping his eyes on the two men.

"Fishbones," Sal started, "How you been?"

"All right," Ferris answered slowly. He looked briefly over to Nicky, who was leaning against the wall and finishing his cigarette.

"We like you, kid. That's why you're here." As Sal spoke, Ferris got the feeling that this wasn't completely true. "Cause we know we can trust you."

When Ferris didn't answer, Sal continued.

"Heard Gino trusts you, too. A real lot. Seems like you went up to that summer house they got, even. That's right, ain't it?"

"Yeah."

"I'm not mad or nothin,' I don't even really like the woods."

'Beach,' Ferris thought, 'Not woods, beach.'

He didn't say anything. He knew Sal was trying to trick him into correcting him. The tall Italian looked Ferris from toe to head, his eyes shining in the yellow light.

"Anyway, we thought since maybe we're all in this together, you'd let us know where the place is, yeah? I mean, one of you ever gets in trouble, we gotta find you, right? Or if I need to get away from some heat, I'd have a place to sit for a while."

"You could ask Gino."

"Gino, bless his heart, he don't always treat us how we deserve."

"I'm sorry, I don't remember where it was. They blindfolded me," he lied.

"You know, I kind of doubt that, kid."

128

Ferris felt the tension starting to build in the small room. He turned to Nicky with an almost desperate look, unable to believe that someone he trusted was doing this to him. Instead of responding with sympathy, Nicky did something quite surprising.

"Look, you little shit!"

It only took a few seconds for Nicky's hand to grasp Ferris' throat, pinning him down to the wooden table. He could feel the sweat of Nicky's palm squeezing into his skin.

"I *know* you've been there, and you know where it is. You know where that fuckin' safe is and if you plan on living to see tomorrow, you tell us!"

Ferris could only stare at Nicky, wide eyed and short of breath. This was a bad dream; it couldn't possibly be real.

"Come on, Nick," Sal groaned. "I was tryin' to do it nice."

If his situation weren't so dire, Ferris would have laughed. Sal, owner of the worst temper in Southport, was playing 'good cop.'

"Well it wasn't fuckin' working, was it, Sal?" Nicky spat before bringing his face closer to Ferris'. The scent of tobacco was still strong on his breath. "Address, now!"

"I don't know!" Ferris choked, making an attempt to twist free. His hands were wrenched tightly on Nicky's wrist, but the man was easily twice as strong as he was. "Nick..."

"Nicky," Ferris repeated, looking him in the eyes. It didn't make any sense. Nicky was always around, laughing, eating, taking care of the boys and drinking with the men. The man Ferris was looking at wasn't the same person. His eyes were cold and narrow, making the idea that this was a nightmare seem even more possible.

"Don't look at me like that," Nicky snapped. "You know how hard we had it? You know how much shit we go through, and for what? They don't respect us. I gave the Giorgettis years of my life, for what? Am I made? No. And they even bring some fuckin' kid to their summer castle and leave us in the dirt."

Ferris' breathing was harsh as he listened and his chest rose and fell in deep, quick swells.

"Gino doesn't even have real power," Nicky continued, "just a bunch of blackmail in a little safe. Anyone could do that, anyone could lead these bunch of shits around. All it takes is balls. Look, kid. You tell me where, and all this will be over. No more troubles, no nothin'. Where was it you wanted to go, Yale? You want a nice condo to come back to when you're done? It'll be covered. Whatever you want, kid."

"Nick," Ferris panted. "I don't know where it is."

He was answered with a hard smack to the face as Nicky backhanded him, sending a few beads of sweat flying. When Ferris made an attempt to catch his breath, it happened again, but stronger. His glasses were knocked from his face, nicking the edge of the table before clattering to the floor. The third slap didn't come, and Nicky stayed his hand as he finished speaking to him.

"Think hard, Fish. Think hard about how much this is worth to you. If we don't find out where that safe is by the end of tonight, we're going to kill you."

Nicky spit out the cigarette butt that he had been biting, letting a few sparks skip across the floor.

"Is it really worth your life?"

Ferris closed his eyes. He couldn't take the sight of Nicky's face anymore. The sweat on Nicky's temples and the familiar, dark stubble on his jaw line were so close he could practically feel them. He knew. The exact address played in his head, repeating like a nursery rhyme. He knew the street number, the way there, and even where the safe was kept. All he had to do was open his mouth and say it. It would only be a few simple words and it would all stop. Nicky would let go of his throat and pat him on the back. He could go home and sleep in his own bed. It would be over.

Demos... Demos wouldn't want him to die over something so trivial, would he? A safe with a bunch of blackmail in it? And Gino, he—

Ferris took in a deep breath. Gino would lose his power – he would end up in jail, or worse. The family would crumble. Ferris remembered exactly what Demos had said to him behind the gas station on the drive to Long Island.

"I think they really trust you."

Slowly, he opened his eyes.

"I don't know."

Nicky was furious. He shoved Ferris further up onto the table, pulling a knife from his pocket.

"Sal, hold his arm out."

The sight of the knife made Ferris' blood drain. There was an echo in his ears, thumping harder and louder with each second. Sal's strong, dry hands held Ferris' arm flat on the table, exposing his wrist.

"So, Fish. Just to show you I really do care, I'm not gonna take your right hand. You're right handed, aren't you?"

Ferris couldn't answer, feeling himself start to tremble. He wanted to throw up.

"Yeah, it'll still hurt. And uh, you probably can't play violin no more without your left hand, could you? That'll be a shame. You made some real pretty music."

There had never been a point in his life where Ferris had been closer to crying. The skin of his eyes felt wet, but he refused to let himself. All he could hear was his own heartbeat. His throat was raw from panting and his eyes had locked onto the knife.

130

Nicky lifted it carefully, positioning the blade just above the tendons in Ferris' wrist. The faint light from the bulb gleamed off of the metal, blinding him for just a moment.

"Last chance."

Ferris made no response. As Nicky pulled back the knife, all Ferris could do was turn away. If he had to feel it, at least not seeing it would help. A bead of sweat broke from his forehead, running down behind his ear and down the back of his neck. As he breathed in, the knife came down hard.

There was a piercing sound of steel snapping into wood as the blade stuck into the tabletop. It took Ferris a second to realize there was no pain; it hadn't touched him. When he found the courage to open his eyes, he saw the blade. It was standing vertically, half an inch from his wrist. At first he thought Nicky had missed, but was surprised to see the man making a call on his cell phone.

"Hey, Gino?" Nicky paused, waiting for a response. "Yeah, we're done. We can trust him."

19

The study hall at St. Basil's was quiet by nature, but the cold silence between the two boys was nothing but awkward. Less than a day ago, Ferris had been thrown down onto a wooden table and threatened with a knife. Now he was going through a book about the Renaissance and wordlessly taking notes. Demos had a worksheet to fill out but was distracted by his friend's distance. They were sitting together, of course – they always sat together. Their usual acknowledgment of one another, however, was absent.

There was a soft chatter in the background as the other students went about their research. Demos found himself staring at his friend, dying for a glance, a word — anything. Ferris said nothing, only spinning a pen around his thumb as he read. Finally, Demos spoke.

"Ferris?"

It took Ferris a moment to look up from his book. His eyes were slow and half-lidded. He didn't answer, only returning the look, waiting. Demos took his time continuing. His words were calm as he spoke; it was clear he had refined them in his head.

"I knew."

Ferris' gaze dropped down to his book, as if unsure of what to say. He remained silent as Demos went on.

"I know you've been wondering if—"

"I figured as much," Ferris finally replied. He turned a page. Demos let out a soft breath, leaning closer to speak.

"If you don't want to be involved with me – er, with *us* anymore, it's okay. I'd understand."

"It's all right," Ferris answered simply. There was no hesitation in his tone.

"Are you sure?" Demos asked, knitting his brow. Ferris hesitated before carefully marking his place, shutting the book to put his full attention on his friend. To Demos' surprise, he gave a slight smile.

"I thought about it for a long time. All night."

Demos didn't speak, waiting to hear more.

"I guess I could be upset," Ferris continued. "It is my nature, after all. To get pissed about everything. But—"

Ferris pulled his glasses off in a rare show of sincerity. His brown eyes were clear in the light of the old academy hall. He turned the frames over in his hands, folding them as he looked up at his friend.

"I promised you I wouldn't be scared."

For a moment, Demos could only stare at him. The fear in his chest melted into relief, warming him to the tips of his fingers.

"Ferris, I—" Demos faltered. He knew what he felt, but wasn't sure how to say it. Ferris looked at him with patience, putting his glasses back on as he let Demos finish.

"It really meant a lot – that you didn't break. I mean, you know I believe in you and... and I trust you. But I still wasn't sure..." Demos trailed off, keeping his voice hushed between them.

"They said he threatened to take your hand," Demos added.

"Yeah, about that. You should think about letting Nicky go. He could have a great career as an actor. I mean, I almost cried."

Ferris laughed gently, reassuring Demos that he wasn't sore about it. Demos frowned briefly, but it passed. His friend's face carried nothing but forgiveness.

"Well, that's what you get for calling my car gay," Demos said snidely.

"Please tell me you didn't actually buy it."

"I'm thinking about it."

Ferris put his face into his palm, sighing slowly. The thought of reconsidering their friendship flashed through his mind. His hand dragged down his face before he looked over to Demos between his fingers.

"How about you promise you won't get it, and we're even."

"Fff," Demos scoffed, dismissing the idea with a wave of his hand. Their conversations never stayed serious for very long.

"Promise he won't get what?" cut in a familiar English accent. Seamus slid into the seat next to Demos, setting down a stack of books that he had no intention of reading.

"A stupid car," Ferris said, opening his book back to the page he had marked.

"*You're* stupid," Demos snapped.

"You been looking at cars without me? I'm hurt," Seamus said, feigning sadness. He had a way with cars and auto shop was one of the only classes he actually attended on a regular basis.

"We've been looking since last Tuesday," Demos admitted, doodling on his worksheet.

"You say that funny."

"What, Tuesday?"

"Yeah, that one."

"How do *you* say it?" Ferris cut in, raising an eyebrow.

"*Choos*day," Seamus articulated, as if proud of pronouncing it correctly. Demos and Ferris looked at each other, unimpressed.

"All right, Limey," Ferris started, twirling a pencil between his fingers, "Say 'Harry Potter.'"

Seamus hesitated suspiciously before replying in forced confidence.

"...Harry Potter."

Demos and Ferris instantly started to snicker, doing their best not to make a disturbance in the study hall.

"What?" Seamus demanded, not getting what was so funny.

"N-nothing," Demos said, biting his lip. There was a pause. "Say it again."

"No. Why?"

"Come on," Ferris smirked, "it's just two words."

"Here's two words for you both. Stupid. Yanks."

This only elicited more snickering from Seamus' two friends. The woman supervising the students gave them a sharp glare, holding her finger to her flattened lips.

"Yeah, go on. Get your laughs at the expense of a poor foreigner," Seamus said softly, his tone bitter.

"I don't know, Seamus. I think you're getting pretty Americanized," Demos said once he'd settled down. "You've started saying 'eraser' instead of 'rubber.'"

"Only because that blonde in fifth period almost slapped him," Ferris added.

"Speaking of fifth period, want to skive off? I'm feeling peckish but don't want to go on me tod," Seamus mused, balancing a pencil between two fingers. It had taken a bit of thinking to put that much obscure British slang into one sentence.

After staring at Seamus for a moment, Demos sighed.

"I take it back. I still have no idea what you're saying."

"I think he wants to cut class," Ferris analyzed, as if translating the behavior of a primate.

"Sure," Demos said, ignoring Seamus, "I need to pick up some cigarettes anyway."

"I'll pass. I don't have a big enough trust fund to get into Yale without good grades," Ferris said, not needing to emphasize his infatuation with a perfect GPA.

"Still going for Yale?" Demos asked, unable to hide his slight disappointment. There was no way Demos was going to attend an Ivy League school, if he went to college at all. His family needed him.

"Yeah. It's Dad's alma mater," Ferris said quietly. He hadn't, as one might think, been pressured into applying. Of all the people he looked up to, his father was the strongest influence in his life.

"Well, good luck," Demos said.

"I'll need it. These kids can't even spell 'Ivy League,' but they probably have a better chance than I do."

"I don't think that's true," Demos said.

"Well, my Dad wants me to get into Cornell but I'm a bloody fool. He'll probably just drop a wad of cash on someone's desk and I'll wake up in a dormitory."

Ferris raised his eyebrows at Demos, as if to say '*see?*'

"What I mean is, you should have more faith in yourself," Demos said, looking at his friend earnestly.

"Well, I'd certainly hate to miss this precious moment, but I've got to visit the gents."

"All right," Demos said, pretending to understand what Seamus was talking about. "See you at fifth, we can go to Mickey's."

Ferris gave Seamus a nod as the Brit left to go find the boy's bathroom.

"Who is he visiting, again?" Demos asked, once Seamus was gone.

"I think he's going to go crap. Or something."

"Ah. Well, I'm going to find some books for my Japanese class. But meet me after school, out front. Uncle Vic wants to take us out."

"Sure," Ferris replied, surprised that he was actually studying. Once Demos had left, Ferris exhaled. Perhaps now he could finally finish his reading. Tentatively, he looked down at his book. He'd barely read a single page.

The real estate agent on the intersection of 22nd and 5th had just finished a very long, hard day. To top it off, he'd been trying in vain for twenty minutes to hail a cab. He was seconds from giving up when a black Lincoln Town Car pulled up along the curb, coming to a careful stop several feet down.

"Oh, thank God," the man exhaled. He was normally wary of gypsy cabs, but he was getting desperate. Pulling the back door open, he slid into the backseat.

"73rd and Nathan, pl—"

He was unable to finish his request, interrupted by the sound of a gun cocking. His eyes were locked on the barrel of a pistol that was aimed directly between his eyes.

"Get the fuck out of my car."

"B-but I th—"

"This is *not a fucking cab!*"

The conversation ended there. The man tripped over himself as he threw the door open, staggering back onto the street. He clutched his briefcase to his chest as he stepped backwards, then ran off. Well, at least this would make a great story to tell someday. He would be sure to leave out the part where he shit himself.

Inside the Lincoln, Victor gave a dramatic sigh as he put away his gun. This wasn't the first time someone on the street had mistaken his vehicle for a gypsy cab. He couldn't even pick his nephew up from school without something ruining his afternoon. It wasn't, however, enough to make him consider a vehicle change. He loved his car. He also loved his gold watch, which he glanced at impatiently. Where the hell were those kids, anyway?

A few minutes later, the back door opened again as two teens rushed into the backseat.

"Sorry we're late, Uncle Vic. Sister Katherine kept me after class," Demos explained. He still had chalk on his fingers from cleaning the erasers.

"Want me to have her taken care of?" Victor offered, ashing his cigarette out of the cracked car window.

Demos laughed, shaking his head. Sometimes, though, it was hard to tell when his uncle was joking.

"So, where are we going?" Ferris asked as he buckled himself in.

"Charlie's rent is due, thought I'd take you kids up for some sundaes or something."

Charles Martin owned an ice cream parlor uptown called 'Sweet Nothings.' Ferris quickly assumed what 'rent' was and then followed that up with the guess that the sundaes would be free. He also figured that Victor wanted to show his nephew the ropes, so to speak. The two boys pounded each other's knuckles in satisfaction of this plan.

The glass doors of the shop opened smoothly, triggering the quaint chime of bells. Charlie looked up from behind the counter, immediately recognizing Victor. He pulled the small white hat from his balding head, giving his guest a nervous smile. The Italian leaned his arm up against the glass display, lowering his glasses to look at the various flavors.

"Afternoon, Charlie."

"Hello, Mr. Giorgetti. These... these your kids?"

Victor turned to look at Demos and Ferris; both were innocently eyeing the menu on the wall.

"Er, sort of. The nerd's a friend of the family."

"Hey," Ferris protested.

"I'm Demos, it's nice to meet you."

"They're uh, they're real nice," Charlie said with a faint smile. "You two want a cone?"

"Amaretto," Demos said instantly.

"Chocolate," Ferris followed, almost interrupting his friend. They'd known exactly what they'd wanted for a while. Charlie dipped the silver scoop in warm water, creating a sweet, heaping stack in two separate waffle cones.

"Thank you," they said simultaneously, taking the offered cones from the man eagerly.

"You look well, Mr. Giorgetti," Charlie said anxiously, fiddling with the scoop before quickly setting it down in realization.

"Please, Charlie. It's 'Victor.' What's the matter with you, anyhow? Usually you're so happy to see me."

136

"Oh, I'm fine. Everything's fine," Charlie said, looking sideways to see if any customers were in earshot. "Uh, why don't we step in the back, for just a little bit? To catch up."

Victor glanced at the boys before looking back at Charlie.

"Of course." Victor pointed at Demos. "Stay put for a minute. I'll be quick."

Demos nodded, sucking a bit of melting ice cream off the side of his cone. He wasn't going anywhere. They both watched the door to the back room as it shut, wishing they could be in on the conversation.

"I wonder what's wrong," Ferris said quietly.

"From the looks of it, he doesn't have the money."

"What's Victor going to do? He's not going to hurt him, is he?"

"I don't know. Charlie's a good guy. But Uncle Vic isn't really patient. Or compassionate."

They exchanged uncomfortable glances before looking down at their ill-begotten desserts. Demos' conscience was far less effective than Ferris' and he quickly went back to eating it. Ferris hesitated, then decided he couldn't just let it melt. It was really quite good, anyway.

In the back room, Charlie was sweating up a storm.

"If you could give me just another few weeks, I could try to get enough together to—"

"Wait a second, Charles. What kind of trouble do you mean? Is the shop doing poorly? You gambled it all away?"

"No. No, Sir, it's nothing like that. It's just, you see, we're just in a tough spot right now. My wife is sick."

"Flu?"

"Breast cancer."

Victor leaned back in his chair, studying the man carefully.

"I thought you had health insurance."

"Well, you see, we do. I thought it would cover her but... well," Charlie struggled, running a hand over his head, "they won't pay. Some loophole in the terms."

Charlie went on to explain the repeated hospital visits, as well as the gleaming price tags that accompanied them. He then outlined, to the best of his ability, his impotent attempts at negotiating with the insurance company.

"I didn't understand it much myself. No matter how many times I—"

"Stop." Victor held up his hand, silencing the old shop owner. "I've heard enough."

His eyes were narrowed in irritation. Charlie looked back at him timidly. Victor's hand raised to reach into his suit's inner pocket. The old man winced at the thought of what was coming, but exhaled when he saw it was only a pad of paper.

"What's the company's name?"

"Shebaro Mutual," Charlie answered slowly.

"Address?"

"I, um," Charlie said, patting his pockets for a wallet. "Here, their business card."

"Charlie, sit up straight," Victor said sternly. The man complied. "All right – we'll look into it."

"I—"

"Once it's settled, you're back on your payments. I don't want to hear any more excuses after this. You got it?"

"Thank you, Mr. Gi—" Charlie stopped himself, smiling. "Victor. Thank you, Victor."

Victor only nodded, standing and straightening the cuffs of his suit.

"And what's the shop open for? Why don't you go spend some fucking time with your wife?"

The Italian walked back into the shop and towards the front door with purpose, his steps quick and even.

"Come on, boys."

Demos glanced behind as they stepped out, checking to see if Mr. Martin was all right. The old man noticed Demos and gave him a brief wave. The teen smiled in return, relieved that he was okay.

As they got back into the car, Demos leaned forward curiously.

"What happened? Where are we going?"

He assumed they were on their way to some place of significance, considering the haste Victor was starting his car with.

"Disneyland," Victor said in monotone, snapping open his lighter to start a cigarette.

Demos sat back in his seat, folding his arms across his chest. Leaning over to Ferris, he mumbled as quietly as he could.

"Every time he says that, someone gets hurt."

"Walt would be proud," Ferris whispered in reply.

Victor multi-tasked as he drove, dialing a number from his cell phone while weaving through traffic.

"Nick? Yeah, I don't care. Look, get over to..." He glanced down at the card as he drove. "481 West 9th St. Yes, immediately. They close at five. I don't give a shit, Nicky. You get your ass down there, now."

He snapped the phone shut and slid it back into his pocket, biting the end of his cigarette in aggravation.

"Demos, tuck back your hair and get out of that uniform jacket."

"But—" Demos objected.

"I don't give a shit if they can see your scar. You'll look tougher, anyway. Push it back."

"Yes, Sir," Demos mumbled, running his hands through his hair to slide it back. He still didn't look very intimidating.

Ferris slowly looked over at Demos. He wasn't sure what was going on, but assumed Victor knew what he was doing. Even if Demos did look a little tougher, he was still just a skinny teenager.

The car came to an abrupt stop in the first space available. They were a block away from their destination — a downtown office building. Victor dropped a quarter in the meter and hurried them towards the entrance of the building. Nick was leaning against the wall, looking annoyed.

"This better be good, Ash."

"I'll make it up to you, you lazy prick."

As Victor walked past, Nicky made a quick gesture and muttered under his breath.

"Cazzo."

Demos exchanged a smirk with Nicky as they went inside. Victor looked briefly to each side, looking for security cameras. This would be easy — there weren't any. Satisfied, he stopped at the receptionist's desk, reading from the business card once more.

"How can I help you?" she asked.

"I'm looking for Mr. Gonyer. Shebaro Mutual."

The woman at the desk looked up at the man addressing her. Though she couldn't quite place where, she was certain she'd seen him before.

"The fifteenth, I believe. Did you have an appointment, Sir?"

"I'm an old friend," Victor said easily, lowering his eyes.

"I'll need some ID, Sir."

"No problem," Victor said, handing over a New York state driver's license. Her eyes widened as they fell on the name and she nearly dropped the card right onto the desk.

"Mr... Giorgetti? Ah, right. Yes, of course. Shall I call—"

"No need. In fact, let's all pretend we were never here. Is that all right, Miss..."

He paused to read her tag, committing her name to memory.

"Miss *Reade*?"

The receptionist swallowed.

"Of course."

Victor smiled, giving the young lady a nod.

"Ferris, wait here," he said, pointing at one of the lobby's sofas as the three walked over to the elevators. Ferris nodded in response and flopped down onto one of the seats. It was probably best that they weren't involving him, anyway. He tried looking out the window to watch cars go by, then got bored and rummaged for a magazine on the table. He could only imagine what could possibly be happening in Mr. Gonyer's office.

Fifteen floors up, the door to that very office was thrown open, slamming against the inner wall. Mr. Gonyer quickly looked up from his desk, staring widely at the three men who had just let themselves in. The largest of them was pulling a torque wrench from his jacket sleeve. A cordless phone was tucked between Gonyer's ear and shoulder and, for a moment, he was speechless.

"...I'll call you back," he said, very slowly, then set the receiver down.

Lacing his fingers, he gave them a quick smile. His teeth were perfectly aligned under a pair of blue eyes and a dark brown cut.

"Can I help you with something?"

"I certainly hope so," Victor said, returning the smile as he sat down in the seat facing the desk. Demos stood at his side, quietly observing.

"You see, Mr. Gonyer, a good friend of mine seems to be having trouble getting his funds from your health plan. I told him it all must have been a misunderstanding."

"I see," the man answered, his voice tense. "His name?"

"Charles Martin."

Gonyer's eyes went to his computer screen, entering in a few keys and reading what came up.

"Yes, hmm." He continued reading, scrolling down a few pages with his mouse. "His wife claims to have breast cancer."

"Terrible thing to happen to such nice people. You can do something about this, can't you?"

Demos was surprised to see the man pause, then grin.

"I'm afraid not, Sir. The treatments they're proposing for Mrs. Martin are too experimental to qualify for coverage under his plan. I'm sure you understand."

Victor's smile dropped, as well as his tone.

"It seems you're the one who needs to understand, Mr. Gonyer."

"I understand completely, Mr...? Ah, I don't believe I got your name."

"Giorgetti."

"Yes, Mr. Giorgetti. I'm quite familiar with scare tactics. I'm sorry to break this to you, but you're not going to bully me, or this company, out of thousands of—"

Without instruction or warning, Nicky punched him in the face. Spit flew from Gonyer's lips as he tumbled back from his seat, choking in surprise.

"Come on, Nicky. I'm sure we can do this without violence," Victor said smoothly, not moving from his seat. He didn't seem sincere.

"I hate when little pricks like him get condescending," Nicky grumbled as he played with the wrench in his other hand.

140

A hand slapped onto the desk as the man made an attempt to pull himself back up. Holding the side of his face, he leaned against the desk and glared harshly at the men in his office. Demos looked back at him emotionlessly.

"You Guinea fucks," Gonyer said, releasing a bit of blood from the corner of his mouth. He'd bitten his tongue on impact. He grasped the receiver of his phone, lifting it to call security. Victor leaned forward calmly, tugging the line from the back of the phone and tossing it to the floor.

"Tell me, Mr. Gonyer. Do you use this company's insurance?"

"Y-yes," he said, backing up towards the window. Nicky stepped closer.

"Are you covered in the event of, oh... I don't know. Falling from great heights?"

It took the man a moment, but something clicked in his head. He turned to notice the open window, then looked back to Nicky. He rushed to step away from the glass but was quickly grabbed by the collar.

"You won't do it."

"Is that so?" Victor asked, adjusting his glasses. Demos continued to watch intently, not interrupting.

"I don't care what kind of deal he has with you. We're a corporation, not some Mom and Pop liquor store you can hassle for loose change. If some old lady loses her tit, then tough shit."

Nicky looked over his shoulder at Victor. Victor simply nodded.

Back down on the first floor, Ferris was flipping through a *Better Homes and Gardens* magazine, stifling a yawn. It was either that, or *Highlights*. People occasionally came and went and the receptionist had gotten a phone call or two. For now, however, the lobby was silent. Ferris turned a page, eyeing an article about curtains in a hopeless attempt to find something interesting. Ah, a recipe for fish.

It was then that a large, blunt object whistled past the window. The body slammed into a small hotdog cart on the sidewalk, shattering the glass display and throwing the vendor onto his back. The umbrella had crumpled from the impact and the pavement was littered with pieces of beef and blood. Cars slammed on their brakes to avoid the debris, clumsily skidding over the tarmac. Ferris looked up from his magazine.

He snapped around to look out the window as the receptionist rushed up next to him. The sight was more than enough to make him cringe. The woman covered her mouth with both hands, holding back a sharp gasp.

"Oh my god," she said weakly, never having seen a dead body before. Though it made him feel sick, Ferris couldn't take his eyes off of the scene.

Once she gathered herself, the receptionist hurried back to her desk to dial 911.

"Yes, hello? There's been an accident on 481 West 9th Street – the Lowery Building. I... I think it was a *suicide*."

Soon, sirens filled the air in the distance. Ferris turned back around, watching the elevator. Where were they? He started to feel nervous, wishing he knew more about what was going on. The buzzing vibration of his cell phone was enough to make him jump and he hurriedly fumbled it from his pocket and brought it to his ear.

"Hello?"

"The car," was all that the voice on the other side said before it hung up. It had been Demos. They must have gotten out through a back door. Ferris quickly walked past the scene, averting his eyes. Nobody really noticed him; all eyes were locked on the bloody mess on the sidewalk. He made his way down the block to where Victor's car had been parked. Sure enough, the three were seated inside, casually smoking. Ferris got into the backseat silently. There wasn't a thing he could think of saying.

"We'll have to find a higher-up," Victor said to Nicky, starting the car.

"Yeah, what if they're all this stubborn?"

"Somehow," Victor started, watching the ambulance lights flashing in the rearview mirror, "I doubt it."

20

A perfectly aligned triangle of pool balls shattered with a sharp crack, the impact sending each ball spinning in its own direction. They slowly rolled to a stop as two dropped into the side pockets.

"Two in the hole and I'm stripes," Seamus said in a rather cocky tone, chalking the tip of his pool stick.

"Yes, we can see that," Demos said, eyeing the layout of the pool table. Seamus didn't respond as he took another shot. It missed, giving Demos his turn.

"I'm still betting on Demos," Ferris said, sitting in a recliner to the side with a magazine. After seeing the young Italian at the shooting range, he had complete faith in Demos' ability to aim. The three were in Victor's basement on a late autumn Saturday, wasting time in lieu of schoolwork.

"You know that hurts," Seamus said. "You have no faith in me."

"Sure I do. I just have more in Demos." Ferris smiled as Demos pocketed his second ball in a row, moving carefully around the corner of the table to aim again. He adjusted the cigarette in his mouth before leaning forward, snapping the stick forward to sink a third.

"He's cheating," Seamus mumbled, taking a drink.

"Oh, like you don't cheat at skeeball at the arcade," Demos said with a roll of his eyes. Not protesting the accusation, Seamus stood up straight as if having a revelation.

"That reminds me. *You*," he said, pointing down at Ferris with the tip of his cue stick.

"Yes?" Ferris answered slowly, looking up from his magazine.

"You're coming with us to Lenny's tomorrow, right?"

Lenny's was an arcade a few blocks from the school. It had recently taken on new management and had been renovated with modern equipment. Somehow, it wasn't enough to keep Seamus from cheating.

"Can't, I'm busy Sunday. You only want me to win at trivia so you can get tickets."

"Oh, no I don't, what a silly thing to—" Seamus hesitated, then gave in. "Okay, I do. But I only need 500 more to get the Billy Idol CD."

"Can't you just *buy* that at a store? Your father is a millionaire for fuck's sake."

"But it's *signed* and there aren't any on eBay," the Brit whined, gesturing his need with his hands. "Come on, you know that trivia gives the most tickets. And you always win."

"I just get lucky."

Seamus snatched up the magazine from Ferris' hands, waving it in his face dramatically.

"You're reading a bloody copy of *Scientific American*. For fun!"

"I told you, I have plans."

"Oh come on, we're mates aren't we? You gotta be there for your mates."

"I'm only friends with you gentiles so you can hide me if there's a World War III."

"Put off your homework, just one day," Seamus pressed.

"It's not homework," Ferris said, holding out his hand in a silent request for his magazine back.

"Then what?"

Ferris considered answering for a moment, then quietly replied.

"Date."

"What was that?"

"I have a date."

Both Seamus and Demos stopped what they were doing, looking up like prairie dogs that had heard a noise.

"*Really?*" they asked in unison.

"Sort of," Ferris muttered, starting to feel embarrassed. "My mother is trying to hook me up with some JAP."

"I thought she wanted you to date a Jewish girl," Seamus said suspiciously.

"No," Ferris sighed. "Not Japanese. JAP. Jewish American Princess. Dr. Eisenberg is our neighbor and he has this daughter, Rachel."

"Oh, she sounds rich. That's not so bad, maybe you'll get laid," Seamus said with a smile.

"Oh shut up," Ferris said, running his hand down his face. "I don't want to go."

"Then don't," Demos said rather simply.

"I have to. Mom gave me that guilt crap about how I don't love her and how she'll never have grandkids."

"She's going to have to accept the truth someday," Seamus grinned.

Ferris only gave another sigh, slouching down in his seat. He wasn't looking forward to the date. Not only did he have no interest in wasting time with some superficial diva, but there was someone else that he would much rather have gone with — someone that he doubted would have any interest in return.

Sunday evening came a little too quickly. Ferris had declined his mother's offer to help 'fix him up,' not wanting her anywhere near his hair or face before the date. He wore a simple sweater over an Oxford shirt, having little concern as to whether he was attractive or not. The café that had been chosen wasn't so bad, but she was late.

He took a glance down at his watch before looking towards the door again. It wasn't that he was eager to see her, but he did want to get this over with and go home. He idly stirred the coffee he had ordered, glancing every once in a while towards the window. After a few minutes, a white SUV pulled up along the curb. A girl stepped out, saying something to the driver before shutting the door and stepping into the café.

Ferris recognized Rachel quickly. They had gone to the same Hebrew school but had never spoken to each other. Even if he had wanted to, she was always surrounded by the same clique of girls. She was pretty in the conventional way, having long brown hair and flawless makeup.

"Um, hey," she said hesitantly, sliding into the chair across from him. She seemed as excited to do this as he was.

"Hi," he said plainly, turning the coffee mug around on the saucer. For a moment he waited for an apology since she was late, but quickly gave up hope.

"So, you want to order something?" he asked.

"I guess, something small. I'm on a diet."

Ferris' eyes drew up from his mug to her face. He wasn't in the mood to tell her how skinny she was, or whatever he was supposed to say, and simply cleared his throat.

"All right," he said slowly. He was already starting to daydream, imagining a rope with which to hang himself, or perhaps a vial of poison. No, that was too Shakespeare.

"Where's the waitress anyway?" she asked, looking over the menu with disapproval.

"She's taking that man's order," he answered, motioning to another table with his thumb. Rachel looked over, watching the exchange with a frown. The customer spoke with a thick voice, taking a moment to understand the waitress' responses.

"Oh great, she's with some retard. This is going to take all night," she said, starting to twirl a bit of her hair on a finger.

"...Excuse me?" Ferris said, raising an eyebrow at her.

"What, does that word offend you or something?"

Ferris waited before answering. He had to take a breath in order to respond rationally. If he snapped at this girl, his mother would probably kill him.

"He's not *retarded*," Ferris said in irritation. "He's deaf."

"How would you know?" she asked, not impressed.

"He can't hear his own voice. It's just how they talk."

"Whatever."

The conversation, if it could be called that, was dead for the next five minutes. The waitress came and took their orders, refilling Ferris' coffee cup and bringing Rachel an iced tea.

"So," Rachel started, trying to pass the time, "Dad said you want to go to Yale."

"Yeah. What about you?"

"Well, my parents want me to go to Cornell or something, but I want to go to Albany."

"Oh?" Ferris asked, surprised that she was thinking for herself. "Why's that?"

"It's one of the best party schools. Well, that's what my college friends say at least. One of them is in a sorority there and I think she can help me get in. She's only been there for a year and already found a husband."

Ferris didn't know how to respond. He wasn't sure if they could possibly have less in common. She didn't take much notice of his silence and continued talking.

"I mean, it's okay here. At least I can go to parties when my stupid parents are out of town. Um, I never see *you* at any, though."

"I don't go to your high school."

"Oh yeah, right. Don't you go to that, um, Catholic school?"

"Yeah."

"Do they have any good parties?"

"I... wouldn't know," he replied, then fumbled for a follow-up statement to mask how bland he was. "Er, those are nice earrings."

"These? My mom makes me wear them. I asked for diamonds for Chanukah, but Dad got me pearls instead. He can't do anything right."

Ferris stared at her, his lips flattening as he struggled not to scowl.

"You poor thing."

Rachel only shrugged and the atmosphere went stale once again.

"I'm going to uh, go to the bathroom," she said, grabbing her purse.

"Yeah." He looked back down at his coffee as she got up. She probably just went to call one of her friends to complain about something. When ten minutes passed and she didn't return, he started looking around the room. He was about to lose his patience when his cell phone vibrated in his side pocket. He normally hated phone calls, but any distraction was welcome. It was a text message.

- WHATS THE CAPITAL OF LATVIA

Ferris sighed. Of course Seamus would try and cheat at trivia. How he could type that fast, Ferris had no idea. With a roll of his eyes, he punched in a quick response.

146

- Riga

A moment later, his phone vibrated again.

- TNX MATE UR THE BEST HOWS THE DATE GOING
- Horribly. And you don't need to type in all caps, you idiot.
- WANT US TO COME RESCUS EYOU
- No thanks.
- OK OMW
- OMW better not be short for 'on my way.'

There was no response. Ferris clenched his back teeth, stuffing the phone back into his pocket. Rachel had been in the bathroom for a very long time. He might as well go too; he doubted she was coming back anytime soon.

As he went around the corner towards the restrooms in the back, he heard her voice clearly from the end of the hall. She was leaning against the wall, speaking into her cell phone. Pausing, he backed up before she could see him.

"I don't know how much longer this is going to take. Oh, God. I know. And you should see what he's wearing. He looks like he's going to like, I don't know, go teach an English class or something. God, everyone in this stupid café is so weird. They dress like they all shop at a thrift store and like, I don't know, are blind." She paused to listen, then laughed. "Oh my God! I know! Oh, oh, and there was some retarded guy and he was like, 'Oh my God, he's not retarded, he's deaf, I know this stuff, okay?' And I was like, whatever. I swear, he's such a loser."

Ferris stared blankly before easing his way back to his seat. He looked to the left, drummed his fingers for a moment, then looked right. Walking out the front door had never been so unbelievably tempting before. His eyes locked on the entrance, willing himself not to make a run for it. Ferris was staring so hard at the glass door that he almost didn't notice Seamus' grinning face appear behind it.

Ferris blinked, knitting his brow. Seamus waved behind the glass, holding up a CD case and pointing to it triumphantly. Demos was standing next to him looking apologetic. Ferris looked over at them, then took a glance back towards the bathrooms. It wasn't a difficult decision to make.

Five minutes later, Rachel came back to the table. She was digging through her purse and took a moment to realize no one was sitting there.

"Um..." She looked around the café, wondering if he went to the bathroom. "Ferris?"

The fresh evening air had never smelled so good.

"And then she was all 'Oh my God, my parents are stupid, they got me pearls instead of diamonds, oh my God,'" Ferris mimicked her voice to the best of his ability, gesturing with his hands.

"Was she hot?" Seamus asked, walking with his hands folded behind his head.

"What? I don't know, I guess. To you, maybe."

"This is it?" Demos asked, looking the CD over in his hands. "This thing cost you 2,500 tickets?"

"Be careful with that!" Seamus said quickly, reaching for it as if it were made of glass. "It was worth every hard earned one of them."

"Hard earned?" Ferris asked skeptically, adjusting his glasses.

"Okay, so you helped me with one question."

"He got lucky," Demos explained, handing the CD back to Seamus. "A lot of them were about soccer."

"Football," Seamus corrected.

"Oh, Mom is going to murder me for ditching that girl."

"Eh, she deserved it," Demos shrugged. "She was in the 'bathroom' for, what, twenty minutes? You can just say you thought she got kidnapped and went looking for her."

Ferris laughed, shaking his head a little.

"I've never been so happy to see your stupid face," he said, looking sideways at Seamus.

"Aw, that's sweet, Fer," Seamus smiled. "I'll take you on a proper date. Hold your chair out and everything."

"As long as you pay," Ferris replied easily.

"You're such a Jew," Seamus teased, elbowing his friend in the arm.

"You're such a retard," Ferris said, shoving him back.

"I'm not retarded, I'm *deaf*!"

Seamus started to run, laughing as Ferris pushed him. Demos continued to walk, smiling to himself as he watched the two start to fight further down the sidewalk.

"Oi, don't, you'll break Billy!"

"Oh, I'll do more than break Billy, prick!"

21

The Levinsteins went back and forth to New York City several times a year. Half of their family lived in the area and Harold often took trips for business. This weekend's occasion was a rather large one; little Isaac Levinstein was having his Bar Mitzvah.

Ferris loved his family. Individually, he was fond of each member and was glad for their support and existence. Together, however, his viewpoint changed dramatically. To him, few things could be as nerve-wracking as a room full of related Jews. The terrible jokes, complaining, and bickering was basically equivalent to being locked in a tiny closet with his mother for five hours. Normally, he got through such events with a handful of aspirin and a forced smile. He could at least be thankful that no one from school could witness the disaster that was his family. This time, unfortunately, something was different.

Slowly, Ferris turned to the left. Seated next to him in the back of his father's car were two people that he still couldn't believe were there.

"I love it here," Demos said, watching buildings go by out the window. "We don't get to go to New York enough."

"Thanks for inviting us, Mr. Levinstein," Emily said, giving the car's driver a smile. Harold adjusted the rearview mirror to look at the kids, returning the expression cheerfully.

"Oh, it's our pleasure. The least we could do after you had Ferris at your summer home all that time."

Ferris could only rub his temples. New York City, sure. His friends? Fantastic. His friends in New York City to see his ridiculous family? No. No, no, no.

Emily was engrossed in the whole event. She hadn't remembered much of Ferris' Bar Mitzvah, being around eleven years old when it had happened. Though lately she had asked many questions about his family, Ferris usually changed the subject when it came up.

"Why does Joseph insist on living on Lexington? Does he know how hard it is to find parking here?"

"Oh, shut your pisk, Harold. They have a lovely home," Ruth said, waving a hand at him in annoyance.

And it began.

"I didn't say it wasn't lovely, I said I can't find any parking! We're going to be late and it's his fault for living here. You want to schlep all over Manhattan, you be my guest."

149

"What, you want he should live in Long Island like your sister? He worked very hard to buy this place, Harold. You complain too much."

"There is nothing wrong with Long Island and… complain? Me, complain? This, coming from you? Ferris, are you hearing this?"

"You're on your own, Dad," Ferris said casually, leaning back in his seat and staring out the window. He learned long ago not to get involved in his parents' bickering.

"See, our son agrees with me," Ruth said, checking her reflection in a pocket mirror.

"When did he agree with you? He's just keeping his mouth shut, is all."

"Which is what you would do if you were smart."

"Ruth, one of these days…"

"What? Come on, what? Want to pop me in the kisser?"

"Oh, like you've kissed anyone with that mouth for ten years."

"Okay Dad, enough. Look, there's a spot."

Emily was biting her lower lip, struggling with the burst of laughter that was bubbling in her chest.

"This woman," Harold muttered, pulling into the spot along the curb. The car came to an abrupt stop next to a meter and its occupants immediately got out to stretch. The drive between New York City and Southport had been a couple of hours long and they hadn't made any pit stops.

"Ferris, you take their luggage with yours," Ruth ordered, gesturing to Demos and Emily's suitcases.

"What?" Ferris asked, pausing as he pulled his bag out of the car. He normally wasn't one to protest helping, but that was a lot of luggage.

"Don't you 'what' me, pick it up and get going."

"But I can't c—"

"You're lucky I don't make you carry all of it, after what you did to that poor girl. Oh, how could I explain to Dr. Eisenberg? Schvitzing in my nice blouse and trying to make an excuse for you? 'Oh, my son, he gets so ill sometimes, he just has to run'… I was so embarrassed!"

"I already said I was sorry," Ferris mumbled.

"I raise you, I love you, I buy you clothes, and what do I get? I get—"

"Babkes," Ferris finished under his breath, already familiar with this speech.

"It's okay, I can carry my—" Emily started, but was immediately interrupted by Ruth.

"No, no. Ferris," she snapped. "Pick them up."

"Fine," he replied bitterly, heaving his own bag over his shoulder before grabbing the other two in either hand. Emily

150

looked guilty at having Ferris carry her things, but Demos smirked in the way only a true friend could. He found all of this very amusing.

"Jesus, Demos, what did you bring? Ten gallons of hair gel?"

"Wine," he answered simply, checking his cuffs for lint as they walked. "I couldn't possibly visit without a gift. They're being kind enough to host us, after all."

"Right, of course," Ferris said with an eye roll.

To Ferris' relief, the doorman of his uncle's condominium brought a luggage cart for them at the entrance. He exhaled heavily as he set the suitcases down, holding his shoulder to twist the socket. There was a man in the elevator to take them to the proper floor and only moments later, they were knocking on Ferris' uncle's door. There was a brief commotion behind it before it swung open, revealing a tall man with graying, curly hair.

"Joey!"

"Harry!"

The brothers embraced as the rest of the family came to the door. They were all meeting at Joseph's home the night before the event for dinner and socializing. It was easy to believe that Joseph was a lawyer. The condominium was a large four bedroom apartment, neatly laid out with wood flooring and white furniture. It had a modern look that was quite different from the comfortable brownstone that Ferris' parents owned. The living room held nearly a dozen people, not counting the new arrivals.

"Aunt Ruth!"

"Goodness! You look fantastic!"

"Oh Ferris, come in here, give me a hug!"

This continued until Ferris had been hugged exactly nine times; he wiped the remains of a kiss off his cheek when no one was looking.

"Harold, you had more kids already?" Joseph joked, inviting Demos and Emily to join them.

"Who is this, Ferris, your girlfriend? Is she Jewish?" asked his uncle Marvin, jumping on the chance to embarrass the boy.

"What? No, she—"

"You're dating a shiksa!" exclaimed Joseph. "What did your *mother* say?"

"Uncle Joe!" Ferris snapped, quickly reddening.

"Who cares, she's lovely!" his aunt piped in as she poured a glass of scotch for Joseph.

"She's not my girlfriend!"

"Oh, really? What a shame," another relative added.

Emily laughed good-naturedly, putting her hand on Demos' shoulder.

"I'm Emily, and this is my cousin Demos. We're his friends."

"So polite! Why couldn't Ferris have introduced us to his friends? Harold, I thought you taught him manners."

Ferris could already feel his blood pressure reaching dangerous levels. Harold began introducing every member of the large family to Demos and Emily.

"Jake here's the oldest," he said, ruffling the red hair of a tall boy with glasses. "Oh, and we can't forget the current Bar Mitzvah boy, of course. Isaac, come over here!"

A skinny thirteen-year-old offered Demos and Emily his hand to shake. He had his father's dark curls and his mother's crooked smile.

"Nice to meet you," Isaac said politely.

"Likewise. Oh, this is for you, Mr. Levinstein," Demos said graciously, handing the man a wrapped box that contained a couple of bottles of fine Italian kosher wine.

"Please, it's 'Joe'! And what did you bring me? A gift! Harold, you never bring me anything! Oh, I love this kid, he's welcome anytime."

"Thank you, sweetheart," his wife said, taking the box from her husband before he could drop it.

There was no shortage of chatter as the evening went on. Demos was already charming one of his cousins while Emily and Ferris sat on the sofa watching everything unfold.

"I'm really sorry about that," Ferris said quietly, still embarrassed at the girlfriend assumption.

"Oh, I didn't mind. But um," Emily said, thinking for a moment, "what's a 'shiksa'?"

Ferris stared back at her for a second, gnawing the inside of his lip.

"I'll uh... I'll tell you some other time."

Emily gave him a strange look, taking a sip from her glass.

"I hope Dad lets us have some free time," Ferris said, changing the subject. "You ever been to Katz's?"

"I've heard of it."

"Sandwich as big as your head," Ferris described, using his hands. "Tastes amazing."

"I bet Demos would have two nibbles and be full," she mused, "and push the plate away dramatically."

"'Oh, I couldn't possibly eat another bite,'" Ferris finished her impersonation in falsetto and they both laughed.

"What's so funny?" Demos asked with a raised eyebrow.

"Nothing," they said together, then laughed again.

"Ferris, Ferris," came a voice from the side. Ferris looked to see Michael, his six-year-old cousin, crawling up onto the sofa next to him.

"Hey, Mikey."

"Don't call me Mikey anymore, I'm Mike."

"Mike? You're six. Mike is an old guy's name."

152

"I *am* old!"

"Yeah, okay."

"Want to hear a joke?" Michael said, practically bouncing.

"No."

"Sure," Emily corrected, leaning in to hear better.

"Okay," Michael started, looking excited to tell it. "What's the fastest fish?"

"What, salt water or fresh?"

"Um... I don't know," Michael said quietly, biting his thumbnail.

"Ferris, you're ruining the joke," Emily said, glaring a little at him.

"Well," Ferris said nonchalantly, "it's a sailfish."

"Wrong! It's a Go-Carp!"

Ferris stared at Michael.

"...That's stupid."

"No, it's not. *You're* stupid!" the child insisted.

"Come here, you little brat," Ferris said quickly, dragging his cousin over to tickle him viciously.

"Stop! I'm not a brat!" Michael squealed, laughing and making a pitiable attempt to get away.

"Don't you watch Discovery Channel?" Ferris said, not letting up. "Your joke is flawed!"

He released his cousin, who immediately ran off giggling, looking for some other adult who wasn't an insufferable know-it-all.

"Hey Ferris," Emily said, getting his attention again. "Knock-knock."

Ferris hesitated before answering.

"...Who's there?"

Instead of answering, she flicked him between the eyes with two fingers.

"Stop being mean to kids."

"Yeah, well his joke sucked. If he wants to go by 'Mike,' he should learn to take criticism like a man."

Emily couldn't help but laugh, covering her face to muffle the volume. Ferris looked over at her quietly. She had a talent for consistently knowing when he was joking and when he was being serious. More often than not, people mistook it for rudeness. His thoughts were interrupted by a slight commotion over by the television. His father and uncle had been trying to operate the projector for the last twenty minutes. Their efforts, so far, were completely in vain.

"There's no picture. It's on, but there's nothing. Piece of crap, this thing. I paid a grand for crap."

"No, no Joey, I told you. You have to turn the projector on before the computer," Harold explained.

"Says who? You? Ah, I don't trust you, you're the one who accidentally taped over my shows."

"That was fifteen years ago. Read the damn manual."

"What? What am I reading? I see nothing here."

"Ah, I don't know, where was it...?"

Ferris watched them with half-lidded eyes. It was like watching raccoons trying to start a car.

"What are they doing?" he asked Jake, who was watching as well.

"Setting up the projector. Well, trying to."

"Projector? What for?"

"Your dad brought a slideshow," Jake replied.

Ferris went silent. A heavy dread came over him like a storm cloud, shadowing the last shreds of hope left in his heart. Slideshows by his father meant music from the '70s, badly taken family photos, and every wipe effect known to man. A moment later, it hit him that Demos and Emily were here; they were going to see old family photos. This could not possibly have been worse.

"Hey, there it is."

"Oh come on, it's only half of the screen. Harold, what did you do?"

"What did I do? I fix it and you whine!"

Ferris had to bite his lower lip to keep from blurting out the answer. It was a simple matter of screen resolution, but he was secretly hoping that they would never be able to figure it out. His eyes darted from Emily to the laptop, then back over to the men. Was it possible to steal it, delete his files, and act like nothing happened? He could even sabotage the projector assembly. Well, they were kind of doing that just fine on their own.

"Did you try plugging it in?" Marvin asked, butting in.

"Oh goodness, what an idea! Why didn't I think of... Yes, we plugged it in, you schmuck!" Joey snapped.

"Just asking, you don't have to yell at me."

"Oh, yelling. You want to see yelling?"

"Shut up, the both of you," Harold said, fiddling with the settings on his laptop.

"Just because you're the oldest doesn't mean you can tell us what to do, Harry."

"Well somebody's got to, you bunch of idiots. Look, there we go. It's working."

"About time!" Marvin sighed, sitting back down in an armchair. "So you gonna show this thing, or what?"

Ferris rested his chin in his palm, leaning forward on his knees. He was not looking forward to this.

The family gathered around the living room once more and the lights went down. The first several photos, thankfully, did not include him. A few were thirty-year-old Polaroids and yellowed portraits. Most of them, however, were of Isaac. The occasion was for him, after all. Ferris was about to feel relief when he noticed a slide of a few cousins as young children. There Ferris sat, five years old, with curly dark hair and thick glasses. It was his fro era.

"Oh, great," he mumbled, hiding his face with a hand.

"Oh wow Isaac, I didn't know you knew Bob Ross!" exclaimed Joseph, triggering laughter from the room.

"Oh come on, Mom was the one who cut my hair!" Ferris said resentfully, gesturing over to his mother.

"No, I think he looks more like Gene Wilder," Jake cut in, not giving his own cousin any mercy.

"Maybe a Harlem Globetrotter," one of his aunts offered.

"Next slide," Ferris demanded with a scowl. He chanced a look over at Emily between his fingers as the slide changed. She was laughing too. They got through the rest of the photos without much incident. Thankfully his father had the foresight *not* to include any naked baby pictures.

"I remember when your hair was like that," Emily said after the lights returned, smiling at him.

"You do?"

"Yeah, you had it for a while. I think you cut it off right after Demos came to the States."

"It wasn't soon enough," he muttered.

"I liked it," she said defensively.

"I'm sure."

"All right, everyone, dinner!" Joseph announced with a single clap of his hands, herding the family into the dining room. Ferris' relatives were quickly distracted by the promise of hot, home-cooked food and forgot to make fun of him for the duration of dinner. The meal was followed by rugelach, some alcohol, and more conversation. Most of the guests went to the hotels they were staying at, but the teens were encouraged to stay the night. Emily stayed in a room with one of his cousins while Demos and Ferris shared an air mattress in the living room.

"I like your family. I don't see what you get so bitter about," Demos said, resting his chin on his folded arms.

"Yeah, you're not the one with embarrassing old photos on a giant screen in front of everyone."

"Well, I've never had a bad haircut," Demos said shamelessly.

"Yeah, well I saw how your mother dressed you," Ferris said, remembering some older photos. "Loafers and knee high socks, and a dainty little ribbon on your collar. You want me to paste those all over school?"

"No," Demos mumbled, averting his eyes in agitation. "Jerk."

"Yeah, that's what I thought," Ferris said, turning over on the bed and pulling the covers past his shoulder. "Night, then."

"Night, Ferris."

The next morning was bright and gray. Ferris sat by a window as his family rushed around behind him, getting things together for the day's event. They were a dozen stories up and he watched the traffic and pedestrians on the street below. It was a cold day and most New Yorkers were wearing scarves and hats.

"Ferris, come have some breakfast."

He looked over his shoulder at his cousin, who was setting a stack of bowls on the kitchen counter. There were a few cereal boxes and some of the family had already started eating. He had expected a more traditional breakfast, but he supposed everyone was too busy organizing for the day.

Ferris languidly pulled out a bar stool at the counter to sit on. He picked through the boxes with a frown. Every cereal was some kind of sugar explosion and he wasn't very fond of sweets. His aunt had probably chosen them with the kids in mind.

"Do you guys have any grown-up cereal?"

"Ooh, Cocoa Puffs!" Harold read excitedly, picking up a box as he came into the kitchen. "Ruth never lets me have this stuff."

"Here you go," his cousin said, finding a box of plain Cheerios in a cupboard and handing it to Ferris.

"Well, at least your dad has good taste," Emily said, pushing some cereal around in her bowl and watching the milk get chocolaty.

"There's nothing wrong with my taste," Ferris said with a glare.

"Yeah, Emily. There's nothing wrong with having the same interests as a seventy-year-old man," Demos added. He was sitting at the counter as well, wrapped in a blanket and sipping a coffee. His body had little insulation and he got cold quite easily.

"No one asked you, *Ghostie*."

"Harold!" came a voice from behind them. "*What* are you doing?"

Ferris' father looked meekly over his shoulder in mid-bite.

"Nothing, Ruth. Just having breakfast."

"You know it's bad for your heart, what did the doctor say? It's all going to go straight to your gut."

"But it has vitamins, look. It says on the box."

"Don't give me that fakakta excuse. Look, your son knows what's good for him."

"Mom, there isn't any more of—"

"Quiet! You trade with your father."

"But—" Ferris and Harold said together in protest.

156

"Do it!" Ruth said with a snap. They both sighed dramatically and switched bowls. Demos smirked, taking another slow sip of his coffee. He could tell it was going to be a long day for Ferris.

The ceremony itself went rather well. The attendees , all dressed formally for the occasion, watched Isaac from their seats. The boy delivered each prayer without stumbling or hesitating, reciting his Torah portion and reading a self-written speech about his experience. The speech caused his mother's eyes to well up with tears; she was unable to believe her child had grown so much. She was, however, infamous for crying at nearly every family event. When it was over, Isaac let out a heavy breath before joining his parents for another embrace.

"Good job, you did better than I did."

"Thanks, Ferris."

"Yeah, you did great up there Isaac," Harold added, to which the thirteen-year-old smiled in appreciation.

"*Ferris,*" Demos whispered, tugging the elbow of his friend's suit anxiously. "*I need a smoke, I'm dying here.*"

Ferris looked at his friend, who seemed a little paler than he normally did. Demos had not found a chance to step away and have a cigarette for an entire 24 hours and was slowly going mad.

"Hey Dad, we're going to uh, go find the bathroom and, you know, powder our noses," Ferris said with a weak smile, pulling Demos away from the crowd and towards the exit.

"All right, but you're missing the food," Harold said, gesturing to the reception's refreshment table and the small complimentary bar.

"We won't be long," Ferris assured him before he disappeared behind a man carrying a tray of hors d'oeuvres.

"Oh, thank God. Man, I was gonna fucking lose it," Demos huffed as he bit the end of his cigarette, lighting it with a match. They'd gone out a back door, through the parking lot, and around the corner to stand in front of a secluded parking garage.

"Yeah, sorry," Ferris mumbled, putting his hands into his pockets. "I told you — you shouldn't have come on this trip."

"Oh, come on," Demos said, tossing his spent match to the curb. "Just a tiny setback, nothing to make me stay home and sulk. Anyway, I'm having fun."

Demos sighed, feeling pleased. It was amazing what one cigarette could do for his mood.

"Seriously?" Ferris asked, suspicious.

"Yeah, seriously. But... are we going to get some time on our own?"

"Well, he's doing the Saturday morning service tomorrow, and then his party. Sunday we can probably go out."

"All right, sounds good," Demos said, heavily exhaling a long plume of smoke up into the air. "You know, you look pretty good in that suit."

"I wear a suit every day," Ferris said apathetically as he adjusted his glasses.

"Well, that's just a school uniform. This one's nice."

"Yeah, well it's no Armani," Ferris said with an indignant tone, gesturing towards Demos' finely tailored suit. Demos had a fondness for the brand and most of his own formal clothing bore the same tag.

"Surprise," Demos said, waving his hand showily. "It's Caraceni! Grandpa bought it for me."

"Yeah I, uh, have no idea what that is."

"They've made bespoke suits for celebrities," he mused, fingering the collar of his jacket thoughtfully. "And, you know, royalty."

"And... you wore this suit to a bar mitzvah?"

"I don't need an excuse to dress nicely."

"Clearly."

"Hey, why don't you let me take you out to get fitted for a—"

"No."

"...Suit," Demos finished slowly, miffed at being rejected so quickly. "Oh, come on. It'll be a gift."

"No. I'm sixteen. I don't need a fancy suit."

"What about for prom?"

"Yeah, like I'd be caught dead at *prom*."

"Quit being such a wet blanket, *Fish*. Or I'll tell Uncle Victor you've been giving his daughter *looks*."

"What?" Ferris said quickly, immediately putting his attention back on Demos. "No I—"

"Yes, you have. I'm not stupid. Look at you, you're even blushing. If you're innocent, why would you be blushing?"

"I'm not blushing!" he snapped, starting to feel even more embarrassed than he had at the slideshow.

"Well," Demos said, pushing some hair out of his eye, "you've been hitting on my cousin. I think you owe me one suit fitting."

"You're blackmailing me?" Ferris groaned.

"It's my nature, of course." Demos gave Ferris a smile that could sink ships.

"I..." Ferris started, raising his finger to make a statement. He gave up, pointing straight at Demos. "Hate you. I hate you so much."

"So we're on? Excellent. Let's make it next Saturday. Wait, we're in New York. We should shop *here*."

"Fine, whatever."

Demos smiled, tossing the filter to the sidewalk as he finished. He loved giving Ferris a hard time, mostly because his friend was so easy to irritate. Crushing the cigarette butt under the sole of his shoe, he instantly pulled out another to light. He needed to get his fill for now, as he had the feeling he wouldn't have another chance for quite some time.

That time didn't come until Sunday, the promised chance to spend a completely unsupervised day in the city. Demos had insisted on shopping in SoHo, while Ferris was set on the Museum of Natural History. Emily contradicted them both with the desire to go to the Museum of Modern Art. They settled on quick trips to all three destinations, dragging each other past designer clothing stores and abstract paintings.

"So what the hell is this, a Brontosaurus?" Demos said, looking up at a giant dinosaur skeleton with his hands on his hips.

"There's no such thing as a Brontosaurus," Ferris said, polishing his glasses with the bottom of his shirt. "It was a misclassified Apatosaurus skeleton."

"I totally had a Brontosaurus in one of my coloring books when I was a kid."

"Well, if you would have read a science book in the past hundred years you'd have figured it out."

"Okay, nerd. No one cares."

"I think it's pretty interesting," Emily said, still staring up at the bones.

"I think I need to go find a bathroom," Demos said indifferently, heading towards the exhibit's entrance to locate one.

"He's just cranky because he didn't get enough time to shop," Emily said, turning her attention from the skeleton to Ferris.

"I'm used to it."

They were alone now and it could stay that way for quite some time. Demos liked to spend at least five minutes adjusting his hair.

"So," Emily said, considering her words before continuing. "You said you'd tell me what a 'shiksa' is."

"Oh, that," Ferris mumbled. He'd been hoping she would just forget about it.

"What's wrong? Is it a slur?"

"Well, not really. Kind of. It's just a word for a non-Jewish girl."

"Oh, you mean like... 'goy'?"

"Sort of. He didn't mean anything by it." Really, all his uncle was trying to do was embarrass him in front of a girl. Ultimately, it had worked.

"I know," she said, giving a smile. "Still, it feels like a bad thing."

"It's not, really."

"Would you date a non-Jewish girl?"

"I kind of have," he said slowly. He wasn't sure if Julie counted. They had 'dated' for a total of maybe twenty minutes. Still, her faith hadn't even crossed his mind when he'd said 'yes.'

"You have? What about when you have kids?"

"I, ah," Ferris said, "I haven't really thought that far ahead."

He put his hands into his pockets, looking at her as he spoke.

"If you look at it this way, your parents would probably be happiest if you married an Italian guy, don't you think?"

"They'd love that," she muttered. "Especially if his family was from Veneto."

"It's kind of the same thing."

"Yeah, I see what you mean."

"You seem really interested in all of this," he said, looking away.

"I'm just curious. I like knowing how other cultures think."

"Ah, yeah. You've traveled a lot, haven't you?"

"Dad used to take us on a trip once a year. A different country every time. But he's too busy now."

"Which place was your favorite?"

"I think... India. I don't know, it was just—"

"Okay, I'm back," a voice interrupted from behind. Demos had returned and his hair was immaculate, as expected.

"Oh, hey," Ferris said, a little disappointed that their conversation had stopped.

"So, we done with the dinosaurs?" Demos asked, looking around the room.

"Are you kidding? We haven't even seen the Deinonychus yet. It's the only one on display in the *world*," Ferris said, gesturing down the hall with a pamphlet.

"I haven't seen you this excited since we went to the Container Store," Demos teased.

"Come on, you can never be too organized."

"That line must make a killing with the ladies, huh?" Demos said with a smile.

"Oh, shut up."

"Come on, let's go look before they close," Emily said, pulling them both down the exhibit hall. Ferris eventually got his fill of fossils, finally allowing them to leave. The three then made their way across the street to their final destination for the day — Central Park.

Though it was getting late in the day, it wasn't quite dark yet. They could still clearly see the outlines of the bare trees and other people walking by on the pathways. There were skaters on a frozen pond near the south, illuminated by exterior lights as they circled the ice. Demos and Ferris were sitting at a small table, content to simply watch.

160

"Here you go," Emily said, returning with a few hot drinks. She handed them each a coffee, keeping a cup of cocoa for herself. They both thanked her and Ferris pulled off the lid, testing the temperature before sipping.

"We have to go back soon, don't we?" Demos asked.

"Yeah. Dad doesn't want to drive too late at night and we have school tomorrow."

"Yeah, that's true," Demos said quietly, still disappointed.

"I'm glad we came," Emily said, looking Ferris in the eyes. Ferris thought about it for a while, his expression softening.

"I'm glad you came, too."

22

The last couple of weeks before winter vacation always seemed to drag the slowest. The students were restless and overworked, trying their best to concentrate for the end-of-semester exams. Ferris somehow managed to keep his focus and take proper notes. Demos, on the other hand, was simply staring out of a window. When the young Italian turned his attention back to his friend, he noticed that Ferris was anxiously rubbing his temples.

"You okay?"

"Headache," Ferris answered simply.

"Take it easy."

"I'm trying."

"Hey, I know what might help. Come with me after class, you could get a free Chanukah present for your mother."

Ferris looked over at Demos, knitting his brow suspiciously. In this context, "free" implied "stolen" and "for your mother" probably meant some type of jewelry.

"I don't know, I—"

"Boys, you have something you want to share with the class?"

"No, Ma'am," they answered simultaneously.

"Good, get back to your reading," the teacher said sternly, writing something down in her grade book. Ferris swallowed nervously, wondering if he'd done something to damage his marks. Demos simply scribbled onto a scrap of paper, passing it over the long desk to his friend. Ferris picked it up, unfolding it to read the handwriting.

Please?

Ferris turned his head, risking a glance at Demos. The teen was giving Ferris his best sad face, looking as if his life depended on this decision. Ferris sighed, writing his response before sliding the paper back.

Fine.

When school was over, they took the subway together to the west side of town. The family had several warehouses and this particular one was between a few factories and mostly out of sight. The boys stood in the open yard, closed in by a tall chain-link fence. Nicky was there to accompany them. A gentle snowfall settled over the pavement, covering the dirt and cement with white.

Demos and Nicky were both smoking as the gate opened to allow a commercial box truck in past the fence.

"Let me guess," Ferris said plainly. "This isn't a truck full of puppies and rainbows."

"Close," Demos said, unlocking the back latch after it parked. The rear door slid open, making a metallic scrape as the contents were revealed. "It's even better."

Ferris craned his head to look inside. Sure enough, there were steel racks of clothing, including women's purses and fur coats. The driver got out of the front cab, slamming the door shut to join them in the back.

"All right, kid. It's done. You got my cut?"

"Hold on, Sal," Demos said, happily sorting through the hangers and estimating their profits. "You'll get paid after we—"

Demos stopped talking, silent for quite some time. He stared at a purse in his hands, eyes still with anger.

"What? After what? The fuck is the matter with you?" Sal asked impatiently.

"The fuck is the matter with *me*?" Demos snapped, practically yelling at the man over twice his age. He furiously threw the bag into Sal's chest, and the man fumbled with it before taking a better look.

"How about this *merchandise*?" Demos' breath was visible in the cold, rising in puffs as he yelled.

"What? This is Coach! What's wrong with Coach?"

"Coach? Look at the bottom of that bag! You think *Coach* would have such shitty stitching? And the leather is all discolored. And if that's not enough, check the fucking tag! Made in *Taiwan*? Where the hell did you hijack this, *Canal Street*?"

"Look, kid. I didn't do nothing wrong. Just cause Ash gives you little practice jobs like this don't mean you can talk to me that way. If you weren't his nephew I'd be kicking in that smug little face of yours so hard—"

"Oh, grow a pair! You did *something* wrong, because this is a truck full of crap!"

"Fuck!" Sal shouted in frustration, ripping the cap off of his head and throwing it to the snowy ground in frustration. "What, so I don't get paid now?"

"Yeah, you'll get paid, once you get your ass back out there and find a truck full of *actual* merchandise."

"Hey, guys?" Ferris said from inside the truck. He'd been looking through the coats curiously.

"What?" Demos barked. He was in a bad mood.

"You think this might be a clue?" Ferris asked dryly, holding up a mink coat with words haphazardly painted along the back.

"Let me see that," Demos snapped, turning back into the truck to take the coat from Ferris. He read the crimson paint for a moment, feeling a little ill as he lowered it.

"Fuck."

"What? What's it say?" Nicky asked, tossing his cigarette aside.

Demos tossed Nicky the coat, trying to ignore his pounding heart.

"*Fuck off, Ghostie*," Nicky slowly read, holding the coat out in front of his body to examine it.

"That Irish prick," Demos seethed, kicking the side of the truck's interior. "Damn it!"

"He must have switched the contents when Sal weren't looking," Nicky deliberated, still looking at the fur coat.

"No shit, Nick," Demos said, getting down from the truck's inside with Ferris and slamming the door shut.

"Seems kind of expensive to replace everything with similar merchandise, even if it's fake," Ferris mused. "I'd have just put in, I don't know, newspapers."

"They did it to rub our faces in it," Demos said bitterly. "To show they had *all the time in the world*."

Demos glared at Sal as he said this. The middle-aged man shrugged defiantly, holding up his hands.

"Hey, look. I did my fuckin' job. Some personal feud you got with this mick ain't my business."

"It sure as fuck is your business, that's why you're coming downtown," Demos said, getting in the backseat of Nicky's car with Ferris. Nicky got into the driver's seat, easily seeing where this situation was going.

"Downtown? I don't have time to go downtown. The fuck are we doing there, anyway?"

Demos narrowed his eyes at Sal, speaking at him sternly.

"We're going to beat the shit out of Brian O'Brien."

With that, he slammed the car door shut. Sal didn't hesitate to get into the car, rushing into the front seat. He shut the door just in time for Nicky to accelerate out the front gates, leaving long, hard tracks in the snow.

Nicky drove an easy thirty miles over the speed limit for most of the drive, only slowing down when they hit city traffic.

"Think we should get Vic for this, kid?" Nicky asked, swerving to drive past a van full of tourists.

"We don't need an army to take care of him," Demos said calmly. He'd relaxed reasonably since they'd been driving, only needing a few minutes to gather himself. "We'll be fine."

"If you say so," Nicky said with a shrug. He certainly didn't mind holding his own in a violent kick-down but wasn't quite sure if the boys would be safe. Demos seemed to know what he was doing, but then again, he was just a teenager.

164

Brian O'Brien lived in a small apartment on the second floor above a barber shop. If he had decided to go for a nice evening stroll, or perhaps pick up a bite for dinner, the entire dramatic drive over would have been for nothing. Mr. O'Brien was, unfortunately for himself, at home that day. The locals on the street watched nervously as the group of livid Italians kicked the building entrance in, then marched up the stairs to demolish his front door with even less grace than the first. The entire raid seemed to be going well until a loud gunshot echoed through the living room and a bullet hole cracked into the wall next to Nicky's head.

"Back off!" came a voice from behind a recliner. It was Brian. Demos didn't move, simply raising his pistol and firing two shots straight into the chair. They easily went through, sending a few puffs of cloth and polyester into the air. Brian panicked and left his hiding spot, overturning a sturdy dining table to hide behind instead.

"Kind of ironic, isn't it Bob?"

"The feck you going on about?" Brian shouted from behind his barricade, reloading his shotgun.

"This is your Beretta, and you're going to die by it. Kind of poetic, right?"

"Get out of me gaff before I blow your feckin' heads off!" Brian retorted, aiming the barrel of his shotgun over the top of the table. A quick shot from Demos sent him back behind the table, trying to ignore the bullet hole in the wall where his head used to be.

"Why don't you come out from behind that little table and have a chat with us? If you insist on hiding, we're going to have to kill you."

"Suck my cock!" Brian yelled, quickly sending another loud shot across the living room. The group ducked as the plaster in the wall crumbled, sending a bit of dust over their jackets.

"I'm losing my patience," Demos said, unruffled by the near-death experience. He gestured towards the table, and both Sal and Nicky rushed it, kicking it aside and grabbing the man by his arms.

"Get off of me, get off!" Brian barked as his shotgun fell to the floor. He struggled impressively as they held him, but Nicky was quite strong and Sal was equally angry.

"Thought you'd make me look like an idiot, did you, you little fuck?" Sal spat, taking the event a little more personally now that the perpetrator was in his grasp.

Demos stepped forward to interrogate their victim, when an unexpected shot burst from a weapon in the kitchen.

"Shit!" Demos said, quickly glancing at the lamp that shattered on the table next to him before ducking behind the sofa.

"Let him go," ordered a woman with a small handgun. She was standing in the room's entrance, biting her lower lip as she glared at them.

Ferris was watching everything unfold from the threshold of the apartment. He certainly wasn't about to get involved, but he didn't want to wait in the car like a child. Demos appeared to have everything under control until now and the sudden shift in power made Ferris swallow nervously. Ferris tried to think of a way out of this, yet somehow, Demos managed to think twice as quickly.

Within seconds, he took precise aim on the woman's hand, pulling the trigger. Blood burst from her wounded thumb as she dropped the weapon, crying out in pain. She doubled over, holding desperately to her bleeding hand.

"Peggy!" Brian yelled, in dread at the sight of his girlfriend bleeding. Nicky took over the task of holding Brian still while Sal yanked the girl up by her arm.

"Come here, you stupid bitch," he muttered, throwing open a broom closet and tossing her inside. He slammed the door shut, firmly propping a kitchen chair against it.

"Let me out!" she screamed, banging on the inside of the door with her good hand.

"I'll tear you apart!" Brian shouted, his face red with rage. Nicky was having a little trouble holding him still.

"Quiet down," Demos snapped, hitting Brian hard across the cheek with the butt of his gun. The action made a thick cracking sound as the metal hit bone, sending bits of scraped skin and blood to the carpet.

"Now you look at me, you piece of shit," Demos said, crouching down to eye level with the restrained Irishman. Brian was bleeding from the face, seething like a trapped badger.

"You can call me cute little names and try to beat me in stupid contests at the shooting range. I don't care. But you don't *fuck with our merchandise.*"

"I'll do whatever the fuck I please," Brian retorted before spitting on Demos' collar. He didn't have the time to take in another breath before the Italian pistol-whipped him one more time, getting more blood on the butt of his gun. Demos stood up straight, taking out a handkerchief to wipe the phlegm from his suit.

"Sal," Demos said thoughtfully. "You're the one he embarrassed, right? Why don't you go ahead and show him how you feel about that."

"Gladly," Sal answered, fishing out a wooden cane from an umbrella stand by the door. Ferris took a step back into the hallway, averting his eyes as he listened to Sal beat Brian senseless.

166

"You little shit, made me look like an asshole!" Sal yelled, knocking his victim upside the jaw with the cane as if he were playing golf. "Thought that was funny, huh? Yeah, *real hilarious!* Fucking mick!"

More blood hit the wall as Sal continued, burning adrenaline like diesel fuel. Ferris cringed at the sound, staring at the wall opposite him in the short hallway.

"That's enough, Sal," Demos said after a minute. He got down on one knee to look at Brian, who was panting for air on the floor.

"Where are the goods?" he asked, his face inches from Brian's. The man only barked a laugh in response.

"Open the closet," Demos asked Nicky, his finger stroking the trigger of his gun.

"Don't you fucking dare!" Brian cried, blood dripping from his chin as he struggled once more.

"The goods, Brian."

The man closed his eyes, letting his head drop as he wrestled with his options. Finally, he opened his mouth.

"Truck's parked behind the laundromat two blocks east," he spat.

"Very good," Demos replied, his eyes gleaming. "I guess we'll let you live. Maybe 'luck of the Irish' isn't an ironic phrase, after all."

Demos smiled good-naturedly, though it was clear his intentions were nothing but malicious. Brian only coughed in response, starting to choke on his own blood.

"One more thing. You ever, ever fuck with us, or our trucks, or the air we breathe, you're going to find yourself thrown out this window," Demos continued, gesturing to the living room window, "with a cane up your pink ass. That clear?"

Brian said nothing, only giving Demos a frigid glare.

"Good, glad we're on the same page," Demos said, standing up again and gesturing for Nicky and Sal to follow him. "Let's go, I'm hungry."

Sal tossed the reddened cane onto the carpet, dusting his strained hands and leaving Brian prone on the floor. They followed Demos out of the apartment, walking past a fairly traumatized Ferris as they went down the stairs.

"I want some fries, I'm fuckin' spent," complained Sal as they got back into the car.

"We'll have to do drive-through," Nicky said, starting the car. "You got blood on you."

Ferris sat back in his seat, taking in a slow breath. He repeated a mantra in his head, reminding himself that he was on their side. Demos had surprised him, though. Ferris didn't think he would let Brian live.

"After we pick up the truck," Demos added, checking the back of his sleeve for any blood stains. "What about you, Fish?"

"I'm... not really hungry," Ferris said slowly, staring at the driver's seat in front of him.

"What? What's wrong? Was it the uh, the Bob thing?" Demos asked, gesturing out the back window with his thumb.

"Nah, I'm fine," Ferris said, still staring.

"All right," Demos said, leaning back in his seat, ashing his cigarette out the window. "If you say so."

As the car drove, Ferris found himself wondering how often this happened when he wasn't around. Above all, he realized just how lucky he was that Nicky and Sal were only testing him before. He didn't even want to imagine how his face might look if they had been serious.

23

Ferris was sitting alone at the Giorgetti manor, reading in a dark wingback chair. The sky outside was cold and white and the atmosphere almost seemed to glow. He could see his breath.

It didn't occur to him that the heat should have been on. He didn't think much of the reason as he marked the book, setting it down to rub his arms. Watching his breath rise, he started to wonder where everyone was. The room was silent. The entire house was silent. The hem of a skirt caught his eye as it passed by the door.

"Emily?"

It was her — he knew it was her. He got out of the chair, approaching the door to look down the hall. All he could catch sight of was her heel going around the corner.

"Emily, wait. Emily?" Moving faster, he followed. He could hear his shoes on the hardwood floor. It was still so cold. He didn't remember the house having hallways this long. As he came to the end of one, he realized it was a dead end. He didn't remember the house having dead ends either. Ferris had lost her.

His eyes lowered, feeling a sense of disappointment. He supposed she must not have heard him. Then, from the corner of his eye, a bit of movement caught his attention.

It wasn't her. There was a dark speck on the wall, moving slowly over the delicate wallpaper. Ferris leaned in closer, discovering that it was a small, black ant. He watched it for a moment before more movement drew his attention from behind. Slowly, he straightened, turning around. The floor was covered in ants. They crawled and clicked over the surface, moving up the walls and towards his feet.

He took a step backwards. There was nowhere to go and his back hit the wall. They swarmed up over his shoes, finding his stomach and arms. He could feel thousands of legs scratching over his skin as he desperately tried to claw them off. They went into his body, biting below his skin and digging beneath his fingernails. Panicking, he opened his mouth to scream, then woke up.

His breath came in deep, raspy pants as he stared at the ceiling of his room. He shuddered, immediately raising his hands to look at them. They were free of ants. With a heavy exhale, he lay his head back.

"What the fuck," he gasped. His hands dragged down the front of his face and he tried to ignore his racing heart. Awkwardly, he felt over the bedside table for his glasses, sliding them up over his nose and looking at the clock. It was five in the morning. There was no point in trying to go back to sleep; he doubted he could even if he tried. The last thing he wanted to do was fall back into that nightmare.

The small light on his nightstand clicked on, giving a dim yellow glow to the bedroom. It was still dark outside. The floor was cold on his bare feet as he walked to the bathroom. His morning routine hadn't changed in years. Correspondingly, his school clothes were the same everyday: a dark gray suit over a pressed white shirt and crimson necktie. He supposed the convenience of not having to pick out a daily outfit justified the lack of individuality.

The tie draped over his shoulders and he lined one end up with the second button on his shirt. He did this like he did most things – without any room for error. The silk looped and tucked as he slid the front down, adjusting the perfect knot below his chin. The Windsor knot was the only type acceptable at St. Basil's. Anything else would have to be redone, or the student would be sent out. Seamus often came to class with some type of four-in-hand or half Windsor, claiming he'd been neglected and never taught the proper way. This excuse only worked the first couple of times.

His thoughts were disrupted by movement from the window. Ants?

It was only snow. Ferris shut his eyes to shake the memory of his dream. He could still see and feel them in his head. Not the superstitious type, he didn't bother trying to interpret the symbolism or meaning. It must have been a simple amalgam of things he'd seen on television or thought about right before bed.

He put on a heavy coat with a hood, gloves, and a scarf. Stanley was already circling around at his feet, eager to go on his morning walk. The dog's curly tail wagged madly as the leash hooked on and the front door opened. He couldn't clear his mind as they walked. Why had Emily been in his dream?

Emily...

All he could remember from the dream was following after her, wanting to see her and be near her. It wasn't just the dream – he felt that way when he was awake. Was it possible that he really felt something for her? The idea made his chest feel tight. Stanley shuffled through the shallow layer of snow, ignoring the salted sidewalk and taking in the scent of a short tree. Ferris stared blankly into space as the dog found something in the snow, playfully biting at a short cigarette butt. The noise finally caught Ferris' attention and he looked down, snapping at the pug.

"Stan, *drop it*," he said sternly. Stanley paused, looked up, then slowly released the bit of trash back onto the sidewalk.

"That's sick, what's wrong with you?"

170

Stanley only panted obliviously, smacking his lips to get rid of the strange taste.

"Idiot. Come on, let's go." Ferris gave the leash a light tug, walking them both back to the house.

Breakfast consisted of a plain toasted bagel with cream cheese. His father had the same, except with a slice of tomato. They shared a pot of coffee.

"You get enough sleep, kiddo?"

"Yeah. I just... I don't know. I'm fine," Ferris said, drinking some of his coffee and staring down at his plate.

"You know if something's bothering you, you can talk to me about it."

Ferris understood what his father was trying to do, but couldn't collect his thoughts into proper words.

"It's okay. Just exams coming up, stuff like that."

"All right," Harold said skeptically before turning a page of his newspaper. It was quiet for a couple of minutes. Ferris didn't know how he could have described it to his father – a dream about ants and cold corridors and an anxious sickness in his stomach. He felt as if things simply weren't right; there was no other way to put it.

"You got uh," Ferris said, gesturing to his chin, "crumb. On your beard."

"Hm? Oh, right," Harold said, dusting it off. "Thanks."

"I'd better get to class," Ferris said, grabbing his bag and putting his dishes in the sink.

"Have a good day, kiddo. Stay out of trouble."

"You too, Dad," he replied with a brief smile.

The school day went by uneventfully. It seemed to drag more than usual and Ferris found himself watching the clock more often than he should have. Like Harold, Demos noticed something different about Ferris' demeanor. Again, Ferris gave a vague excuse. He had trouble paying proper attention to anything until Emily approached him after school. She came up next to his locker, catching his sight by leaning to the side.

"Hey," she said, lacing her fingers behind her back.

"Oh, hi," Ferris answered, shutting his locker and willing himself out of the daze he was in.

"You all right?"

"Yeah, why?"

"You just looked a little, I don't know... mezza morta."

"Long day," he explained, rubbing his temple absentmindedly.

"You doing anything next Saturday?"

He was about to answer that he was going to be studying and working on college applications, but it almost sounded as if she wanted to see him then. Waiting a second, he gave a slight lie.

"Not really, why?"

"The aquarium on the east side has some new sharks. None of my family really wants to go. I thought you might be interested."

"Of course," he answered after a strange pause. This seemed too good to be true. Emily *and* science? Together in the same day?

"Great," Emily said, giving him a smile. "There was something important I wanted to tell you, too. So make sure you're there. Ten a.m., to beat the tourists. All right?"

"Okay," Ferris said hesitantly. "Sure."

She said goodbye and he watched as she left, still trying to wrap his mind around what she had said. Something important. Something *important*? What could she possibly have to tell him? What was it that she couldn't have just said then and there, in the hallway? Was it possible that...?

Ferris shut his eyes, shaking any bizarre hopeful thoughts he might have. He knew better than to get himself worked up over nothing. Still, it was suspicious. He was still in a state of bemusement when Demos came up behind him, giving Ferris a nudge in the side.

"Hey."

"What?" Ferris blurted.

"'Hey.' I said 'hey.'"

"Oh, yeah. Sorry."

"What did Emily say?" Demos asked.

"Nothing," Ferris said quietly, trailing off. He was still staring down the hallway where she'd left.

"Okaaay. Well, I'm heading home. I'll see you tomorrow, all right?"

"Yeah, see you."

Ferris put the last few things he needed into his bag, closing his locker door to head towards the school's front doors. He pulled a pair of gloves out, sliding them on one at a time before stepping out into the cold, December air.

The walk home was supposed to be like any other. He would normally turn left on the sidewalk and walk fifteen blocks to his own street. If the weather was particularly bad he might take the subway, but he normally enjoyed the walk over. Something, however, made him stop. He froze at the foot of the stairs, slowly picking up his head. A voice was speaking directly to him.

"Hey."

It was a voice from someone he'd assumed he would never see again.

Ferris stared at her for a long time. It took him a minute to make sure it was really her standing in front of him on the sidewalk. She looked the same, overall. Her body was a little thinner, if that was even possible. She was wearing a pair of

172

worn jeans and a tattered hooded sweatshirt that was a few sizes too large. Her hair was the same, as were her eyes. One of them bore a dark bruise.

"...Julie."

"You remember me."

He looked away, finally able to tear his eyes from her.

"What do you want?"

"Nothing. I just want to talk."

"No," he shook his head, moving to walk past her. "I don't want to talk to you."

"Please, Ferris. Just five minutes."

"Go home," he said, still walking away.

"I don't have one," she said quietly. Ferris stopped in his tracks. He stared forward, battling internally over his response. He had already been fooled by her once; doing it again would only further prove his gullibility. On the other hand, she certainly *looked* homeless. Of course she looked homeless — it was an act. Still, what harm could five minutes do? If she weren't lying, if she truly had no home, could he really just leave her on the street?

With a sigh, he turned around.

"Five minutes."

They moved to the park across the street where it was quieter. Julie sat down on a bench, looking cold as she glanced up at him.

"What is it?" he asked bluntly.

"I just... I wanted to apologize. About what I did to you."

Ferris was quiet, so she continued.

"A lot's happened to me since I left. I had a lot of time to think. What I did was, well... it was wrong."

Ferris remained quiet, only taking in her words. A small part of him truly wanted to believe her – the rest of him refused.

"So," Julie continued, "I'm sorry."

Ferris watched her, wishing that he'd taken a psychology class that semester. He couldn't tell if she was lying or not. He knew the proper response should have been 'I forgive you,' but he couldn't bring himself to say it. Instead, he said the only other thing on his mind.

"Why don't you have a home?"

"It's a long story," she said, looking down at her hands.

"Go ahead."

Julie took in a quiet breath, gathering her thoughts. As she spoke, she fiddled with the ends of her oversized sleeves.

"I left Brandon. I hitchhiked back to Southport. When I came home, Mom had moved away somewhere."

"There's no forwarding address?"

"No. She might have done it to get away from Dad. I don't know," Julie said, her voice weak. "The landlord didn't know. Nobody knew."

Ferris considered her words, willing himself not to pity her. He reminded himself that it might not be true.

"And why did you leave him?"

"Things were okay, at first. We stayed at hostels and he sold stuff until we could afford a little apartment."

"Stuff? What, pot? Antiques?"

"Pot," Julie admitted before continuing. "Then he just started doing more drugs, selling different things. He got into coke and he started getting mean. I don't know, he just... I was miserable. He made me stay home and clean. And he got possessive and... he was like my dad. We argued all the time."

"He give you that?" Ferris asked, nodding to her black eye.

"What, this? No," she said, giving a short laugh. "I got in a fight with some bag lady."

"Oh," Ferris responded, a little awkward. "So, then you left."

"No. I stayed. I lived with him for two years. I thought, maybe, things would get better. I thought that I loved him anyway. What really made me leave..."

Ferris looked at her questioningly.

"Ah... I don't really want to talk about that," she said quietly. "Sorry."

"It's fine," he said, still studying her. "How long have you been here, anyway?"

"In Southport? A few weeks."

"Where do you sleep?"

"Sometimes the park, but lately it's too cold. I've been at the 12th Street subway station. The women's shelters fill up too fast and they favor women with kids."

"But you're a kid."

Julie laughed again, shaking her head.

"I forget that, I guess."

"Five minutes are up," he said, looking down at his watch.

"Oh, right. Thanks for listening to me. I didn't really have any friends here, you were the closest thing I had to—"

"I'm not your friend, Julie."

She went silent before looking down at her shoes.

"So, goodbye," he said, turning to leave.

"...Bye."

As he walked away, Ferris felt proud of himself for not falling for such an obvious set-up. Her story had been so miserable and pathetic that it couldn't possibly have been real. Brandon got into drugs and her family had mysteriously vanished? It was like a bad Hollywood movie. Still, something bothered him. It tugged at the back of his heart, reminding him of what he might possibly be walking away from. His conscience

174

was difficult to subdue and he found himself thinking about it for the rest of the day. Even the next day at school, it was still on his mind.

"Stupid raisins," Ferris mumbled, pushing some leftover kugel around in a Tupperware container. "Hey, Demos?"

"Yeah?"

"What would you do if you had to, say, keep someone for a while? Maybe a month or so. Not a prisoner. Just, I don't know, a guest. And your uncle couldn't know about it."

"I guess rent them a hotel room?" Demos said, stating the obvious.

"I was thinking something a little more... free-er."

"Hmm," Demos said thoughtfully, tapping the end of his spoon on his lips. "Why?"

"It's hard to explain. You know of something?"

"It would be kind of risky, but yeah."

"What?"

"Well, Uncle Vic had a comare on the side for a while. He bought her a little place downtown. Then something happened, I'm not sure. Aunt Vanni found out, or the chick got deported," Demos said, making vague hand gestures. "Anyway, the condo is empty now. He keeps it as an emergency hideout, or I guess in case he finds another woman. I could probably find the key somewhere."

"Do you think, maybe, I could possibly...?" Ferris asked carefully, rubbing the back of his neck. He was clearly uncomfortable asking such a large favor.

"You want the key?"

"I might not even need it. But, yeah. It would mean a lot."

"Sure. Just promise you won't mess it up or, I don't know, have a wild fucking party."

"Yeah, you know me, always having 'wild fucking parties.'"

"Just be careful. If he walks in there with some hooker, expecting an empty place, and you got a bunch of Mexican refugees in there or something, I'm as good as dead."

"I got it."

"Okay. I'll get them for you after school."

"Thanks, Demos. I really appreciate it."

"For you, anything," Demos said with a smile.

Several hours later, Ferris found himself walking towards 12th Street, anxiously fingering the silver keys in his hand.

"What am I doing?" he sighed to himself, trying to remember his reasoning. The subway station, right – he was going to go there and look for her at night. If she was there, then she had told the truth. If she wasn't, then she was probably warm and safe in some house and didn't need his help anyway. It made sense, somewhat. He stopped at the top of the stairs that led down to the station, wondering if he even wanted to know. After another sigh, he made his way down.

The station wasn't very busy this late at night and some of the entrances were closed due to a lack of attendants. He watched the turnstiles, assuming that if she did come here, she probably just ducked under them when no one was looking. Pulling out his fare card, he swiped it to pass through. It hit him that if she wasn't here, he'd just wasted $1.50 getting into the place. He cursed under his breath.

Ferris walked along the platforms, looking over each person and bench as he passed by. A train came to a stop, letting a few passengers off and on. People walked past him, talking amongst themselves or immersed in books. The floor was dirty, littered with black gum stains and a few candy wrappers. She wasn't on this platform. He found a set of stairs, moving to the next line, heading uptown. Julie was clearly absent from this platform, as well as the next. Ferris pulled back his coat sleeve to look at his watch, trying to figure out how much time he had wasted as he neared the end of the last platform. When he looked up, he saw her.

She was sitting on the end of a bench, legs pulled up against her body. Her face was buried against her knees with the hoodie wrapped around to keep warm. He could see why she managed to get away with sleeping here. She simply looked like a girl waiting for her train. Waiting, well, forever.

It was then, as he watched her on the bench, that he felt a wash of guilt. He'd spoken to her so apathetically. Feeling the keys in his pocket, he stepped up in front of her. After a second, he willed himself to speak.

"Julie."

Slowly, she picked her head up, looking at him in disbelief. He offered the spare coat he had brought with him.

"Come with me."

24

The week was nearing its end and the three boys decided to reward their hard work with a stop at the Sparrow, a local diner. Ferris didn't care to mention that he was the only one who had actually done any work the entire week.

"You know, Ferret," Seamus said, pointing up at the television that was mounted in the corner, "your father looks a lot like Paul Giamatti."

"Yeah, he does," Demos agreed, watching the entertainment report on the screen. "It's kind of creepy."

"Ferret?" was all Ferris could manage to ask, ignoring the comparisons of the actor to his father.

"What, you don't like it?"

"I already have like, three nicknames," Ferris said with an eye roll. "And now two of them are animals."

"Honestly, I always thought you were more of a turtle."

"A turtle?" Ferris asked incredulously.

"Well, I mean, you know. A turtle," Demos elaborated, showing the approximate size of a turtle with his hands.

"I know what a turtle is. What the hell makes you think I'm like one?"

"Steady. Grumpy, but kind of adorable. And the shell. It's hard to get to know you. Well, for anyone but me, I mean."

"Not to mention he's delicious in a soup," Seamus added.

"Yeah, and I spread salmonella like it's my job," Ferris finished.

"Lovely," Seamus said.

"You guys ready?" the waitress asked as she approached, holding a pad in one hand and a pen in the other.

"Cheeseburger with fries," Seamus said, handing her the folded menu. He had learned quite some time ago that asking for 'chips' would result in an entirely different meal.

"The French dip," Demos said, "with coffee."

"Falafel. And an egg cream," Ferris finished. "Thanks."

"Egg cream?" Seamus asked as the waitress left, leaning in with a revolted look on his face. "Is that a beverage? It sounds awful."

"It doesn't have egg in it," Ferris said, a little annoyed as he pushed his glasses up, "or cream."

"Then what the hell is it?"

"It's like chocolate milk with seltzer in it. It's a New York thing, I guess," Ferris said. "Oh, Demos. I wanted to ask you..."

"Yes?"

"Emily hasn't uh," Ferris said, fiddling with a straw wrapper, "said anything about me lately, has she?

"Not really, why?"

"Oh. Well, she said she wanted to tell me something this Saturday when we go to the aquarium. I just don't know what it could be."

"The aquarium? What, you mean like a date?" Demos asked.

"Uh, no, I don't think so. Just for fun. I don't know. Sharks."

"Sharks?"

"Didn't she ask you to go? She said you didn't want to."

"She didn't ask me anything," Demos said slowly.

"Oh," Ferris said. He was slowly making a realization. Emily wasn't just using Ferris as a last ditch replacement. She really wanted to go with him – just him.

Ferris didn't talk for a minute, only looking down and playing with the wrapper. He folded it into a double helix absent-mindedly as he thought about her.

"Bollocks. She's probably going to confess that the entire trip was for a paper she's writing and how she'll want you to help her with it," Seamus said bitterly. "A paper on *sharks*."

"Yeah, probably," Ferris said distantly, flicking the helix across the table with his fingers.

"By the way, you end up using that key?" Demos asked, watching his coffee cup as the waitress filled it.

"Oh, yes actually. I did. Thanks."

"How long you going to need it for?"

"I'm not entirely sure."

"So, are you ever going to tell me what the hell you're doing with that place?"

"You've got to fess up to your amateur pornography shoots," Seamus said. "No one cares if they're bad, we'll still watch 'em."

"Shut up, Seamus. It's, well, you'll probably get mad."

"Mad?" Demos asked, straightening in his seat. He already sounded a little mad.

"Just a… friend. She's staying there until she can get her life together."

"You don't *have* any female friends. Wait. No, it's not—" Demos put his fingertips on his temples, not wanting to think what he was thinking. "You didn't. No way."

Ferris sighed, looking away and not answering.

"*Julie*??" Demos spat, leaning closer across the table. "Are you fucking kidding me? Are you the biggest idiot that ever lived?"

"Who the hell is Julie?" Seamus inquired, looking a bit lost.

"She's—" Ferris started before getting interrupted by Demos.

"She's some bitch from 9th grade who used him for his money and then took the first bus out of town."

178

It had taken Ferris a long time to eventually spill the entire story to his friend, an action he was now regretting.

"And you're shacking her up, why?" Seamus said, puzzled.

"Just shut up, both of you. Let me explain."

"Oh, yeah. This better be Oscar-worthy," Demos said, folding his arms and leaning back in his seat.

"She's changed. She's not like—"

"Oh yeah, never heard that one before. Go on, tell us her sob story," Demos interrupted.

"I'm *trying*. Anyway, she went through a hard time in California. Her boyfriend treated her like shit."

"Oh, like she didn't *deserve* it," Demos snapped.

"Could you just shut up for like, four seconds?" Ferris said, raising his hands in exasperation. "Okay, so she leaves him, comes back to Southport, and her family is gone. Shut your mouth, Demos, I know what you're going to say. I didn't believe her either. Then I randomly went and checked the subway station where she said she was sleeping, and there she was. She's homeless – for real homeless."

"That's karma, Ferris. She deserves every cold night in that subway station for what she did to you."

"She's learned her lesson, okay? Can't you have a little empathy for once?"

"I thought you knew better than this. I thought you were, I don't know, smart."

"I'm not saying I trust her. I don't even really buy her story about her boyfriend. But I can't just leave her there. It's barely thirty degrees outside."

"Well *subway stations* are pretty warm, last time I checked."

"Are you listening to yourself?"

"Are *you* listening to *your*self? You've been completely suckered in. Again."

Ferris gave up, drinking his egg cream through the straw and looking out the window in frustration.

"Look, I don't mean to be a dick," Demos said, "but I just don't want to see you get hurt. It killed you the first time, I just can't—"

"Forget it. You want me to throw her back outside? Fine. It's your uncle's place, not mine."

Demos exhaled, weighing his options. After a minute, he regained his composure and spoke calmly to his friend.

"She can stay. But the second she asks you for money or—"

"I already went over that with her. She's looking for part-time jobs and she's going to buy her own food. I'm only letting her stay until she can find her mother or afford her own rent."

"Good."

"And if I notice a single thing out of place or missing from the apartment, she's on the street. I made it clear."

"All right," Demos said, sounding a little more convinced. "I guess."

There was an awkward silence as the waitress arrived with their food, placing their plates down in front of them. After she left, Demos added a last thought.

"You don't... still have feelings for her, do you?"

"No," Ferris answered, "and anyway, on Saturday—"

Ferris caught himself, stopping before he could finish the sentence.

"What?" Seamus demanded. "On Saturday what?"

"Nothing."

"You think Em's gonna confess her love or something?" Seamus asked, looking slightly annoyed.

"I don't know," Ferris mumbled, suddenly embarrassed. His face felt warm. "I guess it's possible, maybe."

He started feeling stupid, realizing how dumb this would all seem if that wasn't what she wanted to tell him at all.

"Well don't look too desperate, you'll scare her off," Seamus said with a tone of bitterness.

"You know, it's kind of bad to count your chickens before they hatch," Demos started, "but I think that might be it. I think she does like you, Ferris."

Ferris picked up his head, looking Demos in the eyes.

"Honestly?"

"Yeah. Question is, how do you feel about her?"

"Oh, who cares? What is this, Ricki Lake?" Seamus said, annoyed with the entire conversation. Though Seamus' rudeness was a little irritating, Ferris was glad that he didn't have to answer such an embarrassing question.

"You'd better eat that before it gets cold," Ferris said to Demos, changing the subject.

"Yeah, yeah," Demos said, picking up his sandwich. He worried about Ferris more than Ferris worried about himself. Sometimes Demos felt that if he didn't look out for his friend, nobody would. As long as he no longer had a thing for Julie, and as long as she had a job, it would probably be okay. Ferris wouldn't be stupid enough to give her more money, would he?

The next day, Ferris stopped by Victor's spare apartment to check on her, still wearing his school uniform and carrying a small grocery bag. He hesitated before opening the door, worried that the place would be empty and she'd have pawned all the electronics. When the door swung open, he relaxed.

Julie was lounging on the couch, flipping channels on the television with her feet up.

"Oh, hey," she said, looking over the back of the sofa at him with a small wave.

180

"Have you been watching TV all day?" he asked disdainfully, raising an eyebrow at her.

"Mm, no. I went out. Hey, I got a job, too!"

"Really?" he said with a bit of disbelief. "Where?"

"The diner down the street from here. I start tomorrow," Julie said proudly. "Bet you didn't think I would get one so fast."

"No, I didn't," he said honestly. "Mazel tov."

Ferris walked towards the apartment's small kitchen, setting the bag on the countertop as she rolled off the couch and came over.

"I brought you some dinner," he said, pulling a Tupperware container from the plastic.

"I thought we agreed you wouldn't spend any money on me," Julie said hesitantly.

"I didn't," Ferris said bluntly, holding the container up unceremoniously. "Leftovers. Mom made chicken."

"Oh," she said, taking it from him with a smile. "Thanks."

"Yeah. Sure."

She vented the lid and placed the food in the microwave, leaning forward on the counter as she watched it spin. Ferris was about to turn and leave when she spoke up again.

"How was school?"

"It was fine."

"Learn anything... *new*?" Julie said, clearly trying to make conversation.

"Yeah, I guess. Oh, that reminds me. When we find your mother, you have to promise to go back to school."

Julie frowned, tilting her head at him.

"Do I have to?"

"What, you want to be a waitress at a diner for the rest of your life? That's what you aspire to?"

"I thought I'd just marry some rich guy, murder him, and live happily ever after on my inherited funds," she said with a grin, opening the microwave as it beeped. He glared at her and she laughed at his response.

"I'm just kidding. Jeez, take a joke."

He sighed, folding his arms as he leaned back on the opposite counter.

"Isn't there anything you want to do? That you're good at?" Ferris asked impatiently.

"I like playing guitar."

"I didn't know you played guitar," he said slowly.

"Yeah. I'm pretty good at it, too," Julie admitted, poking through the cooked chicken dinner before taking a bite. "Mmm. Your mom can really cook."

"I'll let her know," he said, putting his bag back over his shoulder. "I've got to go, though."

"Wait," she said without thinking, putting her fork down. "Could you stay? Just a few minutes."

Ferris looked at her over his shoulder, waiting before responding.

"Julie… I don't think I'm really, well, ready to talk to you yet. I still can't trust you."

"How did you know?" she asked out of nowhere. It seemed to have been on her mind for a while. "About… what I was doing. And California."

"I went back to get my wallet, since I thought I'd dropped it. I heard you on the rooftop with him. I heard everything," he answered easily as he opened the front door, not hesitating or pausing in his explanation.

Julie didn't speak, looking down at the food in her hands. She tried to remember exactly what she said that night and how he must have felt hearing it.

"…I'm sorry," she finally said, her voice quiet.

"You already said that."

"If you don't trust me, why are you helping me?"

"Because it's the right thing to do," he replied, stepping out the front door and closing it behind him.

"Oh," she replied to the shut door, sighing before setting the food down. Something had made her lose her appetite.

25

It was a fresh new morning at St. Basil's Private Academy and Demos looked eager to start the day. His anticipation seemed to radiate from his speech and Ferris noticed this with suspicion.

"The hell are you so happy about?" Ferris asked, taking a notebook out of his bag. Demos was seated next to him in their morning class and a few students were still drifting in.

"Don't tell me you forgot what today is," Demos replied.

"Our anniversary?"

"No," Demos said, nearly dropping his smile.

"I forgot what today is," Ferris said in a rather frank manner.

"A particular trio is released from juvie and sent back into the halls of St. Basil's," Demos described, gesturing theatrically with his hands, "where they anxiously await their demise at the hands of a vengeful, yet aspiring young—"

"Okay, I get it Mr. Moviefone. Rudy, Zach, and Paul?"

"Precisely! I've been waiting to rip those kids apart since last New Year's. But they were safely tucked away in juvenile hall."

"Shouldn't I be the one wanting revenge? They kicked *my* ass, unless you forgot that already."

"You're too much of a baby to do anything properly vengeful. I'm doing it *for* you."

"Oh, thanks. That's… that's real sweet."

"Anytime."

"But honestly, you really want to start more trouble with these guys? Haven't we been through enough?"

"Ferris," Demos said sternly, taking his friend by the shoulder and looking him in the eye. He spoke quietly, making sure none of the other students could hear.

"They were stupid enough to fight you after we *ran them over with a car*. They nearly killed Seamus and they destroyed your violin. They deserve *anything* I feel like doing to them."

"And what exactly do you feel like doing to them?"

"You'll see. I've got it all planned out."

"So this is what you do instead of homework."

"You're cordially invited, if you'd like to come after school."

"I don't know. Is it going to be anything like the O'Brien thing?"

"Only if they resist," Demos replied with an ominous tinge in his smile.

Ferris spotted the unfortunate students only once that day, in the hall between classes. As he passed them, he chanced a look in Paul's direction. The other teen immediately averted his eyes, lowering his head and rushing past him. Ferris turned to watch Paul depart, raising his eyebrows curiously. Either someone had tipped them off to what was coming, or they weren't as stupid as they looked.

It was after school that Ferris found himself in the backseat of Victor's car, looking out the window and wondering what Demos could possibly have had in mind. He had decided to join them, if only to keep Demos from doing anything too drastic. He kept silent as the car pulled up next to Zach and Paul, who were walking home from school. Ferris didn't say a word as Victor and Nicky rushed out from the front seats to tackle the running boys and remained quiet when the unconscious, gagged teens were thrown into the car's trunk. He simply sat next to Demos, hands folded and eyes blank.

They had driven for half an hour past the city limits when Ferris finally asked a question.

"What about Rudy?"

"He's playing a very crucial part in all of this, don't worry," Demos responded casually. The car came to a stop beneath a large bridge, parking next to the paved riverside. There wasn't a soul that could see them.

Nicky unlocked the car's trunk, popping it open to reveal two whimpering boys inside. They had regained consciousness on the drive over and were now frightened out of their minds.

"Hey, I know you kids," Nicky joked, pointing at them in recognition. "Yeah, you made real nice street pancakes if I remember correctly."

Zach and Paul's eyes widened, realizing that this was the man who had previously run them over with his car. Nicky was pushed aside, replaced by Victor. The man lowered his glasses on the bridge of his nose as he peered down, getting a better look at them.

"Look at these fucking kids. No decency, no respect for their fellow man."

"Look who's talking, Ash," Nicky said with a warm laugh, elbowing his boss in the side.

"Shut your mouth, Nick."

"Sorry."

The boys were hauled out of the trunk, untied and thrown to the dirt. A pair of shovels was tossed carelessly on top of them.

"Okay kids. I've thought about it long and hard," Victor started, framing the ground with his hands. "My herb garden would look spectacular here and I want you two to help me plant it."

Zach and Paul only stared up at Victor, speechless in their dread.

184

"*Dig!*" Nicky elaborated, kicking Zach in the side.

"O-okay," they both stammered, grabbing the shovels and forcing them into the hard dirt.

"Come on, faster. We don't have all night, here," Victor griped, unscrewing the cap of a water bottle.

Paul knew what they were doing. They were being forced to dig their own graves. He kept wishing that this was only a nightmare. He didn't want to die.

"I'm sorry," he said weakly as he tossed a pile of dirt to the side.

"What was that?" Nicky asked, leaning in and pretending to listen harder.

"S-sorry! I'm sorry!" Paul's eyes were wet, and he sniffled to keep his nose from running.

"Sorry? You like that word, 'sorry?'" Victor asked, taking a sip of water from his bottle. "What other words do you like? How 'bout 'kike?' You like that one? Kike?"

"N-no, I—"

"Shut up and fucking dig!" Victor snapped, throwing the plastic water bottle hard at Paul's head. Water burst from the end, getting the boy's shirt and hair wet. It tumbled to the ground, creating a bit of mud as it continued to spill into the dirt. Paul's hands were trembling as he looked up. He let his eyes catch Ferris', and he glared at the other boy with such intensity that Ferris could have sworn he could feel it. Ferris knew though, from the look Paul was giving him; he knew that Paul wasn't sorry.

Demos was leaning against the car, smoking as he watched the digging continue. Ferris leaned back next to him. He was torn on what he should be feeling. Part of him was happy to see it. A couple of cruel, racist bullies being yelled at and treated the way they'd treated others. Yet, despite the bad things they'd done, they were just kids.

"Not deep enough," Victor said when the two had stopped out of exhaustion.

"I can't," Zach panted, dropping his shovel. "I can't do this."

There was a click as a gun cocked, aiming between Zach's half-lidded eyes.

"Pick it up," Victor ordered bluntly.

Zach scrambled for the shovel, holding to it desperately as he started to dig again.

"This is gonna take all fuckin' night, isn't it?" Nicky griped, checking his watch.

"Demos," Ferris asked quietly as they both stood in the background. "You're not really going to kill them, are you?"

"Not really."

"What's that supposed to mean?"

"It all depends on Rudy. I left him a note. He'll just need to find this place before they suffocate."

"Suffocate? You're going to—"

"Bury them alive."

"That's kind of cliché, don't you think?" Ferris muttered, eyes fixated on Paul's digging.

"Okay, so I read 'The Cask of Amontillado' in class the other day and it inspired me. Give me a break."

"What if he doesn't find them?"

"Then uh," Demos made a couple hand gestures, "I guess, they die. But really, he *should* find them. It's not that complicated."

"I don't know," Ferris said, watching as Paul started to sob. "These guys are pretty stupid."

"What, you want to stick around with a shovel and wait in case he never shows?"

"Not really," Ferris admitted.

The digging seemed to go on forever, though one couldn't blame a person for digging his own grave as slowly as possible. Nicky opened the back of a truck that was parked nearby, dragging two wooden coffins from the back.

"Oh, God," Zach said with a crack in his voice, weak at the sight of them.

"Get in the box," Victor said, gesturing at both of them with the gun. They looked anxiously down at the coffins at the bottom of each grave, seemingly unable to move.

"I-I can't, I can't," wept Paul, rubbing his arms as if he were cold.

"Get in the *fucking box!*" Victor shouted firing a shot at the dirt next to Paul's feet. The teen panicked, stumbling back before lowering a foot down into the hole. Soon, they were both lying on their backs, trembling against the wood as the covers slammed shut.

"This is pretty awful, even for you," Ferris said to Demos, folding his arms as he listened to Zach and Paul sobbing.

"They'll be fine," Demos said, waving the accusation off with his hand. Ferris noticed that the covers hadn't been nailed shut, so there must have been some truth to Demos' plan.

"Let's get this over with, I'm getting hungry," Victor said, picking up a shovel and throwing the first pile of dirt onto Zach's coffin. The sound made the boy whimper once more and Victor only rolled his eyes.

"Think they'll rat you out when they get rescued?" Ferris asked, tilting his head a little.

"Nah. They know if we get thrown in jail, about a dozen other Giorgettis will slit their throats. And anyway, we have Chief Blakely on our side."

"Oh, right," Ferris replied, having almost forgotten about the blackmailed police chief. "Well, here's hoping Rudy isn't a complete fuck-up."

"Yeah. It would kind of suck to be responsible for the death of your friends, just because you were too stupid to find them in time."

"Do me a favor and don't ever put me in that situation, okay?" Ferris said warily.

"No promises," Demos said with a smile.

By the time they were done, Ferris was ready to simply pass out in his bed. Unfortunately, he had to check on Julie. The walk over to the apartment seemed longer than usual. He hadn't even bothered changing into clean clothing.

"What the hell happened to you?"

"Me?" Ferris asked, looking back at Julie blankly.

"You're covered in dirt. What, did you go stomping around in the woods or something?"

"Uh, yeah. I guess. Um, how was work?" he asked tiredly, taking off his school jacket and shaking it a bit.

"Good, I got the hang of it pretty fast. I brought you some food, too," she said, gesturing towards the refrigerator with her head.

"Really? I'm starving," he admitted, not realizing how hungry he was until just then.

"Ferris?"

"Yeah?" he replied, opening the Styrofoam container to reveal a tuna salad sandwich. He was surprised she remembered what he liked.

"I know you don't really want to talk to me, but I think we should."

"Why?" Ferris asked, examining the sandwich in his hands.

"How will you ever trust me if you don't get to know me?"

"How do I know what you're telling me is even true?"

"I don't know," she said quietly, looking away. "Forget it, then."

Ferris sighed, putting down his dinner. He supposed he should give her a chance.

"Why don't you start by telling me everything you lied about when we first met?"

Julie picked her head up, looking over at him. She knew that it made sense. Yet, obviously, it was a difficult request.

"Well," she started, trying to figure out where to start. Ferris watched her patiently, waiting for her to speak.

"I dropped out of school. It wasn't a public school, either. They put me in a girl's school for delinquents."

Ferris didn't speak, letting her continue.

"My dad didn't take my money, but I didn't lie about the rest of him," Julie said softly, keeping her eyes averted. "And I didn't lie about liking you."

There was a scraping of a barstool as Ferris stood abruptly.

"I'd better go."

"But—"

"Goodnight, Julie. Thanks for the sandwich."

"Come on, why won't you just *listen* to me?" she yelled, finally raising her voice. He stared at her, expression blank.

"Because you're lying again," he said plainly.

"Why is it so hard for you to believe that someone would actually like you?"

"Because you didn't."

"I said I was sorry, I don't know what else you want me to do."

"I don't know," Ferris said wearily. All of this emotion was too much for him to handle. He sat down on the sofa, exhaling slowly as he leaned back. Slowly, she sat down next to him.

"I didn't lie about much else, other than… not wanting your money. I did want it."

"Yeah, I figured that out."

"But that's it."

Ferris leaned forward, rubbing his temples in irritation. He had to remind himself to stop being so melodramatic and just talk to her like a normal person.

"I'm sorry I've been a jerk, Julie."

She looked at him in surprise, then slowly replied. "I understand why you were."

"I spent some time checking the records for your family. They're hiding better than I thought."

"Yeah, I told you," she said, sounding discouraged.

"You don't think she went into witness protection, do you?"

"I don't know. I hope not."

"I'll keep trying," he said, rubbing a hand over the top of his hair in thought.

"Thanks. It, um, it means a lot, that you're helping me. I mean, this place, how did you even get a hold of it? I knew you were rich, but—"

"I'm not rich. And it's… it's on loan. This place isn't mine, so you need to keep it immaculate."

"I know, you told me."

"Good," he said, looking down at his watch. "I have to go for real, now."

"All right," Julie said, standing with him as he walked to the door. She held the door open for him, leaning on it a little as he adjusted his scarf. "Thanks for staying. A little while, anyway."

"Maybe next time I'll stay a whole five minutes," he said with a faint smile. "See you tomorrow."

188

"Goodnight," she said, closing the door behind him as he left. Julie was certain of one thing — she would need a lot more than five minutes to explain what was on her mind.

26

Ferris slowly walked by the third period math class on his
way to the bathroom. His eyes trailed inside, looking for any
sign of the Paul or Zach. They were supposed to be in there. He
squinted, checking over each head as he passed by. The boys
were absent. Putting his hands into his pockets, he made his way
to the bathroom at the end of the hall. A sick feeling was rising
in his stomach.

At lunch, he waited impatiently for Demos to join him.
Seamus was off somewhere stealing his meal and Ferris was
alone in the classroom where they usually ate. He poked at his
food, constantly looking up at the door to see if it was opening.
When it finally cracked, he opened his mouth.

"De—" Ferris started, then stopped. It was only Seamus. "Oh.
It's you."

"Well, I'm delighted to see you too, Fer!" Seamus smiled,
sitting on top of a desk next to him and sliding a wrapped
burger from his sleeve. "Ah, the bounty of my plunders."

"Why do you keep doing that? You have enough money to
buy a Rolls Royce."

"No, my *father* does. And has. Anyway, it tastes better when
it's stolen."

"Whatever you say," Ferris said, rolling his eyes.

"How's the thing with that homeless bird going?"

"...Julie?" Ferris asked hesitantly.

"Yeah, that one," Seamus said, taking a large bite from his
burger.

"Better, I guess. She keeps wanting to talk to me, but... I have
a hard time being around her for very long. I just get the
overwhelming urge to leave."

"You're afraid to love, I knew it," Seamus said dramatically,
accusing Ferris with his burger-holding hand.

"I'm not interested in her, you know that."

"Oh, right, you want to bone Demos' little cousin."

"God, shut up. You're such an idiot."

"I'm right, though, aren't I?"

"I don't want to *bone* her, I just like her."

"Who don't you want to bone?" Demos asked, finally coming
into the room.

"No one!" Ferris snapped, glaring at Seamus.

"Your cousin, Emily," Seamus grinned, waving at the Italian
as he joined them.

"What?" Demos asked as he sat down, lowering his eyebrow.

"Forget it, just forget it," Ferris said hurriedly. "Anyway, where have you been? I've been wanting to ask you—"

"About our daisy-pushers?"

"Yeah. Are they—"

"He found them. Kind of slow, though. They both suffered some brain damage from asphyxiation. I'd be surprised if they even remembered what happened that night."

"Brain damage?" Ferris asked slowly, setting his lunch down.

"Yeah, they're slightly stupider than they used to be. They'll probably have to go to public school, now."

"Oh," Ferris replied, looking away in thought. He wasn't sure how he felt about that. They weren't dead, but they weren't all right, either.

"And no, they didn't mention us. They either forgot, or are too scared shitless to drop our names."

"I see."

"Oi, you gonna eat that?" Seamus asked, pointing at Ferris' abandoned lunch. He had apparently been ignoring their entire conversation, not interested in things that went over his head.

"Yes. Eventually," Ferris replied, a little annoyed.

"Fine, fine," Seamus said, waving his hands a bit. "Let me starve, see if I care."

"Why don't you go steal another burger and stick it up your ass?"

"Oh, you'd like to see that, wouldn't you?"

Demos laughed as Ferris hit the Brit in the arm. Few things were more amusing than pushing Ferris' buttons.

After school was out, Ferris went down the same familiar stairs, waving goodbye to Seamus by the door. He was about to start home when, once again, someone stopped him on the sidewalk.

"Julie? What are you doing here?"

"I wanted to bring you this," Julie said, raising a bag with some food in it. "I got it from work. You like potato pancakes, right?"

"Uh, yeah, thanks," he said awkwardly, taking the offered bag from her.

"I have another shift tonight, so you don't need to come check on me."

"Oh, all right then."

"So, I'll see you tomorrow?"

"I'm not sure. I have plans tomorrow," Ferris said, remembering Emily. "So probably not."

"Oh, okay. Well…"

"Yeah?"

She placed her hand on his arm, giving him a warm smile.

"Thanks for staying yesterday. I'm glad we got to talk."

"Yeah, don't mention it."

About thirty yards away, still standing by the entrance of the school, Seamus watched the two speak. He quickly figured out that the girl was Julie, recognizing her from the description Ferris had given earlier that week. He was about to start digging in his pockets for a cigarette when a voice made him look up.

"Hey. Is Demos here, yet?"

It was Emily. She and Demos normally met at the front of the school to walk home together. That was, if Demos didn't have other unsavory plans.

"Don't know where he is," Seamus said, turning his attention back to Ferris and Julie. Emily noticed what he was staring at, turning her head to watch as well.

"Seamus, who's that girl?"

"Oh, her?" Seamus said casually, biting the end of a cigarette. He thought about his answer for a moment. Something in him grew cold and he opened his mouth to speak before he could think better of it.

"That's Julie, his girlfriend."

The hands on Ferris' watch read ten o'clock a.m. He lowered his wrist, eyes shifting to the aquarium entrance. He'd made absolutely sure to be on time that day.

The building was well maintained, bearing high, soaring ceilings and decorative glass fixtures. A transparent archway above the doors held a number of tropical fish. He would normally already be studying the sea life, trying to name as many different species as his memory would allow. This morning, however, his attention couldn't fix on anything but the front doors. Each person that passed through was a disappointment, until finally a girl in gray with mousy hair came in past them.

"Emily," Ferris smiled, approaching her as she came in.

"Hi, sorry I'm a little late," Emily said, looking tired.

"Did you get enough sleep?" he asked, walking with her to the ticket counter.

"Not really. It was a long night."

"Oh, sorry," he said, offering payment to the man behind the ticket counter. "Two students, please."

"No, it's okay. I can pay for my own," Emily interrupted, waving him off.

"You sure? I wanted—"

"It's fine," she said bluntly, offering the clerk her money. Ferris went silent, studying her for a moment. This wasn't really going how he'd visualized it. She didn't seem happy to be there. It almost felt as if she had forced herself to come. Would Demos have lied about the way Emily felt? It was possible she just wasn't in the best of moods. She did stay up late, after all.

192

They walked past the main hall, going down a dim passageway lined with glass displays. Each tank was embedded into the wall, lined with coral, rocks, and saltwater fish.

"Do you see it?" Ferris said as they stopped at a small habitat, pointing low in the tank. He was careful not to touch the glass.

"I think so. Oh, there he is. A moray eel."

"Yeah," he said, looking at her briefly before turning back to the eel. "Even the inside of their mouths are camouflaged."

"Cool," she said, unable to help but smile. Something about fish, even a gaping-jawed eel, relaxed her.

They went past more glass windows, stopping to examine each set of fish and sea life as they went. Emily had been wise in deciding to go early. Normally there were so many tourists and visitors that one had to stand on tiptoe and crane their head to catch a glimpse of any fish at all. At this time of day, though, the exhibit was practically empty.

"I love these," Ferris said, getting a closer look as they stopped at a jellyfish tank. "Moon jellyfish."

"Wow," Emily said, staring as the jellyfish floated around slowly, glowing in the tank's multicolored lighting. "They're beautiful."

Emily's mood seemed to be improving, if only a little. She didn't seem to be herself that day. Ferris had the feeling that she would normally have more to say, or at least show more enthusiasm. Then again, he didn't know her as well as he would have liked.

"What the hell is that?" she asked, narrowing her eyes at what looked like a giant underwater tick.

"Ah, that's a giant isopod."

"It's creepy," she said, half-repelled and half-fascinated.

"Yeah, they're pretty gross looking. They eat them in some parts of Asia, though. It's not really that strange, if you compare it to a lobster. Those look like big underwater bugs, too."

"Thanks, now I can never eat lobster again."

Ferris laughed, following her away from the tank. They had already spent two hours in the aquarium. So far, Emily's favorite exhibit was the penguins. Ferris himself was quite fond of the octopus. Both of them, however, were anticipating the final display: the shark reef.

"So, here it is," Emily said, leaning her head back to look at the top of the glass wall. The tank was easily three stories tall, containing 350,000 gallons of water and nearly twenty sharks. They circled the artificial reef, swimming over the visitor's heads. The room was dark, lit dimly with blue from the tank. Bits of light reflected on the walls, shifting with the water as it moved.

Emily appeared to be lost in thought as she watched, staring quietly as the sharks swam by. Ferris did the same but was having trouble with the silence. He looked sideways at her, considering his words before speaking.

"Emily."

"Yeah?"

"You said earlier, when you invited me... there was something you wanted to tell me?"

"Oh, yes. Of course," Emily replied, averting her eyes from the glass and looking down at her hands. It almost seemed as if she had been hoping he would forget about it. She took in a soft breath, making him even more anxious as he waited.

"Chris and I are going steady."

Ferris stared at her for a second before giving a short laugh.

"Why is that funny?" she asked, knitting her brow at him.

"You're... you're serious?"

"Yes, I'm serious."

Ferris' expression dropped as he calculated what she had said. He blinked, then looked away. It felt as if a cold stone had dropped into the pit of his stomach. His chest ached.

"That's what you wanted to tell me?" he finally said, looking back at her. "That's what you wanted to meet me here for?"

"Yes," she said quietly.

"Oh," he replied, finding it quite difficult to talk. "Well..."

"Well?"

"Well, I'm—" he started, wishing his throat didn't feel so raw. "I'm happy for you."

"Thanks, Ferris."

There was a dreadful, awkward silence between them as they both stared at the display. A few sharks swam by before Ferris gave up.

"I need to find the men's room. I'll be right back."

"Sure," she said, not taking her eyes off of the water.

The bathroom was thankfully empty and Ferris stood in front of a sink in frustration.

"Idiot! God, you fucking, stupid, fucking idiot," he groaned, running his hand over his forehead. "What the hell, you really thought she'd—"

"God," he said, this time more softly as he took off his glasses and covered his eyes with his palm. Hesitantly, he looked himself in the eyes. Not only was she not confessing her feelings for him, but she was saying how she felt about *somebody else*. With a slow sigh, he ran some water, rinsing his face.

'Look at you,' he thought. 'You're pathetic.'

He couldn't get the image out of his head; the way she'd smiled and invited him in the hallway at school. She'd been so eager in her voice and warm in her expression. This was it? This was seriously it? Taking in a deep breath, he dried his face with a paper towel before heading back out.

194

"So, you ready to leave?" he asked, stepping up behind her. She looked at him over her shoulder. It was strange, but her eyes almost seemed red.

"Yeah, let's go."

Ferris offered to walk Emily home, relieved when she declined. She headed west, to Little Italy. Ferris went the opposite direction, deciding to make a brief stop before home.

"Ferris," Julie said, picking up her head from the notes she was writing. "Hi."

"Hey," he replied, wearily sitting down on the couch next to her.

"I thought you weren't coming today."

"Change of plans," Ferris said emotionlessly. "I got you this."

He handed her a small aquarium gift shop bag, which she opened to reveal a plush manatee.

"Holy crap, this is so cute. Thank you!" Julie was much too amused to remind him that she couldn't accept things from him. A toy manatee hardly counted as money, though.

"You're welcome. He's kind of fat and dumb."

"Reminded you of me?" Julie said with a smile. Ferris only forced a quick laugh and shrugged, lacking the ability to joke around.

"What's wrong?" she asked, setting the toy down on the coffee table and directing her attention to him. "What happened today?"

"I don't know. It wasn't my best day, I guess."

"Elaborate."

Ferris frowned, looking down momentarily before deciding to answer her.

"Problem with a girl."

"Well, I'm a girl. Maybe I can help."

"This is beyond help."

"Tell me anyway."

"Well," Ferris said heavily, "I could have sworn, I mean I really would have bet my college tuition that this girl liked me."

"But... she didn't?" Julie asked.

"She asked me last week if I wanted to go out today. She said she had something important to tell me. When today finally came, the important thing was that she was 'going steady' with some guy. What does that even mean, 'go steady?' Isn't that phrase from the '50s?"

"Ouch," Julie said quietly. "Dick move."

"I guess," Ferris said, slouching down in his seat. "Did I say something wrong...? Maybe I'm ugly?"

"You're not ugly," she said, sounding disappointed in him.

"There's got to be something wrong with me."

"Well, I was attracted to you."

"Yeah, okay."

"Honestly. I—" Julie bit her thumb, wondering if she should continue. "You might get mad at me for mentioning this, but—"

Ferris looked over at her, his expression apathetic.

"But," Julie continued, "I didn't have to kiss you. I wanted to. And I never told Brandon that I did."

Ferris didn't answer, simply looking away from her.

"You don't believe me," she said, frustrated.

"Not really."

"You're impossible," Julie said, rolling her eyes.

"Look," Ferris said, gesturing with his hand, "if you're just trying to get another manatee, it's not going to work."

"Aw," Julie frowned. She looked sideways, fidgeting with her hands. "Hey, it's okay if I smoke in here, right?"

"Why, have you been?"

"Umm, no," Julie said slowly, clearly lying. Ferris spotted a can of air freshener beside the sofa, picking it up to look over in his hands.

"I guess this stuff works pretty well," he mused. "Still, you shouldn't. This—"

"Isn't your place, I know. There's an ashtray here, and in the bedroom. Whoever's place this is, they smoke."

Ferris tried not to get the mental image of Victor with some woman in the bedroom, smoking after—

"Yeah, anyway," Ferris said, clearing his throat. "You— hey, come on."

Julie looked up innocently, a freshly lit cigarette dangling from her mouth.

"What?"

Ferris only narrowed his eyes at her in response, raising an eyebrow.

"I need it," she explained. "You look like you could use one, too."

He waved her off, denying the offered cigarette. Julie licked her lips, taking a slow drag before exhaling a ring.

"Demos likes doing that, too," Ferris mumbled, leaning an elbow on the arm of the sofa and resting his head on a fist.

"Who's Demos?"

"Some guy who hates you."

"Neat," she replied, putting the cigarette back to her mouth. "I'm adding to my collection."

"Of guys who hate you," Ferris repeated bluntly.

"Yeah. Are you in it?"

Ferris glanced at the wall, thinking about his answer.

"I don't hate you," he finally replied.

"Great, we've gone a step up in our relationship. Maybe in a couple of weeks we'll upgrade to 'neutral acquaintances.'"

Ferris only replied with a slight smile as he watched her finish her cigarette.

"You should be saving your money. Cigarettes are expensive," he said.

"Okay, Mom. I can find them cheap, though," Julie said, putting the cigarette out in an ashtray on the table. She picked up her head suddenly, looking excited. "That reminds me, let me show you what I got."

Ferris' eyes followed her as she got up and went into the next room. There was the sound of a large object being picked up and she re-entered the room carrying a black case.

"You bought a *guitar?*" he asked disdainfully.

"Pawn shop," Julie said with a shrug. "It was cheap and I got lots of tips today."

"You're supposed to be saving for—"

"I know!" Julie said, waving him off as she placed the case on the coffee table and opened it. It was a plain acoustic guitar. It looked like it had seen better days.

"What do you think?" she asked.

"Well, let's see," he said, picking it up by the neck and plucking a couple of times. "Kind of shitty."

"It's really out of tune," Julie explained, "and the strings are pretty worn. Maybe I can—"

"Hold on, let me," Ferris said, positioning it in his lap. He pulled each string, turning the knobs at the headstock as he listened. After a minute, he seemed satisfied with the sound each string made.

"Here," Ferris said, handing it to her.

"I didn't know you played guitar," Julie said hesitantly.

"I don't. Violin," he said, pushing his glasses up on his nose.

"Nerd," she said under her breath, testing the sound of the guitar by playing a few notes.

"Shut up. Play something."

Julie thought for a moment, deciding on a song in her head. Concentrating, she started to clumsily play a song. Ferris made a slight face as she played *Twinkle, Twinkle, Little Star* as poorly as he'd ever heard. He was already trying to think of some kind of response when she abruptly stopped to laugh.

"Just kidding," she said, biting her lower lip.

Before he could speak, she started to play again. Her thin fingers held neatly to the chords as she played, showing a fair amount of skill. Julie strummed easily, looking comfortable with the instrument in her hands. She appeared to have been playing for a long time. The song, though not familiar, was actually quite lovely.

"You're not bad," Ferris said when she finished. "What song was that?"

"I wrote it," Julie replied thoughtfully. "The words aren't done, yet."

"Ever think of playing for money?"

"What, this? That's silly. That's like wanting to be an astronaut."

"Not really," Ferris said as she put the guitar back in its case. "You could start small."

"I don't know. I think I have better chances at that diner."

"Who taught you?"

"I just used some chord and scale charts I got at a tag sale. I think they were 25 cents."

"Nice investment."

Ferris didn't realize it, but he had stayed much longer than five minutes that day. He lost track of time entirely, welcoming the distraction from the afternoon's disappointment. It wasn't until he got home that he remembered how let-down he felt, going back to dwell on what Emily had said. It nagged at the back of his mind. He couldn't place exactly what it was, but he had the overwhelming feeling that something just wasn't right.

27

It was dark. Ferris knew his eyes were open, but he couldn't see anything. He could hear his own gasps echoing off of the flat surface in front of him. It was difficult to figure out where he was. He was lying on his back, feeling side to side for any kind of clue. Wood — everything was wood. The walls were tight around him, smooth and flat under his fingers. The air was stale, scented with sawdust and mildew. Ferris was quiet, but the sound of dirt made him panic.

"Demos?" he shouted, feeling the surface in front of him — the lid of a coffin.

"Demos, let me out!" Ferris cried, inhaling sharply. He knew he should save his breath, but panic was overtaking him. "I'm in here! I'm stuck, *let me out!*"

Ferris' fist banged the lid before he tried to push on it, but it was shut tightly. His breath was coming short, his heart beating so intensely that he could have sworn he could hear it bouncing off the wooden walls. There was the sound of more dirt being shoveled and he forced the weight of his elbow up against the lid.

"Demos!!"

Ferris woke up seconds later, eyes snapping open with a start. He lay still, only panting as he focused on the walls. The sight of the street lights from the window and the cool, fresh air of the room calmed his senses. He swallowed with relief.

"God."

His nightmares had been growing in frequency. Ferris considered a change in his diet, or perhaps fewer aspirin. There was also the option of spending less of his free time with notorious gangsters.

The third option would have to wait. The weather was getting warmer; McPharlin Racetrack was now open. Pietro, Demos' older cousin, was slowly building his reputation as a bookie. He was young, but shrewd. Pietro was normally able to make a profit regardless of a race's outcome, but today the family was shooting for something much larger. Their plan didn't involve their own books; they were fishing from a much larger pond. Of course, the kids had been invited. The presence of youngsters always made the group seem less suspicious, and, aside from that, it was a learning experience.

Located on the north side of the city, the track was only a half hour drive from the Giorgetti home. They parked the car and headed towards the entrance, taking their time as they walked.

"So, Fish, you're good with numbers. Who would you go with?" Victor asked, sucking the end of his cigar. He had replaced his usual cigarettes with something richer, looking forward to the evening's payoff. Ferris had studied the entries program for a long time, still looking through it as he answered.

"Well, for the first race, Gay Bee has a better track record but his last few races have been poor. I think he's just getting old. I'd go with A Horse Named Sue, personally," Ferris replied, fixing his glasses on the bridge of his nose.

"All right, why not. To win?"

"To place," Ferris said after a pause. He was sure, but not entirely sure. "But I didn't bring much money."

"Oh, don't worry, kid. It's on us. Think of it as an early birthday present. Maybe it'll help you pay for Yale."

"If I get in," Ferris said dubiously. "Thanks."

"I'm putting my money on Can't Possibly Lose," Demos said coolly, walking with his hands in his pockets.

"I'm not even going to ask how you chose that horse," Ferris said. "For the final race—"

"Ah, you don't want to bet on the final race," Victor interrupted. He exchanged a look with Nicky, who smiled back at him. Ferris didn't press any further.

"All right," he said simply, looking back down at his pamphlet. They reached the betting windows, waiting as Victor placed the bets for them. He had quite a bit of cash in an envelope.

"Fifty dollars to place on number six. Fifty to win on number two."

"Thank you, Sir," the clerk said, taking Victor's money and giving him two tickets.

"One more," Victor said, sliding an envelope under the glass. "Race nine, five hundred for a superfecta on seven, three, two, and four."

The clerk looked up at Victor slowly, staring for just a moment before taking the money.

"Just one combination, Sir?"

Victor nodded.

"Yes, Sir. Thank you," he said, handing Victor one more ticket. Normally the track betters wagered ten cents to two dollars on an average superfecta. If this man won, he would certainly be taking home a large amount of money.

As they found their seats, Pietro was already waiting for them. He was speaking into his cell phone and writing in a black book, balancing it on a folded leg.

"Hello," Pietro said curtly as he saw them approach. Ferris got the feeling that Pietro was a no-nonsense type of guy.

"Hey Pi," Nicky said loudly as he ruffled Pietro's neatly combed hair.

"Please, Nick," Pietro said with a swat of his hand, quickly moving to smooth his hair back.

"This kid," Nicky said, still grinning as Pietro went back to his phone conversation.

"New England is plus ten. Change your mind? Make it quick," Pietro said impatiently, writing a few more numbers down in his book. "All right, done."

Pietro shut his phone with a quick snap, sliding it into a leather briefcase.

"Sorry about that," Pietro apologized.

"Sure you should be doing that on your cell phone?" Victor asked, leaning back in his seat.

"It's fine, I bought a scrambler," Pietro replied, clearly a step ahead.

"These seats aren't bad," Nicky said, settling down and stretching his arms over the backs.

Pietro had reserved them a private box outdoors, giving them both privacy and a convenient beverage service. Ferris took his eyes off of the race program, looking down below at the horses as they lined up at the starting gate. The seats were full at the track that day, which could only mean good things for Victor. The more money people bet, the more he was going to win.

"Last to load, Moon Child," the track announcer said over the speaker system as the last horse got into position. "All in line, getting set."

There was a shrill ringing noise as the metal gates burst open, sending ten horses rushing forward on the dirt track.

"And they're off!" the announcer continued. "For the opener at McPharlin. It's a slow start for Gay Bee, who's way on the outside."

Ferris and Demos leaned closer to get a better look as the horses rounded the track. Demos had a pair of binoculars which he peered through observantly.

"Look, Can't Possibly Lose is in second," Demos grinned. "And he's closing in."

"Let me see," Ferris said, gesturing for the binoculars. Demos passed them over and Ferris lifted them to watch through the lenses. The horses magnified in his sight, galloping mightily over the track as the minute jockeys balanced above. Sure enough, Demos' horse was now winning.

"Can't Possibly Lose is right off the rail, with A Horse Named Sue on the far off side," the track announcer said. "We have a close duel going around the first turn. It's a break of five lengths back to Moon Child who's way behind the leaders and all alone in third."

"Good thing I didn't bet on Gay Bee," Ferris said, watching as the former champion came up behind, finally making the turn.

"Poor guy," Demos said, taking a drink of water from a bottle. "All alone back there. And gay."

"They're going to the far turn, Can't Possibly Lose has his head in front, A Horse Named Sue right there on the inside. Sugarcube, three off the rail," the intercom echoed above their heads, loud enough to be audible over the scores of yelling race fans.

"Come on, you son of a bitch, keep going," Demos said under his breath, taking the binoculars back and staring intently through them.

"Can't Possibly Lose is being engulfed on the outside by Moon Child, coming to the top of the lane as they straighten away in the upper stretch! On the far off side is Sugarcube, and this thirty to one long shot gets the lead! Here's A Horse Named Sue on the outside making a quick run along with Moon Child, they're coming to the finish! A Horse Named Sue just got up over Sugarcube with second, then Can't Possibly Lose, and Moon Child!"

"Balls!" Demos yelled, hitting the top of the stand railing with his fist. "Third?"

"If you bet to show, you would have won something," Ferris said offhandedly, putting his attention back on the race program.

"Hey, nice work!" Nicky said, giving Ferris a light punch in the shoulder. "You should have bet to win."

"Maybe next time," Ferris replied, watching as the final scores were displayed. "Let's see. Sue's odds were 9-2. Neat. I won $300."

Ferris picked his head up to give Victor a small, appreciative smile.

"Thanks for the ticket."

"No problem, kid," Victor answered easily. "Just don't get addicted to this."

With what Victor was anticipating, the fifty dollar bet was small beans. He took a sip of his scotch, eyes calm as they watched the second race start. They had a long time until the final run of the day, and by the time the races were nearly through, Demos was quite antsy.

"Let's find something to eat," he said to Ferris, getting up from his seat and making sure he had his cigarettes in his pocket.

"While you're up, get me something, too," Nicky said over his shoulder. "And a beer."

"I can't buy beer, Nicky, I'm sixteen," Demos said impatiently. "Just order it."

"Ah, whatever."

"Not a bad Sunday, huh?" Demos asked as they walked past a few displays towards a booth that sold food.

"Yeah. Not bad."

202

"Were you going to tell me how it went yesterday?" Demos asked, finally blurting what was on his mind.

Ferris was quiet as they got in line, waiting behind half a dozen people.

"What?" Demos said. "It wasn't good?"

"No. Not really."

Demos stopped digging through his wallet. He glanced towards Ferris, stunned.

"I don't understand. What did she say?"

"She and Chris are going steady," Ferris admitted quietly, unable to help but sound miserable.

"That's what she told you?"

Ferris nodded, giving Demos a brief shrug.

"What the fuck, I could have sworn—"

"Well, you were wrong."

"I'm never wrong," Demos said shamelessly. "I know Emily."

"You were wrong about Can't Possibly Lose. Seeing that he Can't Possibly *Lost.*"

"I didn't live with that horse for four years."

"You sure?"

"Come on. This is ridiculous. I'll talk to her."

"Don't. Just drop it, okay? Let her do what she wants."

"But that guy is a total dick! He told her she was fat! He bosses her around and gets jealous when people say her art is better than his."

"He's an artist?"

"Yeah, that's how they met. Some art class thing," Demos said with vague gestures. "Artists are assholes."

"Emily's an artist."

"Well, you know what I mean. It doesn't make sense, though."

"How could you be so sure, anyway?" Ferris asked. "About how she felt?"

"Her sketchbook. She drew you all the time. Only crazy, lovesick girls do that."

Ferris stared at Demos, not sure what to think of what he was hearing. It wasn't calculating properly.

"What?" he finally responded.

"Well, not *all* the time. But she's drawn you. I go through her sketchbook when she's not looking. And—" Demos said, raising a finger to make a point. "She's never drawn that dick, Chris."

"Maybe I have a funny shaped head and she's doing studies," Ferris theorized, feeling the back of his hair self-consciously.

"I don't think that's it," Demos said.

"It must be. She's going out with him. Regardless of who she drew however many times, *he's* her boyfriend now."

"I just don't get it. What's wrong with her?"

Demos' train of thought was interrupted as they reached the counter.

"Can I help you?" the woman in the booth asked.

Demos looked up at the menu, trying to remember what the men back in the box seats liked to eat.

"A roast beef sandwich, three hot dogs, and a Caesar salad. Um, fries, some chips, that chicken mozzarella sandwich," Demos said, pointing behind the glass display. "Oh, Ferris, what do you want?"

Ferris was lost in thought when Demos asked him and he blinked before finding the ability to respond.

"Oh, uh, surprise me."

"And a bagel with cream cheese," Demos said. He elbowed Ferris, joking under his breath. "You're a Jew, you like bagels, right?"

"As much as you like 'spicy meatsaballs.'"

"I *love* those."

Ferris took half of the load as they carried their lunches back to the seating area. Nicky was happy to see them; he hadn't eaten in a whole three hours.

"Good job, kids. That looks great. But what are you guys going to eat?" Nicky asked with a grin.

"Yeah right, Nick. Give me that sandwich," Victor said, holding his hand out to take it as he watched the eighth race through the binoculars.

"Thanks, Demos," Pietro said, taking the salad container from the teen. Unlike Nicky, he watched his health.

"The race almost done?" Demos asked as he sat back down in his seat.

"Just about. Ours is coming up after they announce this one's final standing."

Ferris could feel the anticipation in the air. The ninth race was the one that they had all been waiting for and Ferris wasn't even sure exactly why. He did figure out that Victor knew who would get first, second, third, and fourth, in the correct order. The only way he could know that would be to make sure *every single jockey* knew their place. It seemed like quite a bit of work. He doubted they all went along willingly.

"Ah," Victor said, holding his ticket up to read the numbers that were printed on it. He lowered it, watching the horses line up at the gate for the final race. "There they are – my golden geese."

The track announcer's voice echoed above them once more, making brief observations as the horses got into place.

"Here we go," Victor said, leaning forward with his binoculars. The sound of ringing and rattling gates meshed together as the horses ruptured forward.

204

"And, they're off!" the announcer said enthusiastically. "It's the night cap at McPharlin today. We've got The Word with the lead, crossing over to the rail. Merging into second is I Don't Recall, and moving up to third is Fighting Star with Spring and Summer on the outside."

Ferris looked carefully at the horses that were taking their places in the lead. If he remembered correctly, they all bore the numbers that Victor had mentioned at the betting window.

"And up front it's The Word, he's going well on in the lead, up by three. I Don't Recall is keeping himself in second. We've got Fighting Star on the outside, vying for the third spot with Spring and Summer who's at the rail."

A quick glance in Victor's direction let Ferris know that everything was going according to plan. The older Italian had a content smile, something that was quite rare for his face.

"They're on the back stretch now, 3AM Shift is in mid-pack racing in fifth. Up on the outside advancing as they go up the back stretch is Danny Boy, and right behind you'll find That Dirty Bird. He's advancing, just went past Cherries Jubilee, with three or four more lengths back to Easy Street."

Victor narrowed his eyes, moving his point of focus back to the horse that was in sixth. He watched with irritation as it moved up to fifth, nearly catching up to the fourth-place horse.

"The half point at 48 and three," the race caller continued, "The Word still has the lead with I Don't Recall trying to catch up. Coming up behind is Spring and Summer with Fighting Star on the outside. Danny Boy seems to be making a late rush, he's eye-to-eye with Fighting Star, coming up along the rail, and he's passed him!"

"Fuck!" Victor shouted, startling the other men in the box. He stood, his hand in a tight fist.

"Moving up ever further is Danny Boy as they hit the top of the lane. It's The Word up by three, now two, as Danny Boy is gaining on the outside."

"'Fanculo! You son of a bitch! Che cazzo fai?!" Victor exclaimed, crumpling the program in his free hand. He stared with such intensity that Ferris could feel it radiating from the man. Something was wrong. It was very clear that Danny Boy was not supposed to place. For a superfecta, one had to properly predict each horse, in order, from first to fourth. If this unexpected horse made even fourth place, Victor's entire plan would have been for nothing. Nicky leaned back as he watched Danny Boy take third, then second. Ferris and Demos could barely watch as The Word was overtaken at the finish line and cringed in preparation for Victor's response.

"*Fuck!*"

"Ladies and gentlemen, getting set to step into the winner's circle for the first time in his career is Danny Boy," the announcer broadcasted over the speakers, oblivious to the rage boiling inside of Victor Giorgetti's skull. Victor waited. He waited to hear the only thing that was important anymore.

"Winning rider tonight was Eddie Donahue! We'd like to take a moment to congratulate him and the whole team behind Danny Boy."

The jockey's name.

"Eddie Donahue," Victor repeated, eerily calm.

"Marone," Nicky said under his breath. It wasn't clear if it was the situation that made him uneasy, or Victor.

Ferris looked down over the railing as the jockey dismounted, pulling the saddle off of his horse as a stable hand led Danny Boy off. From such a distance, it was difficult to tell if the man's eyes contained pride or fear. Ferris found himself wondering as he watched the jockey leave; did Eddie Donahue realize that the steps he was taking at this very moment were most likely his last?

Victor's eyes followed Eddie as he walked out of sight, out towards the trailers where the jockeys stayed during the racing season.

"Let's go," Victor said, turning to leave the box. Nicky and Pietro immediately followed. Demos and Ferris briefly exchanged glances before going as well. The direction they were going did not seem to be the exit. Ferris' assumption had been correct; Victor wanted to take care of this immediately.

When they arrived at the proper trailer, Eddie was already packing a suitcase. He moved in a frantic rush, throwing a shirt into the small piece of luggage. The other jockeys were at an end-of-day party, having assumed that the unexpected winner was a last minute set-up by the Giorgettis. What man, after all, would be stupid enough to screw with the mafia?

When the door burst open, Eddie's breath caught in fear.

"Get out of my trailer!" he yelled, gathering up what courage he could.

"For such a short man," Victor said, sliding on a pair of black gloves, "you're pretty fuckin' loud."

"You can't keep doing this kind of thing and get away with it," Eddie said. His words were bold, but he was backing up as he spoke.

"Mhm," Victor said, not really listening. "Pietro, shut the door, would you?"

Eddie stared at his only exit as Pietro latched it, picking up his head to look Eddie in the eyes. Pietro's expression was cold, lacking any sympathy.

"So, Eddie. We haven't met, personally. But I do recall sending some men to have a word with you about today's race. Ah, please. Sit down."

"I'd rather st—"

206

Eddie was cut off as Nicky grabbed the jockey by his collar, throwing him down into one of the trailer's benches.

"Anyway, I believe a bribe was involved in your case. Am I mistaken in hearing that you took it?"

"I did," Eddie replied, looking uneasy.

"Which was a smart move, of course. But your part of the bargain, Mr. Donahue, was to lose. Not a very difficult job, really. So."

Victor opened his coat, sliding his hand inside to pull out a small pistol. He pulled out the magazine, making sure it was full.

"What," Victor said sternly, snapping the magazine back into place, "happened."

"I knew I could win that fucking race. I was born to do it. That horse was born to do it. There was no way I was letting us all down by taking your damned bribe."

"How noble," Victor said, unamused. He thought for a moment before handing his pistol over to Nicky. "Nick, take this. I'm going to need your knife."

Both Ferris and Demos were waiting outside the trailer. This was mainly because the trailer was small and didn't lend itself to containing so many people. Aside from that, Ferris had had too many nightmares to expose himself to what was happening inside. He wouldn't be able to sleep for a month. The sound of a scream made them both look up. It didn't seem there was anyone else around to hear it.

"What's worth more to you, Eddie? Your pride, or your only hand?"

Victor had used the word 'only' because the jockey's other hand had been sawed off. Victor was holding it casually in a gloved hand. Eddie only replied with a weak moan, shivering on the floor of his trailer. Nicky had stuffed a rag into his mouth, minimizing any future screams.

"I didn't get that, but judging from the outcome of the race, I'd guess your *pride*," Victor said, slamming the tip of the knife down into Eddie's exposed wrist. It stuck him to the floor as his muffled scream filled the small trailer. Victor grasped the knife, cranking it down until the blade hit cartilage. He then scraped the knife down, sawing to sever Eddie's hand from his arm. It was obvious he would never race again.

Victor dropped the hand, straightening himself and cracking his knuckles.

"Do you know what you cost me, Eddie? How much time and planning that took? How many threats and bribes it takes to make ten fucking jockeys do what they're told? Not to mention the humiliation."

Eddie wept, unable to look at the stumps that were once his hands as they gushed red onto his trailer's carpet.

"What kind of an answer is that, huh? Huh?" Victor kicked him in the side with a black winter boot, rolling Eddie onto his back. "Answer me, you fuck!"

Victor gestured down with a nod of his head and Nicky crouched down by the ex-jockey, giving him a few hard slaps across his face.

"Stop fucking crying!" Nicky complained. "Jesus Christ, you'd think we ended your life."

"You know, Nick. That's not a bad idea."

Nicky looked up slowly as Victor smiled.

The door to the trailer opened abruptly, slamming into the siding as Nicky and Pietro made a hasty exit. There was the sound of broken glass as Victor dropped a bottle of liquor. He struck a match, tossing it as he stepped out of the trailer.

"Go. *Go!*" Victor said sternly, waving the boys off as he stalked forward. Ferris looked up, catching sight of the open door. He immediately regretted his move; the image was embedded in his mind. Ferris clamped his hand firmly over his own mouth, desperately willing himself to not vomit. The body of Eddie Donahue lay writhing on the trailer floor as flames licked the walls. His mouth was jammed with a white, dirty cloth, and his eye sockets were plugged with the thumbs of his own severed hands.

They walked away, silhouetted by flames as they rose up over the chassis of the trailer. The wallpaper crackled as it turned black. By the time the fire trucks arrived, each person present was already safely driving home. Each person, that was, except Eddie Donahue.

28

Between lunch and dinner reservations, Ristorante Giorgetti was mostly quiet. Only soft piano notes and a few voices could be heard in the dining area. Ferris was sitting at a small table, taking the slow hours to work on some assignments. Demos sat at the restaurant's grand piano a few feet away, running his fingers easily over the ivory keys.

The racetrack arson had made the news earlier that week. Reporters and locals were quick to suspect organized criminal involvement, but the chief of police firmly insisted that it had been an accident. Blakely easily claimed that Donahue, having a history of marijuana addiction, simply went back to his trailer for a victory smoke. In his drugged state, there was little he could do to stop or even notice the flames until it was far too late. Not everyone bought the story, but there was not much anyone could do to challenge it. The bizarre positioning of the charred skeleton was left ignored.

The light sounds of *Gymnopédie No. 1* helped Ferris relax as he worked. One of his favorite pastimes was to simply sit and listen to his friend play the piano. The entire afternoon, Demos was playing songs by one of his most loved composers, Erik Satie. Though the music was French, no one seemed to be complaining.

The front doors opened, allowing some of the chilled outside air to come in. Ferris looked up. The moment he saw who it was, the pen he'd been twirling snapped out of his fingers and clattered down to the table. Ferris cursed under his breath.

"Hi, Em," Demos said, still playing the song.

"Hey," she replied, walking inside with a package held close to her chest. Gino had sent her to pick up some cappocolo from the meat shop down the street; he'd spent a good ten minutes explaining exactly how to discern the best cuts. Gino was very fussy. Emily caught a glimpse of Ferris, hesitating before speaking.

"Hi."

"Hi," he answered, not looking up from his notes. Emily said nothing else, heading back towards the kitchen. Before she could go through the swinging doors, however, Victor stepped out and caught sight of her.

"Emmy, there you are!"

"Hi, Dad. I got the stuff Grandpa wanted."

"Good, great," Victor said, taking the wrapped brown package from her. "Come here Pumpkin, you're freezing cold. Let me get you something to drink."

Victor ushered his daughter back into the kitchen, leaving the two boys alone once again. After a minute, Demos stopped his playing, stretching his arms with a curve of his spine.

"You sure you don't want me to talk to her?" Demos asked carefully.

"Yeah, I'm sure."

"If it makes you feel any better, Uncle Vic doesn't like Chris, either."

"Why not?" Ferris asked curiously. Chris was Italian, after all, and seemed well-off enough.

"He thinks the guy is an *impostore*. A fake. He doesn't trust him with Emily. Chris doesn't come around much, pretty much to avoid Victor."

"Oh," Ferris said. He started to wonder what Victor would have thought of him. Possibly too bookish, or too liberal. The kitchen doors swung back open to allow the man in question back into the dining area.

"So you were too busy playing piano to run an errand for your grandfather?" Victor asked Demos, his voice chastising.

"He asked Emily. She looked bored," Demos shrugged, having little passion for chivalry. "She needed some fresh air, anyway."

"This is why you don't have a girlfriend," Victor said, continuing to badger his nephew. Ferris looked up at the ceiling, knowing *exactly* why Demos didn't have a girlfriend. It most definitely wasn't because of his manners.

"But it's cold," Demos said in a pathetic whine.

Then again, maybe it *was* his manners.

"Oh, grow some balls. And when you're done, get back in the kitchen. The mayor reserved the entire place for a last minute dinner party and we're booked to the eyes. I don't know if we'll have enough people back there."

"All right, sure," Demos said, leaning back on the bench and looking smug. "Might take me a while to grow those, though."

"Get your skinny ass back there," Victor snapped, pointing to the double doors. Demos got up quickly, going back to the kitchen without another word.

"Hey, you."

"Yes?" Ferris asked cautiously, looking up from his work.

"I can count on you, right? We're going to need as many hands as we can get. You can make a few extra bucks, too."

Ferris opened his mouth to explain that he had homework, but stopped. Victor was counting on him? The way he worded it made it incredibly difficult to say 'no.' Surprisingly, Ferris found himself considering it. He wanted Victor's approval.

"Of course," Ferris answered.

"Great, perfect. Why don't you go back and give Demos a hand?" Victor said, going back into the kitchen and leaving

Ferris by himself. Ferris looked uncomfortably down at his half-finished assignment, already regretting his decision.

"He conned you into staying, too?" Demos asked when Ferris entered the kitchen. He was already preparing onions, cutting in precise, fast chops with a knife.

"Yeah," Ferris replied, grabbing an apron from a hook and tying it on. "Somehow."

"At least we don't have to wait tables. I heard the mayor's friends are a bunch of dicks."

"What about her?" Ferris said quietly, glancing sideways at Emily. She was sitting to the side, drinking from a mug and looking tired.

"She can help me prep or something," Demos said under his breath. "Uncle Vic would kill someone if she got her hands dirty with dishes."

"Yeah, that's what I'm for," Ferris said, grabbing a rack of used pots.

"Hello, Gino," one of the chefs said from behind Demos. The teen looked up to see his grandfather enter the kitchen.

"Evening," Gino said, walking over to see their progress.

"Grandpa, you're wearing your chef's clothes," Demos said hopefully. "Are you helping tonight?"

"Of course I am. Anything for that jamook mayor," Gino answered. Demos simply smiled at his grandfather, ridiculously pleased to hear it.

"Grandpa," Emily said, smiling warmly as she came over.

"Ah, tesoro, come here. How are you?" Gino said, putting a loving arm around her shoulder.

"I'm good, do you want me to help?"

"No, no, you go sit. We'll take care of this."

Demos made a face that Ferris didn't quite translate.

"But I want to," she insisted.

"All right, here, you help your cousin," Gino said, gesturing over to the counter as he went to go prepare.

"Hands clean?" Demos asked as Emily tied an apron on.

"Yes," she replied with an eye roll. She held them up to show him.

"You sure?"

"*Yes.*"

"Here, make some salad," he said, sliding a head of fresh lettuce over to her.

"I can do other things, you know."

"Maybe when you're older," he teased. A couple of hours later, the mayor's guests arrived. The party consisted of older men in fitted suits and younger women in silk dresses. Several were also politicians, but most were simply members of Southport's wealthy beau monde. They were immediately seated and presented with the best service in Little Italy, not to mention a highly praised wine list.

The host of the occasion wasn't celebrating anything in particular, other than himself. Mayor Palmisano was known for enjoying social events and fine dining more than the average politician. He was also known for organizing such events at the last minute and, in general, being an irritating customer. Though he was a bit of an egoist and lacked passion for progression, the Giorgettis were happy to put up with him. Palmisano's resolute, though criticized leniency on organized crime had been nothing but a blessing.

Ferris couldn't remember seeing the kitchen so busy before. The restaurant had been just as full, but this was an occasion where every customer arrived, and needed to be served, at the same time. Waiters and chefs raised their voices over the clatter of pots and dishes.

"Come on, people, where's my tuna tartar? I've got six orders waiting out there!"

"Two veal fillets, medium!"

Steam and smoke curled up from the multiple stoves and skillets sizzled violently from the heart of the kitchen. Though the other chefs were rushing back and forth, Gino was relaxed. He went by smell, taste, and instinct. The old Italian moved quickly but didn't have a spot of sweat on his brow.

Ferris' work didn't stop. When he finished the wine glasses, there were two racks of appetizer dishes. When those were done, soup plates. Those were followed by more wine glasses. The machine was never silent, in a constant state of churning, beeping, and belting out steam. His fingers were starting to lose feeling from all of the hot water and the constant smell of food made him remember how hungry he was.

He took the time to think, moving automatically. Ferris thought about his abandoned homework assignment and the college applications he needed to fill out. His mind wandered to Julie, wondering if she was also on the job. He thought of Emily.

"These done?"

A voice made him look up and he lost concentration. It was Emily, reaching for a tray of silverware.

"Yeah. Go ahead."

She picked up the tray, eyes downcast as she walked away with it. Ferris sighed. This was ridiculous. The entrees were just now being served but he was already quite ready for the night to be over.

"God, that dick keeps sending his steak back. 'It's not rare, I want rare!' Ma don, this thing is practically mooing on the plate!"

"Take it easy, Greg. Here, give him this one," Gino said, wiping a bit of sauce from the edge of a finished plate and passing it over to the waiter.

"I swear to God, I'm gonna spit on his potatoes."

"Come on, you're givin' me agita, just give him the damn plate," called another waiter.

"Guy's the mayor of Southport, not a fuckin' *Iron Chef*," the waiter griped as he went back through the swinging doors with a tray. Ferris found himself wondering just how satisfying it would be for a man to spit in the mayor's dinner and get away with it but didn't think too deeply on it. What would his mother say?

Ferris didn't take any breaks that night and was relieved beyond belief when the kitchen finally closed. The guests had mostly left and Palmisano himself stepped into the kitchen to have a word.

"I wanted to thank you for doing this on such short notice, Gino."

"Of course, it was a pleasure to serve your guests. I apologize, however, for the issue with your steak."

In the back of the kitchen, a waiter scoffed.

"Oh, that. That's fine. It was worth the wait. But uh, aside from all that, I wanted to talk to you about the bill."

"Yes, so did I," Gino said, removing his apron and setting it aside. He led Mr. Palmisano out of the kitchen into the restaurant's office, shutting the door to give them some privacy.

"What's he trying to do?" Ferris asked Demos, watching the door as he wiped his hands with a dish towel.

"Gino's probably going to give him a big discount," Demos admitted. "We don't have any dirt on him, so the only way to keep him in our pocket is with pathetic ass-kissing like this."

"I guess *you'd* rather just threaten the guy," Ferris mused.

"Whatever Gino decides, I support him."

"I can tell," Ferris replied thoughtfully.

"It's kind of a mutual arrangement. He just tells the press that Italian-Americans are being stereotyped."

"Convenient," Ferris said. He glanced over at Emily across the kitchen. "Kind of like how nobody wants her to do any work."

"Oh, it's not that. Not with grandpa anyway. To be honest, he just doesn't think girls can cook as well." Demos shrugged shamelessly. "Anyway, you hungry? I sure as hell am."

"*Yes*," Ferris said, as if he'd been holding in the desire to beg for food. They joined the other employees near the back where they were eating whatever entrees and desserts were left over.

"Oh, Fish, there you are. I saved you this," Victor said, taking the cover from a ceramic plate. "Spigola al forno."

Ferris looked down at the plate as it was placed in front of him, eyes lowering in an enamored fashion. Sea bass was always so expensive and nobody could prepare it like Gino. It was almost worth doing all the dishes for.

"Knew I could count on you," Victor added, giving Ferris a quick rub on the head.

"What about the lamb, is there any left?" Demos asked expectantly.

"I gave that to Emily," Victor said absently, pouring himself a glass of wine.

"Oh," Demos said, giving his cousin a slight glare from across the room.

"Good thing she didn't have plans tonight," Ferris mumbled off-handedly.

"Well, she did have to cancel something with Chris."

There was a clink of silverware as Victor set his fork down, lifting his head in attention.

"What was that?" His voice was chilling and stern.

"Nothing. I didn't say anything," Demos said quickly, smiling at his uncle.

"You just said—"

"I was joking! It was a joke, come on."

"You damn well better be joking. If she's dating that little shit again, I'm gonna kill him."

Ferris was tempted to just blurt out the truth, as well as offer to drive Victor over to the guy's house, but kept his mouth shut. Before Victor could get any angrier, Gino joined them.

"Mr. Palmisano gives you all his regards. He's gone home for the night."

"Good riddance," a waiter muttered. Gino ignored the comment.

"How's the fish?" Gino asked with a smile, turning his attention to Ferris.

"Wonderful," Ferris answered gratefully. "Molte grazie."

"Prego," Gino replied. His attention turned to his son, asking him over with a finger. "Victor? A word."

Victor stopped eating mid-bite, obediently getting up and following his father to the same office Gino had just come from. Demos exchanged glances with Ferris, nodding towards the door to indicate that they should eavesdrop. Hesitantly, Ferris gave a nod. The door shut and they hurried over to it. Crouching, Demos placed his ear on the wooden door, listening carefully.

"What's the matter, Dad?" Victor's voice was slightly muffled through the door, but it was decipherable.

"What, *exactly*, did you know about Mr. Donahue?"

"I know he took our money and broke the deal. I know I wasted a month planning that day. I know he was a little fuck that—"

"What about his family?"

"What? What *about* his family?"

"Were you aware, Victor, that Eddie Donahue was Mr. O'Brien's brother-in-law?"

There was a long silence.

"No," Victor said, not believing what he was hearing. "No."

"Yes, Victor. In fact, they were quite close."

"Shit!" There was the sound of a fist hitting a desk.

"'Shit' is right. Do you have any idea what your temper started this time?"

"He deserved—"

"*I don't care* what he deserved," Gino said sternly. "O'Brien is going to hit us back. We don't know when, or how, but it's going to happen."

"What do you want me to do?"

"You're going to take responsibility, Victor."

"I see."

"Don't let the kids out late. I have a feeling he's going to go for your family. *Watch* them."

"Shit," Victor repeated. Demos could hear them standing and the boys quickly scrambled away from the door. By the time it opened, they were innocently back in their seats. Victor returned to the table, taking a sip of wine as if nothing of any significance had been discussed. If one looked closely, one would see that he was sweating.

Ferris and Demos didn't have much to say to each other for the rest of the night. They both sat in an uneasy silence, digesting what they had overheard in Gino's office. When Ferris finally went home, he found that he had a difficult time falling asleep. Negative thoughts ran through his mind, unwavering in their provocation. Victor's family was in trouble, and, unfortunately, that included a great percentage of his favorite people.

Ferris had been so preoccupied with the bad news from the previous night that the homework assignment had completely slipped his mind. As the other students passed forward their essays, Ferris stared down at his half-finished paper. His heart started to race.

He had never turned in something late before. He felt anxious for the entire class, fidgeting with his pencil and trying to figure out what he could say to the teacher. After the bell rang, Ferris walked up to the instructor's desk.

"Mr. Nott," Ferris said, holding the assignment in his hands. "I need to talk to you about my—"

"No excuses, Levinstein."

"But I—"

"Just give me what you have."

Ferris exhaled dejectedly, reluctantly handing the single page over to the teacher. The man skimmed the type before looking up at his student with disappointment.

"This had the potential to be a great paper. I'm disappointed in you. I thought you knew how to manage your time."

"I'm sorry, Mr. Nott," Ferris said quietly.

"I'm afraid I'll have to grade this as-is. C-plus."

"… C-plus?" Ferris asked in revulsion, his eyes growing wider. "I can't get a C, my grade will—"

"You should have thought of that when you decided not to do your assignment."

"Please, I can't—"

"That's enough. I'll see you tomorrow."

Ferris stayed in place for a few seconds, too overtaken with shock to move. There was nothing he could do. It was over.

Slowly, he turned to the door, opening it and stepping out into the hallway. Once out of the room, he rubbed his forehead anxiously. Yale had an 8.6% acceptance rate. How was he supposed to stand out against the other 91.4% without a spotless GPA? His heart started racing and he willed himself to breathe normally. The paper got a C-plus. That would drag his class grade down to some kind of B. He couldn't get a B. Ferris had been a straight-A student since kindergarten.

"Shit, shit," he said to himself, feeling another headache coming on. Students herded past him in the hallway, taking no notice of his anxiety. He gave up the battle to take normal breaths as his throat grew raw. His mind was seconds from lapsing into a panic attack when a familiar voice calmed the tension.

"Ferris, are you all right?"

"Demos," he said slowly, looking up at his friend. Taking off his glasses, he rubbed over his eyes apprehensively. "I don't know. I don't know."

"What happened?"

"I… fuck, I didn't finish my paper yesterday. I got a C-plus."

Demos stared at him before laughing.

"What, that's it? I thought your dog died or something."

"It's not fucking funny. I can't get a C. This is ruining everything. I worked so hard to make straight A's, I can't—"

"Look, calm down," Demos said, putting a hand on his friend's shoulder. "It'll be all right."

"No, it won't. I'm going to have a 3.9 or something. How is that supposed to stand out against a hundred thousand other applicants?"

"I'm sure you can still—"

216

"You don't even have to go to college. You don't have to worry about any of this shit, do you? Just fuck around all day and smoke in the parking lot."

Demos' expression dropped, looking irked at Ferris' comments.

"I'm sorry," Ferris said quickly. "I didn't mean—"

"It's all right. You're going to lose it if you let yourself get any more stressed. You should do something to relax."

"Like what? Go to Hawaii? I don't have time to relax, finals are coming up."

"Summer can't come fast enough," Demos sighed.

"I'm starting an internship this summer," Ferris said weakly. "Where Dad works."

"Damn. You're not going to rest until you're dead, are you?"

"I guess not," Ferris replied, trying not to think about how morbid the statement was.

"I have to get to class. Contrary to popular belief, I do attend them."

"Yeah, okay."

"See you at lunch."

"See you."

Ferris watched Demos leave as the other students filed into their appropriate classrooms. The hallway was empty as he stared down the rows of doors, gingerly putting his glasses back on. As the bell rang, he covered his eyes, inhaling slowly.

Ferris wished he had just explained he was too busy to wash dishes and gone home. At the same time, for reasons he couldn't explain, it had been strangely rewarding to hear Victor say 'I knew I could count on you.'

After school, as usual, he stopped to check on Julie before going home. It had been getting better lately; he wasn't as uncomfortable around her anymore. She seemed to have genuinely changed. Ferris still couldn't find it in himself to truly trust her, but he didn't mind staying to talk for a while. At the same time, he hated breaking the same news every day.

"I still haven't found your mother," Ferris said, sounding drained as he sat down on the sofa.

"It's okay," Julie said, as she always did. She sat down next to him, handing him a cup of water as she drank from her own glass. He accepted it gratefully.

"Ferris," Julie said, fiddling with the rim of her glass. "Do you think we could go out today?"

"Out?"

"You always come and stay for a little while, then leave. I think we should spend some time together… you know, out. I'm getting pretty bored here, anyway."

"Where would you want to go?"

"The park?" Julie said hopefully, happy that he was even considering it.

"Yeah, all right. I can do the park."

Heavy coats weren't necessary anymore and Julie put on a light jacket she'd bought at a thrift shop. Ferris was skeptical that she even paid for it. He lent her his scarf; she looked better in it anyway.

"How's work been?" Ferris asked as they walked under rows of trees.

"Okay. Yesterday some dick smacked me on the ass. I didn't have the heart to tell him that I'm sixteen."

Ferris looked at her, frowning a bit.

"Are you sure you want to keep working there?"

"Yeah. They have really busy lunch hours, so I can make a lot of money when I work those shifts."

"I hope you've been saving it," Ferris said.

"I have," Julie replied absently, looking up at the bare tree branches. "And how's school?"

"Shitty," he said, nearly muttering his answer.

"I've never heard you say *that* about school before."

"I got distracted all night, like an idiot, and forgot to finish my assignment. I got a crappy grade and now my entire GPA is ruined."

"It's really that fragile of a system, huh?"

"Yeah," Ferris said, not having thought of it that way before. "It is."

"So…" Julie started, then gave up. "God, I hate small talk."

"Yeah, me too," Ferris admitted. "You'd been gone a while. There's a lot I still don't know about you."

"You, too."

"There's nothing you need to know about me. My life is boring," he lied, having no desire to explain his connections to a local criminal syndicate.

"You never bored me," Julie said, keeping her eyes on the distant scenery. Ferris turned his head, checking her face for sincerity. She didn't appear to be joking.

"Did anything happen in California? That you want to tell me about?"

Julie didn't answer immediately. She stopped walking, standing by a bench before deciding to sit on it. Ferris followed suit, taking a seat next to her.

"Why I left, yeah."

"You feel like talking about it?"

Julie nodded, still needing a minute to think.

"Brandon was always kind of an ass," she finally said. "But I didn't think he'd stoop so low for money."

"What did he do?"

"Got me drunk. Let his friend fuck me for fifty dollars."

218

Ferris stared at her.

"Yeah," Julie continued, "So I left."

Ferris didn't know what to say. A small part of him didn't believe her, or at least didn't want to believe her. It sounded like something she might have made up before, to get pity. On the other hand, this was worse. This was a lot worse. He'd always thought Demos was a pretty terrible person when he wanted to be, but even the would-be gangster would never do something like that. Ferris didn't like to think that such people existed outside of television. It would be easy to just not trust her — to take the story in stride and get on with his day. Something, however, told him that it was real. Something kept him from looking away.

"I'm sorry," he said. "That's... "

He couldn't think of an appropriate adjective.

"That's terrible," he finally said, feeling unsatisfied with his understated wording.

"It's okay," she said. "It's over. Anyway, things are good now. I've got you."

"Yeah."

"That reminds me. I have a present for you."

"You really shouldn't be spending money on—"

Julie silenced him with the presentation of a plain white envelope. Ferris looked down at it, pausing before taking it. He looked at her, then looked inside.

"This is—"

"It's $227. It was actually $226.50, but I didn't want to give you quarters," she explained.

"This is what I gave you."

"I remembered," she said quietly. "I thought about it... a lot. You have no idea how much I thought about it."

"I can't accept this," Ferris said, offering the envelope back to her. She denied it with both hands, shaking her head.

"Just take it. If not for you, then for me. So I can live with myself," Julie said firmly. "Okay?"

Ferris studied the envelope. He couldn't believe she'd actually managed to save it all. Not only had she saved it, but she was giving it away. He didn't need this money; it was the meaning behind it that had any significance. He stared at it before tucking it into his coat's inner pocket.

"All right," he replied quietly. "We're square."

Julie smiled at him, relieved.

"Do you still have enough money to eat?" Ferris asked apprehensively.

"Yeah. I can get food from work, anyway."

"Okay, if you're sure."

"By the way," Julie said, catching sight of a man walking his dogs on the park path, "how's your pug?"

"Stan? I'm surprised you remember him."

"Of course I do. He was cute."

"He's all right. Still fat, though."

"You know, I'd like a dog someday. A big one, like a Doberman."

"Maybe if Stan keeps eating, he'll fit your criteria."

Julie made a sound that sounded something like a giggle, which was the most feminine thing he'd seen her do in a long time. Ferris was still overwhelmed by her gesture. The return of his money meant one of two things – either Julie had truly turned herself around, or she was attempting to gain his trust for something much bigger, and much worse. The trouble was, Ferris had no idea which it was.

29

Beatrice Cotterill, known formerly as Beatrice Aston during her brief marriage, was standing at the door in a red dress. Her dark hair was done up and she had a Prada purse tucked beneath her arm.

"All right, I'll be back tonight," she said inattentively, checking her reflection in a compact as she spoke.

"Yeah, Mum," Seamus replied, flipping a channel on the television. He knew he wasn't going to see her until at least tomorrow afternoon. "Bye."

Seamus' mother snapped the compact shut, sliding it into her purse before going out the door. She'd forgotten to say goodbye. Once the door shut, Seamus leaned over the arm of the sofa, picking up the phone to dial.

"Hey, she's gone. Head over, yeah?"

Demos and Ferris arrived at the apartment door within fifteen minutes. The Aston home wasn't quite the spacious house or brownstone that Seamus' friends lived in, but it was still quite comfortable. Most of the furniture looked as if Seamus had put it together himself with nothing but a hex key and a set of textless instructions. In fact, most of the home's décor appeared to have been chosen by Seamus. The only additions his mother seemed to have made were a large, wooden liquor cabinet and the occasional coat draped across the sofa.

"Anyone want tea?" Seamus asked from the kitchen, already creating an ambiance of cluttering mugs.

"I'll make it," Demos offered as he invaded the kitchen. He was immediately shooed out.

"You taking the piss? Americans can't make tea," Seamus said, turning on the stove.

"I'm Italian," Demos reminded him, a bit insulted.

"Even worse," Seamus replied immediately. Demos glared, but sat down without further argument.

"Do you still have that ugly teapot?" Ferris asked, showing its approximate size with his hands. "You know, the one with the cats all over it?"

"Shut up, Ferret. That was my grandmum's teapot and I'll be damned if I let you insult her good name," Seamus said defensively, pointing at Ferris as he spoke. "I don't come over to your home, all going about and asking where the gold coins and Barbra Streisand albums are."

"Yes, you do."

"Okay, just once. Your mum thought it was funny. If she's got a sense of humor, why haven't you?"

"She thought you were serious. She showed you like, eight albums."

"Big fan, isn't she?"

"No," Ferris mumbled, "my dad is."

Demos, already getting bored, leaned forward on his knees and pulled a small tin from his pocket, flattening a tiny sheet of paper on the table.

"You roll your own, now?" Ferris asked, watching Demos as he placed down some tobacco.

"Sergio showed me how to do it. It's cheaper than buying them in a pack."

"Like you're tight on money."

Demos shrugged, rolling the paper's ends together to compact the contents. For a beginner, he was surprisingly capable. He licked the edge, closing his new cigarette and looking it over carefully.

"Kettle's on. Let me see that," Seamus said, holding his hand out for the cigarette. Demos passed it over without protest.

"Shoddy, at best. You need practice."

"*You* need practice. At not being a dick."

"You need practice at sucking my dick."

"Okay guys," Ferris cut in, holding up his hands, "weren't we going to play cards, or something?"

"Oh, of course," Seamus said. "Anytime you're all ready to start losing, just speak up and we'll start the game."

"You're on, Limey," Demos said, pointing at Seamus in challenge. Seamus responded by taking a pack of cards from a bureau drawer, dropping them into his hand and quickly shuffling with two riffles on the table.

"What'll it be?" Seamus asked as he bridged the cards, letting them cascade back into a single deck. "Poker? Spoons?"

"Egyptian ratscrew," Demos suggested, wanting to play something different for a change. It was then that the tea kettle started to whistle.

"I'll get it!" Seamus announced, as if someone very important had just rung the doorbell. There was the sound of a stove being turned off, followed by the clink of cups.

"How do you two take it?" Seamus called, "We've got... PG Tips, Lemon, Afternoon—"

"Darjeeling with a little milk and sugar," Demos said, peeking at the deck of cards, "if you have it."

"Earl Grey," Ferris added. "Hot."

"*Boring*," Seamus said back from the kitchen. "You'd think you two were my grandmum."

"Are you insulting her good name, Seamus?" Demos said snidely.

222

"No, I'm just calling you a pair of old ladies is what."

"And what are *you* having?" Ferris asked.

"PG with a little Jameson, thank you." Seamus replied, coming back into the room with three teacups miraculously balanced between two hands.

"Do we have to play ratscrew? I was kind of set on the gambling bit," Seamus said disappointedly as he handed his friends their cups.

"No betting. I'm tired of betting," Ferris grumbled.

"Come on, mate. If you need money, just go with the plan I gave you."

"What plan?"

"You know, the busking."

"I am *not* going to play my violin in a subway station, Seamus," Ferris said, shutting his eyes and pinching the bridge of his nose.

"Oh, be a sport. You'd make a fortune! You've seen how many bills get tossed in those open cases."

"I can think of about a hundred reasons why that's a terrible idea."

"And I can think of two hundred reasons why it's a brilliant one."

"Do any of those reasons involve me buying you things?"

"It's possible," Seamus said, starting to deal the deck of cards. Soon, cigarette smoke filled the air and the sound of three hands slapping the same spot bounced sharply off the walls.

"Ow! Asshole," Ferris said, holding his reddened hand.

"Your fault for putting your hand down first," Seamus explained.

"You could at least take off your ring," Ferris mumbled, taking the pile of cards he'd earned.

"I think it adds to the fun," Seamus grinned, sucking on the end of his cigarette. Eventually, Demos and Ferris both became so wary of being hit with the ring that they simply let Seamus win.

The arrival of spring brought the expected pleasant weather and the three took a minute to appreciate it through an open window. Demos and Seamus sat out on the fire escape, watching the city street a few stories below as they smoked. Ferris sat on the windowsill, preferring not to test the strength of the rickety metal platform. The air was cool and damp and the trees beneath them were just beginning to bud. This was their favorite way to spend time together — sitting around and not really accomplishing anything.

Figuring that the wind was still enough, Demos slowly opened his mouth. A curl of smoke rose before he breathed it in with his nose.

"Nice trick," Seamus said, pulling out his cheap lighter and removing the guard. "I've got a new one for you."

He pulled a fresh cigarette from his box, licking the paper on one side.

"What the hell are you doing?" Demos asked, slightly perturbed.

"Just watch," Seamus answered, holding the cigarette down low and flicking his lighter repeatedly over it. After a while, the gray, dusty flint started to build on the damp paper.

"We're all going to die," Demos said under his breath, hoping Seamus wasn't making some kind of explosive.

Ferris remained quiet, having a good idea of what Seamus was trying to do. He was curious to see if it would work.

"All right, watch," Seamus said, putting his lighter back together and striking up a small flame. The cigarette lit before starting to sparkle violently.

"It's the bloody fourth of July!" Seamus announced, exhaling the smoke he'd breathed in.

"Whoa, cool," Demos said, staring at the homemade sparkler.

"Nice," Ferris said, vaguely speculating if smoking lighter flint was bad for you. Then again, these guys breathed in poison ten times a day, so they probably weren't too concerned about it. Watching them do various tricks with smoke reminded him of Julie; she liked to blow rings. He offhandedly wondered if she knew any other tricks.

"It's nice to be out of the house," Demos said, flicking his cigarette. "Uncle Vic is really moody lately."

"You think it's because of what Gino said?" Ferris asked, wishing he didn't have to remember overhearing that conversation.

"That, and I think he knows about Chris."

"Oh," Ferris said, not wanting to be reminded of that either.

"I don't know what Emily's problem is. She was into you, I know it. I just don't get it."

"Forget about it, Demos. You won't shut up about this. Just let it go."

Ferris knew that Demos hated being wrong about anything and he was most definitely wrong about Emily. Seamus was awkwardly silent during their conversation, simply looking away and tossing his spent cigarette off of the fire escape.

"We're always talking about my lack of a relationship," Ferris said. "What about you? You never mention yours."

"I've seen a few people, nothing was worth mentioning," Demos said under his breath. Ferris took note of his friend's use of 'people' rather than 'girls' or 'boys.'

"Just didn't work out?"

"Haven't found the right one."

224

"He's just fussy," Seamus said, finally speaking up. "Can't settle for just anyone when he's had the best."

"Don't flatter yourself, Seamus," Demos said, shoving the Brit in the head. Seamus laughed. Still on the windowsill, Ferris was looking back in at the living room. He was musing, looking at the empty teacups and scattered playing cards.

"Seamus," he started, saying what had been on his mind for a while. "Why do you always wait for your mother to leave before inviting us? Does she not allow friends over or something?"

"Well, no," Seamus said, uncharacteristically quiet. "It just might be a bit awkward is all."

"Awkward?"

"She's a little," Seamus began, gesturing with his hand, "off, I suppose. Spacey."

"You're embarrassed of her?" Demos asked. Seamus didn't answer immediately, as if ashamed to admit it.

"That's not really it. She's not like your families. Your mum is all… sweet and nice," Seamus said, looking at Ferris.

"Yeah, to *you*," Ferris said in irritation. "She drives me up a wall."

"And your uncle, he takes you out and everything," Seamus added, turning his attention to Demos.

"Yeah," Demos replied. "Your mom doesn't really pay much attention to you, does she?"

Seamus shrugged. This wasn't his favorite topic.

"She seemed pretty aloof when I saw her," Demos said, remembering one of the few times she had come home.

"She's got other things on her mind," Seamus said. "Anyway, it's getting a bit chilly. I want some dinner."

Ferris stepped aside to allow Seamus by as he slipped back into the apartment. Demos followed, shutting the window behind him. Seamus disappeared into the kitchen and the noise of cabinets opening gave a hint of his actions. Demos and Ferris didn't press the subject further; Seamus clearly didn't want to talk about it.

"Why don't we just order some pizza?" Demos asked, unsure of how he felt about Seamus cooking.

"It's fine. I got it," Seamus called from the kitchen.

"Want to bet he's going to make us eat hot dogs straight from the package?" Ferris asked.

"I don't even want to think about what he's making."

"Y'know I can hear you both," Seamus said.

"We know," Demos said, leaning on his elbow.

"Twats."

After a few minutes of slow blackjack, Ferris dusted his knees and stood.

"I'm going to go check on him."

"Good idea."

As he stepped into the kitchen, he did a double-take at the kitchen counter. Seamus was dumping a can of Franco-American pasta onto several slices of toast.

"Uh oh," Ferris said nervously. "...SpaghettiO's."

"Supposed to be hoops on toast," Seamus said, almost proud. "SpaghettiO's is all I could get."

"This is a *disaster* on toast," Ferris said, eyes narrowed in scrutiny. He picked up a roll from a pile placed next to the toast. Opening it to see what was inside, he recoiled in slight horror.

"And... you made butter sandwiches."

"It's a roll. With butter on it."

"This is butter with a roll on it."

"Well you can wipe your bit off with a napkin then," Seamus said firmly. "Everyone's a critic."

"Are you even going to cook that?" Ferris asked, watching as Seamus cleaned out the bottom of the can with a spoon.

"I heated it a bit, quit your worrying."

When Seamus was done, despite the butter sandwiches, they each agreed that the meal wasn't bad. 'Spaghetti hoops on toast' wasn't quite ready to be placed on the Giorgetti restaurant menu, but it was filling.

By the time Ferris got home that night, he was tired enough to simply crawl into bed. He almost forgot to remove his glasses. His shirt, aimed half-heartedly at the laundry basket, hit the floor instead. Not having the energy to care, he turned over and was soon asleep. His dreams consisted of peculiar collages containing horses, more ants, and burning buildings. He might have lapsed into stronger nightmares if a strange noise hadn't suddenly snapped him awake.

Ferris' eyes opened, looking up at the ceiling before trailing over to the window. After a moment he recognized the sound. Someone was throwing pebbles at his window. He slid out of bed, grabbing his glasses and opening the window to look out.

"Julie?" he said, whispering sharply. She made a gesture to be let up and he complied with the fire ladder. At the window, he took her by the hand, carefully helping her get inside.

"What's wrong?" he whispered, shutting the window behind her.

"Nothing," she replied. "I just wanted to see you."

"Julie, it's four a.m."

"I couldn't really sleep."

"Are you sick?"

"You're an idiot," she said with a sigh, sitting down on his bed.

"What?" he said, standing in place.

"I came to see you in the middle of the night and you think I'm sick?"

"I don't know. I guess. No."

"Sit down," she said, giving the spot next to her a pat. Ferris made a face, then gave in.

"I haven't seen you for a few days," Julie explained, "so I kind of missed you."

"Sorry. I've been—"

"I know, it's all right," she said, looking around the room. "I remember the last time I was here."

"Me too," Ferris said quietly. He waited for a moment before asking what was on his mind. "Was it true? The reason you were here."

"Yeah, unfortunately. You know, the good thing about not being able to find Mom is that Dad probably can't find her either."

"Yeah, that's true."

"I hope she's doing okay."

"I'm sure she is," Ferris said confidently. He didn't tell her, but he'd already checked the obituaries. He knew it would have been easier to ask Demos for help, since his friend had connections in high places, including the police. He doubted, however, that Demos would want to do anything to help Julie. He was already letting her stay in his uncle's apartment. Going out of his way to do a manhunt didn't seem likely. If the search kept turning up dead ends, though, Ferris knew he might have to resort to pleading.

"You always sleep without a shirt on?" Julie asked suddenly.

"Uh," Ferris said quickly, trying to find something to put on. Julie put a hand on his arm, stopping him from getting up.

"I don't mind."

Ferris was about to protest that *he* minded, when she caught him off guard with a hand on his face. He froze, staring as she removed his glasses and leaned forward to kiss him. At first, he forgot to react, sitting still as her mouth touched his. For a second it almost seemed as if he would accept this turn of events, but he suddenly pulled back, breaking off their kiss prematurely.

"Sorry," he said quietly.

Julie waited before answering, trying not to sound hurt.

"You still don't trust me," she finally said, sounding disappointed. Ferris averted his eyes, unable to handle the look on her face. Trust was part of the issue, but there was something else holding him back. He found it hard to explain, even to himself.

"It's not just that," he said, his voice subdued as he put his glasses back on.

"Then what? I'm too poor? It's because I smoke, isn't it?" Julie said, her voice challenging.

"No," Ferris replied quickly. "It's somebody else."

"Someone else?"

"Emily," Ferris found himself saying before he could stop himself.

"Who's Emily?"

"I mentioned her before."

"The one who dragged you to an aquarium to announce she was going out with some other guy? Isn't she still going out with him?"

"Yeah," Ferris mumbled, embarrassed.

"Oh."

There was an awkward pause between them both. Julie was still trying to figure out why Ferris was hung up on some girl who wasn't single or interested in him. Ferris found himself wondering the same thing.

"How long are you going to wait?" she asked spitefully. "Their wedding? Golden anniversary, maybe?"

Ferris only sighed.

"I know it sounds stupid," he explained, "but I can't change what I feel."

"I guess we really are even, now," Julie said bitterly.

"Don't think of it that way. I'm not your type, anyway."

"You're one of the only people who's been nice to me."

"Then you need to meet some more people," Ferris said, finally finding his shirt and putting it back on. "I'm not an amazing guy. I'm just a normal, decent person. There are plenty of normal people out there. You just seem to be bad at finding them."

"I guess so."

"You're not mad, are you?"

"No," Julie said unconvincingly. She got up off the bed, straightening out her coat. "I'd better go back."

Ferris nodded, opening the window for her.

"Goodnight," she said before disappearing down the length of the ladder.

"Night," he replied, watching her until she was gone. After she'd walked out of sight, he pulled the ladder up and put it away, securing the window tightly. When he got back into bed, he couldn't get his mind off of her words. Just how long was he going to wait, anyway? Ferris didn't want to picture himself sitting miserably at their wedding. He wasn't sure if it was blind hope, or even blinder affection, but he put the thoughts to rest. He would just have to wait and see – a little bit longer, at least.

30

The Kipling Stables were only a 45 minute drive from the heart of Southport and Demos appreciated every chance he had to make the trip. The family only had the time to visit once every month or two. Ferris made sure that he was caught up on every assignment before accepting the invitation out. Luckily, his most recent sleep had lacked any horse-related nightmares.

"Do you like him?" Demos asked, leading his horse out of its stall by the reins. "His name is Luciano."

"After the opera singer, or the gangster?" Ferris asked, polishing his glasses on the bottom of his shirt.

"The singer, of course. Lucky is named after the gangster," Demos said, gesturing to a horse a few stalls down with his thumb.

"Right, of course," Ferris said. "It's a nice horse. Gino bought him for you?"

"Yeah, for Christmas a few years back. He said, 'This horse is small, but powerful. Like you.'"

"Since when are you powerful?" Ferris asked, replacing his glasses and observing the horse critically. The Arabian was, by all means, quite beautiful. He had bright eyes and a dark bay coat, looking well-groomed and well-mannered.

Demos only rolled his eyes, placing an English saddle on the horse's back before securing the straps.

"Do you know how many twelve year old girls would kill to get a pony for Christmas? Did you even ask for this horse?" Ferris inquired, squinting at his friend.

"Yes, I asked for it," Demos replied impatiently. "I rode sometimes when I was in Italy and I missed it."

Luciano shook his mane and Demos patted the horse's face comfortingly.

"You gonna ride, Fish?" asked a voice from behind them. Ferris turned to see Sergio approaching them, leading a larger horse by its bridle.

"Oh, me? No, I'm just going to watch."

"You sure?"

"Yeah, I'm all right."

There was a large, enclosed ring outside, ideal for doing laps or jumps. Ferris leaned on the fence, watching as Demos and Sergio trotted by. He found it curious that the men could be tough gangsters and equestrians at the same time. Perhaps it was the control over a powerful animal that seemed appealing to them. Then again, maybe they just liked prancing around on their days off.

Demos pulled his horse to a stop by the fence, looking down at Ferris as he spoke.

"You bored?"

"No," Ferris said truthfully. "It's nice out here."

Indeed, the stable grounds were lined with old trees and fresh, green grass. The dirt on the ring was slightly damp and smelled like spring. Demos removed his helmet, pushing his hair back to appreciate some of the wind. He was wearing a pair of black boots and a riding jacket, looking ripe for the teasing. Ferris managed to keep his mouth shut, instead focusing on his friend's forehead.

"You know, Demos," Ferris said reflectively, "you never explained how you got your scar."

"Eh," Demos replied, shrugging.

"What, is it an embarrassing story? Was it a cat?"

"No," Demos said, looking up at the trees above them. "It wasn't a *cat*."

"Well then, what was it?"

Luciano stood obediently still as Demos considered his words. He let his hair back down, holding the helmet in his lap with one hand and the other keeping the reins.

"Back in Italy, some guys took me hostage for some negotiation with grandpa. One of them held my face and cut me so I would scream for the phone."

"Did you?"

"No. It wasn't that painful, anyway. I just bit my lip," Demos explained.

"How did you get out? Was it Gino?"

"No," Demos said, his voice suddenly growing quiet. "Dad saved me."

Ferris didn't speak, remaining quiet in hopes of hearing more. Demos never spoke of his father. Luckily, the boy continued speaking.

"He shot every one of them, and then went and found the guy who hired them. He shot him, too."

The horse pawed once at the ground, eager to start moving again. Demos ignored it, lost in thought.

"But he wasn't part of Gino's ring, was he? He was English," Ferris said.

"He didn't associate himself with mobsters. Dad never really admitted what he did, but it was kind of obvious."

"What did he do?"

"He was a contract killer. It's how he met Mom."

Ferris was in suspense, as eager to learn more as Luciano was to get going.

"What happened?" he asked, trying not to sound too curious.

"I'm not really sure. From what I pieced together, he was supposed to kill grandpa. He obviously failed and I think Mom kept them from killing him."

"Why did she do that?"

"I don't know," Demos shrugged as he replaced his helmet. "I guess she fell in love."

Ferris was getting an unbelievable amount of information from Demos that day. Maybe being on a horse let the young Italian's guard down.

"It sounded like he cared about you."

"He didn't," Demos said plainly. "He left."

"Sorry," Ferris said, unsure of what else to say. Demos didn't seem to dwell on it, continuing to talk.

"I'm lucky I only got kidnapped once," Demos said thoughtfully. "I'm worried about the O'Brien thing. Especially Emily."

"Yeah," Ferris said. "She's with Victor right now, isn't she?"

"Yeah, she's safe. So are we. I sort of wish Uncle Vic would tell me about it to my face. If we didn't overhear, we would have had no idea."

"He probably doesn't want to worry you," Ferris guessed, trying to speculate on what was going through Victor's mind.

"I guess," Demos said, leading the reins to turn his horse around. "Luciano's getting antsy, I'm going to do a few more laps."

Demos clicked his tongue, starting the horse back on a trot. Ferris watched him ride off, taking in what he'd learned about his friend. It had taken years, but he'd finally figured out a small part of Demos' history. On one hand, it was strange for someone to know so little about their own best friend. On the other, Ferris doubted there were other people who knew Demos any better.

It didn't seem completely fair that Ferris' life was so simple and clear. He had a mother and a father, both alive and well, who loved him very much. It wasn't any kind of challenge to figure out Ferris' past. Demos and Seamus, however, were much like little islands surrounded by mist and terrible sea monsters. He had to pick apart their histories one page at a time.

Ferris folded his arms on the fence, pondering as he watched Demos' horse break into a canter. Luciano took a small jump gracefully, landing and continuing his run with ease. It was nice to stand outside for a day, away from the city and the people in it who might hurt them. Ferris appreciated the chance to relax, casually watching horses doing something other than race for money. Maybe it was the fresh air, or maybe it was the trees, but his mind felt clearer than he could ever remember.

31

St. Basil's wasn't far from the ocean's edge, making the walk
to the water relatively brief. Ferris stepped under the shadow of
a storage facility, looking out at the water as he waited. Seamus
was supposed to arrive soon, having asked to meet at three
o'clock. Ferris had no idea what it was about, pondering over it
as he listened to seagulls. The ground beneath his feet was
paved. A few weeds grew between the cracks of the deserted
parking area, adding a bit of plant life to the otherwise gray
scenery.

"You all right, mate?" Seamus said as he approached,
carrying a backpack over one shoulder.

"Hey," Ferris answered, turning to face the Brit. "What's with
the drug dealer meeting place?"

"Didn't want Demos to be around. Just wanted to talk to
you."

"Great. You're not going to tell me *you're* going out with
Chris too, are you?"

"Nah." Seamus smirked, though it looked forced. He looked
at the sea, keeping his eyes on a boat in the distance. "So, how
have you been?"

"Weird," Ferris said with a shrug.

"Weird?"

"Yeah. There's too much on my mind."

"Like what?" Seamus asked, turning his attention back to
Ferris.

"Julie came by the other night."

"Anything happen?"

"No. Kind of. She kissed me."

Seamus lifted his head, his attention piqued. He looked more
concerned than happy.

"But I turned her down," Ferris said faintly.

"Why?" Seamus asked, trying to hide the relief in his voice.

"It's hard to say. It was a lot of things. I'm not sure if it's even
trust anymore. But I'm still hung up on Emily."

"You really did like her, didn't you?"

"Still do, apparently," Ferris said, sounding defeated.

"About that," Seamus said, unnaturally downcast.

"What?"

"I've been thinking for a while. Back when you two were
over and talking about her."

"What about it?"

Seamus didn't look like he wanted to answer right away.

"It's what I wanted to tell you," he finally said.

Ferris felt a strange, nervous jump in his heart. This seemed like it was going to be important. Whether it was good or bad, he couldn't tell.

"What is it?"

"I wasn't in my right mind. It was jealousy. I can't keep this to myself anymore. It's driving me mad."

"What did you do?" Ferris asked, his voice growing darker.

"A while back, after we went to the diner, I saw you and Julie in front of the school."

Ferris was dead silent, staring at Seamus.

"Emily saw, too," Seamus continued.

Ferris didn't take his eyes off of Seamus, lowering his head slowly. Seamus took in a breath, waiting before going on.

"I told her Julie was your girlfriend."

The words hit Ferris like a boulder. He couldn't blink or breathe.

"*What?*" he finally managed to say. His hands were both in fists.

"I told Emily that Julie was your girlfriend."

Seamus barely finished the word 'girlfriend' before he found his vision skewing, knocked back with a hard punch to the cheek. He staggered, holding the side of his face. Seamus looked at Ferris, stunned.

"You *what*?!" Ferris cried, glaring with an intensity that Seamus had never before witnessed.

"I—"

"You son of a bitch!" Ferris yelled, grabbing Seamus by his uniform collar and slamming him against a concrete pillar.

"Fer, I—"

"*Shut up!* Do you have any idea what you've *done*?"

Seamus opened his mouth to answer, but Ferris interrupted him.

"You ruined *everything*! Now she's with that asshole, Chris!" he yelled, his eyes dark with anger. "I *loved her*!"

Ferris didn't even stop to realize what he had just admitted, too blind with rage to think properly. His mouth grew dry, not used to raising his voice in this manner.

"You fucked me!" Ferris shouted, still keeping a firm grip on Seamus' collar. His knuckles were white and his hands were trembling. He stared at Seamus for a long time, eyes narrow and teeth clenched. His breath came in a few strained pants before he finally let go, stepping backwards. He hunched, overcome by the truth.

"Ferris," Seamus said carefully. "I'm sorry."

"Go away," Ferris mumbled, holding a hand over his aching forehead. "I don't want to talk to you anymore."

"I—"

"I said I don't want to talk to you anymore!" Ferris snapped, looking back at Seamus with a harsh glare.

Seamus was still, looking as if he desperately wanted to say something, but gave up. Grabbing his backpack from the ground, he looked at Ferris one last time before turning to leave.

Once Seamus was gone, Ferris leaned back against the same concrete pillar. He slumped down, numb. He would have been able to accept the way things turned out if she didn't feel anything for him. That wasn't the case anymore. Demos had been right – she was going to tell him how she felt.

Seamus took everything away.

Ferris was normally against sitting around and feeling sorry for himself. It never accomplished anything and was a pitiful way to pass the time. At that moment, however, he couldn't help himself. He sat there on the dark pavement, face in one hand, feeling more miserable than he had in a very long time.

Ferris was distant for the next couple of days, not speaking during class and avoiding the normal spot for lunch. Seamus hadn't said a word about the incident. Demos didn't know what to do with Seamus, who was eerily downhearted, and Ferris, who was missing altogether. On top of that, Demos had his and Emily's safety to be concerned about. Every car that seemed to be following them home and every suspicious person on the street made him nervous, much to Emily's confusion. Life seemed to have fallen apart and it wasn't clear how, or when, it would come together.

Frustrated, Demos took it upon himself to track his elusive friend down during lunch. Ferris was in the auditorium, where eating normally wasn't allowed. At that time of day, however, there was no one around to tell him to stop. He sat on the edge of the stage, looking very small on such a large platform. He ignored the light footsteps on the stage as they approached, coming to a stop a few feet away.

"So, this is where you are."

At first, Ferris didn't answer, merely poking at the food in his Tupperware container. When he realized that silence wasn't going to make Demos go away, he answered.

"Yeah."

Demos sat down next to him, folding his legs to watch his friend jab his lunch.

"So, what's going on?"

"Eating lunch."

"You forgot where the cafeteria was?"

"No. I'm avoiding Seamus," Ferris replied bluntly.

"Why's that?"

"I guess he didn't tell you," Ferris said, finally looking over at Demos.

"He isn't saying anything."

Ferris exhaled, lowering his lunch. He wasn't sure if he should tell him, but felt that Demos would figure it out eventually anyway.

"The day before the aquarium, he told Emily that Julie was my girlfriend."

Demos stared at Ferris, quickly figuring out what had happened next.

"...Why would he say that?"

"I don't know," Ferris said vacantly. "He said he was jealous."

"That's pretty fucked up," Demos said slowly, before making a realization. "Hey. That means I was probably right."

"Yeah. So now she's dating some idiot and I'm wallowing in self pity."

"Christ," Demos said, rubbing the back of his neck. "Are you going to tell her?"

"There's no point. What's she going to do, jump in excitement and dump Chris on the spot?"

"Yeah, I guess not."

"By the way," Ferris said, "I hit him."

"What?"

"I thought I should admit it. I was mad, so I hit him."

"So that's what that bruise was. I thought he got drunk and ran into a wall."

"It bruised?"

"Yeah."

Ferris didn't respond. He almost felt guilty but then remembered how angry he was. Any thoughts of regret faded and he went back to eating his lunch.

"I guess you're not going to be joining us anytime soon," Demos said, sounding dismayed.

"I don't know," Ferris replied. "I don't want to think about it."

"All right. I won't force you," Demos said, getting up and dusting some stage sawdust from his slacks. "I'll see you around."

"Yeah. See you."

The stage exit shut and the sound echoed across the large, empty space. Ferris looked over to it as it shut, his mouth open as if there was something he'd forgotten to say.

After school, Ferris decided to suck it up and check on Julie. He hadn't seen her since the night she came through his window, unsure of what he would say if he visited. Something gave him the feeling that she might understand what he was going through. On top of that, he had discovered a lead on the location of her mother while searching the previous night. He simply had to hope that she wasn't still upset.

As he walked to the apartment, he found his thoughts trapped in a pit. Nothing seemed to be going right and stress came at him from every angle.

Everyone else seemed to be going on with their day. A man walking five dogs passed by and a few young men were closing up a U-Haul truck on the curb. He pulled out his set of keys, finding the spare he'd made as he got off of the elevator.

If Ferris knew what was behind the apartment door, he might have turned around, gone home, and concerned himself with it some other day. His week had gone badly enough already. In actuality, it wasn't what was behind the door that was upsetting — it was what *wasn't* behind the door.

As he stepped in, he took an involuntary sharp breath. His eyes were still, locked straight ahead.

The sofa was gone. The television, DVD player, and stereo were gone. *Everything* was gone. He might have stood and stared for quite a long time if a noise from the bedroom hadn't caught his attention.

As he looked over, a young man stepped out, flanked by another two carrying lamps and a jewelry box. At the sight of Ferris, he grinned.

"You must be Ferris. Jules said you might stop by."

"Who the hell are you?" Ferris said, his voice coming out more weakly than he'd hoped it would.

"I'm Brandon," the man said, gesturing to one of the others with his hand. "It's nice to meet you."

The lamp in the man's hands found its way over the top of Ferris' head. The pieces fell to the carpet along with Ferris' body, scattering as they hit. His eyes flickered before he lost consciousness, unable to do anything to keep them from removing the last few items of value from the apartment.

If he had been conscious, he might have thought that life was particularly unfair at the moment, been furious with both Seamus and Julie, and possibly committed an act of violence or two on Brandon. Unfortunately, Ferris' eyes were closed, and the only thing he could achieve was a long, silent vision of black.

"She did *what*?" came Demos' voice on the small cell phone, loud enough that Ferris could hold it away from his ear and still understand.

"I was stupid. You were right," Ferris admitted heavily. "You were right."

It had taken Ferris a long time to swallow his pride and call Demos after waking up. He was still sitting on the floor of the apartment next to a few pieces of broken ceramic. There wasn't really anywhere else to sit, seeing that the couch had been stolen.

236

"This sounds a little familiar, doesn't it?" came the static laced voice through the phone.

"I know," Ferris said, keeping his free hand over the bump on his head. He winced – it was still tender at the touch. He couldn't believe he had fallen for her con again. Then again, somewhere in the back of his mind, he'd expected this.

Demos sighed theatrically before speaking again.

"Sit tight. I'm going to come pick you up."

There was a click as Demos hung up and Ferris put his phone back into his pocket. He was surprised that Brandon didn't go through his things or steal his wallet while he was unconscious. They were probably in a hurry.

Demos arrived a few minutes later, pushing the door in and looking around.

"Fuck!"

"Hi, Demos."

"Jesus Christ. They really cleaned the place out," he said, irately running a hand through his dark hair. He didn't panic, however, trying to see if he could rectify the situation before losing his mind. "Did you happen to see the truck?"

"Yeah. A U-Haul. It had a big Venus flytrap on it."

It was a good thing that the truck company they'd chosen had varied, recognizable truck designs. Ferris would never have thought to check the license plate on a random truck on the street.

"Good," Demos said, looking determined as he helped Ferris up, "because we're going to track down every single thing that was stolen from this fucking apartment."

"We are?"

"You want to tell Uncle Vic you were using his place as tramp storage?"

"Okay, we are."

On the way down, Ferris was sure to mention that they were outnumbered and that Brandon's pals were older than they were. Demos didn't seem to care, waving Ferris off as he made several phone calls. He called Nicky, the police, and several other associates, asking if they had spotted a U-Haul with a Flytrap printed on the side. In fact, Demos called every person he could think of, excluding Victor. There was no need to let his uncle know that one of his hideouts had been robbed bare. The boys only waited a few minutes before Demos received a call back.

"It's headed south on 95, just passed exit 19," Demos said quickly, starting the car and speeding out into the city traffic. "I told you that Blakely comes in handy."

"Yeah, yeah," Ferris muttered, watching street lamps flash by as the car barely made a yellow light. The vehicle was an Alfa

Romeo, one gifted from Gino's collection after the boy remained wretchedly undecided despite months of car shopping.

"Sergio," Demos said, having made another call on his cell phone. "Be outside in two minutes. I'm going to pick you up. We're in a rush."

It appeared that Demos was bringing backup and wasn't as impulsive as Ferris had assumed. Soon, they were headed north on the expressway with Demos' older cousin in the backseat. After swearing he wouldn't mention any of this to Victor, Sergio received the details of the situation.

The only good thing about Brandon's rented truck being full of stolen goods was that heavy vehicles moved more slowly. On top of their burdened truck, the group had no idea that they were being tracked by a car with several angry young men. Though they should have been driving as fast as they were able, all the truck managed to attain was a clumsy pace below the speed limit. This was quite unfortunate for themselves, but very good news for the Giorgettis. After a few more confirmations from Blakely's dispatcher, they caught sight of the truck. They followed a few lengths behind, trying to be as subtle as possible.

"I'm assuming a few of those guys are in the back," Demos said, observing the vehicle as they drove. "They've got to stop soon, for food or a motel."

Ferris wasn't looking forward to driving until Brandon's crew was tired enough to stop, but didn't argue. This was all his own fault, after all. Luckily, as a result of moving heavy objects all afternoon, the group tired early. The truck soon made a lumbering turn onto an off-ramp, parking at a poorly maintained motel. The vacancy light flickered in neon pink over a sign that boasted color television. Demos parked around the opposite side, not wanting to be seen until the time was right.

They watched patiently as Brandon went into the office, getting a room key before driving towards the back of the motel parking lot. Ferris slouched in his seat, hoping to avoid being seen. The truck was close enough that they might recognize his face. The doors of the truck opened and a few men hopped out. Ferris froze when he caught sight of Julie. She really was with them. He glared, but only briefly. It didn't take long to realize that one of the men was holding her tightly by the arm.

"Let go, I can walk myself," she snapped, attempting to tug free.

"So we can watch you run off back to Southport? Yeah, right."

"Don't touch me," she hissed, clearly irritated.

Ferris didn't know what to think. He had been so ready to be furious and betrayed all over again that the thought of her being an unwilling victim hadn't even crossed his mind. Was she just in a bad mood, or had the men really abducted her? His mind was reeling, not knowing what to make of her. Demos watched until the last of them had gone into the hotel room, putting his attention on Sergio.

"All right, this will be easy. Just hot-wire that U-Haul and we're out of here."

"Wait," Ferris said, looking up at the hotel door. "What about—"

"We're leaving her."

"But I think they—"

"I don't care, Ferris. She's the cause of all this trouble, she can go straight back to California or wherever the hell they're taking her."

"No," Ferris replied firmly. "*I'm* the cause of all this trouble. I should have been more careful."

Ferris looked Demos in the eyes, speaking earnestly.

"You don't know what that guy is like. I can't let him take her back. Aside from that, I know where her mother is. If you won't help me, I guess I'll just have to knock on their door and ask politely."

"Damn it, Ferris," Demos said, aggravated. He hit the top of his steering wheel, clearly pissed. "Fine. Fine, you big baby."

"Thanks," Ferris said gratefully. "Oh, and... I think these guys deal coke or something. They might be armed."

"Great. That's perfect," Demos said with an eye roll.

The car doors opened and the three stepped out. Demos went to the trunk, popping it open to reveal a discrete paper bag. Inside were several firearms.

"Safety, magazine, trigger," Demos said, gesturing to each part of the Glock before handing it to Ferris. "Got it?"

Ferris nodded as he accepted it, sincerely hoping he wouldn't have to fire the weapon. Sergio took a handgun as well, leading them up the stairs to the proper motel room. He put a finger to his lips when they reached the top, indicating that they should remain silent. Crouching, they listened by the door.

"What, like $500? This is all you managed to save in the time you were gone?" came a male's voice from behind the poorly insulated door.

"Fuck you, Brandon. I had a real job, which is more than I can say for you."

"Shut up, bitch. You're lucky that apartment was loaded, or the trip to come get you wouldn't have even been worth it."

"I didn't *want* you to come get me. Let me go back!"

"Yeah, that's gonna happen."

This was followed by some laughter. Ferris didn't need to hear any more to realize what had happened. Brandon must have found out where Julie was living, driven over to New York, and paid her a surprise visit. He also must have assumed Ferris would take everything the wrong way because of what had happened two years ago. Brandon, though not incredibly bright, had been correct on that guess.

Sergio tucked his gun into the back of his belt, gesturing for Demos and Ferris to get out of sight. Straightening himself, he gave the door a couple firm knocks. The laughter stopped suddenly. After a moment of silence, a suspicious voice called out from the other side of the door.

"Who is it?"

"Management," Sergio said clearly. "A customer left their watch in this room. We'd like to take a quick look, if you don't mind."

"One second," came an irritated reply from inside. There was a hurried shuffling, a hesitant silence, and then the door unlocked. The moment that it started to open, Sergio kicked it the rest of the way in. The door hit the man behind it squarely in the head, knocking him to his back. Before he could even groan, Sergio had pulled out his gun to aim between his victim's eyes.

"Step back. All of you. Hands where I can see them," he commanded firmly, making his way into the room as its occupants backed up obediently. Demos followed suit, but Ferris waited behind. He wasn't sure if he was ready to be recognized yet.

"What is this, a robbery?" Brandon asked incredulously. There was a tinge of nervousness in his voice. He eyed his jacket on the bed, which held his gun in an inner pocket.

"You have quite a bit of our property in that truck of yours," Demos said. "I'll be needing those keys."

Instead of answering, Brandon made a rush for his jacket. His hand barely touched the collar before Demos pulled the trigger. Brandon screamed as he was shot in the foot, crumpling to the carpet. Julie stared down at Brandon as he bled, quickly grasping the seriousness of the situation. Demos gestured with his gun once more, repeating his request.

"Keys."

Frantically and between tears, Brandon fished them out of his pocket. He tossed them to the best of his ability and they fell at Demos' feet with a soft clink. Demos picked them up quickly. They probably didn't have much time before someone in the motel reported the gunshot.

"And her," Demos added, gesturing towards Julie with his gun.

Julie's eyes widened in fear. Being kidnapped by a bunch of drug dealers was bad, but she didn't think she would be any better off with a pair of violent Italian gangsters.

"You don't want me," she started uneasily. "I've got all kinds of STDs and I'm—"

240

"Julie, it's okay," came a voice she was familiar with. Ferris stepped in past Sergio. One hand was held up to calm her — the other held a gun at his side.

"Ferris?" she asked, not understanding what was going on.

"You remember all the times I told you," Ferris said calmly, "that the apartment wasn't mine?"

Julie swallowed, suddenly understanding what was going on. The apartment belonged to mobsters; specifically, ruthless, hostile mobsters. Somehow, Ferris was acquainted with them. Julie's head started to spin.

"It's okay," Ferris said gently, offering his hand. "Come with us."

Julie took one glance at Brandon, then the other men in the room before quickly pushing her way over to him. She took his hand, feeling relief once they touched. Demos gave the room a brief look-over, pocketing the wallet on the dresser before backing out of the room.

"Let's go," he said quickly. They left the room, hurrying down the stairs. Demos tossed the U-Haul's keys to Sergio, who got into the truck alone. A minute later, they were gone.

In response to a call about gunshots, the police arrived eight minutes later to find several convicted felons desperately trying to flush bags of cocaine, one of them bleeding profusely from his foot, and an unregistered handgun. It didn't matter that their truck was gone; they each received a free ride. The back of a police car wasn't their first choice in vehicle, but then again, neither was jail as their destination.

The next morning, the group made an attempt to return the stolen items to their rightful places. Demos turned a picture frame a quarter inch to the left, stepping back to make sure it looked right.

"Okay, we're done," he said wearily. Pointing at Ferris, he rebuked his friend with his remaining energy. "You owe me so, so bad for this."

"I know," Ferris admitted, looking at the restored layout. Julie was sitting in a chair in the corner, looking a bit shaken.

"One last favor?" he asked Demos. His friend replied with a glare.

"What?"

"Drop us off at the bus station."

The drive to the station didn't take long and Demos waited in his car at the curb for Ferris to wrap things up. Julie stood with Ferris in the terminal, holding a small bag and her guitar case.

"So," Julie said with a faint smile, "that's how you got the apartment."

"Yeah. It's actually his uncle's, so…" Ferris trailed off, putting his hands in his pockets.

"Why are we at the bus station? You've had enough of me?"

"No," he answered, digging in his pocket for a folded sheet of paper. He handed it to her with the wallet Demos had stolen.

"This is your mother's address," Ferris said. Julie gingerly unfolded the paper, eyes locked on the address in disbelief.

"Jersey?" she said, voice shaking slightly.

"Yes," he replied, looking up at the schedules on the wall. "There's a ten a.m. bus to Hoboken if you get your ticket now."

Julie didn't answer, simply embracing Ferris gratefully. Her arms went around his neck as she hugged him, speaking next to his ear.

"Thank you."

"You're welcome," he said gently, hesitantly patting her shoulder. She relaxed her hold, looking him in the eyes.

"Good luck with Emily," Julie said with a smile. "She'll figure it out, if she knows what's good for her."

Ferris' expression blanked, not having expected her to say that.

"...Thank you," he finally replied. Julie said goodbye, kissed his cheek, and went to go buy her ticket. Ferris gave her one last wave, watching her for a moment before heading back to the car.

"So," Demos said, starting the car, "don't need the apartment anymore?"

"No," Ferris answered, looking out the window. "I don't."

32

When Ferris first asked his father for a computer, he hadn't lied about needing it for schoolwork. Furthermore, he hadn't lied about needing it for gaming, either. Now that his required essays were neatly typed, stapled, and tucked into his school bag, he was able to take full advantage of the powerful machine. It was time for war.

'*I see you on my border, Hammurabi,*' Ferris typed into the chat window, talking to his cousin Jake. '*You're not fooling anyone with those fanatics.*'

'*what are you so scared of? your cities are fortified, right?*' Jake replied a moment later.

'*I don't think my citizens are ready for a fundamentalist dictator like you.*'

'*they'll be happy. ill MAKE them happy. hey wait what the hell, are you building a fucking spaceship*'

'*Whatever gave you that idea?*'

'*you piece of crap how many parts do you have*'

A voice called up from the first floor, interrupting his focus.

"Ferris!" called his mother from the first floor.

"Yeah?" he replied, cracking open his door to listen.

"Pick up the phone," she screeched. "It's Demos!"

Ferris rolled his eyes at the yelling. He was always told to bring the phone to whoever the call was for, but his own mother always broke the family rule. Nobody tried to stop her. He walked down the hall to his father's study, picking up the receiver from the desk phone.

"Hey, Demos."

"I called your cell like ten times."

"Yeah, sorry. The battery died," Ferris lied. He put the phone on silent when he was 'working.' "What's going on?"

"It's not good," Demos said, his voice worried. There was the sound of other voices in the background, as well as a phone ringing.

"Where are you?" Ferris asked, sitting up straight and knitting his brow in concern.

"The hospital."

A thousand terrible possibilities instantly ran through Ferris' head. Demos was clearly okay, but who was he there for? Had something happened to Emily, or Victor?

"What happened, why are you at the hospital?" Ferris asked, his voice tense.

"It's Seamus," Demos answered, sounding weak.

Ferris went still, not knowing how to respond. He'd forgotten about Seamus during the past week. The shock of hearing that he was in the hospital made Ferris momentarily forget to be angry with him. The grudge took a quick backseat in his mind, giving way to uncomfortable worry.

"What happened?"

"Alcohol poisoning. I think it was intentional."

Ferris tried to swallow but his mouth was too dry.

"Is he okay?" he asked, knowing it was a stupid question. If Seamus was in serious condition, Ferris wasn't sure how he would handle it.

"He's not conscious yet, but they say he should be soon. He's going to make it, but he's still in bad shape."

"Which hospital, what room?"

"St. James. 10-2."

"I'll be right there."

Harold gave Ferris a ride to the hospital, dropping him off at the front with a warm reassurance. Ferris smiled gratefully at his father before going inside the building, finding the proper floor.

Meanwhile, his cousin Jake had typed *'its YOUR TURN, ferris. i'm going to change the timer to 30 seconds!'* into the message box multiple times. Ferris was taking a very long time to play his turn.

When Ferris entered the hospital room, Demos was already sitting beside the bed.

"Ferris," he said, looking up thankfully.

"How is he?"

"Better," Demos said, putting his hand on top of Seamus'. "He wasn't answering his phone, so I stopped by his apartment. He was passed out on the floor."

Ferris' eyes lay on Seamus' unconscious form. He was lying on his back on the sterile, steel bed. It was strange to see someone who was normally animated and confident look so vulnerable. The Brit's skin was unusually pale, appearing almost blue in some places.

"You said you think it was intentional?" Ferris asked softly.

"I'm not sure. He's been really depressed recently," Demos said.

Ferris bit the inside of his lip, having the feeling that he was partly responsible for this. Of course, he hadn't been around to notice Seamus' declining behavior. Ferris had incorrectly assumed that Seamus would brush this off and spring back to normalcy like he always did.

"It was so strange," Demos said, as if reading Ferris' mind. "I'd never seen him like that before."

"I was too hard on him, wasn't I?" Ferris admitted, looking guilty as he sat down in a chair next to Demos.

"Maybe. But Seamus is different. He really attaches himself to people. I don't think he was ready to handle being cut off like that."

"Shit," Ferris said under his breath, running a hand over his forehead. He felt bad enough as it was — what if Seamus hadn't made it? What if Demos hadn't stopped by and found him on the floor? Demos mentioning that the Brit attached himself to people sounded about right. The illusive thought crossed his mind that Seamus might not have always been joking when he flirted with Ferris, but he quickly shook the idea. That was just silly.

Demos and Ferris didn't have much more to say as they sat in the hospital room, waiting for Seamus to wake up. He lay on the bed, more still than the two had ever seen him before. His face looked uncomfortable, hinting at unpleasant dreams. For a long time, the faint hum of machinery and the beeps of equipment made up the only sounds in the room. Finally, Seamus shifted.

Demos and Ferris both picked their heads up, carefully watching to see if Seamus' eyes would open. A moment later, they did. Seamus' vision took a second to focus and the first thing he saw was Demos' relieved face.

"Oh, Demos," he said faintly, his voice a little sore. Seamus took a look down at his own body on the hospital bed, then glanced over at the medical equipment to his side. "What's going on?"

"You drank too much," Demos said, smiling despite his scolding tone. "Idiot."

"Did I really?" Seamus asked before his eyes caught sight of Ferris. He went still, and for a second his friends both thought his heart might stop.

"Ferris," he said slowly.

"You remember my real name. I'm surprised."

"You're here."

Demos stood, taking the opportunity to give the two a chance to talk.

"I'm going to grab some coffee, I'll be right back," Demos said, stretching his arms and giving Ferris a look before leaving the room.

"How do you feel?" Ferris asked, sitting closer to Seamus' side.

"I'm sorry," Seamus blurted, ignoring the question. "I'm sorry, Ferris. I fucked up."

"It's all right," Ferris said gently. "I'm not mad anymore. And I'm sorry, too… for hitting you."

"I'll tell her the truth," Seamus offered, referring to Emily. "Maybe it would—"

"Don't worry about it. If she made a mistake with Chris, she'll realize it on her own. If not, then I guess... as long as she's happy," Ferris said distantly, not sounding too excited about the second option.

"I suppose," Seamus said warily.

"You didn't answer me, though."

"What?"

"I asked how you felt."

"Terrible," Seamus said, waving a hand as if he were at a tea party and not a bright, sterile hospital room. "And thirsty."

"Want me to get you some water?" Ferris asked, moving to stand. Seamus stopped him, putting a hand on his friend's arm.

"It's all right. I'd rather you stayed."

Ferris leaned back in the chair once more, giving Seamus an understanding nod.

"This is the second time I've had to see you in a hospital. You need to watch yourself," Ferris said. It then hit him that both of those times had offhandedly been his own fault.

"What can I say? I live life on the edge."

"If the 'edge' is drinking alone in your living room, then sure."

"About what I said..." Seamus said slowly, turning his head to look at the wall.

"I forgive you. Don't worry about it."

"And all it took was a near death experience?" Seamus asked with a grin. "Fantastic."

Ferris gave his friend a patronizing smirk. He wondered, if Seamus hadn't been in the hospital, how much longer he would have avoided him.

"Hey, Seamus."

"Yeah?"

Ferris stopped to think, trying to figure out the best way to ask.

"When you said you were jealous, was—"

Ferris' sentence was interrupted by the door opening. Demos reentered the room, precariously holding three cups.

"Take it, take it," he said to Ferris, offering the top cup in a stack of two. Ferris carefully took the coffee before it could fall. He and Seamus both promptly forgot their conversation.

"Here," Demos said, handing Seamus a cup. "I got you some water."

"Any fags?" Seamus asked, taking a long sip.

"We're in a hospital," Demos said impatiently, removing the lid of his own coffee to take a small drink.

Seamus looked disappointed, his eyes going from Demos to Ferris, and then to the rest of the room. He was thoughtful for a moment, knitting his brow.

"Where's Mum?"

Demos looked down, not eager to answer that question.

"I gave her a few calls on your cell. She hasn't picked up."

"Must be busy," Seamus mused, finishing his water.

246

"Yeah," Demos said, almost sadly. "Busy."

The Italian walked past the neighboring bed, not paying any mind to the sleeping man in a cast. He stopped at the window, looking outside at the flowering trees and tall office buildings.

"It's a nice day," he said nonchalantly, taking another sip of his coffee.

"Think they'll let me out soon?"

"I'm not sure," Demos said, turning around. "You're underage and you had alcohol poisoning. You nearly died."

"I've been through worse," Seamus said, brushing him off.

"They're going to wait for your mother to arrive," Demos explained, "to have a word with her."

"Damn," Seamus muttered. He could, at times, be naive about his mother's whereabouts and intentions. Even he knew, however, that it would likely be a long time before he set foot outside the hospital.

"So," Seamus said, changing the subject and turning his attention back to Ferris, "we're all right then?"

"Yeah," Ferris replied, pushing up his glasses wearily. "We're all right."

He gave Seamus a faint smile, happy that things were almost back to normal. He was glad to see Seamus, but hoped, quite sincerely, that he would never have to see him in a hospital again.

33

When summer finally came, things seemed to have returned to the usual routine. Ferris studied arduously for the SATs, Demos carried on the family business with a great deal of charm, and Seamus mucked about uselessly. Demos started to forget about the O'Brien threat. It had been months and there was still no sign of retaliation. It was possible that Brian didn't want to risk making a move. Then again, he may have just been waiting for an opportune moment. Either way, the Giorgettis couldn't help but relax a little. Things seemed safe, for now.

One difference in the scheme of things was in Ferris' daily grind. He was now old enough to hold an actual job, taking up an internship at his father's office. He thought that his skills in calculation might be put to the test, or perhaps he would be given some creative challenges, but he was dreadfully wrong. The only important thing he learned on his first week at the job was that the word 'intern' was synonymous with 'secretary.'

"Good afternoon," Ferris lied, spinning a pen between his fingers as he answered the phone. "Crane Markowitz, LLP."

"Yeah, hi," came the voice at the other end of the line. "I'm looking for a Mr. Ken Arnold. I was told by a friend of mine that he was pretty good with small businesses. Sam, that was my friend's name. I think he's been through you guys before. Anyway, he mentioned Mr. Arnold and I thought that maybe he could help me with—"

"Hold, please," Ferris said, trying to hide the fact that he would rather die than listen to this person's life history. He pressed the transfer button on the office phone, deciding to let Mr. Arnold himself deal with the other half of that speech.

"Twenty copies, ASAP," a man said, dropping a stack of papers on Ferris' desk as he walked by. Ferris stared down at them before looking after the man, trying to remember who the hell the guy even was. Grabbing the stack, he made his way to the copier in the back.

"Please work," he mumbled, setting the papers carefully into the feeder before hitting the copy button. The machine sucked in the first few sheets, appearing to be running smoothly. It hummed and churned mechanically, spitting the scanned paper into a tray. On the sixth sheet, however, it jammed. There was a high pitched beep as the copier came to a frantic halt, displaying an error message on its small LCD screen.

"Damn it," Ferris griped, opening the top and tugging the crumpled paper out of the spools. He flattened it with his hands, gingerly placing it back in the tray and hitting enter once more.

It jammed again. Ferris was losing his patience, fixing the problem a second time. He held his breath as it sucked the paper in, only exhaling once it had properly gone through. Three sheets later, there was another error message.

"No paper?" he said incredulously, pulling open the correct drawer to check the level. It was full of paper. He shut the drawer, hitting enter repeatedly.

"Come on, work with me," he muttered, pressing a few more buttons. Finally, it started again.

"Thank you," he said, speaking too soon. It beeped again, displaying the 'no paper' error.

"You piece of crap!" Ferris cried, using all of his willpower to keep from kicking the machine.

This was an entirely different world from the one of protection fees and handguns. Office life seemed so menial compared to what Demos did. Frankly, Ferris thought he might prefer the danger to the tedium of this lifestyle. He didn't understand how his father did it. Twenty minutes later, he dropped the immense stack of copies on the proper man's desk.

"Took you quite a while," the suit said, not looking up from his paperwork.

"Yeah," Ferris muttered. "The copier wouldn't—"

"Okay. Thank you."

Ferris had only been back at his desk for ten seconds when a grating voice drew his attention.

"Hey, intern," called a man in a suit two desks over. "Want to make a Starbucks run?"

Normally, Ferris wasn't wild about fetching drinks for various office assholes, but he was desperate for an excuse to get outside.

"Yeah, sure."

"Here, come get this list," the man yelled, waving a yellow Post-It note with a half dozen beverage variations scrawled in blue pen. He handed it to Ferris, along with a collective wad of cash. Ferris almost smiled when he went outside, ignoring the city heat. He was just happy to be out of the office. The walk to the coffee shop wasn't long, though the line to the counter most definitely was.

"I need a venti skim no-whip mocha, an iced tall vanilla latte, a grande Americano, a tall skim peppermint mocha with whip," Ferris droned, reading from the Post-It with little enthusiasm, "a venti chai, a doppio con panna, and a tall dry cappuccino."

"You need a carrier?" the barista asked, ringing up the order on the register.

Ferris stared at him with half-lidded eyes, most definitely not amused.

"Yes."

With some effort, he managed to get the drinks back to the office without spilling or dropping anything. He gave them their change, taking one of the drinks as he headed back towards his father's office. A knock on the glass paneled door made Harold look up from his work.

"Come in." Upon seeing his son, Harold's expression brightened. "Ferris, how's your work going?"

"Uh, it's all right," Ferris said. "Here, I got you this."

He set the mocha on his father's desk, sitting down in the client's chair to face him.

"Oh, how nice. Thank you," Harold said, accepting the paper cup and taking off the lid. "No whipped cream?"

"You know Mom would kill me."

"Yeah, you're right," Harold said, a little defeated. "So, how are you liking it here?"

"It's okay. Though I'd kind of like to be more... challenged."

"I know this kind of stuff seems demeaning right now, but everyone starts out this way. Don't worry. You'll get to see how the system works, and once they see how bright you are, who knows?"

"Maybe," Ferris said, looking down at his hands.

"You know, if you don't feel this field is right for you, you don't have to go into it," Harold said gently.

"No, it's not that. I'll get used to it."

"You know, you don't have to be like me," Harold assured him. "You've got what it takes to be much greater."

Ferris lifted his head, looking at his father without knowing what to say.

"And I know you will be," Harold continued, giving his son a smile.

"Thanks, Dad," Ferris said, unsure of how to accept such a compliment.

"No, thank you," Harold said, lifting his cup in appreciation. "I was about to fall asleep at my desk. This stuff is so boring sometimes."

Ferris simply smiled. It seemed he had more in common with his father than he thought.

250

34

Ferris was happy to see the end of his work week on Friday night, looking forward to taking the next two days off. The Giorgettis were hosting a small barbecue at the compound that Saturday. Normally Ferris had little interest in swimming pools, but the thought of relaxing and seeing his friends after forty hours of fluorescent lighting and copy machines was almost exciting.

The brick lined driveway that curved across the entrance of Gino's manor was lined with cars. Ferris shielded his eyes from the sun as he stepped out of his father's Maxima. Ruth was wearing an oversized pair of sunglasses and a new, wide-brimmed sun hat. Harold, normally dressed in a dignified, fitted suit, was wearing a colorful button-up shirt and a pair of khakis. Ferris almost felt as if he were at Disneyland.

"Harold, Ruth, you're late! Everyone is out back," said Victor as he let them in past the entrance. "Ferris, Demos is upstairs. He was waiting for you."

Ferris nodded, branching off towards the stairs as Victor led his parents to the backyard. The house was quiet and expansive and the wooden stairs made no sound under his feet as he ascended. He stopped at the door that led to Demos' surrogate bedroom, knocking a few times with the backs of his fingers.

The door opened quickly, revealing an impatient young Italian with a pair of sunglasses tucked above his forehead.

"Took you long enough," Demos said, knitting his brow at his friend disapprovingly.

"Sorry," Ferris replied with a shrug. "Mom couldn't decide on a bathing suit."

"You're… you're wearing jeans."

"Yes, it's what you do with jeans. Wear them. On your legs."

"Aren't you going to swim?"

"I'm not much of a swimmer," Ferris said in irritation, putting his hands in his pockets.

"Well, neither am I, but you've got to at least lie out in the sun."

"I hope *you* are, because you need it," Ferris said with a slight smirk, "Ghostie."

"Get in here," Demos said, glaring as he grabbed Ferris roughly by the wrist. Ferris stumbled a little as he was pulled into the room, caught off guard as Demos slammed the door shut.

"What are you doing?" Ferris asked slowly as Demos started to rummage through a dresser.

"What size do you wear?" Demos asked in annoyance, going through a drawer of clothing. "Here, a medium should be fine. You're not a small, are you?"

"I'm not wearing that," Ferris said plainly as Demos held up a pair of swimming trunks.

"Yes you are."

"No I'm—"

"*Put it on*," Demos said sternly, his tone unnaturally severe. His teeth were clenched and his dark eyes were narrowed. Apparently, this was a serious issue.

"F-fine. Okay," Ferris replied quickly, grabbing the shorts and turning around. Something about Demos' 'business voice' was utterly frightening. He unbuttoned his jeans, moving to pull the zipper when he paused.

"Um, do you mind?"

"Yeah, I'm going. I'll be outside," Demos said. "You better not come down unless you're dressed properly."

"Yeah, okay Mom."

The green swim trunks slid easily over his hips. They were a good fit, unfortunately. If they had been too small he might have had an excuse not to wear them.

"Christ, I'm pale," he muttered to himself, looking down at his legs disdainfully. It wasn't something he'd really noticed before. His skin wasn't as white as Demos' but it was still quite obvious that he'd been working in an office building all summer. Maybe the sun really would do him some good.

As he walked back down the stairs, he glanced idly at the large paintings that lined the walls. They were originals, all ornately framed and meticulously angled. He found himself wondering how many of them were stolen when a splash from the backyard caught his attention. He looked past the sliding glass doors. The entire family, as well as its close friends, were all situated around the pool and deck. Marco, Pietro's younger brother, had just jumped into the water. He was trying to coax his sibling to join him with laughter and a few shouts. Pietro was having none of it, ignoring Marco to continue talking on his cell phone. Hesitantly, Ferris slid open the door to step outside. The smell of cooking beef immediately filled his senses, followed by the lingering aroma of chlorine and beer.

"Your shirt is still on," Demos said, raising his sunglasses to get a better look at his friend.

"Yeah, so? That wasn't part of the deal," Ferris said, sitting down on a lawn chair beneath an umbrella. Demos sat next to him, replacing his sunglasses and taking a sip of his iced tea.

"I said 'dressed properly.'"

"Well, I'm not swimming. This is proper enough for..." Ferris said, trailing off as something caught his eye.

252

"For what? What are you—" Demos looked to the side, noticing that Emily was standing beside the pool in a two-piece. "Oh."

Demos rolled his eyes, leaning back in his seat and crossing his legs in irritation.

"You're pathetic," Demos said idly, poking at the ice in his glass with a straw.

"What?" Ferris said, averting his gaze and making an attempt to act innocent.

"Either ask her out or roll your tongue back up."

"She has a boyfriend," Ferris responded with an exasperated sigh. How many times were they going to go through this?

"So? He's dumb. One time he—"

Demos' sentence was cut off by a girl's cry of surprise, followed by a loud splash. Demos turned his legs just in time to avoid getting water on them.

"Serge, you dick!" Emily yelled at her older brother, who had just thrown her into the pool and was laughing heartily about it. His laughter stopped when he caught sight of her scrambling over the edge of the pool, intently coming after him. Sergio bolted, panting as his little sister chased him along the water's edge.

"Hey! Hey, hey! No running!" Victor yelled, in the middle of turning a steak on the grill. "I'm serious, kids! Cut it out!"

Sergio obediently stopped, only to be shoved bodily into the pool. He hit the water hard, sending a short wave over his aunt who was sunning nearby. She gave a brief shriek, recoiling at the cold water as her husband laughed at her.

"Thanks, Dad," Emily said with a sweet smile as Sergio sputtered to the surface.

"Anytime, Pumpkin," her father replied.

Ferris cringed at the thought of being pushed into the pool, making a mental note not to piss Emily off.

"So anyway," Demos said, "take the shirt off. You look like you're in gym class or something."

"What's with your obsession with my—"

"T-shirt tans are the worst. I mean, *the worst*. If you want to look like a bean farmer, be my guest."

Ferris mumbled something and reluctantly grabbed the hem of his shirt, tugging it off over his head. He snapped it outside-in, making sure to fold it to prevent wrinkles.

"Looks like I was too late," Demos said, not hesitating to tease his friend.

"Oh, shut up. I'm going to cram this shirt up your ass, see what kind of tan that gives you."

"You'll thank me later," Demos said indifferently as he leaned back in his lawn chair. The ice in his glass clinked as he

took another casual sip, looking quite unconcerned with Ferris'
threat.

"Queer," Ferris muttered under his breath. This wasn't the
first time he wished Demos was less concerned with
appearances.

"I heard that," Demos said accusingly. Ferris was likely the
only person on the planet who could call him 'queer' and get
away alive.

"*Queer*," Ferris repeated, this time more loudly.

"Jew," Demos snapped back, lifting his sunglasses to narrow
his eyes at his friend.

"*Queer*."

"*Jew*."

"Hey guys, am I interrupting something special?"

They both took their glares from each other, looking quickly
at Emily. She sat down on Demos' chair, bumping him sideways
with her hip.

"Uh, no. Not really..." Ferris said awkwardly.

"It was nothing," Demos agreed, putting his arm around
Ferris' neck in a friendly manner. "Just regular best-friend talk. I
was actually just on my way to get a burger. You two want
anything?"

"I'm good," Emily replied, having already stuffed herself
with two of them.

Ferris simply shook his head as Demos released him. He
rubbed the back of his neck tenderly; Demos had held onto him
in a suspiciously tight manner.

He and Emily both looked a little uncomfortable for a
moment. They hadn't sat and talked together for a long time.
Finally, Emily decided to break the silence.

"So, you having fun?" she asked, pushing some wet hair
from her forehead. She was still dripping from being dropped
into the pool.

"Hard to say. I just got here," he replied helplessly.

"Why didn't you bring your girlfriend?" Emily said
tentatively, keeping her eyes on the ground.

Ferris watched her for a while, suddenly remembering what
Seamus had said and how it felt to have his hopes crushed like
grapes at a wine festival. His expression was thoughtful, if not a
little sad.

"Emily..."

She picked her head up, making eye contact at the sound of
her name.

"I don't have a girlfriend," he said deliberately.

Emily stared at him, as if waiting for him to continue.

"I've... never had a girlfriend."

Her mouth opened and her eyes went still, locked on him as
if her mind had gone blank. Soon, something clicked in her head.

Ferris wasn't sure, but it seemed as if she understood what had happened. Emily blinked.

"Oh, I-I'm sorry... I thought—"

"I know."

They both fell silent again. The situation was much too complicated to address with more words.

"So," Ferris said brightly to break the tension, "you, uh, you look good today."

"Thanks," she replied, feeling her face suddenly warm. The compliment brought her back down to Earth.

"That's new, isn't it?" Ferris asked, referring to her bathing suit. She'd worn a different one at the summer home in Long Island.

"Oh. Yeah, my old one didn't fit anymore. Hey, what is that? I've never seen it before."

It was then that he noticed her eyes were locked directly on his chest. He panicked, quickly assuming it was a cancerous mole or perhaps an offensive rash. Looking down to see that it was only his necklace, he sighed. He'd forgotten about that thing. It made sense that she'd never seen it before; he hadn't ever been shirtless in front of her.

"Oh, Dad gave it to me. It's Hebrew."

"What does it mean?" she asked curiously, leaning in rather close.

"Life," he answered slowly.

She looked up, noticing how close she was to his face. Their eyes locked for what seemed like a long time. It wasn't long enough, however. A loud, overbearing voice broke the moment as it called across the pool.

"Ferris! Ferris, get over here, you need sun block!"

Ferris groaned a bit, looking over his shoulder at his mother.

"I'm in the shade!"

"You won't be all day! You want to end up like when we visited Bubbe and you couldn't sit down for a week?"

"For the love of Christ," he mumbled, grasping the sides of his head in frustration.

"I thought you didn't love Jesus," Emily said with a tiny grin.

"Well, he's supposed to love me anyway, right? Isn't that what the bumper stickers say?"

"Ferris!" Ruth repeated, reminding him to come over.

"I'll be right back," he said bitterly, getting up and obediently heading towards his shrieking mother.

"Oh, take your time," Emily answered, unable to help but be amused by it all.

Ferris sat unenthusiastically as his mother gave him a generous coat of sun block. He turned his head as she reached for his face, trying to swat her off with a weak wave of his arm.

"Come on, that's enough. I'm not five anymore."

"Teenagers can get sunburned, too. Now you sit still before I give you a smack."

Ferris sighed and went limp as she dabbed his nose. His eyes trailed sideways, looking back at Emily across the pool. She noticed him and gave a small wave, trying her best to stifle a laugh. Ferris only reddened and bit his lip, quickly looking away. This was ridiculous.

"Okay, all done," Ruth said cheerfully. Ferris looked over his own shoulder, trying to see if there were any white lotion spots left on his skin.

"Gee, I don't think you put enough on, Mom. Maybe you should give it a second go."

"Don't be smart with me, bubele. Skin cancer, that's what I saved you from."

"Thank God," Ferris mumbled as he walked away. Emily met him halfway, blocking his path to the chairs.

"Well, you look ready to throw on the grill."

"Shut up, Emily," Ferris said with a glower.

"Oh, come on. Don't be that way. Why don't you come swim with me?"

"That's all right," he replied hesitantly, eyeing the water. "I brought a book."

"You read all day. Why don't you do something else today?"

"I don't think—"

"Please?" Emily asked, putting her hands on his arms. Ferris faltered at her touch but remained adamant in his refusal.

"Sorry."

When Ferris looked Emily in the eyes, he could see the mischief behind them. It made him nervous.

"Don't make me force you."

He could feel her hands rise and took a step backwards. He was too slow, however, and she managed to give him a playful shove towards the pool. She was stronger than he anticipated and before he could stop himself, he lost his footing and stumbled backwards.

"I-I can't—"

He only managed to say two words before his body hit the water, plunging beneath the surface. The first thing he noticed was that it was cold. The second thing he noticed was that he wasn't sure which way was up. He panicked, trying to watch which direction the bubbles from his mouth went. It was no use. He was petrified and disoriented. His body tensed in terror; he wasn't used to being submerged entirely. Not thinking, he gasped involuntarily. Water rushed down his throat and the last bits of air in his body bubbled to the surface.

"Ferris, this isn't funny!" Emily said sternly as she watched his shadow in the deep end. Suddenly, there was the sound of a dropped glass of iced tea. Ruth had risen quickly from her seat, yelling as she found the edge of the pool.

"He can't swim!"

Emily's face fell.

Only two seconds passed before Sergio dove into the water, effortlessly swimming towards the still body near the bottom of the pool. It didn't take him long to bring Ferris to the surface, carefully setting him along the edge. Water pooled around Ferris' body as the party's bystanders stared to see if he would move. Demos' voice broke the silence.

"Out of the way!"

The young Italian pushed his way past the adults, kneeling at his friend's side. He quickly tilted Ferris' head back, leaning in to listen for breathing. There was nothing. Though he was repeating the word 'shit' inside of his head, he remained silent on the outside. The only good thing about this situation was that the voluntary CPR classes offered after school were actually going to prove useful.

Demos lowered his head, pinching Ferris' nose and tightly covering his mouth with his own. Ferris' chest rose with the borrowed air, then lowered. In the background, Harold was calling 911. Emily stood quietly, covering her mouth with a hand as she stared. She wanted to do something but didn't want to get in the way.

Demos gave Ferris another breath, ignoring his own anxious pulse. He remembered what he learned in class: give two breaths, each a second long. He also remembered that only ten percent of CPR recipients ever survived.

Demos' mouth had just pulled back when Ferris' body jerked with a cough. He choked up a mouthful of water from his throat and took in a deep, shuddering breath.

"Thank God," Demos said with a heavy exhale. He'd started to sweat and it took quite a lot to get Demos so tense. He helped Ferris sit up, looking at him intently. "Are you okay?"

Ferris only managed a soft groan, holding the side of his face. His father knelt next to them, offering his son a towel and putting a hand on his shoulder. They both helped Ferris up onto a lawn chair.

"The paramedics are on their way," Harold said comfortingly. He'd done his best not to go to pieces, for his son's sake.

Ferris didn't answer, trying to regain his bearings. He wiped his face with the towel, feeling weak and a little cold. When he looked up, the first thing he saw was Emily. Ferris looked at her for a second, not saying anything as she stared back at him. She looked ready to burst into tears.

"I'm sorry," she blurted, giving him a flustered embrace. "I'm so sorry."

"It's okay," Ferris said, his voice slow. He was too dazed to appreciate the fact that she was holding onto him.

"I almost killed you," she said again, pulling back to look him in the eyes.

"You didn't know. It's fine," Ferris repeated groggily.

"Why didn't you tell us you couldn't swim?" Demos asked, his tone almost accusing.

"I was embarrassed," Ferris said, looking down uncomfortably.

"You idiot," Demos snapped. "You scared the shit out of me."

"...You saved me, didn't you?"

Demos stopped, as if he'd forgotten exactly what had happened. It hit him that he really did save Ferris' life.

"Mh. It's just a good thing I didn't have to do chest compressions. I'm terrible at those."

"Guess I'm just lucky then, aren't I?"

"Yeah," Demos said, putting a hand on top of Ferris' head. "Lucky."

"You okay, kid?" Victor asked, leaning in past Ruth. He was wearing a barbecue apron and smelled like smoke.

"Yeah. Sorry I ruined the party."

"You didn't ruin anything. Just be more careful, my girl's got a mean throw."

Emily made a face as if her father were only making things worse.

"I gathered," Ferris said, having experienced her 'mean throw' firsthand. The sound of an ambulance pulling up in front of the house made the guests' heads turn. Ferris sighed. He hated when things became a big deal.

"Just tell them I'm fine," he said quietly.

"Some water might have gotten into your lungs, it's important that they check you out," his father said as Victor went to answer the door.

"All right," Ferris said, letting his father help him up. He still felt weak.

"I'm coming with you," Demos said quickly as he stood with them.

Ferris would have made an attempt to have Demos stay and enjoy his family's party, but he knew there was no point. He doubted there was anything that could convince his friend to leave his side.

"Me too," Emily said, still looking guilty. "...If you don't mind."

Ferris blinked at her, momentarily taken aback. After a second, he nodded.

When the paramedics came, they gave him oxygen and put him on a stretcher, much to his own dismay. Though he insisted he felt fine, certain procedures were necessary.

258

At the hospital he was diagnosed with good health and sent home. Luckily, his larynx has closed before any water could enter his lungs, not to mention the quick actions of both Sergio and Demos.

"Next time," Demos said as they drove home, "we can get you a pair of arm floaties."

"Or I could just stay in the shade," Ferris suggested, liking his idea much better.

"Maybe we could teach you to swim," Emily offered slowly.

Ferris hadn't considered the idea before and wondered if lessons would do any good.

"I'll think about it," he said before giving her a grateful smile. "Thanks."

Regardless of what he'd said, Emily's expression remained shameful for the rest of the day. Ferris had a hunch that she was going to feel guilty about what happened for quite some time. He found himself wondering what, if anything, could possibly ease her mind.

35

The fluorescent lighting of Crane Markowitz LLP did little to add aesthetic to the sea of cubicles on the fifth floor. Ferris had refined his pencil twirling skills over the past few weeks. There wasn't much else to do. Every so often his supervisor would give him some papers to file or something to fax, but otherwise, things were slow. He'd tried to bring his Game Boy, but his father insisted he leave it at home. A book would have worked wonders, but the commotion outside made it difficult to read.

There had been protesters at the hotel across the street for nearly a month. The unionized employees were on strike. Without much else to do all day, the striking employees had resorted to picketing. While it was possible to picket at a reasonable noise volume, these individuals seemed to think their point could be emphasized with yelling.

"God, if those guys don't shut up soon I'm going to hang myself," snapped a man from behind a cubicle wall. Ferris glanced sideways. At the rate the strike was going, the guy would have to invest in some rope pretty soon.

"Hey, intern," his supervisor said, walking by with a cell phone against his ear. "Call Mr. Foster for me."

"Yes, Sir," Ferris replied, trying to hide the bitterness in his tone.

'Is *it that hard to dial a number yourself?*' Ferris thought as he started punching the numbers. '*And why the hell do you want me to call him for you if you're already on the God damned phone?*'

"Foster speaking," came a man's voice as the phone picked up.

"Hello, I'm calling from Crane Markowitz. Do you have a moment to speak with Ken Arnold?"

"Why, yes. Of course."

"Hold, please."

Ferris rolled his eyes as he put the man on hold, watching his supervisor through the glass of his office door. Still on the phone.

'*Douchebag...*' Ferris thought as he tapped his pencil on the desk, trying to ignore the sounds of yelling protesters from the street outside. A minute later Ferris lost his patience, approaching his supervisor's office door and knocking on the frame.

"Yes?" Mr. Arnold said in irritation, covering the receiving end of his cell phone with a palm.

"Mr. Foster is on the line for you."

"I know, hold on."

Ferris' mouth flattened to a thin line and he moved to step out of the office.

"Oh, and—" Mr. Arnold said, halting his getaway. "Don't interrupt me when I'm on the phone."

"...Sorry, Sir," Ferris said, though the way he forced it left a bad taste in his mouth.

His eyes drifted to the clock. The second hand ticked in a slow, steady curve around the face. He looked back to Mr. Arnold's window. He was still talking. Ferris started to flip the pencil between his fingers. His eyes shifted right, back towards the windows where the sounds of protesting union workers drifted up from the street. He looked at the desk phone; the line with Mr. Foster was blinking. Suddenly, the pencil snapped in half.

Ferris startled himself, quickly looking down at the two pieces in his hand. He took a hasty look around to make sure no one had seen him destroying office supplies, then quietly tossed the broken pieces into the trash. Before he could fret any further, someone approached his desk.

"Can I help—" Ferris paused as he looked up, caught off guard by a girl much too young to need her taxes done. "Emily?"

"Hi," she said unsurely, looking around as if someone were after her. "I'm sorry for coming by unannounced..."

"H...how did you get past the security desk?" he asked incredulously.

"Security desk? Oh, I said I was visiting my 'daddy.' And smiled, and stuff."

Ferris squinted an eye at her. Though the lobby guard's weakness for innocent young girls was annoying and unfair, he couldn't deny he was happy to see her.

"Anyway," Emily continued, "I was in this neighborhood to pick some stuff up for Mom and I remembered you work here. I thought I'd stop by... unless you're busy?"

Ferris stared at her for a second.

"No, no. It's fine," he said, stacking a couple of papers on his desk. "I'm not doing anything."

"Did you eat already? We could get lunch."

"Oh, um..."

Ferris normally ate lunch with his father. Once in a while Mr. Levinstein would have a business engagement or meeting, but it was an otherwise steady tradition.

"I'll be right back," Ferris said quickly, getting out of his chair and heading down an aisle of cubicles.

"Dad?" Ferris asked, poking himself halfway into his father's office.

"Well, hello," Harold replied with a smile, adjusting his glasses as he looked up. "What's new?"

"Someone stopped by, out of the blue. It's Emily. I—"

"Emily is here? Well, what are you doing in my office? Why don't you go have lunch with her?"

Ferris took a moment before responding, unable to help but smile.

"That's a good idea."

"Of course it's a good idea, it's *my* idea," Harold said, putting his attention back on some forms. "Well, go on. Scram."

"I'm going," Ferris reassured his father as he left the doorway, heading back to his desk.

Emily opened her mouth to say something when he returned, but he quickly walked past her to his supervisor's office.

"I'm going to lunch," Ferris said. His tone suggested that the sentence might end with '*And there's nothing you can do to stop me.*'

"I need you to get—"

Mr. Arnold fell silent. His intern had split the scene before he had even gotten to his second word.

In the elevator, the lights blinked steadily as they went down past each floor.

"I've never seen you move so fast before," she said.

"That guy only gives me work when he thinks it'll make me miserable," Ferris griped.

"You looked pretty miserable already," Emily pointed out.

"That lighting doesn't do a *thing* for my complexion, either," Ferris said, mimicking something Demos had once said. Emily laughed, grinning at him as they reached the lobby. As they exited the building, she gave the security guard a cheerful wave. The man tipped his hat in return and Ferris rolled his eyes.

They decided on a hole-in-the-wall Thai restaurant with sun-bleached photographs in the window and a good lunch special. The air carried hints of spices and coconut milk. They chose a small table near a window, sitting beneath a framed elephant stitched in gold. Emily's eyes scanned the menu, looking for her favorite dish. Ferris, without thinking about it, simply looked at her. He liked the way her bangs covered her eyes when her head was tilted down in concentration. Her hands, now trailing down a list of orders, were slender and looked as if they would be very soft. He didn't realize he was looking at her so intently until she happened to look up, catching his eyes. He blinked, looking down at his forgotten menu.

"So, what's good here?" she asked.

"I get the green curry. Dad likes the Pad Thai but I'm not really into peanuts," Ferris explained, keeping his eyes locked on the menu.

"Oh, let's get the curry puffs," she said, pointing to the appetizer list, "and I think I'll get the Pad Kee Mao."

"Hungry?" he asked, giving her a slight smile.

262

"Dad told me to gain some weight. He said his 'Pumpkin is too skinny.' Can you believe that?"

"Don't worry so much about your weight. You've always looked great to me."

Emily went quiet and a small smile grew on her face. Ferris didn't realize he'd even complimented her until he saw her expression.

"Not that I stare at you all day or anything," he added awkwardly. Emily simply tilted her head, looking unconvinced.

"Oh, by the way," she said, changing the subject, "what's the deal with the protesters?"

"Heh," Ferris said, looking amused. "You should know. Your father runs Local 145."

"Local what?" Emily asked, narrowing her eyes at him. Before Ferris could explain, the waitress came to take their orders. Ferris wasn't sure they'd be able to finish that much food but decided to trust her on this one.

"You know, the Union branch, Local 145. They cover the service industry, like maids. Your Dad practically owns it."

Emily gave him a blank stare.

"You don't remember? Huh. Well, his friends run everything, he just tells them what to do. That hotel probably did something to piss him off."

"Oh," Emily replied, looking embarrassed.

"What's wrong?"

"You know more about Dad than I do, and I live with him."

"Oh, no. Demos told me. I'm not psychic. You don't really care about that stuff anyway, do you?"

"I guess not," she said, poking at her water with the straw.

"Um, did you cut your hair?" Ferris asked suddenly, trying to change the subject.

"Yeah, it's a little shorter in the back," she said, glad that he noticed.

"It looks good that way."

"You think so? I'm kind of afraid to have super short hair."

"Why's that?" Ferris asked, leaning his chin in a hand. Personally, he liked short hair.

"I don't know, I guess it's from when I was little. I was the ugliest baby ever. Everyone kept thinking I was a boy so Mom had to put a bow in my hair. Then they just asked why her son had a bow on."

Ferris, unable to help it, started laughing.

"I-I'm sorry," he said helplessly, trying to cover his mouth.

"Oh, shut up. I'm going to jam these chopsticks up into your brain."

"Such a violent little boy," Ferris said, still laughing. Emily brandished the wooden chopsticks at him threateningly when the waiter approached the table with two plates. There was an uncomfortable silence as the waiter placed the food onto the table, then quickly stepped away. Once he was gone, they both started to laugh.

"Did you see that guy's face?" Emily's asked.

"He probably thought we were idiots."

"Or like he was going to call the police," Emily said, taking a bite of her lunch. "Oh, wow, this is good."

"Yeah, it's not bad for $4.95," Ferris said, picking up a piece of chicken with his chopsticks.

"I got my schedule in the mail yesterday. Though I guess we don't have any of the same classes."

"Probably not," Ferris said. They were in different grades and had different interests. He doubted she would have enrolled in Advanced Placement Calculus.

"It took me a long time to pick my classes," Ferris continued. "My teachers were trying to pressure me into a certain direction, but I would rather die than take French Existentialism."

"Yeah, that sounds like hell."

"And I still have to do some projects over the summer for Economics."

"They can do that?"

"Sure, if it's an Honors class."

"What do you have to do?" Emily asked, looking around in her noodles for another piece of chicken.

"Last night I had to look up what a 'primate city' was. It's just a gigantic financial superpower in a country," Ferris said, sounding disappointed, "and not a city of apes like I was hoping."

Emily laughed and Ferris was surprised to see that she was almost done with her food.

"What about you? Looking at any schools?" he asked.

"I want to go to art school. If I were a boy Dad would lose his shit, but he probably assumes I'll just marry some rich guy and be a happy painting housewife. So they support me."

"Well, that's… nice. I think," Ferris said hesitantly.

"I'm going to apply to SPA once I get my portfolio together."

"…Spa?" Ferris asked, making a strange face.

"You know, Southport Arts. Don't tell me you've lived here your entire life and haven't heard of it."

"Oh, oh right. Of course," Ferris said, feeling stupid. "I thought you already had a portfolio."

"It still needs work," Emily said, fiddling with her chopsticks.

"But your stuff is amazing, I—"

"My biggest fan is my dad," Emily interrupted. "My biggest client is also my dad, who hangs my paintings up all over the house like they're Rembrandts or something."

"Hey, that's saying something. Your dad is fussy about paintings."

264

"I made one of them when I was five," Emily said with an impatient hand gesture. "It's a bunch of baby ducks."

"I saw that, in the hall upstairs? Instant classic."

Emily gave him a look that meant she didn't want to be patronized, but at the same time appreciated his humor. When the waiter brought the check, Ferris quickly gave him some bills. As he walked away, Emily frowned at Ferris from across the table.

"You really shouldn't have. That would make this a date, and—"

"Friends can pay for friends," Ferris said simply. "It's just five dollars."

"Plus the appetizer," Emily mumbled, then sighed. "Okay then, thanks. But I owe you…"

"Fine, make me a painting," he said with a shrug.

"It's just going to be baby ducks."

"I was hoping so."

36

Ferris slept in late that Saturday, taking advantage of the rare opportunity to do so. Around one p.m., his eyes opened. A thin strip of sunlight draped over his temple from a crack in the curtains. His pupils constricted on contact with the light. Squinting, Ferris sat up, letting his vision adjust to the room. He took his time getting dressed, having a cup of coffee despite the heat outside.

His seventeenth birthday had recently passed, though it was going to take some time for him to truly feel older. He wasn't one for parties, but his friends always insisted on surprising him with one. Though being the center of attention was the last thing he wanted, Ferris, more or less, appreciated the gesture in the end.

Ferris put his coffee down onto a coaster, sitting on the living room sofa with his legs folded. He looked through a photo book that Emily had given him as a birthday gift. The pages were large and full-color, printed with macro shots of exotic insects and wildlife. It wasn't the sort of thing he would ever think to buy, but now that he had it, he loved it. Demos, unashamedly rolling in the profits of his career, had bought him a PlayStation 2, completely crushing Seamus' self-proposed claim of "best gift." Seamus had presented him with a box set of VHS tapes for some British show called *Dr. Who*, whatever *that* was.

Ferris was eyeing a photo of a feather-horned beetle when a vibration from his pocket made him jump. His cell phone had startled him and he hastily dug it out to see who was calling. It was a text message from Demos.

Meet us in the park in 30 min?

Ferris thought about it for a second. He had nothing else to do that day, though he didn't want anything to do with the sweltering weather. He typed back with his thumb, though not able to do it as quickly as Seamus or Demos could.

Sure.

He grabbed his bag on the way to the front door. His hand had nearly touched the doorknob when his father's voice stopped him.

"Ferris, you got a letter in the mail."

Curious, Ferris looked over his shoulder as Harold handed him a slightly crumpled envelope. The handwriting on the front was nothing but feminine chicken scratch. There seemed to be some kind of cute animal drawn next to his address.

"Know who it's from?" Harold asked offhandedly.

"Doesn't say. I'll read it later, thanks."

"You need a ride? I was going to stop by Victor's in a minute anyway."

"That's all right, we're meeting in the park."

Ferris tucked the letter into his bag and said goodbye to his father, stepping outside. He immediately regretted this action. The air was hot and humid, sticking to him like plastic wrap. He made an uncomfortable groan. Summer was his least favorite season. At least the subway cars were air conditioned.

The stop was a few blocks away and Ferris quickly appreciated the slight drop in temperature as he went underground. He swiped his card just in time; he could see the headlights of the oncoming train shining against the tile wall. Rats scattered back into the walls as the train came to a gradual, screeching halt over the rails. There weren't many people out that day and there were plenty of open seats. Ferris took one, pulling the letter out of his bag with interest. He turned it over in his hands, briefly examining the envelope before cutting the top open with a finger.

Dear Ferris,

You gave me your address a while back, so I figured it was a hint for me to write to you. If not, then tough. You have to read this anyway.

I wanted to say thanks, again, for helping me find my mom. She was so happy to see me that she couldn't stop crying. I'm really glad I went home. Shannon is still a bitch, but I can deal. Mom got a job with a department store and she's associate manager or something. She doesn't have to have more than one job now, and New Jersey is cheaper. Jersey kind of sucks. (I'm still getting used to the smell.) But she's happier here, so I am too.

I'm back in school now because you made me promise. Ass. It's boring, but I'm coping. I guess. These guys at school have a shitty little band and they want me to play guitar for them. Maybe if I join they'll suck a little less. I'm thinking about it. I've made a couple of friends though. You were right about me needing to meet better people. These guys are pretty nice. Still, they're not you. I hope you're not rolling your eyes.

Ferris caught himself rolling his eyes.

Anyway, just thought I'd say 'hi' and stuff. Hope you're doing all right. Write me back if you find the time between encyclopedia volumes. Nerd.

Lots of love,
Julie

267

There was an address written along the bottom in the same messy handwriting. Ferris folded the letter and placed it back in the envelope with a strange sense of accomplishment. So, she hadn't forgotten about him yet — it was a nice feeling. He didn't expect to ever hear from her again and was glad to know she was doing so well. The fact that she'd gone back to school was especially nice for him to read. He would write her back when he went home. Just as his thoughts were winding up, the train stopped at the appropriate station. The doors chimed as they slid open.

Foley Park wasn't far from the station's exit. He sat on a bench, idly watching a line of people waiting to get ice cream from a small stand. Quite a few people were walking their dogs and Ferris decided to keep the place in mind for Stanley. The pug loved romping around in the grass, but many parks didn't allow dogs on the turf. In the distance, he spotted Demos, who raised his hand in silent greeting. Ferris returned the gesture, waiting for the other teen to approach the bench.

"Seamus not here yet?" Demos asked, looking around as he took out a pack of Blackjack cigarettes. He was clearly too lazy to roll his own that morning.

"No, not yet," Ferris said, then scoffed. "I don't know how you can do that in this heat. It's like a thousand degrees out here."

Demos only shrugged, sucking on the cigarette as he lit it. He sat down next to Ferris, leaning back and crossing a leg over his knee.

"How's work?" Demos asked, looking as if he'd stayed up too late last night.

"Okay, I guess. I won't miss it when school starts."

"It's not really the same without you around," Demos said. If Ferris didn't know any better, he might have thought Demos' voice held some spite in it.

"You'll have to get used to it. This is my last year here, remember?"

"Oh yeah," Demos said, his voice slow with realization. "College."

Demos' expression took a turn for the worse. Ferris was about to make an attempt at consoling him when a British accent cut in.

"Hey, this guy giving you trouble?" Seamus asked, jerking his thumb towards Ferris.

268

"Hi, Seamus," Demos said, quickly changing his expression. He smiled, offering Seamus a cigarette which was accepted gratefully.

"You could always go to college too, you know," Ferris offered, though his point was weak.

"Ferris, you're going to *Yale*," Demos said bitterly.

"I haven't been accepted yet. I might end up at Harvard or Brown."

"*Harvard* is your safety school?" Seamus asked, sounding disgusted.

"Their school of business has a 5% higher acceptance rate than Yale," Ferris said under his breath, looking off to the side as if embarrassed to be with the two.

"You've certainly done your research," Seamus said. "You applied yet?"

"I think I finished my application, but I haven't sent it in yet. Dad thought I should drop his name, but I don't know…"

"Why not?" Demos said, seeing nothing wrong with the proposal. "He's an alumnus, it might help."

"I just want to get in on my own, not through connections."

"If you say so, goody-goody. You're still going to visit, right?" Demos asked. He knew the answer, but simply wanted to hear Ferris say it.

"Of course. Passover, Yom Kippur, Thanksgiving, summer break," Ferris said, counting off on his fingers.

"Great. You'll stop by and be cranky from fasting all day."

"Fasting doesn't make me cranky," Ferris protested.

"Yeah, really," Seamus said. "He's always that way."

"Shut up, Seamus."

"That reminds me, I wanted to show you this thing last night but you weren't online," Seamus complained. "What was your email again?"

"Ironman 26?" Ferris said, as if it were obvious.

"I didn't know you were into Marvel," Demos said idly, flicking some ash off of his cigarette.

"It's a joke. You don't get it?"

Demos and Seamus simply stared at him.

"F and E are the first two letters of my name."

The two continued to stare at him.

"Table of elements?" Ferris asked hopefully. He sighed, then elaborated.

"Fe is the symbol for iron. And its atomic number is 26," he explained, his tone annoyed. "Come on, it's funny, right? You don't get it?"

"Give up, Ferris," Demos said, pushing some stray hair out of his eye.

"I don't know what's worse," Seamus said thoughtfully. "Your reference to a comic book character or a chemical element."

Seamus gave Ferris a grin.

"Well, either way, you're not getting laid," he finished.

"I hate you both," Ferris mumbled, upset that his joke went over their heads. He mumbled something under his breath that sounded like *'wasted on idiots like you.'* Ferris started considering a new screen name when Demos stood up and stretched.

"Well, I don't want to sit out here all day. Let's catch a movie."

"Yeah, wouldn't want you to lose your porcelain complexion," Ferris added, not holding back on his snide tone.

Demos narrowed his eyes, not wanting to admit that Ferris was right. He was more the type to burn before tanning, anyway. As they left the park, Ferris shielded his eyes with a hand, looking up at the sky. The sun was a taskmaster, beating down on concrete and skin without mercy. Cicadas in the trees creaked and chirped overhead. A dark, cool movie theatre sounded more than ideal at the moment. Seamus and Ferris didn't protest further, following the pasty Italian down the street to the nearest cinema.

As they moved down the sidewalk, they passed a homeless man on a bench. There was a saxophone case next to him — it appeared to be all he owned. He held out his hand to catch Demos' attention.

"Excuse me, could you spare one?" the man asked, making a smoking gesture with his fingers.

"Yeah, sure," Demos said, digging a cigarette out of its pack and handing it over. He offered the old man a light.

"Thank you, Sir. Thanks a lot," he said gratefully, puffing a bit on the new cigarette.

Demos nodded briefly before they continued down the road. From the corner of his eye he noticed Ferris giving the man some change.

"You're so strange," Ferris said offhandedly when he caught up to them.

"What? I was being nice."

"You never give them change or food, but you always give them cigarettes."

"I know what it's like to need one," Demos said with a shrug.

"I think you're secretly trying to kill them all."

Demos held a finger up to his lips, as if Ferris had discovered his secret and he was shushing him.

"Well give me one, then," Seamus cut in.

"You already got one."

"Oh, come on, you—"

"You're not homeless, Seamus," Demos said, rolling his eyes. He was about to add something to his sentence when his walking slowed. Ferris noticed that Demos was glancing sideways, though trying to be subtle about it. Ferris raised an eyebrow at his friend, who only replied with a brief mutter.

"That car is following us."

Slowly, Ferris turned to look towards the street. A black car was parked on the opposite curb. The window hurriedly rolled back up as it pulled into the road and drove away.

"What the hell?" Ferris asked, nonplussed.

"This is the third time I've seen that car," Demos replied. He sounded irritated.

"Who do you think it is?"

"I don't know," Demos said, dropping his cigarette butt to the ground and crushing it with the toe of his shoe. "Maybe Bob, maybe cops."

"We're not doing anything illegal," Seamus said casually, not completely understanding the gravity of the situation. He was aware of Demos' family business, but didn't realize how deeply involved his friend was.

"Come on," Demos said quickly, nodding towards the movie theatre. "Let's get inside."

Ferris followed without any complaints. He had the feeling that Demos was more worried than he was letting on.

The film was a typical summer action thriller, meeting the required quota of explosions and guys wearing sunglasses. The three hadn't gone in anticipating anything deep and were rewarded with a couple of hours of mindless entertainment. They stopped worrying about the mysterious black car for a short while, distracted by Raisinets and overly dramatic close-up shots of a death scene.

"Well, that was gay," Seamus announced as they exited, folding his hands behind his head.

"What did you expect? Le Ballon Rouge?" Ferris said, rubbing his temples. He could feel another headache coming on.

"At least one titty shot," Seamus said woefully.

"Give up, Seamus. We all know you're a fag," Demos said coolly as they pushed through the exit doors.

"Oi, shut up."

Ferris popped a couple of aspirin into his mouth, swallowing hard before glancing around for the car again. It wasn't anywhere in sight. They turned onto the city street, walking with their backs to the sun. They passed a subway entrance and a couple curled together in the shade of a building. The pair had a cup and a cardboard sign. It seemed that the warm weather drew the homeless out in droves. A minute later, Demos turned to Ferris with an amused look.

"You say *I'm* inconsistent? You gave the saxophone guy some money but you didn't give those two shit."

"They have each other," Ferris said bitterly. "He didn't have anyone."

Demos stared at his friend, not sure how seriously he should take the comment.

"Someone sounds lonely," Seamus teased.

"That was deep, Ferris. You should put that in some song lyrics," Demos added as he lit up another cigarette.

"Fuck you."

Seamus and Demos only laughed the way they usually did when they pressed Ferris' buttons. It was just so easy. They ended their day with lunch at a cheap Mediterranean restaurant. Other than the suspicious black vehicle, the day wasn't particularly special. Even so, Ferris made sure to remember it clearly. Summer wouldn't last forever and this was one of the few afternoons he had left with Limey and the Ghost.

37

The summer between their junior and senior years went by surprisingly fast, though Ferris didn't shed any tears at the end of his internship. At least, by his last day, the protesters had stopped. It seemed that Harold's talk with Victor had been effective. This was their final year of high school before they became adults; they were now in the 12th grade. They were taller than the incoming freshmen and supposedly wiser. Being an upperclassman offered a different view of the school. By now, it almost seemed to belong to them.

The first day of classes at St. Basil's came on a rainy September day. The ivy vines that grew along the sides of the brick were thicker now. Demos, Ferris, and Seamus were standing out front as other students walked in past them, motionless in a river of dark gray and crimson.

"Well, one year left. Let's get it over with," Demos said, putting his schedule back into his briefcase-style bag.

"Surprised we made it this far," Seamus added. He snapped his gum, moving it to the other side of his mouth.

"Personally, I'm surprised you haven't been deported," Ferris said, deadpanned.

"How could you say that? I'm God's gift to this country," Seamus said with a dash of charm in his smile.

"Hope you came with a receipt," Ferris said under his breath as they went inside.

Though it was rare that the three of them had a class together, they shared an equal talent, or lack thereof, in art class. Each was pathetically below average when it came to painting or drawing, but the class was required for graduation.

The students were situated around a setup of oranges and tin cans, attempting to paint the scene in oils. Ferris found himself wishing that Emily was just there to do it for him.

"How's this?" Demos asked, tilting his canvas to give Ferris a better look.

"What is it?" Ferris asked after a minute of hesitation. Demos looked insulted.

"We're all painting the same thing."

"That doesn't look like a can. Or an orange. Are you trying to do cubism or something?"

"Well look at yours, *Renoir*. It looks like you ate five tubes of oil and threw up on—"

"That's uncalled for," Ferris said sharply.

"At least we're not as bad as Seamus."

"I don't know," Ferris said, looking over at Seamus' canvas, "I think his is better."

Seamus' canvas was, of course, blank. He was slouched against the back of his chair, head rolling back as he slept through the last twenty minutes of class. His mouth was wide open and Ferris found himself tempted to put something in it. He started to wonder if oil paints were poisonous when the instructor's voice interrupted his thoughts.

"Seamus Aston?" she said, her tone bitter. There was no response from her sleeping student.

"*Mr. Aston*," she repeated, her voice firmer. Again, no response. A few of the girls giggled to themselves.

The teacher folded her arms as she addressed her class.

"Could someone give Sleeping Beauty a kiss so we can continue?"

Ferris promptly gave Seamus a smack on the back of his head.

"I'm not—... what?" Seamus stammered as he righted himself, blinking until his vision focused.

"Good morning, Seamus," the teacher said. "Nice of you to join us. Mind sharing your painting with the class?"

"Ahh..." Seamus replied hesitantly as he glanced over at his blank canvas. "Right. I call this one '*The Duchess*,' and it's symbolic of the political—"

"That's enough, Seamus. Do the assignment."

"Right, Miss."

Demos smirked as Ferris took the blank canvas, pretending to scrutinize it for a moment.

"Look," Ferris said, angling the white gesso surface so Demos could see. "Looks just like you."

Demos' smirk dropped and he narrowed his eyes.

"No, no, I need to paint the *fabulous* haircut in... what's your color? Ebony? No, *raven*," Seamus added.

"Are you guys even friends?" One of their classmates cut in, her voice skeptical. "All you ever do is make fun of each other."

"We're best friends," Seamus answered easily. "*Forever*."

"*I don't even know them,*" Ferris whispered. The girl rolled her eyes and went back to her painting.

"Stay up all night looking at porn?" Demos asked the Brit, raising an eyebrow. It was normal for Seamus to fall asleep in class, but it was also normal for him to go to bed at four a.m.

"No, I was playing with my bird."

Demos and Ferris both went silent. After a moment, Ferris slowly asked a question.

"Is that some… British term for…?"

"No. My *cockatiel*," Seamus cut in quickly.

"You don't have a cockatiel," Demos said warily.

"I do so. Dad finally managed to get the proper paperwork to have him shipped over. Crackers was so happy to see me. I hadn't been with him in years."

"Crackers?" Ferris asked, unimpressed.

"Leave off, I named him when I was six years old."

"I didn't know birds lived that long," Demos mused, concentrating on the dimples on a particular orange.

"Cockatiels generally live to be fifteen to twenty years old," Ferris said easily.

"Thanks, Britannica," Demos said, keeping his attention on his painting.

"You two should come see him, he can whistle David Bowie."

"Sure, if you make us tea again."

At lunch Ferris found Seamus and Emily sitting near the back of the cafeteria. He set his paper bag down on the table, wondering what kind of kosher surprise his mother had come up with this time.

"Here you go," Emily said, handing a tray of nachos over to Seamus. He accepted them eagerly, crunching without much grace.

"Thanks, Emmy."

"Hey, don't do that," Ferris said, giving Emily a look.

"What? He was hungry."

"Don't *feed him*. He's like a stray dog, now you'll never get rid of him."

"Hey, don't get on her case just for being nice. You could take a lesson from her in manners," Seamus said sternly, talking and chewing at the same time.

"I'm sure," Ferris said, pulling out a plastic container. Its contents were bright orange. "Oh God, tzimmes. I hate carrots. She *knows* I hate carrots."

"It's why you have thick glasses," Seamus lectured, pointing at him with a nacho. "Carrots help you see."

"Can you even remember the last time you ate a vegetable?"

"Hey, where's Demos?" Emily asked suddenly, looking across the cafeteria.

"Haven't seen him," Ferris said, looking as well. He pushed his chair out, standing to abandon his lunch. "I'll go make sure he didn't get lost or something."

"Grab me a Coke, would you mate?"

Ferris ignored Seamus' request, navigating through the expanse of wooden tables to find the exit. He didn't see Demos in any of the seats — perhaps he was smoking outside. Cool, damp air hit his face as he pushed open a side door. He'd forgotten it was raining.

Demos and Seamus' favorite place to smoke was around the side of the building below a set of bleachers. The seats were situated against a wall so the space below them was conveniently obscured from view. The ground below was always littered with cigarette butts. Ferris came around the corner, craning his head to see if Demos was there. Seeing a figure, he opened his mouth to speak. He stopped, however, when he saw that he was mistaken. There were two figures.

Demos had his back to the wall, furiously kissing the redhead who was pinning him. His arms were passionately wound around the taller boy's neck as they huffed and tugged. Reddening, Ferris immediately turned back behind the wall, safely out of view. His expression blanked. It was difficult to get the image out of his mind. He'd recognized the other boy. Aaron Fisher was another senior at St. Basil's, but he had never seen the two together before. After a minute Ferris bit his lip, making the decision to return to the cafeteria. He only took a few steps before a voice stopped him.

"Get a good look?"

Ferris swallowed, slowly turning to look at Demos. His friend was straightening his tie nonchalantly, giving Ferris a half-lidded look. Aaron had left in the other direction.

Instead of apologizing, Ferris felt an impulsive accusation escape from his mouth.

"You didn't tell me you were dating him."

"Didn't think you'd care."

"You do this a lot?" Ferris asked, his tone still tinged with accusation.

"Sort of. This one's the most serious so far," Demos said, then smiled. "I really like him."

The smile caught Ferris off guard and he dropped the subtle anger.

"Oh."

Ferris didn't know what else to say. He never really thought about Demos' promiscuity or relationships; the Italian was very good at hiding them.

"Do me a favor," Demos asked gently. "Please don't tell Seamus."

"Um, sure."

"He gets jealous," Demos elaborated.

Ferris' head was spinning. He didn't know who dated who, or when, or whether or not he even cared.

"You should tell me this stuff, you know," Ferris blurted before he could stop himself. "We're friends."

Demos considered him for a moment, his eyes thoughtful.

"All right," he finally replied, smiling as rain sprinkled down on his uniform. "I will."

The corner of Ferris' mouth raised slightly, returning the expression.

"Let's get inside, I'm hungry," Demos finished, walking past Ferris with his hands in his pockets. As Ferris followed his friend in, he started to wonder how many relationships Demos had been through before this, or if he could even count them on his fingers.

Ferris frowned at Demos' back. Though nothing had technically gone wrong, the event had left a bad taste in his mouth. He'd always thought that he knew Demos better than anyone, but today it seemed as if he barely knew his friend at all.

38

The Southport zoo was bright that day and the sun was high overhead. Ferris was there alone, walking from one display to another and taking notes. A glare filled the lenses of his glasses and he shielded his eyes with a palm, finding shade through an indoor primate display.

"Aye-aye," he mumbled to himself, scratching words into his notebook. "*Daubentonia madagascariensis.*"

He adjusted his frames, peering closer at the bizarre lemur. The animals were nocturnal, sleeping cozily in the dark display. One was napping near the glass, giving him a close look at its peculiar physique. It had bushy fur and long, gangly fingers. The animal was famous for its extended middle finger, which looked like a frightening, crooked twig. Suddenly, the finger tapped the glass. Ferris blinked as the Aye-aye stared at him, wondering if he'd inadvertently woken it up.

"Hello," he said hesitantly. It leered at him with glowing, round eyes.

"God, you're ugly."

Ferris looked up at the rest of the display, noticing the rest of its family. There was a young lemur clutching its mother sleepily.

"Yet even you can get a girlfriend," Ferris added bitterly.

A shrill, electronic beeping interrupted his self-pity and he looked around in irritation.

"What the hell?"

"Shouldn't you answer that?" came a voice from behind the glass.

Ferris turned sharply, staring at the Aye-are in disbelief. It opened its mouth once more, revealing tiny, beaver-like teeth.

"It's for you," the lemur emphasized plainly. Ferris' mouth opened as he gawked at the talking animal. Then, without warning, he woke up.

Ferris sat up abruptly at his desk. He was in his bedroom. Unfinished science homework lay scattered under his arms and the page of an open book stuck to his elbow – the chapter on lemurs.

'*Of course,*' he thought, with a roll of his eyes. The beeping hadn't stopped. He scrambled awkwardly for his cell phone as it chirped, quickly bringing it to his ear.

"Hello?" he answered, his voice scratchy. His throat was dry from the inadvertent nap.

"Ferris? Are you busy?" came Emily's voice from the other end of the line.

Ferris' eyes drew sideways to the clock on his desk. It was two a.m.

"What? Emmy... do you know what time it is?" he replied groggily, rubbing his hand over his forehead.

"Did I wake you up? I thought you would be studying," Emily said, her voice nervous. "Wait, did you just call me 'Emmy?'"

"What? No. No, of course not. Go to sleep, okay?"

"I... I can't. I'm in a little trouble."

"What's wrong?" he asked, sitting up straight.

"Um, it's a long story. I'm at 98th and Brenton."

"98th and... what? What the hell are you doing there? Who's with you?"

"No one."

The area Emily mentioned happened to be a relatively awful part of town. The most he'd ever done was drive through it on the way to the airport. He wouldn't even consider getting out to ask for directions, not to mention standing alone on a street corner at two in the morning.

"I'm coming to get you. Stay out of sight and put your phone away," he said quickly, grabbing his jacket and heading out the door. His first instinct was to panic a little, but scaring her wasn't exactly his plan.

"Okay," she said quietly, sounding relieved. "Thanks."

Ferris said goodbye and hung up, stuffing the phone into his pocket as he grabbed his father's keys from the hook near the door. He waited, but only for a second. It didn't seem that his parents were awake. In theory, he would be stealing his father's car in the middle of the night, but it was for a good cause. At least, that was what he kept telling himself. He pressed a few numbers on the keypad near the door. The alarm shut down.

The Nissan's engine started with a low rumble and Ferris quickly looked up to see if any house lights had turned on. Thankfully, the noise hadn't woken them up. The car's CD player immediately started up with the engine, loudly playing a song by the Moody Blues.

"Shut up," he mumbled, switching the stereo off. Questions ran through his head as he pulled out onto the street, wondering how Emily could possibly have gotten herself into this situation. His heart started to pound, worried that something might happen to her before he arrived. The car sped up.

He knew he was getting close by the change in atmosphere. Towering high rises gave way to short apartments with chipped paint. Half-empty bottles littered the sidewalks and the closed shop doors were covered in haphazard graffiti. The streets were empty aside from the occasional wandering bum.

The car pulled up along the curb at the designated crossroads. A street light flickered overhead, but Emily wasn't in sight. He waited for a moment, thinking she might approach at the sight of the car. The street remained empty. Getting out to look for her was at the bottom of his 'Things I'd Love to Do,' list, but it didn't seem he had any other choice. His hand paused on the door handle. Maybe he should bring something to defend himself with, just in case. Ferris felt around underneath the driver's seat, hoping to find a crowbar of some sort. There was nothing but a forgotten candy wrapper. He moved to the glove box, trying to remember if his father had a Maglite. He felt beneath the owner's manual, touching over a cold, metallic handle. Suddenly realizing what it was, he withdrew his hand.

He blinked, staring at the gun in his father's glove compartment in slight shock. Sure, Harold dealt with mobsters, but it was paperwork.

Just paperwork, right?

His head started to reel when he remembered there were more pressing concerns at hand. He put the gun in his pocket and stepped out of the car, locking it.

Ferris' eyes darted over the street and the shadows, listening carefully. It wasn't as if he could just start yelling her name. He bit his lip, trying to ignore the nagging feeling that something bad had happened to her.

Down the street, he could hear a glass bottle breaking. The sound made him anxious and he turned the corner with his eyes over his shoulder.

"Ferris!"

He turned, feeling an immediate wash of relief as Emily embraced him.

280

"You're here," she said, keeping her voice low.

"Not for long," Ferris replied quickly, tugging her back towards the car. He kept looking around, not wanting to let his guard down just yet. He obviously wanted to talk to and check on her, but they had to get off the street first. His lungs didn't release his breath until they were inside the car. The doors locked with a heavy click and he started the car, turning to her with a glare.

"What the *hell* are you doing out here? Do you know what could've—"

"It's not my fault," Emily said, rubbing the back of her neck. She tried to look out the window as they drove but Ferris' voice demanded her attention once more.

"What happened?"

"Chris kicked me out of the car."

There were a few seconds of dull silence before Ferris spoke up.

"*What?*"

"We were arguing about something. He just slammed on the brakes and told me to get out."

Ferris found a similar urge to slam on the brakes rising in the back of his mind. He kept himself from snapping, simply gripping the steering wheel harder.

"What the *fuck* is wrong with him? What the *fuck kind of thing* is that to do? Jesus Christ, shit. "

Emily had never heard Ferris speak so angrily before and needed a moment to take it in. His vocabulary lacked variety when he was mad.

"I'm going to kill him," Ferris said in a tone that made it believable.

"It's fine, I deserved it. I said some really awful things to—"

"No, I don't give a shit what you said. You could have been killed out there. It's two in the morning, you don't dump a teenage white girl out on fucking Brenton Street. I don't care how bad your *feelings* are hurt. Son of a bitch."

"You're kind of hot when you're mad," Emily said, catching him off guard. Ferris faltered, reddening at her words.

"Don't tease me," he mumbled.

"I'm not," Emily insisted.

"What were you fighting about, anyway?"

"Just... stuff. It's not important."

Ferris sighed. He wished she would tell him, but it wasn't his business.

"Well... I'm glad you're okay."

Emily gave him a grateful smile which he caught from the corner of his eye. She leaned forward, turning the stereo on at a low volume. By the time 'Nights in White Satin' had finished, they were parked on the corner of her street.

"Thanks for coming to get me."

It was obvious why she couldn't call her father for help. It also was unlikely Demos could sneak out of the house without being questioned by Victor.

"I'll always come and get you," Ferris said without thinking, "if you need me for anything."

Emily was silent, looking down at her hands. After thinking for a while, she looked back at him.

"You know, it's okay if you call me 'Emmy.'"

The door opened and she stepped out, already formulating some excuse to tell her father if she was caught on her way in.

"Goodnight," she said, smiling at him.

"Night," he replied as she shut the door.

The car was stationary for a while. Ferris was staring out the window when he remembered the gun in his pocket. Slowly, he pulled it out, turning it over in his hands. He put it back in the glove compartment, shutting it with a firm click. 'Tuesday Afternoon' had started to play, but he turned the music off. He would need a lot of silence to think on the drive home.

39

A cold autumn morning welcomed Ferris as he stepped outside, adjusting the strap of his school bag. He had stayed up until five a.m. polishing an essay and was feeling immensely weary. Not only was he too weak to walk properly, but being groggy had the tendency to put him in a sour mood. The chilly air did little to wake him up. It was clearly going to be one of those days where he took the subway to school.

His eyes were red behind his glasses as he stared at the card vending machine. This was normally a smooth procedure, but the letters on the screen didn't seem to want to focus. After fussing with the options, he managed to get the machine to spit out a fare card.

It was difficult to get a seat during the morning rush — it was almost difficult to get on the train at all. Ferris stared blankly as he held a pole, trying not to care as a large woman pressed him against it. The man in front of him flapped the folded pages of his newspaper, intently reading an article. At first Ferris' eyes gazed dully at the other side of the paper. After a moment, something on the page itself snapped him into a momentary state of alertness. It appeared to be a photo of his father.

Curious, Ferris knit his brow and leaned in closer. The letters were difficult to read at that distance and the train was rocking its passengers back and forth. A word in article's title caught his eye.

Consigliere.

Being best friends with a young gangster led to Ferris' thorough research of the Italian mafia and its structure. Consigliere was a term given to the family's top advisor. It was a rank given only to deeply trusted men. If Ferris remembered correctly, the rank was voted on. There was no way that Harold, his own father, could possibly...

The doors chimed open and the man with the newspaper left the train, leaving Ferris pining to read the rest of the article. He tried to think of how close his father and Gino were and how much time Harold spent out of the home. Until the moment he found the gun in the glove compartment, Ferris had naively assumed that his father was a simple bookkeeper. How the hell did some newspaper know more about Harold than his own son?

Ferris was so deep in thought that he nearly missed his stop. He scrambled to slip through the doors but was a second too slow. They shut firmly on his schoolbag. He cursed, tugging angrily before finally kicking at the door and stumbling backwards onto the station's platform. He stood in a bewildered stupor as businessmen pushed past him to get to work.

The more he thought about it, the more it fit. The special treatment the Levinsteins always received, the devotion his father had for Gino, and the amount of trust they gave to Ferris himself. Because his father wasn't Italian, Ferris always assumed he had no place in the true rankings of the Giorgetti family.

He found Demos in front of the school. Ferris was eager to ask him about the situation, but it would have to wait. Class would be starting soon.

"Hey," Demos said plainly, putting his hands into his pockets. "You look tired."

"No shit. Where's Emily?"

"Chris was giving her a ride today."

"Oh," Ferris said flatly, turning his head to look away. That was the worst answer he could have possibly received, other than 'she died.'

"Did you hear the good news?" Demos asked, changing the subject with an anticipating smile.

"She's getting married?" Ferris replied bitterly.

"What? No. The world doesn't revolve around your stupid crush."

"Shut up, what's the good news?"

"Nicky's getting made! They announced it this weekend. I've never seen him so happy… he's been dying to hear this for years."

"Why didn't they?" Ferris asked. "He's a good earner."

"The books were closed. He was always secretly pissed about it."

Ferris remembered Nicky's fake interrogation and had no trouble believing that. The man probably didn't even have to act that much.

"Well, that's great. I'm happy for him," Ferris said honestly, though his weariness added an unintentional tinge of sarcasm.

"He's having a little party tonight. You should—" Demos paused, glancing up at something. "Oh, Emily's here."

284

Hesitantly, Ferris looked over his shoulder. Emily was stepping out of Chris' car, giving him a quick kiss on the cheek. Apparently she wasn't mad about being abandoned in the middle of the night. Ferris narrowed his eyes unconsciously. Demos moved to approach the car. Ferris had no desire to go near Chris but followed his friend like a duckling anyhow.

"Hey guys," Emily said, slinging her bag over her shoulder.

"Hey Emmy," Demos replied, giving Chris a glare over her shoulder. It was clear that he wanted to have a few words with the boy, but couldn't do anything of the sort in Emily's presence.

"Have a good day," Chris said warmly, leaning to give her a wave out the window. Chris went to a different high school and still had a bit of a drive before he got there.

"Bye, Chris. Thanks for the ride."

The three turned to go into the school when a voice caught their attention.

"Hey, Ferris."

Ferris looked slowly, wondering what Chris could possibly want with him.

"Yeah?"

"Could you stay a sec? I need to ask you something."

Ferris exchanged glances with Demos and Emily.

"Come on, let's get to class," Demos said to his cousin, taking her by the elbow as they went towards the building. Ferris and Chris were alone.

Chris got out of his car, rounding the bumper before stepping up to Ferris. He was a good looking guy; his active physique and indie-rock haircut made Ferris annoyed and jealous at the same time.

"So, how you doing?" Chris asked nonchalantly, keeping a hand on the hood of his car.

"What do you want?" Ferris asked impatiently, not even remotely in the mood for feigning civility.

"I wanted to thank you for taking Emmy home the other night."

Ferris hadn't expected those words, and blinked.

"Oh, um," he started, unsure of what to say, "right."

"You probably think I'm an asshole, huh?" Chris asked with a laugh.

Ferris' eyes went half-lidded. He supposed that this was an appropriate time to humor the boy and assure him that it was okay.

"Yeah."

Chris' laugh cut short and he cleared his throat, tapping his own chest.

"So," he started, his tone becoming more serious, "you didn't tell anyone about that, did you?"

"No…" Ferris said slowly, starting to see where this was going.

"Good," Chris replied, "Let's keep it that way."

"And why, exactly, should we 'keep it that way?'"

Chris stood up straight, leaving his car and stepping up to Ferris. He seemed even taller up close.

"Look, I'll be frank with you."

Ferris didn't reply, only folding his arms in weak anticipation.

"I know you've got some pubescent hard-on for my girlfriend," Chris continued, "and I'm sure you masturbate furiously to the thought of her every—"

"That's *enough*," Ferris interrupted quickly, reddening in embarrassment.

"Don't even bother, I've seen how you look at her and how she talks about—"

Chris shook his head, stopping his tangent.

"Anyway, just give it a rest, okay? Really, she's not interested. I'm taking good care of her."

"She can take care of herself," Ferris blurted before he could stop himself.

"What was that?" Chris asked, craning his head as if he misheard.

"Nothing. Look, I'm not going to steal your girlfriend. Don't you have your own school to get to?" Ferris said, trying to remain calm despite his pounding heart. He started to wonder how Demos kept his cool so easily.

"Oh, I'm not worried about *that*," Chris said, irritatingly confident. He got back into his car, shutting the door with a slam.

"Remember," Chris said, holding a finger up to his mouth as a reminder to keep quiet.

"Yeah," Ferris said dryly.

"It was nice talking with you."

Ferris' mouth opened to give some kind of witty retort, but the engine rumbled and the car skidded off down the road. His pulse was rocketing in anger and he wished there was something in his hands he could break.

"Fuck you," he said under his breath, though the car was long gone. It was fairly pathetic.

"Ugh, asshole!" Ferris shouted to no one, grabbing his forehead in frustration. He kicked a tree, suddenly wishing he smoked so that he could have a cigarette to feel better. It was then that he noticed that everyone had gone inside for class. He was out front all alone.

"Shit, I'm late!" he griped under his breath as he rushed up to the building.

The other students had just started the morning prayer with the voice on the intercom as he hurried into the classroom. The teacher gave him a disapproving look as he made his way to his desk. He was still fuming from his encounter with Chris, using a mantra to keep himself from snapping a bunch of pencils.

"Our Father, Who art in heaven," the other students said in unison. "Hallowed be Thy Name."

The teacher gave Ferris another look as he sat silently. He reluctantly clasped his hands, mouthing the words as the students continued the prayer.

"*All around the mulberry bush,*" he said silently, glaring up at the chalkboard, "*the monkey chased the weasel...*"

Even faking the prayer was difficult. There were so many things on his mind that he nearly forgot the words to his replacement rhyme.

"And lead us not into temptation, but deliver us from evil," his classmates finished.

"*Pop goes the weasel.*"

They said "Amen" together and the instructor asked them to sit and open their English books to the chapter they had left off on. Ferris couldn't get both the newspaper article and Chris' words out of his head. Apparently Nicky was having some kind of party that night, too. He started to hope there would be alcohol there, a desire that was relatively new to his mind.

Of course, the last thing that Nicky's celebration lacked was booze. Ten hours later, the evening had come. A hired bartender poured and shook drinks with finesse, choosing not to discern between those who were above or below 21 years of age. Gino had graciously offered use of his luxury yacht for the night, an opportunity Nicky was unlikely to pass up. In actuality, Gino loved any chance to show off *La Veloce* and didn't like for her to sit neglected for too long. Most of the guests were on the upper deck where the music and drinks were.

Ferris was standing on the main deck's edge with a glass of white wine, looking out over the city as it went by. It sparkled at night, considerably more beautiful from far away. The party seemed too sumptuous for Nicky Morello, an overweight Italian from New Jersey who couldn't remember to close all of the buttons on his shirt.

"You're missing the fun," Demos said, coming up next to Ferris and leaning on the railing. He raised his glass to his lips, drinking some of the scotch he'd ordered.

Ferris glanced back to the dining area where a song by Louis Prima was playing loudly over the speakers. The sound was muffled from where they were standing, allowing them to focus on the view and the cool night air.

"I would have thought he'd prefer a strip club," Ferris said distantly, "or a pizzeria."

"Probably, but he's having the time of his life."

"He's waited years for this. I hope he doesn't blow it by getting drunk and falling off the boat."

Demos laughed lightly, only because he could picture it happening. They had nearly finished their drinks when two others stepped out down the deck from them. The woman lit a cigarette, talking casually to the rather large man next to her. Ferris recognized the woman as Gina, one of Demos' cousins from Italy. He'd met her briefly on the trip to the summer house the year before. She had the same severe, aloof aura and wasn't exactly the most approachable of people. Even now, at night, she wore a pair of large sunglasses. The man next to her was familiar, but Ferris couldn't remember meeting anyone who was bald.

"Hey, Demos," Ferris asked quietly, "is that...?"

"Benny? Yeah. You didn't hear?" Demos replied, watching the pair as he spoke.

"Hear what?"

"That's one of the reasons they're in the States. Chemo. He's been getting treatment for his stomach cancer."

"Oh... Jesus. I'm sorry," Ferris said in a soft tone, not knowing what else to say.

"It's all right."

288

Ferris hadn't spent a lot of time with Benny but remembered him as being kind and inquisitive. Benny normally had a head full of dark, thick hair. It was gone now, along with his strength and pride. He didn't even appear to be standing straight anymore.

"Let's go say 'hi,'" Demos suggested, turning to approach his cousins as Ferris followed.

"Ah, Demos," Benny said with a smile, giving them his attention. He still had his accent. "And Ferris."

"Buona sera," Demos said, trying not to let his expression soften too much.

"Ciao bello," Gina replied coolly. She cupped her elbow in one hand, leaving the other free to pull the cigarette from her dark red lips. "Come va?"

"Non mi posso lamentare," Demos answered, finishing the last of his drink.

"You don't think... we should speak English? For your friend," Benny cut in gently, nodding towards Ferris. Demos opened his mouth to explain, but Ferris got to it first.

"Sto studiando molto l'italiano," Ferris said quickly, explaining that he'd been studying.

"Che carino," Gina said flatly before giving her cigarette a long suck. Ferris assumed she was being sarcastic, but didn't like being called 'cute' either way.

"Your English is very good," Ferris said, ignoring Gina. "Better than last year."

"Thank you," Benny said, smiling, "...very much. Your Italian is good, too!"

"So, you've moved to the States now?"

"Yes. Papà is helping to run the restaurant. Whole family is here now."

Gina and Benny's father, Roberto, was notoriously powerful back in Italy. Ferris wondered how well he'd fare now that he was in Southport.

"How do you like it?"

"It is... very cold."

Ferris and Benny both laughed, yet Gina remained stoic. It seemed a little ironic to Ferris that Gina was much more intimidating than her gigantic, muscular brother. She also seemed like she'd rather die than continue talking to them.

"Andiamo, Benny," Gina said, taking her brother by the arm and leading him back indoors. She gave Demos one last look but didn't say goodbye.

"Buona serata," Benny said before he disappeared, leaving Demos and Ferris alone on the deck once more.

"Did I say something wrong?" Ferris asked after a moment, giving the entrance a blank look. She had done the exact same thing the last time he spoke with her.

"No. That's just how she is."

"I don't think she likes me."

"Actually, it's me she doesn't like," Demos said, confident in his response.

"How do you figure?" Ferris said, turning to look at Demos curiously.

Demos lifted his chin as he watched the spot where Gina and Benny had disappeared inside.

"She wants in on the business. They won't let her because she's a woman."

"You're probably more of a woman than she is," Ferris teased, leaning back on the deck's railing.

"Precisely. She could theoretically do anything I could, but gets left behind. I might even be made someday and I'm not even a full Italian like she is. Uncle Victor says if I work hard enough they might be willing to overlook my father. That doesn't normally happen. So, she hates me."

"Well," Ferris said, adjusting his glasses as he watched the city go by, "she certainly doesn't have your charisma."

"*Nobody* has my charisma," Demos said without a trace of modesty.

"Well, what do you think? Would you let her in?"

"No. Women just don't get involved in this stuff."

"You never know, you could use that to your advantage. Element of surprise," Ferris said. "This is the year 2001, after all. Women do all kinds of things. They even vote now."

"No shit," Demos laughed, feigning disbelief.

"Maybe if you gave her a job or two, she'd hate you a little less."

"I don't know. I doubt she'd want to take orders from *me*. And, aside from all of that... if she got hurt, her father would kill somebody."

Demos looked down at his empty glass disdainfully.

"I'm going to get another drink. You should mingle."

290

"Wait," Ferris said suddenly, stopping Demos with a hand on his arm. He had been looking for the right opportunity to ask Demos about his father's position.

"Hm?" Demos asked, looking over his shoulder with half-lidded eyes.

"Before you go, I need to ask you something."

"What is it?"

"It's about my dad. I... saw this article in the paper. I wanted to know—"

"Oh, so you did see it," Demos said, his expression unchanged. "You should ask him yourself."

Demos gave Ferris a reassuring smile before heading inside. Ferris stood alone on the deck, wondering how Demos managed to always stay two steps ahead of everything.

He took one last look at the scenery before going inside as well. His senses were immediately overwhelmed by music, chatter, and the smell of alcohol. Nicky was surrounded by a group of other men, all laughing at a joke that Ferris had just missed.

"You know what this room needs," Nicky started, emphasizing with his hands, "is a pool table."

"That's the worst idea I've ever heard," Victor said plainly. "This is a boat."

"But it's such a smooth ride!" Nicky declared, sliding his palm across the air in a straight line. His voice held a tinge of drunkenness to it.

"You flatter me," Gino said, humoring Nicky this once.

"Dad," Ferris said, approaching the men and keeping his eyes on his father. He knew it would be polite to let the men talk, but he was dying to get his question off of his chest.

"Hey, kiddo. Having a good time?" Harold asked.

"Fish," Nicky said, a little louder than necessary. He gestured to a teenage girl on the other side of the room. "Have you met my niece? I think you'd like her."

Nicky winked in a way that only a drunk man could.

"Uh, maybe later," Ferris said with a feigned smile. He turned his attention to his father. "Dad, could I talk to you for a second?"

"Excuse me a moment," Harold said addressing the others. The men gave him a nod before going back to their conversation about how ridiculous a pool table on a boat would be.

They walked to the other side of the room together, standing by a glass wall.

"What's on your mind?" Harold asked, rotating his wrist to clink the ice in his glass.

"Well," Ferris said, starting to wish he'd come up with an outline for this conversation, "I was wondering… I feel like there's something you're keeping from me. I think I'm old enough to know."

Harold looked thoughtful for a moment, as if trying to remember.

"Ah," he said finally, picking up his head. "All right, I'll admit it."

Ferris waited, surprised that it was that easy.

"I did join Mensa, but it was thirty years ago and it was just to impress a girl. Did you find the ring in my desk?"

"What?" Ferris blinked. His voice dropped, disappointed. "N-no, that's not it. I saw this article…"

"I know," Harold smiled. "I'm just giving you a hard time."

"I get enough of that from Demos, Dad."

"True."

"So you know what I'm going to ask?"

"Yes," Harold said wistfully. "I saw the article, too. Did you read the whole thing?"

"Actually, I… I only saw the headline. And your photo," Ferris admitted, slightly embarrassed.

"I see. Well…"

Ferris flattened his mouth, feeling tense at the anticipation.

"It's true. Gino asked me last week."

"Oh," was all that Ferris could manage to say. It felt as if his blood was draining.

"Are you upset, Ferris?"

"No," Ferris said quickly. "No, it's just… it sounds dangerous."

When the words came out of his mouth, Ferris immediately regretted saying them. He sounded like his mother.

"I know what you must be thinking. I thought about it for a long time, too. But Gino and I are very close. I want to be there for him."

Harold paused, giving Ferris some time to let it sink in.

"Has a friend ever needed you?" Harold said, already knowing the answer. "Even if it was dangerous?"

Ferris nodded slowly, immediately thinking of Demos. He hadn't thought of the situation from that point of view. When he considered the lengths he would go to for Demos, his father's decision seemed obvious.

"I wouldn't put you or your mother in harm's way," Harold assured him, putting a hand on Ferris' shoulder.

"I know," Ferris said, looking his father in the eyes. "So, how did the paper know before I did?"

"Lucky guess," Harold shrugged. "Maybe a waiter couldn't keep his mouth shut."

"I see."

"I'm sorry, Ferris. That you didn't hear it from me."

"It's all right... I know I'm still kind of young."

"You're really not. Look at you, you're going to college soon."

"Yeah," Ferris said, having forgotten. He waited, then spoke again. "Hey, Dad?"

"Yes?"

"I'm proud of you." Ferris gave his father a rare smile.

"I think it's my job to be proud of *you*, isn't it?" Harold said, looking a little surprised.

"I've always thought—"

A voice interrupted Ferris from across the room.

"Harry, come on, we're having a toast!"

Harold didn't respond, putting his attention back on Ferris. "What were you saying?"

"It's okay, Dad. Go ahead," Ferris said earnestly.

"All right," Harold said, putting his hand on top of Ferris' head. "Have another drink, kiddo."

Ferris nodded as he watched his father rejoin the men, taking a glass of wine with them for another 'Salute!' Ferris had always wanted to be just like his father, now even more than before. He watched as the men went back to talking, becoming lost in thought. If his father influenced the most powerful man in the city, and his mother controlled his father, then was Ruth the shadow queen of Southport? It was probably a good thing that she wasn't at this party. The men were having such a good time that this would make a much bigger headline than Harold's article. Ferris could imagine it already: *Jersey Gangster Knighted into Giorgetti Ranks.*

Something like that, maybe more dramatic. Ferris was thinking so deeply that Demos was able to step up beside him unnoticed.

"So, how was your talk?"

"Oh," Ferris said, suddenly aware of Demos' presence. "It went well."

"Good."

"Hey," Ferris said, keeping his eyes on Gino and Harold. "You think we'll be that close when we're old?"

"I'm counting on it," Demos said, looking at Ferris with a smirk. Ferris didn't reply, only thinking back to what had happened earlier that night.

It was true. Demos always was two steps ahead.

40

The weather was inviting that day, prompting Demos and Ferris to walk to Ristorante Giorgetti in lieu of the subway. They were passing a basketball court behind a tall chain-link fence, taking it easy to absorb the scenery. Ferris was holding a cherry sucker in his mouth while Demos dangled a yo-yo awkwardly from his finger.

"This thing is impossible. I don't get what's so fun about it," he griped.

"Let me see that."

Demos passed the blue yo-yo over bitterly, wondering what Ferris could possibly do with it. His frown didn't leave as he watched his friend slip the plastic toy down from his palm with ease, tugging it back up with a flick.

"Aren't you the one who's supposed to be good at this kind of thing?" Ferris asked snidely.

"Yo-yos aren't guns. That thing is a kid's toy. Congrats on mastering that, by the way. You should put it on your resume."

Ferris only laughed. Demos was used to being the best at everything and his vanity didn't do well with even the smallest of failures.

"You sound like that one time you lost at Mario Kart," Ferris said, still rolling the toy up and down in the air.

"Emily cheated! She's a girl. Girls can't drive."

"I'll let her know you said that."

"Give me that," Demos snapped, grabbing the yo-yo from Ferris' hand. He stuffed it into his pocket and immediately lit a cigarette. Ferris scoffed.

"All right, princess. You did win it in class, after all."

"I just answered one question right, and it was about Italian history. What about you, genius? I haven't seen you win any useless crap from class contests."

"Yeah..." Ferris said, taking the sucker out of his mouth. "I think I'm losing my touch. I got a 92 on my calculus exam."

"Oh, go cry about it," Demos said, rolling his eyes.

"I'm serious. I usually don't get below a 98."

"What's 76 times 49?"

"3,724," Ferris answered after thinking for just a moment.

"You're fine."

"But calculus isn't multipl—"

"You're *fine*."

"But you don't—"

Ferris was interrupted by a basketball as it rattled noisily off of the chain link fence. He stopped momentarily, startled by the sound. A few elementary school-aged boys jogged up to the stray ball, laughing amongst each other as they continued the game. Demos hadn't blinked an eye, only sucking bitterly on his cigarette as he continued walking. Either he'd either seen it coming from a mile away, or his senses were deadened by his mood.

A few blocks later, they reached the restaurant. They were about to step inside when a voice caught Demos' attention from the side.

"Hey, kid," Sal said sharply. He'd been leaning against the wall under a shadow. "I need to talk to you."

"What do you need, Sal?" Demos asked nonchalantly.

Sal dropped his cigarette to the ground, stubbing it out with his shoe. He jerked his head to the side, motioning for them to go around to the back of the restaurant. When Ferris moved to follow, Sal stopped.

"Not him."

"Then I guess you don't really need to talk to me," Demos said, looking off to the side. Though Ferris didn't really feel a need to be there, he couldn't help but feel pleased.

"Fine, whatever. Bring your boyfriend. Just keep it down," Sal said under his breath, turning the corner of the building.

The alley was lined with boxes and a dumpster, quiet but for a few pigeons on the roof.

"You know Bazzini's?" Sal said, quickly getting to the point.

"The barbershop? Yeah. What about it?"

"They ain't paid up for a month."

"So? You're Sal. Go knock over some tables and yell."

"That's the thing. Vic's been telling me to keep it down lately. Says my temper attracts too much attention," Sal said bitterly.

"So what do you want me to do about it?"

"Well, if you were there he might not mind so much. You know, if it was your idea."

"So *I'm* the one who gets the blame."

"Whatever, sure. You gonna help me or not?"

"Sal," Demos said, giving the older Italian a sweet smile. "I wouldn't miss one of your tantrums for the world."

Bazzini's was located within Little Italy, so the drive over was relatively short. Sal pulled his Cadillac up along the curb a block from the establishment. His '81 Eldorado was easily recognizable and he didn't want to give his victim a running start. Still, the sight of Salvatore Viggiano in the shop's doorway was enough to make the proprietor drop his electric razor. Mr. Bazzini quickly stepped backwards, rushing towards the back room and abandoning his customer in the barber's chair.

"Hey, hey!" Sal snapped, quickly following after him. Demos and Ferris watched from the outside as Sal yanked the man back by the collar of his shirt, dragging him past the entrance and out onto the sidewalk. The customer, hair only half cut, looked over his shoulder in bewilderment. The barber started to beg.

"Come on, Sal, come on. Don't do this, I told—"

Bazzini's body was thrown into a set of garbage cans, sending trash and plastic tumbling down with a crash. He pushed himself up onto his hands, only to be picked up and punched across the cheek. He dropped to the pavement, panting on his back. Down the street a few pedestrians ran the other way.

"Sal... Sally, listen—"

Sal held an empty trash can in mid-air, prepared to break open Bazzini's head.

"Don't call me Sally," he snarled, moving to bring the can down.

"Hold it," Demos said calmly, raising a hand to stop him. Ferris exhaled, not in the mood to see a murder that day.

Sal looked over his shoulder at Demos, glowering. He had no choice but to halt his beating; this was supposed to be Demos' idea this in the first place.

"Mr. Bazzini, is it?" Demos asked, walking around Sal and crouching down next to the barber. The man didn't answer, but Demos let it slide.

"Did your check get lost in the mail?" Demos asked.

"I-I don't pay you guys no more," Bazzini said weakly, spitting up some blood in the process.

"I wasn't aware that was an option."

"Mariani's got my shop now. And I'm gonna tell him about this," the barber coughed.

Demos' expression dropped. The Marianis were one of the other crime families in Southport. Generally, they kept to their territory north of the river. It was rare that they challenged the authority of the Giorgettis, mostly because the Giorgetti family held much greater influence.

"Wrong," Demos said coldly, managing to bring back his smile. "You pay us. I don't care what they promised you. This shop, and every shop on this fucking street, is ours."

Bazzini opened his mouth as if to protest, then noticed that Sal was still holding the trash can.

"F… fine."

"Good," Demos said, patting the man's cheek. He stood up straight, smoothing down the front of his Oxford shirt. He motioned with his head for Sal to set the trash can down.

"Oh, one more thing," Demos added. "Next time a Mariani comes poking around here…"

He raised his hand to the side of his head like an imaginary phone.

"You call us."

The barber nodded quickly, eager for the conversation to be over.

"We'll be back in one week. Have everything you owe us, or move out of the country."

"One week," Bazzini repeated, nodding again.

"Let's go," Demos said, turning to walk away from the mess they'd left. Sal followed, but not before giving the man a swift kick in his stomach for good measure. Ferris watched as the forgotten customer rushed through the door and down the street, leaving a wake of hair clippings. It was a safe assumption that Bazzini wasn't going to finish that haircut anyway. Ferris gave the groaning barber one last look before he put his hands in his pockets, turning to follow Demos. He was bothered — not by the fact that he'd just seen a man nearly killed with a trash can, but that he was now utterly desensitized to it. He hadn't even cringed this time.

Somehow, he didn't see this as a good thing.

41

Under the shadow of the Midtown Bridge lay rows of buildings, gray from the recent rain. Street lights flickered on one by one, rolling in a domino effect down the street. Ferris was, as usual, following Demos towards another dark evening in some smoky room. Near the end of the block sat a walk-up which housed a gambling lounge in its basement. The establishment was by no means young but had only recently come under Giorgetti acquisition.

The two boys went down a set of nondescript stairs to the lowest level of the building. The correct door lay at the end of a long, dim hall. Halfway down, Ferris paused to straighten a doormat with the toe of his shoe. Demos noticed from the corner of his vision, rolling his eyes at the unnecessary fussing.

The silence in the hall was broken the moment the door cracked open. The room was thick with smoke and chatter.

"Is Nicky homeless yet?" Demos asked, sliding into a chair to join a card game. Ferris sat next to him, but only to watch.

"I'll have you know I'm on top tonight," Nicky said defensively. "You sure you wanna play? Your poor piggy bank..."

Demos' "piggy bank" actually consisted of several bank accounts, one of which was overseas in Switzerland.

"I could never break my piggy bank open, Nicky. I did name him after you, you know."

"I'm touched," Nicky mumbled, shuffling the deck easily with thick, calloused fingers. He dealt the cards around the table and Ferris watched each player take their hand. Roberto and Sal were familiar, but several of the players were new faces.

"Ferris," Demos said, looking down at his cards expressionlessly. "Could you get me a drink?"

Ferris paused, his expression inscrutable. After only a second he nodded, pushing his chair back to walk towards the bar.

"Scotch on the rocks," Ferris said plainly to the bartender, who immediately began to prepare the drink.

A minute later the cold glass was set on the poker table with a clink. Demos thanked Ferris without taking his eyes away from the game. Ferris made it a point not to look at his friend's hand. His own expression might give everything away.

"Ma' don," sighed one of the men in relief as he pulled in a pile of chips. "Looks like I can keep the deli after all."

They laughed, but they knew he wasn't joking.

"How's business been, anyhow?" Nicky asked, flicking a blue poker chip with his fingertip.

"To be honest, fuckin' great. Haven't seen a mick around in ages."

Demos' expression dropped and his brow knit in thought. He was quiet for a moment before speaking.

"O'Brien's been so quiet lately…"

"That's a good thing," Nicky grinned. "Gave up after we kicked his ass, right?"

"No," Demos said slowly, still thinking. "It's not like him. It's making me nervous."

"Relax, drink your scotch," Nicky said reassuringly. Demos picked up his drink, eyeing the ice before taking a sip. When the glass left his lips, he sighed. It only took another two hands before it was empty.

"Want another?" Ferris asked bluntly, eyes locked on the glass. Demos hesitated to answer, as if making a realization.

"Oh, ah…"

"It's all right," Ferris said, giving a slight smile as he picked it up.

He was at the bar once more, leaning against the polished wood as he waited for the bartender to find a fresh bottle of scotch. Idly, he listened to the conversations around him. One man was lamenting over a woman who had left him; another had just landed a new job. Victor's voice, however, caught his attention like no other. His back was towards Ferris, but the tone was clearly recognizable.

"They got Parker, too."

"This is the second one in a week," came another, unfamiliar voice.

"This can't be a local guy. No one in Southport is that good," Victor said, his voice low.

"You don't want to know who the rumors pin…"

"The Russian?"

"No," the man said. "Belmont."

Ferris froze, trying to remember why the name was so familiar. It didn't hit him immediately, but his gut still tensed with apprehension. No... of course. Belmont. Killian Belmont.

Demos' father.

He turned his head away from the men, feeling the need to stay undiscovered. The glass appeared in front of him and he quickly took it back towards the poker table. Ferris was glad that nobody was looking at him as he sat back down next to Demos. His expression was troubled.

His first instinct was to tell Demos, anxious from the drama of the moment. It was, after all, big news. The more he thought about it, however, the less he wanted to speak. It was only a rumor. Demos didn't have a wild track record of wanting to talk about his father. He usually changed the subject when Mr. Belmont was brought up and even seemed irritated at the thought of him. Ferris suspected that Demos might be annoyed by the fact that his father was in town. It probably was, most likely, just a rumor.

As Ferris' thoughts mulled heavily in his head, cards continued to flutter across the table. They clicked against the wood as they were shuffled. Roberto snuffed out a cigar in a large glass ashtray.

"Let's see what you have," Nicky said, eyeing the backs of his cards.

"Full house," Demos said coolly, splaying his hand out for the table to see.

The deli owner mumbled something bitterly and Roberto dropped his cards down in frustration. Demos tried not to grin as he pulled in his winnings. Nicky started to consider an age limit at these games. The only thing worse than losing was losing to a teenager.

"You want to jump in?" Roberto asked Ferris, noticing that he looked bored.

Ferris didn't answer immediately, a little surprised that he was being talked to.

"Actually, I have to get going."

"Aw, you sure? If you give me thirty more minutes I can pay for your first year at Yale," Demos offered.

"No, I'm serious, I—" Ferris stopped before explaining that he had an exam in the morning. He was talking to a bunch of gangsters.

"I got shit to do," he finished, looking at the time on his cell phone for good measure.

"Yeah, beat it," Nicky said. "Your bedtime's coming up."

Demos gave Nicky an icy smile, knowing that the older man was simply sick of losing. Nicky looked away, raising his eyebrows innocently.

"All right," Demos gave in. "I'll get you tomorrow."

With that ominous warning, he folded the thick wad of bills into his wallet and left the table. Ferris trailed behind.

"Night, kids!" Nicky called after them, lighting up a fresh cigar.

Ferris' hands were in his pockets as they walked back down the same hallway, eyeing the peeling floral wallpaper.

"So, how much did you win?"

"A few hundred. Want to stop for dinner? My treat," Demos said, pushing open the building's front door.

Ferris opened his mouth to answer when a white light suddenly blinded him. There was a click and a churn before he heard the pounding of footsteps. The moment his eyes adjusted he could see a man running off down the street, a large camera clutched in his hands.

"Hey!" Ferris called, instinctively angry. "Hey, what the fuck!"

Before he could think about it, he was chasing the man. Demos stood blankly on the stoop, watching as his friend rushed off down the sidewalk.

Ferris wasn't an athlete by any means, but he was in much better shape than the middle-aged photographer he was pursuing. He grabbed the man's collar, stopping him against a wall.

"Give me that!" Ferris demanded, holding his hand out for the camera. They were both breathless.

Without speaking, the man offered it, his hands trembling. Ferris snatched it in annoyance, turning the digital screen on to view the images. There was the one of him and Demos at the entrance of the gambling lounge. There were a few more from earlier in the day of Victor and Nicky. He gave the man a brief glance, noticing that he was still afraid. It suddenly hit Ferris that he must have thought he was a mafioso like Demos and Sergio. Might as well take advantage.

"Please, don't have them hurt me, I didn't—"

"Shut up," Ferris snapped, snapping the memory card out and putting it into his own pocket. "What are you, a reporter? The police?"

"Just the *Southport Daily*," the man said sincerely. "Just a little article, I swear. Nothin' bad."

"Are you some kind of idiot? Taking photos of people from two feet away?"

"I... I accidentally left the flash on," the reporter admitted sheepishly. "You weren't supposed to see."

"Well, here's some advice. Stick to writing about the farmer's market. It's a lot *safer*," he said, clenching his teeth at the last word.

"Y-yeah."

"And keep your flash off," Ferris said, tossing the camera back to the reporter.

"You got it," he replied, exhaling.

"Get the fuck out of here."

The command wasn't necessary and only a moment later, he was gone. Demos approached from behind, his shoes making no sound on the sidewalk.

"My hero."

Ferris looked over his shoulder.

"Look what you've turned me into."

"What? You're assertive. I like that," Demos said with a shrug.

"He was terrified of me."

"You did chase him down the street, you know."

Ferris scratched the back of his arm, realizing that Demos was right. He wasn't normally the type of person to run after complete strangers. Something about Demos' presence made him defensive.

"Yeah," Ferris said under his breath.

"You don't have anything to worry about," Demos said, his expression calm. "You know you wouldn't have actually hurt him."

Ferris didn't respond, but he knew Demos was right. It was just an act and it had worked. After a while, he nodded.

"I think you need some sustenance," Demos said, putting his hand around his friend's shoulder. "How about that noodle place we passed?"

"Sure," Ferris said. Demos was very good at changing the subject. "I'm glad that your newfound fortune is going towards a bowl of cheap ramen."

As he spoke, Ferris fingered the memory card in his pocket. He wondered what else was stored on it, and if the reporter was who he claimed to be.

"Well, I'd take you out for lobster but it's not *kosher*," Demos explained, embellishing with his hands.

Ferris' worries and curiosity would have to wait, obviously, until after dinner.

42

As Ferris' senior year progressed, so did the pressure to get accepted to his desired school. While Demos and Seamus were barely picking away at their homework assignments, Ferris had already completed them along with a dozen scholarship essays. After hearing the news that one of Yale's admissions staff would be in town, Ferris extended an invitation to one of his violin recitals. Though his intended major was not music, he had hopes of securing a scholarship through his playing.

Upon hearing of Ferris' plan, Demos immediately asked if he could attend.

"No," Ferris said plainly, scratching behind Stanley's ears as they sat on the couch. "I'll be nervous enough without *you* there, too."

"Since when do I make you nervous? We play together all the time and you never invite me to your recitals."

"I don't know," Ferris said hesitantly.

"If you keep saying no, I'm just going to ask your mother. I know she'd *love* for me to join them."

Ferris looked annoyed, glaring sideways at his friend. At times he wished Demos didn't know him and his family so well.

"All right, fine. If you really want to. You might get bored, though."

"I love listening to you play," Demos admitted. Ferris didn't argue the point; he felt the same way about Demos' piano playing. Stanley rolled onto his back in Ferris' lap, hoping to get his belly rubbed.

"Hi, Stan," Demos said in a slightly higher pitch, leaning in to scratch the pug's exposed stomach. "You're such a cutie, yes you are."

"Please, my Mom does that baby talk enough. He doesn't need you doing it, too."

"But look how much he loves it. Yes, he does. He loves it so much!" Demos smiled, ruffling the dog's head. Stanley responded with his default expression: a big, lopsided grin. Ferris rolled his eyes, handing the pug over to Demos as he got up from the sofa.

"You take him, I've got to get dressed for tonight."

"Are you going to wear a bowtie?" Demos asked hopefully.

"See, this is why I don't want you to come."

Demos didn't respond, only looking at Ferris expectantly.

"Yes," Ferris sighed. "I'm going to wear a bowtie."

"Fantastic," Demos smiled before turning his attention back to the fat dog in his lap. "Who's the cutest, fattest puppy? Yes, it's you. It's you!"

Ferris groaned at the display before trudging up the stairs. He went into his room, shutting the door as he began to prepare for the night. The sweater and shirt he'd worn earlier that afternoon came off, replaced by a spotless white dress shirt. His suit and bowtie were black. He picked a piece of lint from his shoulder in front of the bathroom mirror, turning to make sure there weren't any missed specks. His hair was short, yet he meticulously combed it back anyhow. When he looked up from polishing his glasses, Demos' reflection was behind his in the mirror.

"You look good," Demos said, examining his friend thoroughly. "Wait till Emily gets a load of you."

"Emily?" Ferris said slowly, squinting at Demos in the mirror as he replaced his glasses.

"Oh," Demos said offhandedly, holding up his cell phone. "I invited her."

"You did *what*?"

"She accepted, of course."

"God damn it, Demos. Do you know how much pressure there's going to be on me tonight?"

"What are you worried about? You're going to look *and* sound amazing."

Ferris couldn't continue chastising his friend after such a compliment, falling silent in embarrassment.

"You should ask me first next time," he said under his breath.

"Like you'd have said 'no.'"

"You're damn right I would have said 'no.'"

Emily had planned to join them at the music hall at the start of the event. Unfortunately, the Levinsteins were running a little late. Ferris rushed to the back room with his violin case, leaving Demos to find her on his own.

The concert hall was larger than one normally used for student recitals. Ferris had remained a member of the Youth Symphony Orchestra, and still, for the last several years, held the rank of first chair. It was he and two other students who occasionally had featured recitals and these were held in one of Southport's older auditoriums.

"There you are!" his conductor exclaimed at the sight of Ferris, ushering him backstage hurriedly. "You're late."

"I know, I'm sorry," Ferris said as he was awkwardly led behind the curtain. "Traffic."

"It doesn't matter, as long as you're here. The girls are already in place, go join them."

'The girls' were the conductor's other prize pupils. They often shared performances with Ferris and the three were acknowledged as quite the compatible trio. They greeted him as he sat down next to their seats, rosining his bow and double-checking his violin's sound. Thankfully, it was as well-tuned as it was when he left the house.

Ferris tried not to think about the fact that someone who could decide whether or not he attended his college of choice was sitting in the audience, watching his every move. If he could impress the admissions member, he might greatly raise his chance of acceptance. He swallowed, ignoring the tight feeling in his chest and the slight prickling in his hands. All he could do was his best.

A woman introduced them before the curtain rose. The auditorium was dark but for the stage lights washing over their seats. Ferris always found that these lights obscured his view of the audience. Perhaps, tonight, it was best that way. In unison, the three lifted their bows, then began to play.

The piece was by Vivaldi, set specifically for three violins. Ferris ignored the audience, his heartbeat, and his anxiety. His hand held lightly to the bow, doing the only thing it was meant for at this point in time: playing the violin.

The music was rich and sweet, carrying over the concert hall clearly as the audience listened. Ferris' calloused fingertips pressed from one chord to the other, firmly holding each note as he ran the bow smoothly over the steel strings. Soon, he was so lost in his playing that he simply forgot to be nervous. When the piece ended, only the sound of loud applause brought him back to his senses. He relaxed; it seemed to be going well.

They followed the piece up with Pachelbel's *Canon in D*, as well as a few sonatas, bringing the performance to an end. Ferris felt a wash of relief upon lowering his violin. Unless something happened without his notice, the night had gone relatively trouble-free. Somehow, the desire to find his friends came up in his mind. He wanted to see what they thought.

Before he could leave the stage, however, a voice asked for his attention. He turned to look at the man next to him, who was dressed smartly in a brown suit.

"Mr. Levinstein, I don't believe we've met in person," the man said. "I'm Mr. Yardley, we spoke earlier."

Ferris closed his violin case, shaking the man's offered hand in a slight state of shock. He hadn't expected him to actually come speak to him about the performance.

"Yes, thank you for coming," Ferris said, finally gathering himself and giving the man a polite smile.

"It was my pleasure, honestly. You did a wonderful job tonight."

"...thank you, Mr. Yardley," Ferris said in minor disbelief.

"I'll be sure to tell the board about your performance. I took the chance to review your application."

Yardley paused, lifting his chin in curiosity.

"You're quite sure that you want to apply for Economics and Mathematics? I believe you would do just as well in our music department."

"Oh, ah," Ferris said, caught off guard by the question. It had never even crossed his mind to take up a career in the violin. "Yes, I'm sure. It's been my goal for a long time, Sir."

"I see. Well, I apologize for making this so short, but my time in the city is limited tonight."

"Of course, I understand. Thank you again for attending," Ferris said earnestly.

"Quite welcome," Yardley said, giving Ferris a nod. "It was a pleasure meeting you."

"Yes, likewise."

Ferris watched the man exit the backstage area, standing in a bit of a stupor. This didn't feel right. Nothing in his life ever went this smoothly without some kind of disaster getting in the way. This all seemed too good to be true. Was it possible that his luck had simply turned around?

Still deep in thought, Ferris packed up his things, saying goodbye to the two girls before leaving to find his guests in the entrance hall.

"Ferris, that was great," Demos exclaimed as he approached. He put a hand on Ferris' arm, looking genuinely impressed.

"Thanks," Ferris said, turning to catch sight of Emily. She smiled at him.

"It was beautiful," she said. For a moment she struggled with her words, trying to think of the right way to say what she felt. "It- it really... well, thanks for letting me come."

"Oh, right," Ferris replied, not caring to mention that he didn't 'let her' attend at all. "Thank you."

Her compliment meant even more to him than Yardley's had and Ferris felt his face warm just a bit. Ruth and Harold praised him just as highly, giving their son an affectionate congratulations. Ruth followed it up with an embarrassing kiss on the cheek before Ferris could do anything to stop her. All the while he looked off to the side, anxiously expecting the entire concert hall to burst into flame. This was just too perfect.

"Ruth, Harold!" called a woman down the hall, raising her hand in greeting. Ferris' parents excused themselves to go chat with a friend of the family, a lawyer and his wife who lived down the street.

"Well," Demos said with a sigh, putting his hands into his pockets. "I need a smoke. Why don't you two catch up?"

Demos gave Ferris a brief smile before turning to leave, pushing the glass doors out to the chilly evening air. He hadn't given Ferris much of a choice.

"So," Ferris said slowly, putting his attention back on her. They hadn't had a chance to talk alone for a while. "How have you been?"

"Good. You know, the usual. Art, homework, adolescent despair."

"Sounds lovely."

"And how about you? How are things?"

"Oh, eh. Applications, scholarships, SATs, that sort of thing. It's running me into the ground."

"I can tell," Emily said, watching his eyes. "You look exhausted."

"Do I?"

"Don't work too hard. Please."

"I'll... try," he lied.

"You're lying."

Ferris blinked, then sighed. "Okay. I'll take a day off or something."

"Promise?" Emily asked, holding out her pinky.

"Sure," he replied, hooking her finger with his. Now that he'd made a promise, he was going to have a hell of a time doing nothing productive for 24 hours. This was going to be worse than fasting.

"Maybe I'll help you pass the time," she said, mostly in order to keep an eye on him.

"I'd like that."

"Then it's a date."

'If only,' he thought. 'If only.'

43

It was noon on a cold Wednesday and Ferris' eyes were locked upwards. He tried to see the bright winter sky through the slats of bleachers and cigarette smoke but soon gave up.

"Would you guys hurry up? The tables are all going to fill up," Ferris complained, directing his irritation towards his two friends. If they took any longer getting to lunch, there wouldn't be anywhere to sit.

"And the record for longest eye-roll of all time goes to Mr. Levinstein," Seamus said, ignoring Ferris' request and blowing smoke from his nostrils.

"Fine," Demos said, flicking his smoldering cigarette butt to the damp ground. "Let's go."

Ferris had indeed been right in his worrying, as the last empty table had been occupied by the kids who played Dungeons and Dragons. There were a few empty seats next to some of the wealthier boys, but Ferris wasn't keen on taking them. Demos moved to sit and Ferris reluctantly followed.

The trio's reputation at St. Basil's was a bit complex. Demos' natural charisma automatically made him popular, yet nobody dared to get too close because of the rumors about his family. Seamus was well-liked, if one didn't count the ever-growing pile of angry ex-boyfriends he'd created. Ferris was simply an insufferable pundit who probably would have been better suited with the D&D kids three tables over. Unanimously, however, the girls of St. Basil's all thought Seamus had a great ass.

Many of the boys, specifically the ones who were their new table mates, did not.

"Have you heard the one," started one of the boys, setting the table for a joke, "where a Jew, a Brit, and a wop walk into a bar?"

"Blimey, are we that diverse?" Seamus asked Demos, sounding impressed with himself.

"We're like... the Planeteers," Ferris added. "We need to find a black kid."

The boy who'd started the joke, realizing that it wasn't upsetting them, gave up. The three of them, for some reason, kept the conversation going.

"Sorry Ferris," Demos smiled. "There weren't any Jews on that show. You're off the team."

"How do you know Captain Planet wasn't—"

"Totally not circumcised," Demos said with a wave of his hand.

"Oh, come on. Like you would know that."

"It's not *natural*. He loves *nature*. He has a giant boner for nature."

"Okay, there was a line," Ferris said, looking put-off. "You just crossed it."

"An uncircumcised boner," Seamus added.

Ferris put his palms over his ears, groaning in disgust.

"I'm not hearing this."

"And it's *blue*," Seamus grinned.

"And you wonder why no one wants to sit with us," Ferris said, glancing sideways at the students down the table.

"I'm impressed," Demos said, looking down the table. "A year or two ago you'd have beat the shit out of those boys."

"What're you talking about?" Seamus demanded.

"You were a huge bully, Seamus. Don't tell me you forgot how we met," Ferris said.

"Oh, come off it. Or we can relive that event if you want."

"Let's change the subject," Ferris muttered.

"All right then," Demos said, lacing his fingers. "Current events."

"What, you mean the NATO summit?"

Demos stared blankly at Ferris over the tops of his fingers.

"Uh… no. More like senior prom."

Ferris put his chin in his hand, lacking any sort of excitement. Though prom was many months away, the theme of "Some Enchanted Evening" had been chosen and the students were already making plans.

"I'd rather talk about boners," Ferris mumbled, unimpressed.

"What, you're not going?" Seamus asked, swallowing the last of his sandwich.

"*You* are?"

"Of course we are. I get to wear a tux and take bets on prom queen," Demos said indignantly. "And you are, too."

"No."

"Oh, come on. Why not?"

"It's a pointless display of disposable income and dance skills, both of which I lack."

312

"Oh, it'll be fun. We can get trashed before we go and your date will have a hot dress."

"Like I could get a date," Ferris said, pushing his untouched lunch back into the paper bag as he stood. "I'm going to class."

Demos exchanged a glance with Seamus as their friend left. He clearly wasn't going to class, seeing that it didn't start for another ten minutes. The real reason Ferris didn't want to go to prom had apparently surfaced.

"Um, back in a mo'," Seamus said quickly, pushing his chair out and trailing after Ferris.

The dial on Ferris' locker turned back and forth as he attempted to open it, tugging on the handle and muttering to himself.

"Piece of shit, come on."

The metal door rattled but didn't open. Ferris was tempted to kick it when a voice stopped him.

"Oi, something the matter?"

"Damn thing always sticks," Ferris said under his breath, not looking at Seamus. The Brit twirled the dial a few times, letting it click under his fingers before popping it open.

"There you are," Seamus said with a flourish of his hand.

"Thanks, Fonzie."

"That's not what I meant, though."

"What?"

"You're crabby. I mean, even more so than usual."

When Ferris only shrugged, Seamus took matters into his own hands.

"You know, I could hook you up with plenty of—"

"That's okay," Ferris interrupted.

"No, honestly, I know some girls who'd love to—"

"Really, it's okay."

"Then why don't you ask Emmy?"

"What? No. She has a boyfriend."

"You could go as friends, lots of people do."

Ferris went silent, having a miniature revelation. They could go as friends. He could spend the entire evening with her and she'd be in a dress and…

"Eh?" Seamus pressed, nudging him. "Ask her, then."

"I'll think about it."

The other students started to leave the dining hall to return to class, filling the hallway with motion and chatter. Emily came down the stairs from the second floor, heading towards her

313

locker. She hadn't been with them during lunch in order to work on an art project. There was a dab of missed paint still on her elbow.

"And there she is," Seamus said, hands on Ferris' shoulders. "Go on, then."

Ferris looked down the hall where Emily was, wondering if he should. He watched her take a book from her bag, replacing it with another.

"Okay," he finally said.

"Fantastic, see you later," Seamus said with a pat on Ferris' cheek before disappearing into the crowd. Ferris sighed before making his way over.

"Hey."

"Oh, Ferris. Walk with me," she said, shutting her locker and leading him down the hall. "So what's new?"

"Um, nothing," he mumbled, which wasn't particularly what he'd planned on saying. After a pause, he added another word. "You?"

"Third period is killing me. How the hell can you spit geography facts out like nothing?"

"I played a lot of Carmen Sandiego when I was a kid."

"Well, I played Sim City but I'm no mayor."

"If it makes you feel better, I need your help with my cultural survey essay."

"Oh yeah?" she said, looking a little smug.

"Yeah. I've only been to like three countries, and Canada doesn't count."

"Too busy to travel, huh?"

"I… guess. But I want to." He hesitated, then continued. "I wanted to ask you something else, if you've got a minute."

"Sure," she said, stopping by the door of her class. "What is it?"

"Well, everyone's talking about, you know, prom."

"Yeah. I didn't take you for the type to care."

"I don't. Well, I do. Kind of. I mean, I'd care if you went with me."

Emily suddenly looked uncomfortable.

"Are you asking me to go with you?"

"Yeah," Ferris said, trailing off. Her expression wasn't promising.

"But," he added quickly, "just as friends. That's it. Just for fun, you know?"

314

To his surprise, her expression didn't change. She stared away from him, biting her thumbnail.

"Ferris... you know I can't."

"But it wouldn't mean anything," he emphasized, starting to lose his nerve. "There's no reason we can't just—"

"Yes there is," she said bluntly. "He'd get jealous. You know what he's like."

"But he doesn't even go to our school," Ferris said, slowly feeling self-conscious for pressing so much.

"Ferris, I can't, okay?"

He kept his eyes on her and it gradually sunk in. If he pushed it any further he'd only be embarrassing himself. He hadn't imagined that she would say 'no.' It seemed as if they were close enough by now that something like this would be okay. Apparently, things were different.

"All right," he finally replied. "Sorry."

"It's fine."

Ferris wished that his face didn't feel so heated. He couldn't remember the last time he'd felt this awkward.

"Well, I better get to class," she said, opening the door.

"Yeah. See you."

The door shut behind her. He was stunned as he walked back towards his locker. All he could focus on was the regret swimming around in his head.

"So, how'd it go?" Seamus asked, leaning against one of the lockers. He'd been waiting.

"Thanks for the *advice*," Ferris snapped, walking past him without slowing down. Seamus stared after him, a bit bowled over.

"It wasn't on purpose," he insisted, raising his voice as Ferris turned the corner. Seamus sighed, now in the hallway by himself.

"...Honest."

Ferris hardly paid attention in his next few classes. He was disillusioned, unconsciously staring out the window in lieu of the teacher. By the last class of the day he was drawing circles in his notebook, wearing down the lead of his pencil with endless loops. It was impossible to concentrate.

Prom. What a stupid idea. Just a bunch of debutante formalities and bad music. It was a good thing she'd said no, or he might have spent an entire night embarrassing himself.

315

When the classroom door creaked open, he didn't look up. The visitor didn't catch his attention, in fact, until she said his name.

"Ferris Levinstein? You're being called to the office," said a woman with her hair in a tight bun.

He picked his head up, staring at her for a moment. There were a few 'ooo's' from the other students, as they usually murmured when someone was in trouble. Silently, he pushed his notebook into his bag and left the room.

He wasn't normally the type to be called to the principal's. One time they wanted to congratulate him on a high statewide test score – perhaps he'd done well on an exam. He followed the office woman as her heels clicked on the floor. The wooden door had a glass window that read "Principal." He turned the knob, opening it to reveal the head of the school at her desk. She was a stern-faced nun with a habit. The Asian man seated near her desk, however, wasn't familiar.

He was sitting with one leg crossed over the other, holding a cup of tea as he chatted with the principal. His brown coat was long and unbuttoned to reveal his dress shirt and tie.

"Ferris," he said, setting his cup down to stand. "Pleasure to finally meet you."

Ferris shook the offered hand, his expression blank. He had no idea who this man was.

"You know me?" Ferris asked slowly.

"Oh, I know all about you."

The man's next words made Ferris' heart skip a beat.

"Detective Lee, Southport Police Department," he said, flashing a police badge. "I have a few questions for you, if you've got a minute."

"Do you need anything before we start? Some water?" the detective asked, now sitting on top of the desk. He had asked Ferris if he'd prefer the principal to stay in the room, but the last thing Ferris wanted was a nun glaring at him while he got interrogated by a cop.

"No thanks," Ferris said warily, feeling that everything he said was being recorded and analyzed. He was sitting in the chair across from the desk, one normally used for the parents of misbehaving teenagers.

"Can I call my parents?" Ferris asked suddenly, desperately needing some advice from his father.

"That won't be necessary — you haven't been arrested. We'll be finished before your class is over, don't worry," the detective said as he finished his tea.

Ferris held back a sigh. He was starting to wish he knew less about math and more about law. This didn't feel right.

"So, Ferris. Do you have any idea why you're here?"

"I was only a Communist for like, a week. It was a phase I went through," Ferris said, monotone.

"Try again," Lee said, not smiling.

"Pen I stole from the bank?"

"Think bigger. Not necessarily something that *you* did."

"Do I win something if I guess right?" he said, his voice still vacant.

"I'll let you go back to class."

"I give up," Ferris said. "Why am I here?"

Lee flattened his mouth, studying Ferris. Ferris looked back, doing his best to keep a blank face. In actuality, he was astoundingly nervous. He watched the detective, taking note of his large, square glasses and slicked back hair. A few strands were loose over his forehead. He was thin and looked like the type of man who was stressed all the time.

"Do you know anything about the mafia?" Lee finally asked.

"Sort of."

"Do you know any gangsters? Do you think you could list some names?"

"Well, there's Michael Corleone and his family. I'm not sure if Tony Montana counts since he was from Cuba. Do you mean mafia like, the Italian one, or just crime lords?"

"Cute," Lee replied curtly. The corner of his mouth bent to a brief smile.

Ferris looked back as if he had no idea what Lee was talking about.

"I know you're trying to protect your friends," the detective said, "but there's no use playing dumb. We've been watching you for a year now. You gave my cameraman quite a scare."

Ferris remained still but felt a bead of sweat run down the back of his neck. The room felt hotter. No wonder the rest of that memory card had been full of photos of prostitutes and drug dealers.

When Ferris didn't answer, Lee elaborated.

"You may have noticed a black car or two."

Ferris averted his eyes. The playing field was uneven now. He had no idea exactly how much this man knew. He also noticed that the detective was taking notes.

"I find it hard to believe that you've spent a good five years of your life with infamous criminals without knowing about it."

A newspaper was slapped down on the table in front of Ferris' seat.

"You do recognize this boy, right?"

Slowly, Ferris looked down at the paper. There was an article about mob activity with a candid photo of Demos and Victor. He remembered the article — it was the one Demos had complained about because his hair looked bad in the picture.

"Yes." There was no use in lying about that.

"Has he ever done anything... illegal, Ferris?"

Ferris' skin prickled. He had several options here. First, he could lie. This seemed like the obvious choice, but if this ever went to court he could be imprisoned for false information. He could also plead the fifth and refuse to answer. This option, however, was as good as saying 'Yes.'

"I don't know," Ferris said slowly.

"I see."

Lee stood up, walking to the side in thought.

"Ferris," he finally said. "Do you have any idea how your father became so close to the Giorgetti family?"

For once, Ferris had no idea what the answer was.

"No," he replied honestly. If this detective knew and Ferris didn't, it would be pretty annoying.

"He had a best friend at Yale. Jack Frischman, a law student."

None of this was familiar to Ferris. He tried not to look too interested.

"Frischman graduated with honors and was a working defense attorney in record time. He was legendary. Frischman was... also the family lawyer for the Giorgettis. He introduced your father."

Ferris looked down at the table, wondering why he'd never been told any of this before.

"You're probably wondering why Dad didn't tell you this story," Lee said quickly, catching onto Ferris' expression. Ferris didn't respond.

"Frischman's wife was killed in a mob war. The police offered him and his son protection if he'd testify as a witness. He refused, of course. Very noble."

Ferris had a feeling this story wasn't going to end on a 'very noble' note.

"But since he'd spoken to the cops, the Giorgettis assumed he'd snitched. His body was found with a rat stuffed into his mouth. His son was dumped into the Midtown river a few days later. He hadn't really done anything wrong."

"Well," Lee continued with a shrug. "I mean, other than dealing with the mob."

Ferris looked to the side.

"You might think this is glamorous and fun right now. I mean, you *are* a teenager. The guns and danger probably appeal to you. Maybe you're getting money."

Lee put his hands flat on the table, leaning in closer.

"It's not worth it. Trust me."

Ferris remained silent.

"Think about it. You want to go to college, get a job, maybe have a family? Do you really want this life? Because I promise you, your loved ones *will* die."

"Is that a threat?" Ferris said defensively.

"Of course not, Ferris. It's a warning. We can take care of you if you help us."

"What, exactly, do you want me to do?"

Lee pulled up his briefcase, opening it with a couple of clicks. He pulled out a large photo print which depicted a bulletin board. Pinned on the board were dozens of black and white photos, indicating a criminal hierarchy. Gino, of course, was at the top of the pyramid. Below were Victor, Nicky, Sal, and many others. Ferris could even see his own father pinned up near Gino's portrait. A few of the pictures were in the wrong place. Ferris compulsively wanted to correct them, but he knew that was exactly what Lee wanted him to do.

This was all wrong. Demos had always insisted that they had the chief of police in their pocket. Why was such a thorough investigation on the Giorgettis being allowed?

"Does this make any sense to you?" Lee inquired.

Ferris stared at it, not answering. His eyes locked on a photo of Demos.

"I promise you, we'll make sure your entire family is safe. We won't indict your father."

Demos' photo had been taken from the side. The boy was looking at someone in front of him, biting a cigarette. There was confetti in the background. Ferris remembered that day — they'd gone to the Chinese New Year parade downtown. It would have been easy to take a few snapshots with the crowd and the noise. They'd both eaten too many Chinese sweets and had gotten stomachaches.

"Well?" Lee asked.

Ferris put his attention back on Lee, his eyes empty, but dark.

"I don't know any gangsters," he said flatly.

After a bit of silence, the detective nodded. He slipped the print back into his briefcase and shut it.

"You can go back to class now," Lee said bluntly, removing his glasses to clean them. Awkwardly, Ferris stood. Before he reached the door, Lee passed him a business card.

"If you change your mind."

As he walked back towards his class, Ferris' head was spinning. Was that all it took? It seemed too easy. There had to be more to it than that. Ferris looked down at the business card in his hand. There was an official seal next to some text. Southport Police Department, Seong-min Lee, Detective.

Once outside the office, he crumpled the card in his hand and tossed it into a hallway trashcan.

Half a mile from the school, at the 21st Precinct station, Lee was looking over the notes he'd written from their conversation. Behind him, an irritated voice snapped him to attention.

"You better not have done what I *think* you just did." The section chief, a woman in a severe business suit, was standing with her arms folded.

"Depends on how well you're thinking today," Lee said casually, cracking open a can of Diet Coke.

"I should report you to Blakely. You know damn well he shut down the Giorgetti case. *Indefinitely*."

"What he doesn't know won't hurt him."

"Jesus Christ, Lee. Just because your wife left you for a Kkangpae—"

"They didn't steal my wife," he said, annoyed. "She was one of them. And thanks for bringing that happy memory up, I appreciate it."

"You clearly have some kind of gangster vendetta and I'm not going to tolerate it. You want your department shut down?"

"No," he said, his voice tired.

"Why don't you go after the Marianis instead?"

"They're ants compared to the Giorgettis," Lee protested.

"Perfect. You can get your revenge on mobsters while staying in a nice, safe little playing field. Everyone's happy."

"I'm not going to compromise my—"

"Lee, stop. This isn't about being a hero. This is about keeping your job."

The detective gave a very slight nod, not looking her in the eyes. The chief sighed.

"Good, glad we had this talk," she said, her tone only a little dry.

"By the way," she added, looking at her watch, "isn't your daughter out of school now?"

Lee sat up abruptly in his seat, panicking.

"Suki! I forgot!" he said, scrambling to get his keys. "*Shibal*, I'm an idiot!"

"Way to stay on top of things."

"She's going to be so mad at me."

"Lee, she's five years old."

"She hits hard!" he insisted, grabbing a stack of folders and rushing past her.

"You forgot your—"

The chief sighed, giving up. He was already gone. She looked at the badge he'd left on his desk among scattered paperwork, wondering how he ever got anything done. He forgot a lot of things; she was quite sure that he would conveniently forget their conversation as well.

The atmosphere at the Levinstein home wasn't much better.

"Oh, you're home. Dinner's almost ready," Harold said, looking up from his paper.

"Dad," Ferris said, his voice weak. "I need to talk to you."

44

Harold's office was set near the back of the home on the second floor. Its décor was dark and sophisticated, consisting of walnut bookshelves and leather wingback chairs. Harold was seated in one, watching his son carefully as he recounted what happened in the principal's office.

"And then he pulled out this photo of a big bulletin board with everyone's pictures tacked up like a family tree. And… and you were on there."

Harold only nodded, waiting for Ferris to continue.

"I think he wanted me to fill in the blanks, but I didn't say anything. I swear, Dad."

"I know you didn't. It's okay."

"Is it true? What he said about your friend in college."

"Some of it," Harold said. His voice was calm but held a tinge of anxiety.

"Did they kill him?"

"Yes. But—"

Ferris knit his eyebrows, wishing he'd heard otherwise.

"Jack did cooperate with the police," he said sadly. "It got several men arrested."

"What about his son? Did he do anything?"

"No. He didn't do anything."

They were both quiet for a moment, then Ferris spoke.

"But they killed him, too."

"Yes."

Ferris looked down at his hands.

"Ferris, have you told anyone else about this?"

"No, just you."

"I think we should wait before telling them. To be on the safe side."

"But… they trust me," Ferris said defensively, looking up at his father.

"Of course they do. But," Harold raised his eyes to a wall of books, thinking, "they trusted Jack, too."

"What if they find out from someone else? Then they'll definitely think I gave out information."

Harold didn't answer immediately, mulling over the idea for a while.

"You really want to tell them, Ferris?"

"I think they should know that someone's after them. I can tell Demos, see what he thinks."

Harold seemed to relax at the idea of just telling Demos, nodding slowly.

"All right. Tell him first and do what he says."

Ferris nodded, keeping his eyes down. He always felt like the Giorgettis were his second family and that he could trust them with his life. Now, however, something uncomfortable was creeping up the back of his throat. It made his palms prickle. He wanted to deny it, but it was unavoidable.

There was fear.

"Was Jack really your best friend?" Ferris asked slowly.

"Yes." Harold stood up. His eyes were hidden by a glare on his glasses. "He was."

It didn't seem like his father wanted to talk about it and Ferris didn't press any further. Their thoughts were both cut short by a yell from the kitchen. Ruth was nearly ready to throw their cold, abandoned dinner in the trash.

Ferris waited until school was over before speaking to Demos. As they waited by the front door of the Sparrow Diner for Demos to finish his cigarette, Ferris tensely pushed his hands into his pockets. He looked up and down the street, clearly antsy.

"Hold on," Demos said, taking his sweet time finishing his cigarette.

"It's... important," Ferris emphasized, narrowing his eyes.

Demos shook his head very slightly before glancing sideways. He was looking at a pair of men on the curb. Ferris held his tongue, trying his best not to sigh in frustration. Finally, the men left.

"All right, go on."

"It was just a couple of guys, they probably couldn't even hear us," Ferris griped.

Demos only shut his eyes, slowly shaking his head once more.

"They were plain-clothes cops."

"What?" Ferris blinked.

"Didn't you see the way they were standing? Feet spread apart, arms folded. Back so straight you could swear there was a rod up their ass."

"That's what I wanted to talk to you about," Ferris said slowly. Demos only raised an eyebrow. "They've been following you. Someone's on your case."

"I know."

Ferris stared at Demos, not sure if he heard him correctly.

"The black cars, the photographer, the stalker-cops who can't act casual to save their lives," Demos elaborated.

"You knew, this whole time?"

"Of course."

Ferris narrowed his eyes.

"But do you know *who*?"

"From that cute, irritated look on your face, I'd say you're going to tell me."

Ferris glared harder.

"No wonder everyone wants to kill you," Ferris muttered.

"Are you going to tell me or not?"

"A detective pulled me out of class for questioning."

Demos' smug expression dropped, replaced by a calm frown.

"What does he know?"

Ferris continued, glad he was finally being taken seriously.

"It's hard to say. Their hierarchy chart wasn't accurate, but he knew a lot about your guys' past. I thought Blakely was supposed to—"

"He *is* supposed to keep anyone from investigating us. This guy must be going under his nose. Did you get his business card?"

"Um... I threw it away," Ferris said sheepishly.

Demos glared at him.

"I was emotional, give me a break."

"Did you at least get his name?"

"Yes. It said Seong-min Lee."

"He'll be easy to find," Demos said, starting to walk down the street. He pulled his cell phone from a pocket, punching in a phone number with his thumb.

"Find? What are you doing?"

"Nothing," Demos said casually, holding the phone up to his ear. He waited a moment. "Hey, Nicky? You near a phone book? Well get near one. Yeah, I'll wait."

Demos tapped his foot a few times, looking up at a sign.

"Lee, Seong-min. Seong... min. I don't know. S-U-N-G? No? S-O-N-G?"

Ferris watched as Demos finally managed to get the name right, feeling uncomfortable. Finding out where this man lived couldn't mean anything good. Demos shut his phone with a snap, putting it back into his pocket.

"I need the car, we're going home," Demos said curtly, walking straight through the other pedestrians on the sidewalk. Ferris picked up his feet, rushing to follow.

"Oh..." Demos said suddenly, slowing down.

"What?"

"Did you tell anyone else about this?" he asked, looking Ferris straight in the eyes.

"Just Dad."

"Good."

Demos resumed his pace, dropping the subject. Ferris swallowed.

It didn't take them long to get to the house. Ferris stood back as Demos loaded a suspicious paper bag into his Alfa Romeo.

"Please tell me that's a packed lunch."

"Just trust me," Demos said. "Get in, you're driving."

"Of course," Ferris said with a roll of his eyes, opening the car door and getting in.

The home of Detective Lee was nowhere near their familiar neighborhoods. They crossed the river, driving north until they nearly passed Southport University. The street was average — not quite poor, but nothing like the multimillion-dollar brownstone that the Levinsteins owned. Ferris started wondering if detectives made less money than he thought. It was a little ironic that a man who devoted his life to doing the right thing was rewarded with a third story walk-up with chipped paint on the stoop. At the same time, the Giorgettis owned a gated manor, a summer house, and two yachts.

For some reason, they had been waiting by the curb for twenty minutes.

"Awesome. We accomplished a whole lot of nothing and wasted a tank of gas. Time to go home," Ferris said, reaching to start the car.

"Hold it," Demos said, putting out his hand. His window was facing the apartment that matched Lee's address and he was carefully watching the street.

"This is pointless. We don't know his schedule. He might not even live here anymore." Ferris sighed. "What are you trying to accomplish?"

"I'm casing the place."

"Okay," Ferris said, his tone deadpan. "You're going to rob him?"

"Hey, what did you say he looked like again?"

"Um, Asian guy. Shorter than me, but taller than you."

"Big glasses?"

"Yeah."

"Brown coat?"

"Yeah, but I never told—"

Ferris paused, leaning over. He adjusted his glasses, trying to see out of Demos' window. Sure enough, the detective was walking down the sidewalk towards the apartment. He was holding a little girl's hand.

"Patience is a virtue," Demos said.

"I'm going to kill you," Ferris muttered.

"Okay, later," Demos said, cracking the tinted window and rustling through the paper bag. He pulled out a small pistol with a silencer on the end. Ferris' eyes widened and he immediately put his hand out, taking hold of the gun's barrel.

"Don't you dare," he said, glaring.

"Ferris, let go."

"No."

"We need to nip this issue at the bud," Demos said, his voice eerily calm.

"I thought you weren't supposed to kill cops."

"And I thought Blakely had us covered. Looks like nobody wants to follow the rules."

Ferris looked back out the window, watching as the little girl reached up, asking to be carried. The detective leaned down, hefting her up in his arms. He looked tired, but happy.

"He has a daughter," Ferris said, not letting go of the gun.

"I'm not going to hit her," Demos assured him.

"I can't believe you sometimes. He's just doing his job."

Demos jerked the gun away, giving Ferris a cold stare before aiming back out the window.

"And I'm just doing mine."

The gun cocked and Ferris hardened his voice.

"Demos, stop."

At first there was no answer. Demos kept his aim on Lee's movement. He watched as the detective pulled out a set of keys, keeping the girl up with one arm and fumbling with the lock with the other.

"*Stop.*"

It was silent for a moment, then the gun lowered.

"If I get arrested because of him—"

"You'll be fine," Ferris said, relieved. "We'll figure out another way to take care of this."

Demos turned his head, watching Ferris unsurely.

"I promise," Ferris added.

Demos nodded silently, putting the gun back into the bag. Ferris sighed, then started the car. He had absolutely no idea how they would get out of this situation. Hoping it would just "blow over" probably wasn't a viable course of action anymore. Demos noticed Ferris' discomfort and said the one thing that could possibly make it worse.

"I trust you."

No pressure.

Ferris didn't answer, giving Demos a brief glance before turning back to the road. He had no doubt this would keep him up all night.

A week had passed and Ferris still hadn't come up with a sensible way of solving the problem of Detective Lee. His lack of sleep showed clearly in his face. Eyes half-lidded, he attempted to concentrate on what the teacher was saying at the head of the class.

"And let's say that behind these three doors there are three options. Behind one door is a first edition, autographed copy of Euclid's Elements. The other two have cars or something."

"Can we pick a car?" one of the students cut in, drawing up a few titters of laughter from the class. Ferris started to allow himself to get lost in probability and numbers, pushing his more unpleasant thoughts to the back of his mind.

"Yes, very amusing," the teacher said, though clearly not amused. "Anyway… after you choose one door, the game show host removes one of the two remaining doors that doesn't have the book. You have the option of switching doors. Thoughts?"

"It doesn't matter, the odds are still the same," answered a boy sitting next to Ferris.

"Anyone else?"

"Actually…" Ferris said, as expected. The instructor looked at him expectantly.

"Mathematically, there's a 2/3 chance of winning if you switch doors."

"Care to explain?"

"Well… you start with a 1/3 chance of choosing the correct door. When one door is removed, the entire 2/3 probability is left to the remaining door."

The teacher sighed.

"Yes, very good. That was going to be my lecture this afternoon."

"Then can we go early?" one of the students asked.

"No."

There were a few collective groans.

"Why don't you all test this problem out by doing a tree of possible outcomes? Pair up."

Though Ferris wasn't popular, he never had any trouble finding a partner for class activities. He normally just did all of the work himself and being teamed up with him meant an easy A. Almost immediately, a girl slid her chair up next to his.

"Hey, Ferris."

He was relieved to see her. Beth was one of the smarter students in the class, meaning he wouldn't be stuck doing the work himself. She was also one of the few black students in the entire school. St. Basil's was famous for many things, but diversity wasn't one of them.

"So, how's it feel being a know-it-all?" she asked with a smile.

"Oh, like you didn't know the answer," Ferris said, rolling his eyes. "You just kept your mouth shut to save face."

"Maybe," she said, writing the problem in her notebook.

They both started to write, though Ferris' thoughts kept wandering to every horrible thing that was currently plaguing his life. Beth's hushed voice brought him back to the moment.

"Hey, you've heard about prom, right?"

"Hasn't everyone?" he whispered back.

"Well, I was wondering…"

Beth bit her lip and Ferris could have sworn that she looked suddenly shy. Was she going to ask him to go with her? The thought of going with someone else hadn't even crossed his mind. Well, she was cute and all...

"Do you know if Seamus has a date yet?"

Ferris was quiet for a second.

"Um, I don't know," he said, going back to his work. The pencil scratched over the paper in his notebook as he wrote. "You should ask him yourself."

"Oh, all right."

Ferris nearly snapped 'I'm not his secretary,' but had just enough tact to keep his mouth shut. He bitterly thought back to when Seamus offered to hook him up with someone. Apparently the Brit was so devastatingly charming that he had girls to spare. Of course.

Finally, the bell rang.

Once in a while Ferris would take Stanley to a small dog park after school. The fat pug needed all the exercise he could get. Demos would bring his own dogs as well — two greyhounds that he'd recently adopted. He'd kept their racings names: Public Enemy and King Tut. This time Seamus tagged along for no reason other than to play with dogs for free.

Stanley wiggled in Ferris' arms as they went through the short gate leading to the dog run. It was hard not to constantly look around for cops. He carefully set the dog down, unhooking the leash and letting him go. A herd of small dogs immediately rushed up to smell the newcomer. The pug tumbled off to play with a walleyed grin.

Ferris sat down on a bench to watch, slouching with a brief sigh. Demos sat next to him, crossing one leg over the other.

"You think I can smoke here? There aren't any signs."

"I wouldn't," Ferris said, looking over at the potentially crotchety old women with Pomeranians.

The greyhounds pranced around elegantly while Stanley, in contrast, rolled around in the gravel with a black pug. Seamus, who was sitting next to Demos, had become friends with a Shih Tzu. The dog crawled over his lap, licking his face. Seamus was delighted.

"I've never seen that other pug before..." Ferris said, wondering who it belonged to.

"Hey, what do you think?" Seamus asked, nudging Ferris with his elbow. He was looking across the way at a girl with a Chihuahua.

"Um, I don't know. It looks kind of like a big rat."

"The girl, fool."

"Oh," Ferris said, shifting his attention. He squinted. "She's wearing sweatpants with 'Brat' written across the ass."

328

"And?"

"Yeah, right. You know, when girls draw all that attention to their ass, it's like when a chimpanzee is in estrous and her rear turns bright pink to attract—"

"That's enough of that," Demos said, disgusted. "No one wants to hear about monkey sex, and you—"

"Chimps aren't monkeys, they're apes," Ferris said, cutting Demos off. He almost sounded offended at the mistake.

"Big fucking difference."

"There's a huge—"

"Excuse me, is that your pug?" a voice cut in, stopping their argument.

"Um, yeah," Ferris said, looking up. The voice belonged to a teenage girl with glasses.

"Oh, he's cute. It looks like Gertie has a new best friend."

"The black pug is yours?" he asked. Seamus nudged him. Ferris didn't divert his attention, simply kicking Seamus in the heel to get him to stop.

"Yeah," she said. "They're being such snobs... ignoring the other dogs to play with another pug."

They both laughed lightly. Ferris waited for her to chastise him for having an overweight dog, but it didn't come. Normally the other dog park regulars were outrageously snooty when it came to dog care.

"Are you new? I haven't seen you before," he said, making conversation.

"Yeah, I used to go to Foley Park but it got too crowded."

"That's kind of far..."

"I don't mind the walk. Oh, what you said earlier about chimpanzees..."

"Oh, uh," Ferris said, nearly reddening, "you heard that?"

"Yeah, I think the same thing sometimes. And that sports are kind of just like... chimp dominance displays."

"Making noise and knocking sticks around to show the other guys that you're the best?"

"Yeah," she grinned, offering her palm. "I'm Sue."

Ferris shook her hand politely.

"Ferris."

"Nice meeting you," she smiled, heading back towards her dog. Once she was gone, Seamus leaned in obnoxiously.

"Hot, yeah?"

"Cut it out."

"You like her, I can tell. She's smart. You're in *love*."

"Shut up, Seamus," Ferris sighed. "Why don't you go ask Chihuahua girl for her number?"

"Why don't you ask *Sue* for *her* number?"

"Oh, please."

"For God's sake, Ferris," Demos said, butting into the conversation. "For once I'd like to see you do something other than mope around when it comes to girls."

"I don't '*mope around*,'" Ferris insisted.

"Fine, prove it."

"Fine!"

"*Fine*."

Ferris stood up, glaring at his friends for a moment before walking over to the new girl.

"So," he said, walking up next to her, "you usually here after school?"

"I'd like to be, but I've been studying like crazy the last few weeks for midterms."

She studied? That was promising.

"Well, maybe we could study together. It might go faster."

"Oh?"

"Yeah. Want me to give you a call sometime?"

She stood still for a moment, examining him thoughtfully. A second later, she pulled out an old receipt and clicked a pen, writing briefly on the back.

"Here."

Ferris couldn't believe that had actually worked. He was already dying to say something along the lines of 'Ha! In your face!' to Demos, but he had to finish the conversation. His eyes glanced down at the receipt, attempting to memorize the number: *314-159-2653*

"Thanks, I'll—"

Ferris stopped, reading the number more carefully. After a second, he looked back up at her, raising an eyebrow.

"Nice," he said bluntly, passing the paper back. He wasn't very amused.

"What?"

"That's not your number. That's Pi."

She was quiet before a slight smile crept over her features.

"Congrats. You passed my idiot test," Sue said, writing on the receipt once more. "Here, this is my real—"

"That's all right," he said, holding up a hand. His expression hadn't changed. "I don't really need more testing in my life."

"Oh..."

"Maybe next time."

"Sure," Sue said, taken aback. She managed a little smile. "See you around."

Ferris knelt down to pick up Stanley, carrying the pug back to the bench where his friends were. He started to dig around in his bag for the leash when Demos put a hand on his arm.

"Holy shit."

"That was amazing," Seamus added.

"I can't believe you did that."

Ferris stared at them.

"What?"

"You just completely rejected that hot girl," Demos explained.

"Denied."

"Did you see her face?"

"What are you talking about?" Ferris asked, clipping the leash onto Stanley's collar. "I said 'maybe next time.'"

"I never knew you could be such a fantastic asshole," Seamus said, hooking his arm around Ferris' neck. "I'll leave you alone about girls from now on. Promise."

"Yeah, right. You'll start again in three hours."

"Four," Seamus said defensively.

Demos called his dogs over, giving each of them a treat. He wanted to get out and have a cigarette.

"By the way," Ferris said as they left the enclosed dog run, "Beth asked me if you had a date for prom."

"She asked *you*? Low. Well, she's gonna have to get on the waiting list."

"Lucky girl."

"Oh! Don't worry, mate. You're still number one," Seamus assured him, grabbing Ferris by the hand to show his sincerity.

"Cut it out," Ferris snapped, shaking his hand free.

Demos lit a cigarette, looking tense. Ferris knew that he wanted to talk about the detective, but it would be better to wait until Seamus was gone. Ferris wasn't looking forward to saying that he still had no ideas.

School and girls aside, he was going to have to come up with something quick.

45

"Okay, that wasn't bad. Try again."

Ferris nodded at Sergio, keeping his fist tight and taking another hit at the punching bag. There was a rattle as the chains holding it up shivered. He stepped back into position, his feet unsettling some dust on the scuffed floor of the gym. Unlike most of the city gyms, Tommy's didn't have yoga or Stairmasters. Its patrons were mostly interested in two things: lifting weights and boxing. Sergio was a loyal member and, of course, it showed.

"Let your torso drive your arm. Draw it back quickly."

Ferris nodded again, flexing his fingers under the wrappings. He punched again, aiming past the punching bag. He never imagined that he'd be doing something like this. Yet there were countless things that he never imagined he'd do, but had, thanks to the Giorgettis. Benny was sitting at a table with his father, quietly watching the lesson. Normally Benny would be lifting weights, but his treatments had left him even weaker than before. Roberto was sipping a glass of whiskey.

"You sure this is necessary, Serg?" Demos asked, leaning against the boxing ring and puffing on a cigarette. The smoke drifted up in the dim afternoon light.

"Someone has to protect your skinny ass when I'm not around," Sergio replied bluntly. This was, after all, his idea.

"You want me to protect him? I'm just doing this to get all my lunch money back," Ferris griped.

"You're kind of skinny," Sergio admitted, "but at least you're not a girl scout like Demos."

"Hey," Demos snapped.

"But I think with some practice, we could tone you up a little," Sergio finished, ignoring Demos.

"Guys," Demos glowered. He hated being ignored more than he hated being insulted.

"Shouldn't you be selling cookies or something?" Ferris asked over his shoulder, unable to help but smile. Demos only rolled his eyes, looking bitterly in another direction.

"All right," Sergio said, adjusting Ferris' stance. "Try again. Breathe out as you throw the punch."

Ferris' fist was inches from the punching bag when the doors slammed open dramatically. He faltered, jerking upright as every head turned towards the entrance.

"Papà..." came a quivering, female voice. Everyone held their breath, only for a second, as they watched Gina step in with a dramatic black eye. Roberto's chair knocked over as he stood, rushing over to his daughter.

"What happened?" he asked firmly, his brow tense as he placed both hands on her face. "Who did this?"

Gina shook her head, biting her lip.

"It's okay, dolcezza. You can tell me."

"The kitchen boy, Eric," she finally answered between sniffles. She spoke English more often now, but still had an accent. "At the restaurant. He was drinking, I just tell him to work faster and he... he—"

"Shh, don't you worry," Roberto said, patting her pale cheek. "You wait here with Demos. We'll take care of it."

"Papà, are you going to hurt him?"

"Of course not," Roberto said, for posterity. He sat her down, putting his jacket around her shoulders. He nodded at both Benny and Sergio. A moment later, they were gone.

The room's dead silence was soon broken by a few dull, slow claps. Gina looked over at Demos with disdain.

"What?" she asked.

"Nice show."

Gina only glared at him, waiting for Demos to explain himself.

"Your makeup is smudged," he finally said, his tone cold.

Coolly, Gina pulled out a compact to examine her reflection. Indeed, the black and blue surrounding her eye had smeared in the corner.

"So I am caught," she said plainly, fixing the blotch before snapping her compact shut. Her tone was eerily different from her innocent victim act earlier. "You want a medal?"

"What did he do? Look at you funny?"

"Maybe," she said, putting her trademark sunglasses back on. She sipped at the whiskey her father left behind. "Of course, only you are gay enough to notice my makeup, Demos."

"And only you would be manipulative enough to pull something like that, *Gina*."

"Do you guys need a minute alone?" Ferris asked, feeling awkward.

Gina, for the first time that day, looked at him. She lowered her shades, examining him from head to toe.

"What is with the... get-up?" she asked, referring to his A-shirt and hand wraps. It had taken her a second to remember the phrase.

"Sergio is training him," Demos answered between his teeth.

"In bocca al lupo," Gina smirked, rolling her eyes.

"Crepi," Demos replied, his tone growing nastier by the second.

"You know I can understand you," Ferris grumbled. "And I know what sarcasm is, too."

"Your father is going to kill him," Demos said, his voice dark. "You know that."

"Not my problem," Gina said, sipping more whiskey.

"Gina."

"Are you going to tell on me?"

Demos only glared at her. Tattling would be pointless now, and even then, Roberto would probably trust his own daughter over his nephew. He lit another cigarette.

"Give me one," she demanded.

He handed one over, his expression pissy. She held it between two fingers, glancing sideways as she waited for him to light it. A minute later, he reluctantly obliged. They both puffed angrily, looking in opposite directions.

Ferris was about to go back to practicing when he heard a muted ringtone from across the room. Curiously, he made his way across, digging through his bag to find his phone. It was vibrating madly, displaying an unknown number.

"Hello?" he said, holding it up to his ear.

"Ferris… is this Ferris Levinstein?" came a tinny voice. It was uncomfortably familiar.

"Yes, who is—"

"It's me. You remember me, don't you?"

After a second of thought, he connected the voice to a name. "Detective? I'm hanging—"

"Wait! Wait," Lee said, cutting him off. "It's not about that."

"Then why are you calling me?"

"I need your help. I…I'm out of options. I don't know what to do."

It was hard to tell over the phone line, but it sounded as if the detective's voice was cracking. This felt like some kind of trick. His speech sounded nothing like the confident lecture he'd given at the police station.

"What's this about, Mr. Lee?"

"Lee. Just… Lee."

"What do you want, Lee?"

"I need the Giorgettis. I need you to… convince them to help."

"And why the hell would the Giorgettis lift a finger for *you*?"

"It's not about me, Ferris."

There was an audible sigh on the other end of the line. Ferris waited.

"The Marianis took my daughter."

A few minutes later, their call ended. Ferris stared down at the cell phone in his hand, ignoring his dry throat. The detective had explained the situation to the best of his ability. He sounded genuinely tense, as if he'd been watching a tiger circle him as he spoke. Though he had made his best attempt to be clear and calm, his voice occasionally shook.

334

"I'll see what I can do," was all Ferris had responded with before hanging up. What else could he say? Maybe this was all a plan set up by Demos and the girl was actually in the other room playing with some Legos.

"What was that all about?" Demos asked from across the room, his tone suspicious.

No such luck.

Ferris didn't answer immediately. He'd seen Lee's daughter, though he didn't mention it to the detective. She was tiny, as most five-year-old girls were, and had been wearing a pink raincoat. He didn't want to imagine her dead. It might all be an act — did cops play this dirty?

Ferris nodded Demos over while Gina feigned disinterest, sucking the last bit of her cigarette.

Off in their newfound corner, Demos folded his arms as he waited for Ferris to explain.

"I have good news and bad news," Ferris said under his breath, keeping his eyes on the opposite wall.

"Good news."

"I've found a way out of our 'situation' with the detective."

"Bad news."

"You might get blood on your suit," Ferris said.

"Elaborate," Demos pressed.

"I guess he was after the Marianis too, since they took his daughter. They're holding her unless he personally kills Blakely, I guess since he has security access to the station. He won't do it. He said he'd drop our case and burn the evidence if we help him get her back."

"Christ," Demos mumbled. The Marianis knew exactly where to hit the Giorgetti family. Blakely was their puppet and his death would weaken them significantly. What exactly were the Marianis planning?

Demos was thinking hard. Of course they had to take up the offer; they had no choice. Unfortunately, it was just going to be the two of them. None of the other Giorgettis knew about the problem with the detective and it would be troublesome if anyone found out that a cop had interrogated Ferris. This was messy and complicated.

Ferris watched him think. It was obvious why Lee was asking them for help instead of his superiors. Demos knew more about the inner workings of the underworld than a dozen cops put together – not to mention the Marianis had threatened to kill the girl if Lee spoke a word to the other cops. Luckily for the detective, they'd neglected to mention anything about ratting to the Giorgettis.

"Are you sure he was serious?" Demos asked suddenly. "No offense, but you have a habit of trusting people a little too—"

335

"I believe him," Ferris said, looking his friend in the eyes. He meant it.

Demos nodded, looking towards the exit.

"Let's go."

"Wait," came a stern voice from across the large, empty room. Ferris blinked. He'd forgotten about Gina.

"What?" Demos asked impatiently.

"I'm going, too."

"Like hell you are."

"You bring me or I tell Papà everything," Gina said, dead serious.

"You bitch."

"Maybe we can use her," Ferris offered as he put his shirt back on.

"No one will take us seriously if there's a girl with us," Demos snapped.

"Three is better than two."

"They do not know my face," Gina added. "I can find where she is."

"How exactly do you plan on doing that?" Demos sneered.

Gina lifted her purse, slipping her hand in to remove a small black pistol. She lowered her head, her glare steady in the filtered light.

"How do you think?"

Less than half an hour later, Demos and Ferris were waiting in a car parked across from a gentleman's club. Frank Mariani was the owner of the establishment and Gina had gone in requesting a "job interview."

"This was a stupid idea," Demos muttered. "And now I'm going to have to tell Uncle Roberto that I got his daughter killed."

"Give her a minute," Ferris said, surprisingly calm. Gina certainly had a better chance of getting Frank alone than they did.

"She doesn't know what the fuck she's doing," Demos continued, still irritated. "She knows more about Prada shoes than she does about... anything else."

Ferris decided not to mention that Demos knew just as much about shoes as Gina did.

"Relax."

Demos complied by folding his arms and glaring at the dashboard. Ten minutes later, Gina casually strolled out the front door and into the back seat of their car.

"The girl is at the butcher's on 90th. Frank is unconscious, maybe for one hour. Drive quickly. He will warn them when he wakes up."

336

Demos stared at her in the rearview mirror. He couldn't tell if she was looking back; she was still wearing her large, dark shades. Gina's face lifted coolly over her long neck as she waited for a response. He didn't answer, only starting the car with a twist of the keys. The engine rumbled and the car pulled quickly into traffic, heading north towards 90th Street. Ferris turned his attention to his cell phone, dialing as he watched buildings go by.

"Detective? I think we can work something out."

The conversation was brief and Lee had agreed to meet them down the street from the shop. Ferris had never heard someone sound so relieved before. He wondered how his own father would react if he were kidnapped.

The detective was waiting for them in an empty auto shop, dressed in a nondescript jacket and looking anxious.

"So you're the one that's been following me around with those creepy black cars, huh?" Demos asked shamelessly, one hand on his hip.

"I'm afraid so."

"Stalking a minor," Demos emphasized, leaning in a bit.

"Demos, cut it out," Ferris said impatiently.

"Of course," Demos smiled. "Let's get to business."

"Do you know anything about the building?" Lee asked, ignoring Demos' catty remarks.

"They're probably keeping her in the back, maybe with the meat," Demos speculated. "Do you want to do this tactfully or by force?"

"Is a tactful way possible?"

"Not really."

"Let's just do whatever it takes," Lee said. He obviously meant it.

"Are you heavy?"

Lee pulled back his coat to reveal a gun tucked alongside his chest.

"And you're Asian, so you know karate, right?" Demos said icily.

"Korean, taekwondo. And no, not every Asian person is a martial arts master," Lee replied bluntly.

"You don't really look like you belong in an Italian pork shop. Maybe you should wait outside."

Ferris was getting annoyed at the attitude that was choking the atmosphere, but Demos did have a point. The Mariani goons probably knew what Lee looked like. If the detective took one step into the shop, there would definitely be gunshots.

"Actually, he's right. Maybe you should wait."

Lee looked uneasy.

"It'll be okay," Ferris reassured him. Lee didn't know how much he trusted a couple of teens to save his daughter's life, but he didn't have much of a choice in the matter.

"All right. If you take too long, I'm going after you."

"Fair enough," Demos nodded. With that, he turned to leave with Ferris and Gina at his heels. Lee stood alone, watching them disappear and hoping to heaven that this hadn't been a mistake.

The door to the butcher shop opened with a soft chime. The man behind the counter was cutting thin slices of ham with a machine.

"Can I help you?" he asked, his voice heavy.

"Hmm," Demos said thoughtfully, looking over the display of cut deli meat. "I don't think you have what I'm looking for up here. I'm going to have to go in the back."

"Sorry, customers aren't allowed in back," the butcher replied, still cutting ham.

"Don't play dumb with me," Demos said. "I just want to have a word with a few of my *friends* back there."

"Look, I don't—"

The gun at the butcher's forehead cocked as he turned to face it.

"Be a dear and open the door."

They left Gina pointing a gun at his head while the two went into the dimly lit bowels of the pork shop. There was the expected scent of cold meat and skin. Ferris shuddered unconsciously. The first room was empty, housing only a scuffed table and hanging sausage links. There were two doors to choose from: an office and the meat locker. Demos nodded towards the latter and they went through.

The silence was eerie. Ferris expected there to be at least one guard, but it was empty. Large, frozen carcasses hung in rows, swaying slightly as they walked past. It was dark. Only a couple of weak bulbs lit the room, hanging from the ceiling and casting shadows along the walls. Ferris had never seen an entire pig's corpse before and now wished he never had. The room smelled like concrete and blood. Breath escaped their mouths in small, lingering puffs. Why couldn't Demos have chosen the office?

Something at the end of the room caught Demos' attention and he rushed forward. Ferris followed close behind. Upon hearing their footsteps, the small figure spoke.

"If you don't let me go, my Daddy's going to put you in jail forever," she said angrily, shivering against the cold, dry air. She was blindfolded, sitting on the floor with her wrists and ankles tied firmly.

"It's okay," Demos said, kneeling next to her. "We're friends of your Dad."

338

Just as Ferris was beginning to think that this was all too easy, a gunshot echoed across the low ceiling. The bullet narrowly missed Demos' head, piercing the wall behind him. They both split, ducking behind separate carcasses as another shot rang out.

They should have checked the office.

"Are you fucking kidding me?" came a voice from a few meters away. "He sent some kids do to his dirty work?"

The voice stalked closer; the footsteps were loud against the cold, stained floor. Ferris panted, wishing that the only thing between him and the smoking gun wasn't a slaughtered pig. He could hear Demos sidestep and fire. The shot missed, hitting cold meat instead of living flesh. Ferris fingered the trigger in his hand but couldn't see a target. He listened, greeted only by shadows and scuffles. There was a grunt and something fell. The sound of a weapon sliding across the floor scraped his ears. Ignoring his instincts, he rushed from his hiding spot to see if Demos was okay.

The sight that greeted him made his stomach drop. Demos was on his knees, one arm twisted behind his back as the Mariani held a gun to his temple. The man locked eyes with Ferris, telling him without words not to come any closer. The hanging bulb was swaying, painting stark shadows over their eyes. Ferris stopped, swallowing.

"Put your gun down."

Ferris put his gun down, holding up his hands.

"Now, just—"

The man didn't finish his command. There was a knife up in his ribs, making it difficult to speak. Instead, he gurgled. Demos' expression was blank as he pushed the Mariani off of him, wiping the knife clean on the gangster's shirt. His eyes caught his gun, which had skidded several feet away. Picking it up, he sighed with disdain.

"It's scratched."

Ferris' hand had nearly reached his own weapon when another gunshot snapped him to attention. The bullet skimmed the edge of a pig, piercing the wall. He turned quickly, eyes catching the butcher's outline in the doorway of the meat locker.

"Shit," he said under his breath. If the butcher was here, where was Gina? Demos moved to fire, but the crack of bone on bone faltered his movement. The butcher wobbled, then fell. Behind him was Lee, hand flat in a post-strike position.

"Fine. I learned it in the army. Did you find her?" he asked tersely.

Ferris pointed towards the back of the room. Lee immediately pushed past them. Demos and Ferris dusted themselves off as they listened to the reunion.

"Daddy!"

"Oh Suki, thank God you're okay."

"I'm cold."

"It's okay, come here."

The detective wrapped his daughter in his jacket, picking her up carefully. He shielded her eyes from the bodies on the floor, rubbing her back to keep her warm. Near the entrance, Gina was unconscious on the floor. The butcher must have hit her pretty hard.

"Ferris, could you get her?" Demos sighed.

Ferris hesitated, then knelt to lift her with both arms. There was a bruise on her temple. Well, at least she could attribute it to her story about the kitchen boy.

Back at the garage, Lee set his daughter down along the backseat to sleep. He touched her hair, listening as Demos rambled.

"And no photos, no articles, no more stalking."

"Yes, I know."

"Shred that whole chart. Shred it three times."

"I will."

Demos paused, noticing that Lee was far more concerned with the little girl than with his demands. He exhaled.

"Maybe you should get her a tougher babysitter."

"Maybe I should just be a traffic cop," Lee said quietly. "What was I thinking?"

"Come on, don't be like that. Just, you know, stay out of trouble."

"I'll try."

The drive home was quiet. Gina was knocked out in the back and Ferris was staring out the window. Demos broke the silence with a question.

"What's on your mind?"

"You don't think this will start a turf war, do you?"

"I don't know. They're not powerful enough to strike back. But if they get Blakely... who knows?"

"Well, at least we have a detective on our side now."

"If he stays a detective. He looked like he wanted to kill himself."

Despite his worries, Ferris was glad that he didn't have to worry about any of the Giorgettis going to jail. Demos could handle gangsters, but a jury? It was hard to tell.

A few days later, a suspicious package arrived at Ristorante Giorgetti. The bouquet of peace lilies was set on the table, addressed to no one in particular. All that was attached was a simple, plain note card. Demos smiled as he fingered the tag, reading its short message out loud.

"Thank you."

46

Harold's car came to a slow stop in front of Ristorante Giorgetti. It was a dark, rainy night and the street lights highlighted pillars of steam rising from the sewer grates. He passed his keys to the valet as Ferris got out of the passenger seat. Several men were standing in a circle under the front awning, smoking and talking in low voices. Nicky gave Harold a nod, while Sal offered Ferris an unsettling wink.

"Are they all here for the meeting?" Ferris asked quietly, not wanting to draw too much attention from the restaurant's patrons.

"Yes," Harold answered simply, keeping his hand on Ferris' shoulder as he led his son to the back hallway. There was a private room reserved for parties and, of course, business.

Demos was waiting for them at the room's entrance. He gave Ferris and his father a nod before carefully turning the knob. The door opened soundlessly.

The room was long and elegant, lined with dark, floral wallpaper and cherry wainscoting. A wooden table took up the majority of the floor space, easily large enough to seat a dozen men. Gino was already seated near the center with Victor and Roberto on one side. Across were several older men that Ferris had never seen before. Demos' lips nearly brushed Ferris' ear as he whispered to him.

"Angelo Mariani."

Ferris' eyes fought not to widen as he stared at the boss of the Mariani crime family. He was clearly no angel. He had a heavy brow over a wide nose, carrying a menacing air regardless of his expression.

Harold took the seat to Gino's left. The men who had been smoking outside gradually filed in, filling the remaining seats. Normally boys Ferris and Demos' age wouldn't be allowed in an official meeting, but the issues involved them. They were allowed to stand back against the wall with Sergio and Pietro, watching over Gino's shoulder.

Angelo picked up the glass of Johnnie Walker Blue he'd been served, swirling the liquid as he spoke.

"Gino," he said in a low smoker's voice. "Your generosity, as always, is overwhelming."

Gino ignored the backhanded remark, simply giving Angelo a cold, professional smile.

"It's a pleasure to have you, especially on such short notice."

"Is it really necessary to have this many of your men tonight?" Angelo said, returning the smile to reveal a row of perfect teeth. The ratio of men in the room was a clear representation of the power each family held over Southport. The reminder hurt his ego.

"Dear Angelo, there is nothing to be afraid of."

The Mariani boss momentarily looked as if he were about to snap but somehow maintained his demeanor.

"You should know by now, Gino, that I am not afraid of you."

Gino leaned in, his bright eyes locked on the man across the table.

"And that," he said, his voice lacking empathy, "is your biggest mistake."

A vein in Angelo's neck bulged. Before he could respond, Gino continued.

"My grandson informed me that you've been stepping out of line, Angelo. Muscling a shop under our protection..."

"Your territory is too big," Angelo blurted, making a fist around his glass of scotch.

"We reap what we sow."

"The Marianis were in Southport long before we were," Victor added. "You had plenty of time to make your mark on this city."

"You didn't," said Gino. "We did. You're going to have to deal with that."

"This isn't *your* city," spat the hard featured man sitting next to Angelo.

"We've gone over this," Victor said, pushing his index finger into the table. "You stay on your side of the river."

"The Irish are on our side of the river!"

"Then you better fucking learn to like Guinness," Victor sneered. Gino held up his hand, gesturing for Victor to stop. His son grudgingly obeyed.

"There's more to this than territory, Angelo."

Mariani simply narrowed his eyes, waiting for Gino to spit it out.

"You went after Blakely."

"I did no such–"

"*Angelo.* You blackmailed a cop."

"What does that have to do with Blakely? We did it for ransom," the man replied quickly, ignoring the nervous sweat on the back of his neck.

"He's lying," Ferris said suddenly, his voice low.

"The fuck did you just say?" snarled the man to Angelo's left.

"That's a lie," Demos repeated, stepping in for Ferris. "He kidnapped the detective's kid to make him kill Blakely."

The Mariani goon choked on his own anger, nearly getting up from his seat. Angelo stopped him with a soft hiss.

"One of my men is dead, Gino."

342

The blue eyed Italian didn't respond, knowing that there was no way of proving that the Giorgettis had done it.

"You need to watch your kids," Angelo continued. "If they keep poking their noses in other peoples' business... well."

He locked his eyes back on Ferris, glaring.

"I don't want to see anything bad happen to them."

Out of nowhere, Harold stood, scuffing back the chair he was seated in.

"You stay the fuck away from my son."

His hands were flat on the table as he leaned in, giving the Mariani boss a venomous glare.

"Harold," Gino said in a weak attempt to calm his consigliere.

"If you so much as *look* at him again," Harold said in a pointed tone Ferris had never heard before, "I'll rip that smile right off your fucking face."

Ferris was stunned, not blinking as he watched the back of his father's head. Harold didn't say 'fuck,' or threaten people, or speak in a voice that sent chills up his spine. Ferris couldn't remember ever seeing his father so angry. The fact that it was all on his behalf made Ferris' face warm.

For a moment, Angelo stared back in shock. After digesting the words, the Mariani crime lord simply smirked.

"Gino, you need to learn to control your men."

Gino put a hand on Harold's arm, who soon complied by sitting once more. Harold didn't remove his eyes from Angelo's face. Similarly, Angelo made sure to remember Harold.

"I trust you won't be making any more attempts to extend your territory?" Gino asked after a minute of uncomfortable silence.

"If you can keep your children from getting into our business."

"You made it our business, too, I'm afraid."

"Go back to Italy," the hard featured goon snapped.

"It's a little late for that," Victor said with a detached smirk. "Maybe you should get together with the Irish, you two would make a lovely couple."

"This meeting is over," Gino said, putting one hand out on the table. "I hope this will be the last one we need."

Angelo didn't respond, only giving the Giorgettis a tart smile. He finished his drink, setting the glass down onto the table with a hard clink.

"Goodnight, gentlemen," Angelo said icily. He stood and Pietro held the door for him and his men. It shut behind them with a gentle click, leaving the Giorgettis casting anxious looks at each other.

Demos sighed, relieved that none of the Marianis had mentioned Gina. Though he didn't care if she got caught, he knew that he would be blamed for letting her come along. It was a tough decision, telling Gino everything that had gone down with the detective and Ferris. It had to be done. If the Marianis were after Blakely, the situation was much bigger than the two of them. The fact that their meeting had accomplished absolutely nothing didn't help the sick feeling in Demos' gut.

Ferris was still watching his father, unsure of what to say. Instead of speaking, he simply put a hand on the man's shoulder. When Harold turned to look, he was greeted with a tight smile and a pair of worried eyes.

Outside, Angelo got into the backseat of his car as one of his men started the engine. He watched the restaurant windows, his eyes glazing under the yellow light.

"The Irish," he mused, speaking to himself. "That might not be such a bad idea."

47

The ocean seemed to go on forever. The air was warm and the water was chilly, causing Ferris to shudder as his head went under. He brought himself back up, breaking the surface with a short gasp. He wouldn't go past the depth where his feet could touch the ground. Demos and Emily still hadn't gotten around to teaching him how to swim. Next summer, perhaps.

He rubbed the salt water out of his eyes, looking up at the sky. The sun was almost gone, rippling gold in its reflection on the water. Darkness had already begun to cast itself over the far edges of the beach. Better head back.

As he waded through the dark water, his foot happened upon a large, soft object. He stumbled past it, looking back with a furrowed brow. Deciding to ignore it, he went further, only to feel a similar object bump his shin. It slowly surfaced, bobbing alongside him. A log? It was hard to see without his glasses. No, it looked more like a person. What was a fully clothed person doing in the water like—

It was a dead man.

Ferris took in a quick breath, sloshing water as he stepped backwards. Before he could rush away, more bodies began to surface. They were pale and blue, wide eyed and bloated with water. Standing silently in the distance was Demos, legs submerged and indifferently gazing back. He had a gun in his hand. An Italian leather shoe floated past his leg before Ferris grabbed the sides of his head.

God, no. Not this dream again. Not this—

He woke up abruptly. His hand went to the side of his neck, ignoring the cold sweat.

"Breathe," he reminded himself. His body complied. There was no reason to be flustered; he'd had plenty of dreams worse than this. Hell, he'd even seen a guy with his own thumbs shoved into his eye sockets in *real life*. No big deal, really. Before he could take another deep breath, there was a knock on his door.

"What?" he called groggily. His mother popped her head in.

"Emily is here to see—" Her eyes widened behind her cat-eye glasses. "You're still in bed? You lazy thing, get dressed!"

Emily poked her head in behind Ruth.

"You forgot about our appointment? Ferris, I'm hurt," she said with a smile.

"Look at that, a nice girl comes to see you and you hurt her feelings. Shame on you."

"Get out of here, both of you!" he groaned, pulling his comforter over his head. There was a bit of giggling before the door clicked shut.

How could he forget that Emily was coming today? She had made him promise to take a day off back at his violin recital and was here to spend some time with him. He glanced over at his alarm clock. It must not have gone off.

"Piece of shit," he mumbled as he stumbled out of bed and tugged on a pair of jeans. Stanley yawned at the end of his bed, rolling over to go back to sleep. Ferris dressed haphazardly, opening the bedroom door and looking from side to side. There were voices downstairs; his mother must have given Emily some tea and about a thousand cookies. He wearily made his way to the bathroom.

A few minutes later, he somehow made it down the stairs and seated himself next to Emily. His head lay back on the top of the sofa as if he were too tired to hold it up properly.

"I can't believe you slept this late," she said before putting an entire cookie in her mouth.

"Isn't this my day off?" he retorted, keeping his eyes shut.

"Yeah, yeah," she said after swallowing. "What do you want to do today?"

"Sleep."

"Ferris," Emily warned, her tone dangerous.

"Um, let me think."

His mother came in from the kitchen, setting a mug of coffee down in front of him. He immediately reached for it, taking a sip despite the temperature. He let out a short, happy sigh.

"You functioning yet?" Emily asked, amused.

"Give me a second. And let's go to your house."

Though Victor Giorgetti's home wasn't the most exciting of all places, Ferris did feel comfortable there. If he was going to take a day off, he might as well spend it in a place he felt at ease. He was also determined to finally beat Emily at Mario Kart.

"Okay," she said. "As long as you don't mind Demos and his boyfriend sucking face behind us."

"Eh, I guess."

As far as Ferris knew, Demos was still dating Aaron Fisher. He supposed the two took whatever chances they could get to spend 'quality time' together. Before they could head out the door, Ruth made sure to give Emily a large Tupperware container full of spare cookies.

"Thanks for coming out," Emily said quietly as they walked. "I'm glad you're not… mad at me."

Ferris waited before answering her.

"It's fine, I didn't really care about prom anyway."

"I know, but I felt bad. I'm sorry."

"Don't worry about it. You can't help what Chris is like."

346

The answers came easily to Ferris' mouth, though the rejection still made him feel ill when he remembered it.

"Have you asked anyone else?"

"I'm not going," he said bluntly, not realizing how much he sounded like a drama queen.

"Oh, come on. You'd have fun."

"Forget it," he said quickly, then looked down. "What about you? Are you going to his?"

"Yeah. I'm not going to know anybody at their school."

"You'll still be the best looking one there."

"Aw. Are you trying to butter me up for something?"

"Maybe I can take your guard down so I can kick your ass on Rainbow Road."

"In your dreams."

When they got to the house, Victor and his wife, Vanni, were packing up a few last things to head out of town for a wedding. It was no wonder Demos was going to invite his boyfriend over; the teens were going to have the house to themselves.

"I'm going to get some drinks, why don't you check and see if Demos is up yet?" Emily said, stretching her arms behind her head.

Ferris nodded, heading up the stairs. Poking his head in past Demos' cracked bedroom door, Ferris saw his friend still asleep in bed. The room was dim. Demos' thin frame was rolled onto his side, rising and falling slowly with his breath. Ferris carefully backed out of the room, not having any intention of waking Demos up. The Italian was very crabby when woken up unexpectedly. Ferris ignored the fact that he wasn't any more pleasant himself.

A short walk down the hall revealed Emily's bedroom with the door wide open. Ferris had only been in Emily's bedroom a few times before. He found himself looking around absently, glancing at the vintage bedspread and Chinese acupuncture chart on the wall. She had collected a great deal of things from her travels, but everything was arranged in a more or less neat manner. There was a set of brass owls and a lantern made from textured rice paper. Her décor was a large contrast to his own minimal, neutral, and meticulously organized layout. Somehow, he liked it.

His eyes dropped to her paints and brushes, looking over a painting that was half finished against an easel. There was a long, tan brush that had snapped in half and he picked it up to read the name.

'Arches, Pure Kolinsky, 10.'

Ferris wondered what had happened to it – was it expensive? He set it back in place and his eyes caught a tabletop full of watercolor tubes. They were all out of order.

Well, that wouldn't do. He started rearranging them with an unnecessary amount of determination. A minute later, a voice caught his attention from the room's entrance.

"Are you spying on me?" she asked, holding two glasses of Coke.

"You have a lot of stuff," he blurted before he could stop himself.

Wow. *'You have a lot of stuff.'* He'd have to save that golden line for later. Why weren't girls all over him, again?

"Not everyone can be obsessively organized," she said as she handed over a glass. He took a sip.

"I'm not obsessive," he mumbled, his voice barely audible.

She didn't answer, only pointing to the watercolors which had been arranged in a perfect rainbow order. He blinked at her innocently.

"Did you do this?"

"Don't be silly," he said, averting his eyes and taking a sip of his drink. "Let's go play Mario Kart."

He walked brusquely past her, leaving her to roll her eyes in the doorway.

Once the game started, the snarky remarks only got worse.

"Damn it," Ferris said grumpily as his go-kart was flattened into a round pancake on the track. "What the hell, did you just lap me? I hate you."

"Maybe you should learn to drive, Fishface."

"Shit!" he said, driving into a pit of lava once again. "Forget this, let's just do battle mode, okay?"

"What are you kids playing?" Victor asked as he walked in from the kitchen. "What is that, the racing thing?"

"Yeah," Emily said. "You want to try?"

"Me? Yeah, let me see that," Victor said, taking one of the controllers from her and sitting down next to them in his recliner. "So what do I do? Which one makes you go?"

Emily explained the basic functions of the game as Ferris tried not to laugh. At times, nothing made an adult seem more out of their element than a video game. Victor, who was normally in complete, brutal control, was currently a little lost.

"What, what was that? What hit me?" Victor said angrily, gesturing to the screen with his hand.

"Turtle shell, the spiked ones are—"

Before Emily could finish her sentence, Vanni cleared her throat.

"Honey, we're going to be late."

"Ah, come on."

"*Vicky*," his wife said with emphasis. Victor winced at being called '*Vicky*' in front of the kids, handing the controller back to Emily.

"Bye, Pumpkin," he said, kissing the top of his daughter's head before the couple went out the door.

"I kind of wish they were staying," Emily said wistfully. "Now Demos is going to call his boy toy over."

"Maybe if we're lucky, he'll stay asleep," Ferris said, selecting Luigi again.

"If only," she replied, choosing Wario and starting the game. Ferris played better in battle mode, but not by very much. He was down to one balloon when Emily spoke up out of nowhere.

"I wanted to ask you earlier," Emily said, keeping her eyes on the game. "Do you, um... know anything about Orthodox guys?"

"Jews? A little. Why, what happened?"

"Uh, there was this guy. Dad was renting a space out and the owner met with us. But—"

"Let me guess," Ferris interrupted. "He wouldn't shake your hand?"

"Yeah. How did you know?"

"Orthodox Jews can't touch anyone of the opposite gender, outside of family," he explained. "It throws a lot of people off."

"Oh, God. I thought I did something to piss him off or... I don't know."

"Don't take it personally. I'm sure his wife wouldn't shake *my* hand."

The corner of Ferris' mouth quirked, as if amused.

"You probably think it's weird, don't you?" he asked.

"Not really," she said, though her tone was unsure. "As long as you don't start recoiling at the sight of my hand."

"I already do that."

"Oh, you jerk. Eat lightning," she said spitefully, shrinking his character down to gnome-like proportions. Ferris was ready to toss the controller down in frustration when Demos came down the stairs. He was rubbing an arm over his eye, drawn downstairs with caffeine in mind.

"Oh, Ferris. Hey."

"Morning, Princess," Ferris said, looking over his shoulder.

"You suck at this game," Demos observed wearily, watching the television screen with half-lidded eyes.

"He doesn't suck," Emily said. "I'm just really awesome."

"And modest," Ferris added curtly.

"By the way, Aaron is on his way over."

Ferris and Emily both groaned.

"What? It's not like you haven't made out with Chris while I was trying to watch TV," Demos sneered.

Trying to keep from getting jealous, Ferris swallowed the bitter taste in his mouth.

"Fine," he said. "I'm innocent in all of this. Give me a break."

"Are you sure you won't like it? How long did you stare at us behind the bleachers, anyway?" Demos said with a self-satisfied grin.

"I fucking hate you."

"You love me," Demos yawned before stalking off to the kitchen. The espresso machine hadn't even started to drip before Ferris lost once again.

"Yeah, well I could destroy you in Pacman."

"That's not a two player game."

"This is my 'relaxing day off' and I'm going to start hemorrhaging."

"Ew, do it outside."

Ferris mussed her hair and she started to smack him away. Their battle was interrupted by the doorbell.

"That was fast," Emily said, looking towards the entrance.

"I'll get it," Demos said in a sing-song voice, walking past them to answer the door.

Aaron Fisher was the tall, ginger-haired son of a heart surgeon. Ferris was sure that he would be a hit with the ladies if he weren't, well, gay.

"Let's go up to my–"

"Hey, are you playing Mario Kart?" Aaron said, interrupting Demos with an eager look towards the TV.

"Yeah, you want to play?" Emily said cheerfully. Demos scowled.

Aaron joined them and Demos reluctantly sat next to him on the couch. To Emily's relief, Aaron wasn't better than she was. The three boys together, however, were slowly beating her to a pulp.

"No fair, you guys can't gang up on me. This is free-for-all," Emily said in irritation.

"Boy power," Ferris said plainly.

"Fuck you guys!"

Near the end of the game, Demos' hand was slowly edging up Aaron's knee. Aaron forgot how to drive and within seconds the two were on each other, kissing feverishly. Emily pointed inside her open mouth, making an ill expression.

"You guys are losing," Ferris said, but they didn't hear him. Shrugging, he turned up the volume. He didn't want to hear them make out to his left. He wasn't sure if he was jealous or just genuinely uninterested but didn't want to think about it either way.

With the game back to one-on-one, Emily slaughtered the boys' stationary characters and proceeded to attack Ferris without any mercy. Within seconds, it was all over.

"Great, just when you might finally lose, my team has to go all gay," Ferris scoffed, then turned off the TV.

"You could always join us," Demos said coyly.

"Go get a room."

Ferris' advice was actually quite wise, if not a little late. If the two boys had actually been in Demos' room, they would have heard the front door open in time to stop whatever inappropriate things they were doing. Being in the living room, they only had seconds to react as the front door swung open and Victor laid eyes on the sight of two boys in lip-lock. There was silence in the room, as if each of them had forgotten how to breathe.

The blood drained from Demos' face. He and Aaron instantly pushed away from each other, eyes locked on the furious man in the doorway. The whites of Victor's eyes flashed behind his glasses and he took a deep breath through his nose.

"What," Victor said, his tone eerily quiet, "the fuck is going on here."

"I... I–" Demos stammered, at a complete loss for words. With all of his intuition, he hadn't considered that his uncle Victor would return to the house so soon.

It seemed that Demos' uncle wanted to move but was paralyzed by his own fury. They could hear him exhale through his teeth. His breath trembled, as if he were preparing to erupt.

"You," he said, locking eyes with Aaron. He straightened himself, taking a step forward. Aaron immediately leaned back in fear. "I'm going to fucking—"

Victor's threat was cut off by Ferris' voice as the teen stood between them.

"I'm sorry, I'm really sorry," he said immediately, holding up his hands. "It was my fault. We were playing 'truth or dare' and I dared them to."

Victor's eyes shot over to Emily, who nodded quickly in confirmation. It took the man a moment to consider the excuse, eyes flickering from one boy to the other. Finally, his stare settled back on Ferris.

"You think this kind of shit is funny, kid?" he demanded, his voice still boiling. "Making my nephew a faggot?"

"No, Sir," Ferris answered, trying not to stammer.

"You ever pull this kind of shit under my roof again and you will *never* step back in here. You fucking got that?" he said, bringing a pointed finger between Ferris' eyes. Ferris' posture weakened as his stomach tried to burrow beneath his other organs.

"Yes, Sir. I won't. I'm sorry," he said, his voice weak. Victor swallowed hard, stalking to the kitchen to grab the wedding gift that he'd forgotten. He stopped in the doorway, hissing in another breath. Slowly, he turned to look at the teens.

"Both of you, go home."

The door slammed shut.

Demos looked like he was about to start shaking. He buried his face in his hands, not speaking. Aaron hesitated, then stood. He was pale and his eyes were glazed. Within seconds he was out the door, not saying goodbye to any of them. It shut with a click that seemed to echo in Demos' head.

Ferris and Emily exchanged looks before turning their attention to Demos.

"Demos?" Ferris said after a minute, putting a hand on his friend's back. "Are you okay?"

Demos slowly took in a breath, letting it fill his chest before exhaling. When he picked his head up, his eyes were glassy.

"Ferris... thank you. I'm–" He stopped, having difficulty speaking. "I'm so sorry."

"It's okay."

"If you weren't here I don't know what I—"

"It's fine. He'll forget about it."

"No, he won't. He's always suspected and now–"

"He believed me. It's okay," Ferris repeated. "He was mad at me, not you."

"I'm sorry, you didn't do anything wrong," Demos said, his voice cracking.

"I think hanging out with you is pretty wrong," he teased. Demos gave a slight smile.

Ferris reluctantly got off of the sofa, rubbing one of his arms.

"I guess I'd better go."

"This was supposed to be your day off," Emily said, disappointed.

"I promise I'll go home and sleep."

She looked down dejectedly. Ferris put his hand on the doorknob, giving Demos a reassuring smile.

"It'll be all right."

The door closed behind him, leaving Demos hoping to God that those words would ring true.

352

48

Harold rarely had the chance to go home early from work. On the off-chance that he did, he always took the opportunity to pick Ferris up from school. The silver Nissan rolled up alongside the curb, stopping a few feet short of his son. The boy's breath was coming up in thin clouds. Aside from his uniform, Ferris' only defense against the cold was a thin striped scarf.

"Hi, Dad," he said, getting in the passenger seat and pulling the door shut.

"Hey kiddo, how was school?"

The car pulled back into traffic, passing a number of other students who were waiting for their own respective rides.

"It was okay... Mr. Nott accepted my extra credit report," Ferris said, breathing warm air onto his hands. "And I got hit in the head with a volleyball in gym."

"Oh, good," Harold said, smiling as he watched the road. "I mean, your history class. You were really worried about your grade."

"Yeah," Ferris sighed. He didn't continue the conversation. He'd been listless the entire day. The fact that Demos didn't show up at lunch or to any of their classes didn't help Ferris' anxiety. There was a cold feeling in his chest that refused to go away. The entire disaster with Victor had only been yesterday, but it felt like he'd been fretting for ages.

"Hey Dad," he said. "Can you drop me off at Demos' house today? I think... he might be sick."

"Sure thing."

The car changed direction, heading further east. It was quiet for another minute.

"You feeling okay?" Harold finally asked, unable to keep himself from prying any longer.

"Hm? Oh, yeah. I'm fine."

Ferris kept his gaze out the window, watching people on the sidewalk with lowered eyes. There were so many things he wanted to tell his father but wasn't sure if he should. He frowned, focusing harder on the scenery. A few blocks later, he opened his mouth.

"Can I ask you something?" A stupid request, but Ferris felt that his question needed some cushioning.

"Of course. What's on your mind?"

Ferris bit the inside of his cheek.

"Well," he said, trying not to swallow too hard, "how do you feel about homosexuals?"

Harold raised an eyebrow, a little surprised by the question. He could only wonder what might possibly have brought it up. Briefly, he chanced a look over at his son.

"Not me," Ferris muttered. "I'm not gay."

"Well, could you be more specific?" Harold asked.

"Do you think it's wrong?"

"I don't really think it's my place to decide if it's 'wrong' or not."

"Dad, quit being vague."

"All right, sorry." Harold thought for a moment, looking off at the far end of the road. "Well, you know, I don't see what the fuss is all about. I had a gay friend once. He was just like anyone else I knew."

"You did?" Ferris asked, trying to mask his astonishment.

"Yes," Harold said. "Jack."

Ferris turned his head back to the road, staring at the flickering white lines. Jack Frischman – his father's best friend from college, the man the Giorgettis had murdered and dumped in the river. Ferris fought a shudder.

"Oh," Ferris said, his throat dry. "I didn't know."

"Kiddo, really. It's okay if you're gay. I mean, as long as he's Jewish."

"Dad! I'm not gay. Seriously, cut it out."

Harold only laughed.

It didn't seem fair. Ferris had liberal parents but was as straight as an arrow. Demos, who was more fabulous than the cast of *La Cage aux Folles,* was living with a stiff necked Roman Catholic who owned 24 guns.

The car parked in front of said Roman Catholic's home. Demos was sitting on the curb a few yards down, face buried in his arms. Harold put a hand on his son's arm just as he was getting out of the car.

"It'll be fine."

Ferris looked back for a second, then gave a slight smile.

"Thanks, Dad."

The door shut and the car drove off, leaving the two alone on their side of the street. Ferris rubbed the back of his neck before walking over, sitting down next to his friend. He didn't speak at first, letting the Italian feel him there.

"Ferris," Demos said, his voice muffled by the sleeves of his hooded sweatshirt.

"I'm here."

Slowly, Demos picked up his head. His eyes were red.

"What happened?" Ferris asked, leaning in. "You weren't at lunch."

"Aaron dumped me," Demos replied, his voice barely a whisper.

354

Ferris opened his mouth but didn't say anything. Though he'd seen it coming, it still rubbed him the wrong way. While trying to come up with a response, he noticed that Demos was nearly shivering.

"It's cold out here, why don't we–"

"I don't want to be around them," Demos interrupted, referring to his family. It explained why he was sitting on a dirty curb instead of a nice leather chair.

Ferris put a hand on Demos' back.

"What did he say?"

"He's too scared. He said it's not worth it."

"Weak," Ferris said under his breath.

They both stared down at their shoes.

"You *are* worth it," Ferris added. "You know that."

Demos turned to look at his friend. Ferris, who was more concerned with books than with relationships, had never left Demos' side. After years of murder and fire, here he was, next to him on the curb. After rubbing a sleeve over his wet eyes, Demos rested his head on Ferris' shoulder. The older boy didn't protest, simply watching the house across the street.

"Thank you," Demos said quietly. They were still for quite some time, comfortable in the other's silence. The trees creaked with a cold wind that flushed over the houses. A car or two drove by before Ferris spoke again.

"Tell your uncle that you're staying the night. Mom is making brisket."

Demos smiled for the first time that day.

"I love your mom's brisket."

49

It had finally become cold enough to snow in Southport. Most of it had been removed from the streets, but soft white piles still coated a few cars. Gold lights wrapped the bare tree branches, illuminating the streets. It was getting late, but most stores extended their hours during shopping season. Though the sun had gone long ago, the boys had just started their day.

"So what do you want for Chanukah?" Demos asked, already holding a few shopping bags as they weaved through the crowds.

"We don't have to get you eight things, do we?" Seamus asked warily.

"No, just… get whatever. You know me," Ferris said with a shrug. Demos had a tendency to show off when he bought gifts for others. Ferris began to wonder if maybe he should have requested something cheap.

"All right then, I'm getting tiaras for the both of you," Seamus said with determination, putting an arm around each of their shoulders. "For my princesses."

"Speak for Demos, I look awful in sparkles," Ferris muttered, picking Seamus' arm off with two fingers.

"Oh, come on. I can picture you in one right now. Just lovely," Seamus said as he framed Ferris' face with his hands.

"*Please* don't do that."

Their conversation was interrupted by a man dressed as Santa Claus as he offered Ferris a pamphlet.

"Oh, 'scuse me, sir. Would you be–"

"No," Ferris said abruptly, waving off the paper. The man gave up, moving on to the next person on the street.

"Way to get into the Christmas spirit, Scrooge," Demos said.

"I hate Christmas."

"We noticed," Demos said, flicking open his lighter. He brought it to the cigarette in his teeth, sucking to light it. Ferris did hate the holiday season, but it hadn't stopped him from getting a new video game for Seamus and an engraved cigarette case for Demos. He wasn't normally one to encourage Demos' smoking, but Ferris didn't see his friend quitting anytime soon. Not to mention Demos had not-so-subtly hinted at wanting one about six times.

"Oh, oh. Here, let's stop here," Seamus said with a crooked grin. He was staring at a candy store. The entrance was glowing with color and sparkles. The entire scene reflected in Seamus' eyes as if he were a still a young boy.

"Sure," Demos said. "I need to pick some stuff up for grandpa's party anyway."

"You think they got wine gums?" Seamus said.

"If I knew what they were, I could tell you," Demos replied.

Ferris didn't have much of a sweet tooth and browsed the rows of bins idly as his friends got down to business. Seamus lifted a lid to sneak out a piece of chocolate, popping it quickly into his mouth before moving on to the next bin.

"Seamus," Ferris scoffed, tapping the 'no tasting' sign with his finger. "If you're going to steal could you at least use the scoop? Who knows where your hands have been."

"Want to find out?" Seamus said, wiggling all ten of his fingers.

"Augh," Ferris shuddered, turning to go find Demos. As he left, he could hear Seamus popping open more lids. Ferris rolled his eyes.

"Hey," Demos said, grabbing his friend's attention with a wave of his hand. "What do you think?"

Ferris stepped over, looking at the candy over Demos' shoulder.

"Should I get these," Demos said, gesturing to a bin of brightly colored coconut haystacks, "or the licorice?"

"Come on, Demos. Coconut? Think of your poor family."

"What? Everyone likes coconut."

"Emily hates coconut."

Demos squinted at his friend with suspicion.

"So what *does* she like, then?"

"Gummy bears. Well, anything gummy. Chocolate, too."

"Why do you know this?"

"Demos, you *live* with her. Isn't it obvious?"

"God, your crush is bad," Demos sighed, putting a hand on his forehead.

"What are you talking about?" Ferris snapped.

"Nothing," Demos said, dumping a scoopful of chocolate covered cherries into a bag. He paused, then narrowed his eyes at Ferris.

"Or does she hate cherries, too?"

"Cherries are fine."

"Thanks," Demos said curtly, closing the bag with a hasty twist-tie. He looked down in thought. After a moment, he cast a glance at the taller boy.

"Hey, Ferris?" he asked slowly.

"Yeah?"

"What's *my* favorite candy?"

"Black licorice and... Galatine, those little Italian milk candies," Ferris said, showing the approximate size with his fingers.

"Oh."

"What, why?"

"Just wondering if I had anything to be jealous about," Demos said with a teasing smile.

"Well fine then, what's mine?"

"You don't like candy. You don't like anything. You're a hateful old man in a teenager's body."

Ferris tapped the tip of his nose.

Seamus' search for the candy of his childhood went fruitlessly. Despite the half pound of 'free samples' he'd consumed, he still managed to leave depressed. Demos paid the cashier with a credit card and soon they were back on the street.

"Carry this for me, would you?" Demos said shamelessly, handing the new shopping bag to Seamus. The English boy took it without question, though he did get tempted to reach inside. They passed a few more stores until one of them caught Ferris' eye. He'd been waiting for the art store; he still hadn't bought Emily a gift.

"Hey guys, I need to get something for Mom. I'll catch up with you in a second," Ferris said, gesturing to the jewelry store next door.

"We can go with–"

"No, really. Go ahead."

"Well, okay. See you."

Ferris exhaled. He didn't want to put up with the two of them making fun of him as he tortured himself over what to get for Emily. The moment they were out of sight, he slipped into the art shop.

The store wasn't quite as crowded as the others. Shelves of paint, pencils, and things Ferris couldn't even recognize lined the aisles. As he paced past the inks, he began to wring his hands. He didn't know the first thing about art. Why were there five different brands of marker? What was the difference? He started to think that this might have been a bad idea when an employee picked up on his distress.

"Is there something I can help you find?" she asked, giving him a patient smile.

"Yeah," he mumbled. "I'm a little lost."

"What are you looking for?"

"Well, a gift. There's this… a friend of mine is an artist. I want to buy her something nice, but I have no idea what to get," he replied honestly. This was the stupidest he could remember feeling in quite a while.

"Ohh," she said, now understanding the situation. "Well, do you know what she works in? Is she a painter?"

"Yeah. She likes all kinds… lately she's been using watercolors."

"Oh, great. We have a lot of new watercolors in. Right this way."

Ferris started to feel better as he followed her past the aisles. At least now his gift would *probably* be useful.

"We have these tubes in a variety of colors, or you can get a set. The watercolor brushes are right here, too."

Ferris' eyes ran objectively over the rows of brushes. Something caught his eye, however, and he stopped to pick the brush up.

"Arches, Pure Kolinsky," he said aloud, trying to remember why it seemed so familiar. His eyes narrowed until suddenly he had it.

"This is it! She had this brush on her easel, but it was broken," he said, almost excited. "I think she'd need a new one, right?"

"Oh, lucky of you to remember that. Do you know which size it was?"

"It was a ten."

"Ten... ten," the employee mused, running her hand past the different sizes. "Ah, here we are."

She handed him the brush with a smile.

"I can wrap that up for you, if you'd like."

"Sure," he said, relieved that they had it. "How much is it?"

"That size is $98."

Ferris froze. He stared at her, lowering an eyebrow. He couldn't possibly have heard her correctly.

"What?"

"It's $98. They're pure red sable brushes with blond oak handles. These are the best quality you can get."

Ferris was speechless. He now fully understood the term 'starving artist.' It was entirely impossible for him to comprehend a little paint brush costing nearly a hundred dollars. Maybe if it were made of gold or something...

"Is it too much? We have a lot of great watercolor sets if your budget is a little lower," the staff girl said cheerfully.

Ferris stared at the brush in his hand. He rolled it between his fingers, thinking quietly. He shut his eyes, speaking before he could change his mind.

"No, it's okay." He opened his eyes. "I'll take it."

"You sure?"

"Yeah."

"Great! I can ring you up right over here," she said, leading him towards the front register. Ferris did his best not to sigh deeply as he handed her his charge card.

'She needs it. Just think of how happy she'll be,' he thought to himself. He'd just have to cut down on his book fund for a couple of months. No big deal. The girl rang him up and he turned down the bag, not wanting to show his friends that he'd been in an art store. Instead, he put the box inside of his messenger bag, trying to avoid looking at the receipt.

"Thanks for your help."

"No problem. Have a good night, Sir."

When he met back up with Demos and Seamus, he managed to look blasé once more.

"What'd you get your mom?" Demos asked, fingering the fabric of a tie.

"Some earrings." It wasn't a total lie. Ferris had bought his mother a pair of earrings about a week ago.

"I could have found them cheaper," Demos said, not caring to ask how much they'd cost in the first place.

"You mean 'stolen.' That's okay. Mom is picky."

"Hey, I'll take some earrings if you got 'em," Seamus said, elbowing the Italian.

"Your ears aren't pierced," Ferris said.

"Oh, not for me. I think I could get Maria in the sack with a nice little gift is all."

"Oh, right. I forgot I was talking to you," Ferris said, though he was distracted. He couldn't stop thinking about the small package in his bag. It was as if it weighed twenty pounds. Gino's Christmas party was coming up in a few weeks. Ferris could only hope that by then Emily wouldn't have completely given up on watercolors.

50

The main hall of the Giorgetti compound was filled with music and chatter. The room was massive. A gold chandelier hung from the lofty ceiling, decorated with tasteful red ribbon. Candles, holly, and tinsel made the large hall seem to sparkle. The hundred or so invited guests were dressed elegantly, talking against the sound of a popping champagne cork. Gino had hired a small group of classical musicians to play string renditions of Christmas songs. They were currently performing *Tu Scendi Dalle Stelle*, one of Gino's personal favorites.

Demos was standing next to the grand piano, wearing a suit as black as its finish. He sipped a tall glass of red wine, watching as Southport's social and political bigwigs made conversation. Seamus and Ferris were bickering behind him. It was rare for Seamus to cross over into the world of his family, but this was Christmas — everyone was invited. With the anticipation of free alcohol, Seamus had readily accepted the invitation.

"Oi, come on. Just one kiss, would you?" Seamus pleaded.

"No freaking way," Ferris said, his tone utterly flat.

"But the mistletoe is right there," Seamus said, gesturing above their heads. "You have to."

"I'm a Jew, I don't have to follow your asinine rules."

Seamus sighed dramatically.

"I hope you're happy, Fer. You've destroyed Christmas."

"Now I just need to get Easter and my work will be done," Ferris said, finishing the last bit of spumante in his glass. Seamus reached around to pluck the empty glass from his friend's fingers.

"I'll just fill you back up, yeah?" he said with a smile. "Back in a bit."

If Seamus couldn't use the mistletoe trick, the least he could do was get him drunk. Ferris stepped up next to Demos, putting his hands into his pockets as he watched the crowd.

"Hey," Ferris said, squinting at a small man who was speaking animatedly with Victor. "Is that the ice cream guy?"

"Charlie Martin," Demos clarified. "And that's his wife."

There was a woman who looked to be in her fifties next to the man. She was wearing a blue silk dress and smiled as she spoke.

"She looks fine," Ferris said, remembering that she was supposed to have cancer.

"Yeah, the insurance company covered her treatments after all. I'm kind of glad, too. I didn't want Uncle Vic to pop a blood vessel."

"Uh huh," Ferris said, taking off his glasses. "That sounds messy."

He took a cloth from his pocket, wiping the lenses and then holding them up to the light to make sure any smudges were gone. He was trying not to think about the small wrapped paint brush in his pocket. He'd given his gifts to Seamus and Demos earlier. Seamus, in return, had given Ferris a handmade macaroni valentine that was ten months late because it had been lost under his bed, plus a David Bowie CD. Demos said he would give him his gift "later." Ferris couldn't help but feel nervous by the way Demos had phrased it.

"I haven't seen Emily," Ferris said offhandedly, despite having thought of nothing else for the past half hour.

"She's going to be a little late. You don't want to know where she is."

"...With Chris?"

Demos quirked his mouth as if that had been obvious. Ferris sighed.

"Wait'll you see what she got you," Demos said, trying to lighten the mood.

"What is it?"

"Like I'm going to spoil the surprise."

"I hope it's a new best friend."

Demos ignored the quip, setting his empty glass down on a passing tray. He looked across the hall, noticing Seamus had been distracted on his way back and was talking to a pretty brunette by the Christmas tree.

"I need a cigarette. Let's go to the lounge for a second."

Ferris nodded, following his friend through the crowd and past the staircase. There was a long hall lined with dark wooden doors. Demos' hand dropped onto a gold knob, pushing in the door to reveal the manor's parlor. It was quiet, housing a small bar and a few chaise lounges. There were glass cabinets and walnut shelves that held a few sculptures and liquor bottles. Demos pulled a cigarette from his new silver case, holding it lightly between his lips as he moved towards the back of the room to look through a drawer. To Ferris' surprise, the Italian pulled out a gift box wrapped in silver paper with a green ribbon.

"I'm not sure if you'll like this..." he said, handing the package to Ferris. He struck a match, lighting his cigarette. "But I thought you should have it."

"It's not a body part, is it?" Ferris asked tentatively, turning the gift in his hand to look at each side. It was heavy.

"Just open it."

Ferris gave his friend a look before tugging off the ribbon, cutting the tape with a finger. Beneath the paper was a solid case with a latch. When he opened it, his breath momentarily left

362

him. He set it down on the bar, hands flat on either side as he stared.

"Demos, I..."

"Keep it. Just in case."

It was a small black handgun. There was a set of ammunition and a spare magazine.

"It's light," Demos explained, "and not too powerful."

"I don't know if I... well—" Ferris said, still staring at it.

"You never know. Hold on to it. For me, okay?"

Ferris waited before nodding, closing the case and turning to face his friend.

"Thanks, Demos."

The Italian only smiled. They put the gun back into the drawer, deciding to pick it up later. Demos stubbed out the remains of his cigarette in a glass ash tray and they left the room together. Back in the main hall, the party was exactly as they had left it. Seamus approached them with a plate of hors d'oeuvres, stuffing a piece of shrimp into his mouth.

"Where's my drink?" Ferris asked, putting a hand on his hip.

"Yer what? Oh yeah, that..." Seamus replied while chewing.

"You're fired."

As Seamus started to protest, Ferris' eyes caught a pearl colored dress past a group of politicians. His expression softened as he watched Emily talk to her brother. Her dress was long with an empire waist and Victorian lace. She was laughing at a something Sergio had just said and Ferris noticed the purse she was holding when she adjusted it.

"Oi, Ferret. You there?"

"What?"

"I asked if you still wanted that drink."

"Oh... it's okay," Ferris said, squinting. He didn't remember her having a Louis Vuitton bag. "When did she get that purse?"

"Chris must have gotten it for her," Demos said, looking at the same bag. She certainly didn't have it that morning.

"Oh."

Ferris was starting to feel ill. He didn't know much about women's accessories, but he at least knew that the brand she was carrying would have cost Chris several hundred dollars. Of course, Ferris hadn't bought the brush in some attempt to wave his wallet around, but he had inwardly hoped it would show how important she was to him. Of all the things he could have bought, he was about to hand her a dinky little paint brush that she may or may not have even needed. This wasn't how he'd pictured this happening. Up until now, Chris simply seemed like a jerk who didn't think of anyone but himself. This time, however, he'd gone and dropped hundreds of dollars on a gift for his girlfriend. Maybe Ferris had been wrong about Chris. Maybe it would be best to keep his gesture to himself.

He didn't want to think about it anymore.

Ferris pulled the gift from his pocket, stuffing it in Demos' hands.

"Give this to her. Say it's from you, okay?"

"What?"

"Just do it, all right?" Ferris said, turning towards the staircase. Demos lifted a hand to stop him, but was interrupted by his uncle. A firm hand went around Demos' shoulders as Roberto led him towards the piano.

"Demos! Your grandfather wants you to play us a song. Go on, go sit."

Demos glanced over his shoulder, briefly catching Ferris' form trudging up the stairs. He opened the piano and traced his fingers over the keys, trying to remember the notes for *Fantaisie-Impromptu*. It would be best to give Ferris some time to think. Hopefully, he would figure it out on his own.

Upstairs, Ferris found the bedroom that he usually slept in when he stayed at the manor. There was a large four poster bed and a fireplace. Heavily, he sat down on the windowsill. His knees drew up under his chin, the same way he would sit as a child. Snow was falling in thick flakes and the sounds of the party were muffled by the door. As he looked out the window, he knew very well that he was just feeling sorry for himself. He couldn't, however, bring himself to quit.

Demos played three more songs before his family allowed him to stop. He turned around on the bench, taking another glass of wine from one of the wait staff. Emily approached, giving her cousin a smile.

"You've still got it," she said.

"Thanks," Demos said shamelessly.

"Um... you haven't seen Ferris around, have you? I've got something for him."

"Well..." Demos mused as he fished the gift from his suit pocket, offering it to her with a twirl of his wrist.

"What's this?" she asked, taking it curiously. "You already gave me a cell phone."

"No clue. It's from Ferris."

"Ferris? Why didn't he give it to me himself?"

"I don't know. Open it."

Emily tore the paper off and her eyes widened as she caught the logo on the case. Opening it eagerly, she stared at the brush inside. Emily opened her mouth, momentarily speechless.

Demos didn't understand what the big deal was and blinked as she picked it up with two fingers.

"...He got this for me?"

"Yeah. He told me to give it to you and stormed off upstairs. I think he's on his period or something," Demos mumbled. Emily frowned, then looked over towards the stairs.

364

Ferris' eyes were so fixated on the falling snow that it took him a moment to notice the door cracking open. He didn't turn his head, knowing from the soft tread that it was Emily. He felt her walk past him, setting down a large shopping bag and sitting on the windowsill by his side. She didn't speak at first, looking out the window with him.

"I was looking for you," she said, her voice quiet. He didn't respond. She ignored his detachment, looking down at the paint brush case in her hands.

"Did you get this for me?"

"Demos told you?" he asked, glancing at her with irritation.

"Why didn't you give it to me yourself?" she said.

Ferris turned his attention back to the window.

"Ferris, answer me."

His eyes flickered down, his expression unchanged.

"It's not important," he said.

"But I really liked this. It was thoughtful of you..."

"Yeah," he scoffed, "but you could buy like five of those with that purse."

"Is that was this is about?" she asked, narrowing her eyes.

"No," Ferris lied.

"What am I supposed to do with a Louis Vuitton purse?"

"I don't know. Show off how much your boyfriend loves you?"

"You think love is affirmed by price tags?" she snapped. He didn't have an answer for her.

"Fine," she said, standing up. "I thought you were better than that. I thought you knew what was important, but I guess I was wrong."

She tossed the bag she'd been carrying into his lap.

"Happy fucking Chanukah."

Emily stormed out, slamming the door shut behind her. Ferris stared at the door, then looked down to the bag she'd given him. Tentatively, he reached in to pull out its contents.

As his eyes locked on the oil painting, he felt his stomach wrench. On the small, stretched canvas lay hundreds of intricate brush strokes. They formed a pale fish skeleton among curled waves with flourished white crests. He nearly dropped it as he rushed to the door.

"Emily, wait!"

Ferris' hands gripped the frame of the door as he called out after her. She stopped at the top of the stairs, eyes locked on the first step.

"I'm sorry," he begged. "Wait, please."

Her eyes shut and he could only hope that her thoughts weren't spiteful.

"Come back. I need to talk to you," Ferris said gently. Emily's eyes shut more tightly. Finally giving in, she turned to face him.

"Okay," she mouthed, barely speaking.

Once she was back in the room, Ferris shut the door. With a flick of his wrist, he locked it. With the things he had to say, he didn't want anyone to barge in unexpectedly.

Emily sat on the bed and he hesitated before sitting next to her. He looked down at his hands, wringing them for a moment.

"I didn't mean it," he started. "You know I'm not like that. I guess I was just..."

Ferris exhaled.

"I was jealous. I'm sorry."

"It's okay," she said quietly.

"It's not okay, it was stupid. I guess it's just... when I saw it, I thought... I thought maybe Chris really did care about you. More than I thought," he said, then caught himself. "Not that that's bad. I mean... you know."

"Ferris," Emily said, still holding Ferris' gift in her hands. "I really needed this brush. It meant a lot to me, that you even knew that."

"It meant I was sneaking around your room like a creep," he mumbled.

"No," she smiled. "I lent it to Chris and he broke it. I couldn't tell Dad so... I just told him I broke it. He said I wasn't responsible enough for expensive brushes anymore."

"Oh." Ferris was surprised. He figured Victor was the type to forgive anything his precious daughter might do.

"So... thanks."

"You're welcome," Ferris said, then looked back at the windowsill. "And um... thanks for the painting. No one's ever done something like that for me before."

He turned back to look at her, giving a slight smile.

"I really love it."

"I'm glad you like it," she said. Her eyes softened before she bit her thumbnail. "You honestly thought the purse was a better gift?"

"Well... he was really thinking of you."

"That's the thing, Ferris. He wasn't. What do I care about brand name purses? The fact that he got it for me just shows he doesn't know anything about me."

"But you love him, right?"

She didn't reply. Ferris fidgeted. He opened his mouth, then closed it. He took in a deep breath before he tried opening his mouth again.

"Emily..."

She looked at him.

"I know it's not my place, and I'm sorry. But I can't take this anymore," Ferris said, raising his hands. "If he doesn't know anything about you... why are you with him? I just don't get it.

366

He treats you like garbage, he's a... sorry, he's a total prick, and you're not even sure if you love him."

"I don't love him," she said plainly.

"Then why? I know you're not stupid. You could do better than him. And I don't mean me, I mean anyone. *Anyone* would be better than him. What's—"

Ferris gritted his teeth, then blurted out the rest of his sentence.

"What's wrong with you?"

Emily's eyes were locked on her hands. She was silent, but Ferris let her be. Whatever she had to say was turning around in her mind and he could wait for it to settle. She shifted, breathed, and brought her gaze up to him.

"You have to promise not to tell anyone what I'm about to say."

"I promise."

Ferris' breath was short. He didn't think there would actually be an answer to his question. She fussed with her hands, then began.

"I met Chris a couple of years ago in an art program. He was all right. Sometimes he'd ask me out but I didn't really feel like it."

Ferris watched her speak with complete focus, taking in every word as if it were gold.

"Sergio would pick me up after class, and Chris' brother would come get him, too. Serg and Tito never really got along. One day they got into a fight in front of the school. Like, a real fight. Tito got his ass kicked and had to get a cast."

Ferris only nodded, not risking interruption with speech.

"Turns out... Tito works for the Marianis. Chris told me they were going to jump Sergio. They were going to find him on the weekend and..." Her voice was weak and she left the sentence in the air. "Well, Chris said he'd stop Tito if I went out with him and did whatever he wanted."

Everything clicked in Ferris' mind – every question, concern, and night spent staring at the ceiling in confusion was answered with a few short sentences.

"I didn't want anyone to get hurt..." Emily took in a soft breath as if it was difficult to even think about. "I thought Chris would just get bored with me after a few months. But he didn't. He won't let me talk to other guys, watches everything I do, and now buys me superficial gifts to convince himself he's the best boyfriend in the universe. He even tried to make me grow my hair out but—"

"So... the aquarium," Ferris said, finally speaking. His voice felt dry.

"I was going to tell you the truth. I was going to tell you everything. But... you know."

"...Yeah."

Emily smiled to herself, biting her lower lip.

"You know I've had a crush on you since we were kids," she admitted. "But by the time you noticed me, I was already with him."

Ferris swore in his head.

"Then I guess... all this time, you knew how I felt."

"How *do* you feel about me?" she asked.

He glanced from side to side. This was obviously the ideal time to say it. If not now, then never. It was difficult, however, to make his mouth work correctly. Instead, he swallowed.

"Emmy..."

"Yeah?"

"I... I think about you all the time," he said, already embarrassed. "I always felt stupid for it, but I couldn't... I couldn't just forget about you. I'm happy being your friend, but sometimes I can't help but remember that I—"

Ferris's chest seemed as if it was going to close in around his heart. His throat was raw from the difficulty of his words. The toughest ones hadn't even surfaced yet.

"Well, I... I love you." Slowly, he caught her eyes. "You know that, don't you?"

The look on her face answered him. The corners of her mouth rose and her eyes were warm. She nodded.

"So," he said once he managed to tear his eyes away from hers, "what now?"

"I don't know," she said, her expression changing. Something about her seemed lost. "What can we do?"

Ferris stopped to think, but it didn't take long for him to respond.

"Fancy an affair?"

Fancy? He really needed to spend less time with Seamus. Emily's eyes widened. For a moment, she stared at him, trying to figure out if he was being serious or not. As she studied his face, she found herself leaning closer. Just when he thought that she was actually about to kiss him, she looked away.

"If we got caught..." she said, trailing off. Her mouth was set in a soft frown.

"Are you worried about your brother?" Ferris asked, trying to hide his disappointment.

"I'm worried about you."

"Emmy," he said, voice low. "If you knew how many times I've been close to a painful death around Demos..."

"Is that supposed to make me feel better?" she asked with a quirked eyebrow.

"I don't care."

"What?"

368

"I don't care what he might do to me," Ferris said, determined. "And he won't find out. I promise he won't."

"How can you promise that?" Emily asked, sighing. Ferris put a hand on the side of her face, making her look at him.

"Are you happy like this?" Ferris said, keeping his eyes locked on hers. After a second, she shook her head.

"Well, neither am I," he said, eyes lowering. "Please don't tell me 'no.'"

"I won't."

She took each side of his head with her hands, curling her fingers to feel the texture of his hair. There were only inches of space between their faces, and then none. Ferris' head tilted when she kissed him, shutting his eyes. He wasn't as nervous as he'd thought he might be. This was different from other kisses; he had been waiting for this one for years.

They each took in a short breath for the second they were apart. Emily quickly closed the gap once more. She tasted like white wine and her mouth was warm. Ferris' brow knit as she pulled him down on top of her, not releasing his mouth from hers. Outside the window, snow continued to fall. The world went on as usual, but for Ferris, time had simply stopped.

Downstairs, Seamus was trying to coax Demos into a fifth glass of wine.

"No," Demos complained, batting the half-drunken Brit off of him. "I'm not going to look like a fool in front of *these* people."

"Like you care what a bunch of stuffy politicians think a' you," Seamus grinned, waving a glass of champagne under the Italian's nose. Demos frowned. It was usually Ferris who got the full brunt of all this hassling. Where was Ferris, anyway? He looked towards the stairs, guessing that the two were still talking. Demos' eyes narrowed in thought before Seamus put a hand on his shoulder.

"C'mon, let's dance."

"God, kill me," Demos said with a roll of his eyes as he was dragged off towards the musicians.

Back in the room, Emily's dress was in danger of being damaged. It was halfway unzipped and haphazardly folded beneath their bodies. She was gripping the back of Ferris' previously crisp white shirt while he kissed her throat. His suit jacket was somewhere on the floor. Breathless, she pulled him up for another long kiss on the mouth. When their lips broke apart, he took in a deep breath.

"Uh, maybe..."

"Not yet," she said, finishing his sentence.

"Right."

They had both gotten slightly carried away in the moment. It was only now that they remembered there was a party going on downstairs.

"Well, I do have a condom," she mused, glancing sideways towards her purse. Ferris had managed to keep his calm up until then, but could now feel his face burning as he tried to form a reply. She bit her lip to keep from laughing.

"What?" she asked.

"U-um…"

"Oh, really?"

"Quit making fun of me," he finally snapped, still completely flushed. Smiling, she leaned up to gently kiss his jaw.

"I love you, too."

Ferris quieted, lying next to her. Emily's arms wrapped up around his neck, bringing their foreheads together again.

"We can't tell anyone," she said. "Not even Demos."

"Okay."

"I'm serious. If you tell him, I'll kill you," she said, cutting her fingers across her throat.

"Got it."

The party had been going on for hours and Ferris had missed nearly half of it. Victor was standing by the open bar looking at his watch. Demos could have sworn he could see his uncle's eye twitch. It honestly was getting hard to believe that Emily had simply gone to 'powder her nose' for 45 minutes.

"I'm going to go look for her," Victor finally grumbled.

"Wait, don't," Demos said, not wanting Victor to stumble in on the two having a private conversation up in an isolated bedroom.

"What? It's been nearly an hour," Victor snapped.

"Emily is just—"

"I'm just what?" Emily asked, stepping up behind them.

"There you are!" Victor said, half relieved and half angry. "Where have you been?"

"Oh, just… girl problems," Emily said under her breath. With the pained look on her face, she was really playing the part.

"You poor thing, let me get you some aspirin," Victor said, his mood changing dramatically. He put his hand on her shoulder, leading her away with a sympathetic expression. Demos let out the breath he'd been holding.

"What was that all about?" Ferris asked, coming up next to Demos. He stood casually, as if he hadn't just spent the past five minutes scrubbing lipstick off of his neck.

"What the hell did you guys discuss, the meaning of life? You're lucky I kept Uncle Vic from storming up there in—"

"Nothing. I apologized for being a dick and then we just caught up."

"Okay," Demos said incredulously. "If you say so."

"She gave me a nice painting."

"Oh, you liked it? Good. She spent forever on that thing."

"I could tell."

"What about my gift?" Seamus whined.

"Your stale macaroni valentine will hang forever in my heart and nothing shall ever replace it."

"That's what I thought," Seamus replied with a smug grin, wrapping one arm over Ferris' shoulders. "Now, about that drink."

51

It was March. For the last few weeks, Ferris had been rushing straight to the kitchen each day after school. Food wasn't the target of his attention, however, as he was always drawn to the flat spot of marble on the end of the counter. This was where the mail was usually set. He would repeat the same routine of scooping up the letters, flipping through them without breathing, then slowly setting them down as he bit back his disappointment. Occasionally he would find an envelope with his name on it, but the return address never read 'Yale.'

Jake, his cousin, had already been accepted to NYU in his hometown. The teen had to plead incessantly to get permission to stay in the school dorms. He didn't want to live with his parents forever. Ferris had also been accepted to several schools, including Brown, his safety. The anxiety that was starting to build inside of him was impossible to express in words. Demos and Seamus could absolutely not relate.

"Slow down, it's not like getting the mail faster will get you into school faster," Seamus griped, frowning as he attempted to keep up with Ferris. They had planned to go to a diner together – after Ferris checked the mail of course. Demos already had plans.

"I know, but some kid in class got his letter from Yale yesterday," Ferris said between breaths, trying his hardest not to break into a run. "It should be here."

"He get accepted?"

"No," Ferris said, unsure of whether to be smug or worried. The other boy's grades had been fairly impressive.

"Oh come on, it's just gonna be some eensy letters on your resume, what difference does it make?"

Ferris slowed down for a second, giving Seamus a hard look.

"If you had any idea," he panted, "how hard I've worked for this."

"God, I know. We all know. Go on," Seamus said with a roll of his eyes, urging Ferris on with a light push to his back.

The front door of the Levinstein home opened abruptly, startling the fat pug who'd been napping nearby. He didn't have time to bark as Ferris kicked off his shoes and walked through to the kitchen. There was a familiar flipping sound as he picked through the mail, followed by a sigh.

"Damn it."

"Oh, sweetie, you're home," Ruth said, coming in from the living room.

"Yeah," Ferris said. From the tone of his voice, he might as well have been dead.

"Something came for you," she said, waving a large envelope. Ferris' head picked up instantly, staring as if he'd seen a ghost. He didn't say a word as she handed it to him, only biting his lip. It was big – the size of a manila folder. The front bore his address, as well as that of Yale University's.

Seamus meandered up beside him, swiping an apple from a bowl on the counter.

"Hey, that's it," he said, taking a noisy bite.

Ferris wanted to say something to Seamus about ruining this potential 'moment,' but his mouth stayed shut. He opened the envelope and pulled out the papers inside. Taking a breath, he looked down to read.

Congratulations on your admission to Yale College, Class of 2006! Announcing the good news to a candidate is the absolute best part of my job—

"Yes! Finally, *yes!*" Ferris roughly grabbed the nearest living thing, which happened to be Seamus, deliriously kissing him on the cheek before rushing out of the room. Seamus' eyes followed him out before taking another bite of his apple. The crunching noise was all that was left in the kitchen as Seamus heard Ruth congratulating her son. Seamus had never seen Ferris speak that quickly, loudly, or happily in the years they'd been friends. He took a mental note of the event.

"I gotta be around for more acceptance letters," he said to himself before swallowing.

Ferris went to the study to call his father. By the time their conversation was over, Seamus' apple had become a core. Ferris came back into the kitchen just in time to see him throw it into the trash.

"I'm guessin' your dad's happy, yeah?"

"Yeah. He wants to take me out for dinner."

"Oh," Seamus said, battling between disappointment and support for his friend.

"I told him tomorrow. We have plans already," Ferris said with a faint smile.

"Excellent," Seamus said, throwing an arm around Ferris' shoulder. "To the Sparrow, then?"

"Sure. Let me call Demos," Ferris said, pushing a few buttons on his cell phone. Demos' 'business' could wait until later.

Twenty minutes later, the two were seated in one of the diner's red booths. Ferris was stirring a coffee while Seamus pondered the menu.

"What do you think, should I go French and get the 'roast beef au jus?' Or maybe Mexican and get the quesadilla."

"Well, you can't get good Mexican food in England, and God knows when they're going to deport you..."

"Quesadilla it is."

"Hey, you pronounced it right," came a voice from behind them. Demos approached their booth, sliding in next to Seamus. His slender hands folded neatly on the table. Though Ferris' college acceptance had not, in fact, been more important than a potential loan-sharking investment, Demos put the meeting off anyway.

"What? I've always said it right."

"Kwes-uh-dilla?" Demos asked with a raised eyebrow. Seamus waved him off.

"I was *joking* when I said that."

"Sure you were," Demos said before turning his attention to Ferris. "Well, well. Congratulations."

"Thanks," Ferris said after a sip of coffee.

"We're proud of you."

Ferris put down his cup.

"You don't look proud," he said plainly.

"What do you mean?"

"Your voice sounds like I just told you I have cancer."

"Well..."

Seamus cut in, leaning forward in his seat.

"Well you're gonna be gone. I'll probably end up somewhere. Dad might make me go back to London or something. We'll be all... apart. The three of us, you know?"

"It was going to happen no matter what school accepted me. I explained this before."

"But aren't you gonna miss us?" Seamus asked, sincere for once.

"Well—" Ferris said, caught off guard. His voice grew more subdued. "Well, of course I will."

"We were a good team, us three," Seamus insisted. "But you'll just make some new friends at school. Some snotty, smart ones too, I bet."

"Give me a little credit, Seamus. You know how bad I am at making friends."

"I don't know. You've changed."

"I have not."

"You have," Demos said, speaking up.

"Can't you just be happy for me?" Ferris sighed, fiddling with his coffee mug.

"We are," Demos said, his voice sincere. "You really deserve this, Ferris."

"You honestly think so?"

"Of course. And the admissions guy was really impressed with your violin recital, too."

Ferris nodded, then paused. His eyebrows knit as he thought back to the night of his recital.

"...I never mentioned Mr. Yardley to you."

"Oh," Demos said, blinking. "Yeah. Met him briefly. Seemed like a nice guy."

"When did you meet him?" Ferris asked slowly. His eyes were starting to narrow.

"Uncle Vic and I saw him... you know, just a quick chat."

Ferris' eyes tightened at the corners, his mouth feeling suddenly parched. He was frozen, hands set in tight fists next to his mug.

"You... you didn't," he said, his throat bobbing as he swallowed.

"Hey," Demos said, reaching out to put a hand on top of Ferris' fist. "We just wanted to give you a little edge, you know?"

"Did you threaten him?" Ferris snapped. His voice was starting to rise.

"Not... in so many words..."

Ferris threw off the hand that was touching him.

"I can't *believe* you," he said, seething. "I told you I wanted to get in on my own merit. You knew that!"

"Ferris, we did it for you," Demos said softy, trying to calm his friend's nerves.

Ferris' heart was pounding now.

"I've been studying my ass off since kindergarten so you could wave a gun in some guy's face and *cheat* me in?! Does hard work mean nothing to you? Haven't you earned a single fucking thing in your entire life? The honest way?"

He stood, ignoring the heat in his face.

"You're proud of me? Of what? What did *I* fucking do?"

He tossed a few bills down onto the table and left. The diner's door shut with a soft jingle. After a bit of silence, Seamus folded his hands behind his head.

"Hooo boy."

"Shut up, Seamus," Demos said, putting his face into his hands.

Harold's second floor office was dreadfully silent. Ferris was seated in the leather office chair, chin down on his folded arms as he stared at the phone. Mr. Yardley's business card lay flat on the desk, tempting him to simply call.

They didn't understand. Yale wasn't just something he wanted for resume padding. It had been something to work for, to prove to himself that he could get by without his family's influence – that he could accomplish something on his own. Harold had been accepted years ago without dropping any names. Ferris had known, or at least had hoped, that he could do the same. He picked up the acceptance letter that he'd received only hours before. The elation he'd felt when reading the same text earlier was now gone. There was only one way to go from here.

He picked up the phone, dialing the number on the business card. He waited, then pressed five to speak to a human being.

"Hello, Office of Undergraduate Admissions."

"George Yardley, please."

"One moment."

There was a minute of silence, then a man's voice.

"Yardley speaking."

"Mr. Yardley, this is Ferris Levinstein. I'm not sure if you remember me..."

"Oh yes, the violin recital. Of course. Can I help you with something?"

"I received my acceptance letter..." Ferris said, fiddling with the paper in his hand.

"Good to hear."

"But I have to turn it down."

"I'm sorry?"

"I won't... be attending Yale. You can give my spot to someone on the waiting list."

There was a pause.

"Would you mind if I asked what this is about? You did seem... quite interested in attending. We gave you a couple of scholarships, if you read the—"

"Yes, I saw. I just—" Ferris sighed. "I feel that... the circumstances surrounding my acceptance were not entirely my own doing."

There was another pause.

"Are you by any chance referring to Mr. Giorgetti's visit?"

"...Yes," Ferris said quietly, trying to keep the shame out of his voice.

"Well, Ferris. I must say I was disappointed to see them. There was no need for further negotiation – you'd already been accepted by that point."

"...I had?" Ferris asked, sitting up straight.

"Yes, of course. I informed them of this but they seemed very intent on... speaking with me anyhow."

Ferris stared for a moment, then shook himself back into proper thought.

"Er, I'm sorry. I didn't have anything to do with—"

"I'm sure you didn't," Yardley said earnestly. "You seem like an honest, hardworking young man. We would not have accepted you if you weren't."

When Ferris didn't reply, the man inquired further.

"Do you still wish to decline your—"

"No! No... it's fine. I'm coming," Ferris said, exhaling in a bit of relief.

"Excellent. I'll see you in the fall. Was there anything else?"

"No. Thank you, Mr. Yardley."

"Anytime. Goodbye."

They each hung up and Ferris slumped down in the chair. He shut his eyes, biting his lower lip to try to subdue the smile that was emerging. Seconds later, the door cracked open.

"I told Mom not to let you in," Ferris said quietly, opening his eyes halfway to watch Demos come in.

"I, um, was listening."

"I gathered."

"I'm sorry. I didn't know it was so important to you," Demos said, sitting in one of the chairs facing the desk. "We should have asked first. I just... wanted to look out for you."

"It's okay. I overreacted. I was just embarrassed, you know? It's like winning the Olympics and then finding out you were on steroids the whole time."

"I didn't think of it that way..."

"I know."

"So, you're not mad anymore?"

"No. Last time I got in a big fight, I made Seamus take the booze train straight into the hospital."

"I could drink him under the table."

"What?" Ferris said, sitting up. "You're like twenty pounds."

"I'm Italian."

"He's British," Ferris said before remembering something. "Oh, I told Seamus I'd have dinner with him. I'm going to have to make it up to him."

"Don't tell him that. He'll just feel you up."

Ferris smirked.

"You know," he said, folding his arms as he leaned forward on the desk, "I really am going to miss you two."

"So you're still going to Yale, then."

"Yeah," Ferris said, then smiled. "No thanks to you."

52

West from Little Italy lay a shopping district with dozens of towering department stores. Ferris usually avoided places such as these, having no interest in crowds or one day sales. Few things could actually bring him into one of these stores for half a day, and one of them was Emily.

"What do you think?" she asked, turning around to show him the long blue dress.

"It's too bright," he complained from the bench where he was seated. Emily had been stepping in and out of the dressing room stalls, getting his opinion on each outfit. She needed one for prom. Ferris certainly didn't mind; he got to see his girlfriend in a bunch of dresses.

"But I like it. Not everyone can be a miserable rain cloud like you," she said, lifting the back to examine the matching shoes.

"Hey, you asked what I thought."

"My mistake."

"They all look pretty good," Ferris admitted. "I just wish you were going with me."

"I wish I was, too," she said, her expression dropping.

"I should just pick the frumpiest one so he gets to see as little of you as possible," Ferris mumbled.

"Then what are we doing here? I could just get a potato sack from the restaurant."

"Yes, let's."

Ten minutes later Emily decided on a long, black dress and they left the store with a shopping bag. It was April and a spring rain was spattering over the street. They shared an umbrella that was barely big enough for the two of them. Ferris offered to hold the bag for her, despite her insisting that it wasn't heavy. After a block, she reached to link arms. A car drove by and she drew back, frowning.

"I hate this," she said under her breath. "We can't do anything in public."

Ferris now had a faint idea of what it was like to be Demos.

"We just have to make up for it in private."

"I like the way you think," Emily said, listening to the rain as it fell over their umbrella. "If we can ever get time alone."

She thought back to the house with Demos and her parents, as well as Ferris' home where Ruth was nearly always present. They'd only really had a house to themselves two or three times.

"Mom and Dad are going on a short anniversary trip next weekend, actually," she said. "You should, you know, stop by. For a bit."

He smiled and she returned the expression. They walked for another couple of minutes before she spoke up again.

"I've been meaning to ask you something..."

"Yeah?" Ferris replied, glancing at her.

"Well, we need to talk about your going away to college. You'll be pretty far."

Ferris looked forward for a moment, thinking.

"I'll understand if you want to break up," he said quietly. "I'll only be in Southport a few times a year."

"That's not what I meant. I thought *you'd* want to break up. You'll be meeting so many new people, and all..."

"No, of course not," he said firmly. "What about you?"

"I waited for years to go out with you, I can wait another four."

"Are you sure?"

"I'm sure."

"So we're going to have a long distance relationship," Ferris mused.

"Looks like it."

"We can do it," he said, giving her a brief smile. "I'm positive."

Their sentimental moment was disrupted by a man waiting in the shelter of a bus stop.

"Hey, chick," he called out, adjusting a thin jacket over his protruding belly. They both ignored him. As they passed by, he raised his voice.

"Nice ass."

Ferris immediately opened his mouth to say something, but Emily did it first.

"Nice tits," she replied without missing a step. The man didn't respond, only scoffing as he turned away. Ferris made a sound that was something between a laugh and a snort.

"Remind me never to mention your ass," he said.

"You didn't seem to mind it last week."

Ferris reddened and shut up.

By the time prom actually came around, Ferris was the only senior at St. Basil's without plans for the night. He'd decided not to ask anyone else and turned down Demos and Seamus' repeated offers to take him. It wouldn't have felt right to take some other girl and he certainly didn't want to go alone. Seamus ended up going with a tall blonde and Demos with a short brunette. Ferris knew it was solely because it was the closest the two boys could get to dating themselves. While the others were in tuxedos and limos, Ferris was sitting on his bed re-reading *Moby-Dick*. He sipped at the teacup next to his bed, idly setting the book down in his lap. His eyes wandered towards the window. He started wondering exactly what his friends were doing and if they were having a good time or not. Wasn't this the

most important night of most young people's lives? He fingered
the pages of his book, flipping them without thinking.

The school had rented out the Stanhope Ballroom for the
event and Ferris was sure that it must have been impressive.
Trying not to dwell on it, he looked back down to his book. It
was his own choice not to go, after all. He'd sternly proclaimed
how stupid he thought the entire thing was, hadn't he?

Five chapters later he was reaching for the teacup again, only
to find that it was empty. Just when he considered getting up for
a refill, a noise caught his attention from outside. It was a honk.
Honks weren't terribly abnormal on a city street, but this one
repeated itself two more times. Sitting up, he peeked through the
blinds.

Seamus' car was parked in front of his house. The headlights
were bright and the motor was running. Another honk made
Ferris wince, holding up his hands in an attempt to shut him up.
He rushed out of his room and down the stairs. Hastily, he
tugged on a pair of shoes and grabbed his keys.

"What the hell are you guys doing here?" Ferris asked,
peering over his glasses as he approached the car. Demos was
leaning out of the passenger seat window, coaxing Ferris over
with a wave of his hand.

"Got dull real quick," Seamus said, lowering his head to look
out the window. There was lipstick on the collar of his shirt.

"Seamus got our dates plastered and they passed out."

"Of course," Ferris muttered. "Where are they?"

"In the trunk," Demos said, deadpanned.

Ferris stared at him for a few seconds before Demos' mouth
quirked into a grin.

"Their friends took them home. We're going to the beach."

"Get in," Seamus grinned, holding up a carton of beer bottles.

Ferris took a look back at his house, then to the car. A smile
crept over his face and he got into the back seat. The door swiftly
shut and the car rumbled off down the street.

Though most of Southport's shoreline was taken up by docks,
there was still room for several beaches. Rawson Beach was busy
during the day, but at night it was practically deserted. Dark
waves lapped the sand and a sparkling city skyline illuminated
their backs. Three pairs of shoes and socks lay discarded on the
dry sand. Demos and Seamus were walking briskly through the
water, half-drunk and kicking the waves at each other. Ferris
watched them from several yards away, ankle deep in the cold
ocean. He would have been content to simply observe, but
Seamus sent an arc of salty spray across his shirt.

"You little punk," Ferris fumed. The Brit only laughed. His
snickers halted abruptly when Ferris shoved him down into the

surf. Seamus' feet flew up as he landed on his back with a heavy splash.

"Oh no," Seamus choked between laughs. Water dripped from his hair. "My tux."

Ferris, feeling a bit of guilt, offered a hand to help him up. Seamus took it, then pulled his friend down on top of him. There was a terrible splash and Demos couldn't help but lose his cool and start laughing as well. Ferris spit up a mouthful of sea water when he surfaced, unable to see with all the droplets on his glasses.

"I'm going to kill you."

"You're the one who had to go all *Boston Tea Party* on my arse," Seamus said, nearly giggling as he tried to wrestle Ferris back into the water.

"Well, guess who won *that* war," Ferris threatened as he struggled to stay above the surface, flattening a hand on Seamus' face. The laughter was becoming unbearably contagious. Before he knew it, Ferris had joined the two in laughing for no apparent reason. Their voices were the only sounds on the beach that night.

After lying back on a blanket for an hour, they were still nowhere near dry. Seamus had tossed his shirt and jacket on the hood of the car to dry. Demos cracked open another beer bottle, offering it to Ferris. He took a sip as they each looked up at the sky.

"Can't remember the last time I saw stars," Seamus said, uncharacteristically thoughtful as he drew a bottle from his lips.

"If you think about it," Demos said, "all the city lights are like stars, but on the ground. Like the sky is upside down."

The three were quiet for a second before Ferris and Seamus simultaneously started to laugh.

"I need to start writing down all the shit you say," Ferris snorted.

"Why don't you make that into a haiku?" Seamus suggested, snickering all the while.

Demos tossed a handful of sand in their direction. The two recoiled, shielding their drinks.

"Hey, come on," Seamus sputtered, dusting sand out of his hair. "It's a compliment. You're such a wonderful poet."

"And you didn't even know it," Ferris added. They both started to laugh again.

"You know what else I am? A dead-eye shot. And you guys are slow moving targets."

"Ooh, scary," Seamus snickered, chugging what remained of his beer. Ferris flopped down onto his back. Even though it was night, the sky still glowed with light pollution.

"Prom night turned out better than I thought," he said to himself.

"What are you talking about?" Demos said. "You're dripping wet and covered in sand."

"Like I said," Ferris replied, "better than I thought."

53

Seamus poked the lemon in his water with a plastic straw, watching it bob up and down at his whim. Ferris was seated next to him with a coffee, scribbling something in a small green notebook. Demos had just arrived, setting down his tiny cup of espresso and giving his two friends a tired smile.

"You didn't wait too long, did you?"

"It's fine," Ferris said, still writing notes. Demos was usually either punctual or fashionably late. He was never early. "So, what's in the bag?"

Their attention turned to the red shopping bag Demos had placed next to his feet.

"I got you guys something."

"A gift?" Seamus said, perking up. He loved free things, regardless of what they were. "For us?"

"Yes, for you," Demos said in a tone that sounded as if he should pinch his friend's cheek for embellishment. The bag made a crinkling noise as he dug inside and two small books were set neatly on the table. They had plain black covers made of cloth. Seamus immediately grabbed one to flip through it.

"Oh, photos," he said with a grin. Inside the book lay various snapshots and Polaroids of the three of them throughout the past year. Hesitantly, Ferris reached for the remaining book to thumb through the pages. He was not the most photogenic of all people.

"Oh, great. You got me when I passed out at the Halloween party?" Ferris groaned.

"That's the best photo in there," Demos said defensively, "and the one of Seamus as a trash can or a butt plug or whatever."

"I was a Dalek, okay? I told you a dozen–"

"Yeah, okay. Trash can."

"Who's this chick?" Ferris asked, tilting the book to show a shot of Seamus and a redheaded girl.

"My girlfriend," Seamus said offhandedly, "for a week."

"You expect me to keep up with that?"

"Well, she was the one who gives 'the best head at St. Basil's,'" Seamus said, almost proud. "Remember?"

"Yeah, I doubt it," Ferris mumbled.

"What would you know, virgin?" Seamus said, leaning in over the table and grinning in the cocky way he always did.

"I'm not a virgin," Ferris said bluntly. Two seconds later, he snapped his hand over his mouth.

"What?" Demos demanded, his eyes narrowed. "Who?"

"No one. It was a joke."

"No, who? Tell me."

"Yeah," Seamus said, putting both hands on the table. "Who was it?"

"No one. I was kidding. I'm a virgin," Ferris muttered.

"What?"

"*I'm a virgin,*" Ferris said sharply. A moment later he realized everyone in the café was staring at him. Reddening, he slumped down in his seat.

"Are you sure?" Demos asked with a raised eyebrow.

"Of course I'm sure. You'd think I would notice something like that."

Demos stopped pressing, but clearly wasn't convinced. Ferris suppressed a sigh. If he disclosed his relationship with Emily, she'd kill him. That was a close one. It was hard not being able to talk to anyone about sex, but at the same time, he would have been too embarrassed to bring it up anyway. Seamus would have been the perfect person to ask, but the Brit was too nosy.

Ferris had almost asked him a few months ago, when things with Emily were starting to get to 'that stage.' He was pacing inside his own mind with anxiety, sitting on the edge of Seamus' bed with his fingers tapping the sheets. Every so often he'd open his mouth, start to ask Seamus something, then shut it in awkward silence.

"How do I–"

"What do I do if–"

"How do I know when–"

He couldn't finish his sentences. If he asked, then Seamus would pry with 'who, what, why?' Everything had to be kept secret. Nobody could know — especially not Seamus. Ferris was in the middle of a sentence when Seamus' cell phone rang.

"Just a second," Seamus said, stepping into the other room to answer it. It was probably one of his many girlfriends.

In fact, 'one of his many girlfriends' had left traces of herself all over the bedroom from earlier that week. There was a stick of women's deodorant on the dresser and a St. Basil's uniform skirt on the floor. A few feet over lay a bra. What the hell had this girl left in, a garbage bag?

Every few seconds, Ferris would catch sight of the bra from the corner of his eye. Those things were so strange. Sure, they closed with those metal hooks or whatever, but how did girls fasten them without looking, and backwards? It was hard not to worry about whether or not he'd be smooth about it when the time finally came with Emily. He'd been meaning to briefly look at one but it was too embarrassing to do in a store. Maybe he could just quickly see how it hooked. He wasn't being weird. No, this was research. This was science.

Before he could think about it anymore, he picked the bra up by the thin strap. He held it with two fingers as if it were a dead

384

rat. Who knew where the thing had been? It was white with blue flowers and had lace trim along the edges. Ignoring his good sense, he turned it over in his hands and examined the hooks. There were rows of them, like a shark's teeth. Creepy.

"You need help getting that on?" Seamus asked from the doorway. Panicking, Ferris dropped it in mid-fumble.

"Wh-no, I was just–"

Seamus raised an eyebrow, grinning in amusement.

"Look," Seamus said, picking the bra up casually and sitting next to Ferris on the bed. "Hooks like this, and if you do this you can open it with one hand. See?"

"Yeah," Ferris replied. This wasn't awkward or anything. "I see."

"Go on, try."

"It's okay, I get it."

"Try!"

"I get it!"

Ferris shook the three month old memory, going back to the photo book in his hands. Trying to change the subject, he flipped to the very end.

"You left one blank spot," Ferris said, now at the last page. "You run out of pictures?"

"That's for our graduation photo — which hasn't been taken yet."

"I still can't believe they're graduating Seamus. He attended, what, three classes all year?"

"Oi, I did my schoolwork. Sometimes."

"Which you copied from me."

"Hey, I didn't copy everything from you."

"I know. You occasionally copied Demos, who in turn copied from me," Ferris said, stirring his coffee. "Q.E.D."

"What?"

"Just eat your muffin."

Seamus grumbled, now purposely ignoring his muffin out of spite.

"Thanks," Ferris said to Demos, sliding the photo book into his bag. "Looks like it took you a while to put together."

"It did," Demos said shamelessly. "And you're welcome."

The final photo for the book was taken a few weeks later, in early June. The boys had black graduation gowns and the girls wore red to represent the school colors. Most of the students were moving on to different universities. Only a few, like Demos, would never open a school book again. St. Basil's had rented out the city's music hall for the graduation ceremony. It was massive, filled with friends and family of the graduating students. The Giorgettis had bought a 'few' extra seats to accommodate their large family, requiring much more than the allotted two. Surprisingly, Seamus' mother had managed to come. She was his only guest.

The graduates milled around backstage to wait for their names to be called. Meanwhile, the principal was giving the audience a few words before handing out diplomas. Ferris and Demos had decided to walk out together. Seamus was paired with the redhead despite having dumped her twice before. He would probably get back together with her halfway through the ceremony and then break up once more before they went home.

"Congratulations," came the simple word as Ferris was handed his diploma in a black leather folder. He shook the man's hand and Demos did the same. The process took about half an hour, but the students finally seated themselves in front of the stage.

"Don't you have a speech to give, valedictorian?" Demos asked, elbowing Ferris. Traditionally, the school's valedictorian said a few encouraging words to the graduating class. Instead of being up on the stage, however, Ferris was seated comfortably next to Demos with one leg crossed over the other. He shrugged.

"I decided to give that honor to the salutatorian," Ferris said with an almost disturbing nonchalance. "You know I hate public speaking."

"But you would have given the best speech ever," Seamus said, disappointed. "'Fuck you guys,' then you'd flip them the bird and walk off stage."

"Yes. That's exactly what I would have said."

"Don't roll your eyes at me, I know you were thinking it."

Ferris only smiled. They stopped talking as the second-highest ranking student in the school stepped up to the podium with a typed speech in her hands. As Beth spoke of the future and the past, Ferris grew more relieved that he had given the responsibility to her. Though he would have been able to come up with something decent, he found himself supremely disliking the way bullshit tasted in his mouth.

When the ceremony was over, the students stood together.

"Fuck you guys," Ferris said with a bitter smile, tossing his cap into the air to join the others that had flown up. His attention immediately went back to his friends, not caring even slightly as to where the hat landed.

54

It was early June, the day of Ferris' birthday. He had nothing planned. It was obvious by now what would happen on this day; Demos had planned a 'surprise' for him each birthday for the past six years. Harold was missing. The two were probably off putting something together at that very moment. Ferris licked the edge of his thumb and turned a page of his newspaper. A moment later, his cell phone rang.

"Hello?"

"Hey kiddo. What are you doing?"

"Hi, Dad. Not much."

"Why don't you meet me at the restaurant in a couple of hours for lunch?"

Real subtle.

"Sure," Ferris said, suppressing a smile. They'd used Giorgetti's before – it was convenient for private parties. After hanging up, he looked at the time on his cell phone. He was fairly certain that if he went right now, he could catch them in the act and effectively ruin his own birthday party. Maybe that would teach them.

Ferris wheeled his bike out onto the sidewalk. This was the last summer he'd really be using it; he wasn't bringing it up to Yale. The ride from his house to the restaurant was familiar. He barely needed to pay attention to the turns and buildings, practically going by muscle memory. This June was particularly hot and the breeze from riding did little to help. As he neared the block of his destination, the heat intensified. For a moment he was puzzled — then he saw the smoke.

The bike came to an abrupt stop across the street from Ristorante Giorgetti, skidding on the pavement. It hit the ground with a harsh clatter as he rushed closer.

The restaurant was burning.

Ferris' throat tightened, swallowing a mouthful of air. It was dry; fire had sucked out the oxygen and moisture. He stared, the flames reflecting in the lenses of his glasses. Black smoke billowed from the windows and flames roared over the walls. The sky was filled with a snow of drifting ashes.

He might have stared for an eternity if the sound of gunshots didn't draw his attention to the street. His head snapped left, catching sight of a group of men situated next to a car holding firearms. He quickly recognized one of them as Brian O'Brien. The man's bright blue eyes were staring straight back at him. Only a single curse word was able to run through Ferris' head before Brian motioned with his arm, sending two men in his direction. Taking a step backwards, Ferris stumbled and froze. Within seconds he was thrown to the ground. The pavement scraped his cheek and his breath escaped in a heavy gasp. With gritted teeth, Ferris struggled to throw them off. Sergio hadn't trained him long enough; he was clearly no match for the older, stronger men. From the corner of his eye he noticed where Brian was aiming his gun. Their weapons were locked on the restaurant's entrance; the other exits must have been blocked off. Ferris stopped moving, now only gawking in horror.

Harold and Demos had to be inside.

When the door was thrown open, Ferris' heart stopped. A coughing waiter took three steps out before his body was riddled with bullets. Ferris cringed at the sound of gunshots, averting his eyes when the body fell. Moments later, the host joined the body in front of the door.

Ferris' silent prayer that his friend was elsewhere crumbled when he saw the Italian's small frame stagger outside. His chest tightened and he stared helplessly, preparing to watch Demos die. For some reason, however, there was no gunshot. Demos coughed harshly, tripping over the bodies and barely able to stand. He was grabbed from each side. As they dragged him towards the car, his body went limp. Demos was out cold.

"We got 'em, let's go," Brian said with a commanding bark, nodding his men towards the car. The passenger door barely opened before a gunshot shattered the window.

They each turned back towards the restaurant in a panic. In the smoky doorway stood Harold, a pistol at arm's length. The other hand was holding a white handkerchief over his mouth. His glasses obscured his eyes, but it was clear that he was livid. Harold fired once again. This shot didn't miss, piercing one of the men through the chest. The man fell backwards onto the car before crumbling to the street.

The moment Ferris had been dreading arrived as Brian lifted his pistol. Three shots rang out, two hitting glass and one embedding itself into Harold's body. He staggered, grasping the doorframe as he slid down in the threshold.

"*Dad!*" Ferris screamed, making another attempt to struggle. He was ignored. Brian stalked forward as the men kept their weapons aimed at the windows. The moment Harold lifted his head, a boot to the shoulder knocked him back inside. Brian slammed the door shut before jamming a charred piece of wood

388

across the frame and knob. He paid no attention to the bodies piled in front of it.

"Angelo had special orders for you," Brian said to the door. "You're gonna burn with the building."

"Dad!" Ferris repeated, throat raw.

"Shut up."

The butt of a gun met Ferris' temple and his world went black.

Half an hour passed. A bump in the road knocked Ferris into waking and he immediately called for his father in a half-conscious haze. He stared into the dark, panting for air. His hands and ankles were tied firmly together. Demos was in front of him, still passed out.

"Demos?"

There was no reply and Ferris' eyes darted to each side. They were both on their sides, shoved into the car's trunk between an empty gas canister and an oil stained rag. Victor had once told him that he should kick out a rear light if ever trapped in a car's trunk, but he had no control of his legs. There was nothing he could do.

The sound of the road beneath them and his own fearful breathing filled his ears. He tried calling Demos' name again, but he was still out cold. Ferris exhaled, shuddering.

"God, Demos, wake up," he repeated, his voice weak. There was still no answer. Ferris shut his eyes, trying to think of a way out. His mind barely formed a sentence before there was a faint screech of brakes. They'd stopped. The car lifted as he felt the weight of four men step out. There were muffled voices, all Irish but one.

"You got them?"

"Yeah. They're in the trunk," Brian replied.

"Nice work. And the restaurant?"

"Gone."

"Good. Never liked that place. Terrible veal, don't you think?"

"I could say if I ever fuckin' ate there, Angelo."

"Hah! Right. Well, get the kids. Throw them inside."

The moment Ferris heard a key start to fiddle with the trunk's lock, he instinctively shut his eyes. Light streamed over their bodies as the musty trunk odor was replaced with hot, summer air. There was a scent of concrete and oil.

"Scrawny as I remember them," Angelo smirked.

"They went down easy. You coulda got a bunch of girls to do this job."

"Then what the fuck am I paying you for?" he laughed before turning to go. The gravel under his feet crunched as he left.

Ferris continued to feign unconsciousness as they were both lifted roughly from the car. The trunk slammed shut. A crack of his eyelid told Ferris that they were at a warehouse. The surrounding area was nothing but lots, pavement, and chain-link. His heart sunk.

Even if he were to scream, there wouldn't be a soul around to hear it.

55

A slap to the face brought Demos back to consciousness. He gasped quickly, eyes forced open by the sudden pain. When he shifted to move, he found his arms bound together. He was seated on an old chair in the middle of a deserted warehouse. Piles of oil drums and steel littered the vast interior. The sun was nearly gone; only faint streams of light filtered through the small, high windows near the ceiling. They bathed the floor in color, making it seem like dusty gold.

"Cop on," came a man's voice. "Gettin' real tired of watchin' you sleep."

When Demos managed to pick up his head, his eyes widened at the sight of Brian O'Brien.

"Yeh, it's me," Brian grinned, rotating a knife in his hand. "Long time no see, eh Ghostie? And what was it you used to call me..."

He lifted Demos' chin with the tip of the knife, leaning in close enough to feel the boy's breath on his face.

"'Bob', wasn't it?" Brian continued.

It was taking Demos a moment to remember what had happened. His eyes flickered as his mind went backwards in the day. It was Ferris' birthday. Demos had been cooking in the kitchen, sautéing some mushrooms in a pan. Harold had been talking on his cell phone behind him. Then, the sound of broken glass — a flaming bottle had been thrown in through the front window, shattering in an explosion of glass and petrol. Two more had followed it. Smoke had begun to billow into the kitchen. Demos had tried the side door, but it wouldn't budge. He'd begun to cough but felt a hand on his shoulder. Harold had led him towards the front door, only to pull back at the sound of gunshots. It was then that Demos remembered Ferris, hoping that he would see the flames and stay away.

"Ferris?" Demos said weakly, his throat dry.

"Don't remember you ever callin' me that," Brian said in disappointment. "Ah, wait. I remember. That was your boyfriend, wasn't it?"

Brian gestured to a body on the floor.

"Him, yeah?"

Demos jerked against the ropes, his breath short as he focused on his friend's back.

"You *fucking*—"

"Relax the cacks, he's not dead," Brian said, turning Ferris over with his foot. He lay on his back, groaning slightly. There was a small, dark bruise on his cheekbone.

"What the fuck did you do to him?" Demos snapped.

"What, that? That's nothin'. We wanted to wait till you were awake for the real fun."

"What?"

"Ain't it obvious?" came a female voice from the side. They both looked towards the source. The woman's eyes were dark, looking at Demos as if he were spoiled meat. Her hand rested on a stack of crates; it was missing a thumb.

"You remember Peggy?" Brian said with a smile. "My girl."

"You..." Demos said slowly.

"Yes, me," she said, stepping forward. "You didn't think Brian was really the brains here, did you?"

Demos didn't have an answer for her, so she continued.

"He's a damned fool," Peggy said, running a hand over Brian's hair as if he were a dog. "Sweet, but a fool. Came home one day, so upset, saying a skinny little Italian took his gun. I told him I'd take care of it."

Her hand dropped as she took a step closer to Demos' chair. Shadows peeled back from her face, revealing dark brown hair that draped over her shoulder.

"Got to say, I underestimated your temper." Peggy raised her hand, wiggling her fingers. All but one — her missing thumb. Demos glared, but his eyes shined with fear.

"So that's what this is?" Demos spat. "Revenge?"

"Aye, Ghost. This is good old-fashioned revenge."

"Then what do you want with him?" Demos said, nodding his head down towards Ferris.

"Ah, you'll see," Brian said, lighting a cigarette. He held the end between his dry lips as he continued. "It's not you we're going to hurt."

"What?" Demos said, his voice breathless and confused.

"When you tore up Brian, I had to listen," Peggy sneered. "I had to listen to you beltin' him and then hear him moan for an hour afterwards. Nothing I could do. Do you know what it's like, Ghost? To listen to your loved one suffer, unable to do a damned thing about it?"

Peggy's sneer drifted into a smile.

"Well, you will."

"But he didn't do anything!" Demos gasped. "He's not a part of this."

"Exactly. He didn't do anything. Just stood and watched in the doorway," Peggy said. "He's as cold and heartless as the lot of you."

Demos' eyes widened with the realization of what was going to happen if they weren't rescued relatively soon. He swallowed.

"That's what I like to see," Brian said, sucking in on his cigarette. "Fear."

"Stu, Peter!" Peggy called to the side. "Get over here."

Moments later, two men joined them. One of them was holding a golf club.

"Well now," Peggy said, tossing a handful of dark hair over her shoulder. "Have at 'im, boys."

She left, disappearing behind a wall of crates while the men joined Brian. They circled Ferris like sharks, looking for just the right place to strike. Daring a look, Ferris weakly cracked open his eyes. Brian grinned back down at him.

"Guys, look. He never hurt anyone," Demos pleaded. "I can get you money, whatever you want."

"Hear that, boyos?" Brian said, dragging Ferris up to his feet. "He'll give us money! We can add it to the pile the Marianis dropped off this morning."

Demos' stomach did something strange; he was starting to feel sick.

Ferris wobbled, barely having the strength to stand. It didn't last long. He was punched hard across the mouth, thrown back into Brian's arms. He was held up as one of the men brought his fist into his stomach. Ferris gagged, shutting his eyes tightly.

"Stop!" Demos shouted. His voice fell upon deaf ears.

The sound of shoes scuffled over the floor as Ferris was beaten. He didn't make very much noise; he didn't have the energy to. When he hit the ground, his glasses clattered to the side. Noticing them, Brian lifted his boot and stomped down on the black frames. They snapped under the impact, now only a pile of plastic and broken glass. Pleased with himself, Brian grinned and looked back at his victim. Ferris was breathing hard, making a sad attempt to right himself with a fist on the floor. One of the men lifted the golf club.

"Stop!" Demos begged. He was shaking. "Jesus Christ, stop! Stop, please!"

Slowly, Ferris looked over towards his friend. He had told himself not to make eye contact but couldn't help it. The sight of Demos, usually so strong and calm, now reduced to a begging child, made Ferris feel depressed. The golf club came down, meeting him just below the cheekbone. His vision flashed white. A mouthful of blood and a single molar flew with the club's momentum. His body rolled once before he landed on his back, gasping. Ferris could feel the soft, raw texture of his gums where the tooth had been knocked out. Blood spilled from the open hole, filling his mouth with the thick taste of pennies. He choked on it, coughing to keep it from seeping down his throat.

Ferris curled in on his stomach, spitting onto the dusty floor. Droplets of blood appeared in a curved row, dripping from his lower lip and chin. Demos stared forward, eyes glassy and throat raw. He was fixed hard to his seat, simply breathing and staring. His mind had shut itself off; he had left his body. Ferris didn't look at him.

"Run," Demos finally whispered, letting the word escape dryly past his lips. A boot kicked Ferris over and another one met his stomach. Amidst the buzzing in his head, Ferris could hear Demos repeat the word. 'Run.' His eyes lifted, darting around for a glimpse of light. On the other end of the warehouse was a faint, pale rectangle – an open door. It seemed like it was miles away, but Ferris knew better. He tried to think of how long it would take him to run there, or if he even had the energy to stand. His mind was spinning. No, it was burning. Burning with light and blood and muddled laughter. One voice stood out to him, making the only sense amongst all of the noise.

"Run."

From somewhere in his body, the last trickles of energy surged into his hands, lifting him up off the ground. His legs moved, stumbling forward, standing. Without thinking, he started to run. Each scuff of his shoes on the concrete echoed; each step seemed to take an hour. The white door was closer now. How soon could he find a phone, call for help, and wait? Would Demos be all right – would they survive before the Giorgettis arrived?

Ferris would never find out. Strong hands grasped his shirt and he tripped down onto the floor. He fell onto his chest with a body on top of him, knocking out his breath. When he looked up, the door seemed as if it were shrinking away. It was still so far.

"Well," came Brian's voice from above him. "I wasn't going to do this, originally."

Brian pulled a knife from a leather sheath as the other man held Ferris down firmly.

"Stu, pull up his pant leg. Don't matter which one."

Ferris shuddered as he felt the air on the bare skin of his ankle.

"We're going to have to do something to keep you from runnin'."

Ferris couldn't see, but he could certainly feel as the knife slashed the thick base of his Achilles' tendon. The muscle snapped and his calf bunched, popping under the skin and sending a scream up through his throat. From somewhere to the side, he could hear Demos shouting something. Brian's attention turned to the Italian. He smiled, pleased at the way the teen's voice was heaving and cracking.

"Throw them both in the back room. We'll kill him tomorrow."

Ferris shivered before going limp, unable to make sense of the words. His eyes fluttered shut, finally overcome by the pain. He passed out for the second time that day, going still on a bed of concrete and blood.

56

The room was small, barely the size of a broom closet. Like a closet, there was no window. A faint glow of light filtered in through the crack under the door. Demos was sitting, back against the gray bricks and head drooping. Hair hung over his face, hiding his features from the walls. In his lap lay Ferris' head. Demos had spent the past hour tending to his friend's wounds. Their captors had thrown in a first aid kit, claiming they wanted Ferris to live through the night. There were no scissors; he'd torn at the bandages with his teeth, covering the gashes with faded white gauze. They had everything planned; it was all a sick, well-organized game. He shouldn't have shot off Peggy's thumb.

Demos ran his thin, shaking fingers down the side of Ferris' face. Accidentally grazing a bruise, he stirred Ferris into opening his eyes. Ferris' eyelids lifted slowly, one of them half-shut from a swollen bruise. Pain greeted him from every corner of his body and he winced, curling his fingers.

"Ferris…"

"Demos?" Ferris replied, his voice stale.

"I'm sorry," Demos whispered, smoothing back Ferris' hair with his hand. He didn't bother asking Ferris if it hurt; he knew that it did. "I'm so sorry."

From under a dark bruise, Ferris managed to give a faint smile. "It's not your fault."

Ferris' attempts at comforting his friend didn't seem to work. Instead, a wet trail ran down from one of Demos' eyes, then the other. He didn't bother brushing the tears away, only biting his lip.

"They're looking for us, Demos. They'll find us."

The thought of the adults triggered a flood of flashbacks. Instantly, Ferris remembered his father.

"Dad," Ferris said suddenly, his voice cracking.

"What?"

"Dad," he repeated, trying to sit up. He failed. "He was trapped inside… Oh, God. Dad, he–"

"He's okay," Demos assured him. "He's smart, I know he found a way out."

Ferris was on the verge of breaking down, but Demos' voice calmed him. It was one of the few things that could. His body stilled and he lay his head back onto Demos' leg.

"I hope you're right," he said shakily.

"I'm always right."

Ferris didn't have the energy to argue. He didn't want to think about his father dying, trapped between crumbling walls and fire. When a tear hit his temple, his eyes darted up.

"Demos," he said gently, forgetting his own worries. "It's all right."

"No, it's not."

"They're going to find us. Maybe even tonight. All we need to do is hold out. It'll be fine."

"You're not usually the optimistic one," Demos sniffed.

"Someone has to be."

Ferris shut his eyes, letting his head drop to the side in Demos' lap. He tried not to think about the searing pain from his ankle. Even if they opened the door right now and let him go, he wouldn't be able to walk. It wasn't even possible to stand. Unless he found a surgeon relatively soon, he may end up crippled in his right leg for life. These should have been the least of his worries; he hadn't listened when Brian said that they would kill him in the morning.

"Was anyone else inside?" Ferris asked, barely moving his lips. His friends would have gone to the party, but were they early?

"Some kitchen staff," Demos replied. "Not Seamus or Emily. Stop worrying."

Ferris made a weak nod; it was the only good news he'd heard all day.

"I bet you'd kill for a cigarette right now," Ferris said softly after a minute of quiet.

Demos didn't reply, but a smile tugged at the corner of his mouth. Ferris always knew what he was thinking.

"Did I ever tell you," Demos said, his voice slow, "why I started smoking?"

He took Ferris' silence as a 'no.'

"Dad used to sit at the table in the kitchen... clear everything off and set down tobacco and papers. He would roll cigarettes – so carefully and perfectly. I'd sit and watch him do it. That dark, sweet scent... it would be in the air and on his hands. I loved that smell."

Ferris' eyes were still as he listened, forgetting their situation for just a moment.

"When I moved here, when I was lonely, I'd break open Uncle Vic's cigarettes, roll the tobacco in my palm and put my face in my hands. He was so mad when he caught me."

Demos' eyes tightened, squinting at the wall. His smile was laced with shame.

"Dad... I hate that asshole. But, I don't know, it made me feel better. I guess it sounds stupid..."

"It doesn't," Ferris said.

"It still makes me feel better," he said. "The smell. But—"

396

Demos' eyes dropped, trailing to the dirty concrete floor. "I'm not lonely anymore."

"Good," Ferris said, his voice barely audible. He could remember Demos in the past with someone's blood on his shirt, hands shaking as he tried to light a cigarette. It seemed different now – somehow, more innocent.

"Ferris," Demos said. "I didn't get to say 'Happy Birthday.' It's probably past midnight."

Ferris didn't answer. He'd forgotten that he was eighteen now. All he could do was hope that it wasn't the last birthday he'd ever see.

57

When Ferris woke up, he could feel the surface of a table against his back. He wasn't in the dark closet anymore. His eyes slowly gathered his surroundings; it was the same area of the warehouse where they'd beaten him before. When he tried to sit up, he noticed that his hands and legs were tied down. His shirt was missing – and so was Demos.

"Comfy?" asked Brian, his head leaning over to block the ceiling. Ferris' eyes flicked left and right.

"Where's Demos?" Ferris asked, voice at a near panic.

"Oh, it speaks," Brian said, straightening himself. "Don't worry, he's around."

Brian's eyes trailed to the microphone set discreetly on the table next to them.

In another room, somewhere else in the building, Demos sat in a corner. There was nothing with him save for a small speaker set on a chair and a camera hung from the ceiling. The setup was crude and the equipment was cheap; he didn't expect any better from the O'Briens. He knew he was being watched but didn't care. His eyes were fixated on the speaker. Brian's voice came through the grill, laced with static, yet still loud.

"Glad you made it. Wasn't sure if you'd bleed to death or what. The Ghost did a pretty good patching job, I have to admit. Kind of for nothing, though. If you'd died last night you wouldn't have to go through all this."

Back in the warehouse, Brian was gesturing towards the table with the microphone. Beside it lay a knife and an electric hot plate. On top of the hot plate was a kettle filled with water.

"If you think I'm doing all this for a cup of scaldy…" Brian started, then laughed. "Nah. It's for you."

Brian casually raised the heat on the hot plate.

"They say a watched pot never boils, so it might be in your best interest to keep your eye on this one. You're not going to like this at all."

The kettle was starting to steam. As the vapors thickened, Ferris' heart began to thump. Brian didn't have to explain himself; it was fairly clear was the boiling water was for. Ferris' eyes locked on it, begging silently for it to go cold. There was a faint reflection of the walls in the silver finish of its body. If he had his glasses on he would have been able to see the fear in his own eyes. Peggy sat nearby, smiling as she watched Demos through a small, black and white television.

"Yesterday was for Brian. You let him live, and so did I," Peggy said to the screen, unable to keep in her smile. "But today... today is for Eddie."

Peggy's smile widened as the kettle began to whistle. It was shrill, screaming with a voice full of hot air and steam.

"And Eddie's dead."

Brian clicked off the hot plate and lifted the kettle. Ferris swallowed. This wasn't a game and it wasn't some test with Nicky — it was real. They were going to kill him.

Demos stared hard at the speaker. He didn't move, even forgetting to breathe as he listened. The earlier whistling of the kettle had brought him up next to the chair, hands on the edge as he sat helplessly on the floor next to it. Now it was silent. The silence killed him more than the noise had. He wanted to be there, to see Ferris and speak to him. In this room, deep in the basement of the warehouse, there was nothing he could do. His thoughts were harshly interrupted by a scream. Demos' eyes snapped up and his hands began to shake. He gripped harder to the edge of the chair. Ferris was screaming on the other end of the wire and it came through the speaker like a sound from the belly of his nightmares.

"Ferris," Demos whispered, now holding the speaker with both hands. He could hear his friend panting. The breaths were hard, cracking with pain. Ferris sounded as if he were clenching his teeth, sucking in air as his chest heaved. Demos could practically see it in front of him – Brian's grin, gently tilting the kettle down to pour boiling water, layers of flesh peeling back as the scalding liquid gushed over it. Ferris cried out again. The scream petered off, dissolving into quick, sharp groans.

"*Stop!*" Demos yelled, not caring whether or not the camera was gathering any sound. "Stop it! I'll do anything – I'll give you anything! Stop, please!"

His eyes welled up, obscuring his vision.

"I'll do anything, I swear... stop. God, please stop! What do you want? I'll do anything you want," Demos repeated, growing raw in the throat. "Anything."

Peggy gazed casually down into the television screen, resting her head on a fist.

"Demos. Sweetheart," she said, looking pleased as punch. "You're already doing it."

"*Fucking stop it!*" Demos shouted, straining his lungs. Bile threatened to rise up through his throat. His body weakened, curling against the chair. There really was nothing he could do; he was going to listen to Ferris die.

Moments later, he heard another voice. It was Ferris, but it wasn't a scream. He was speaking to him.

"Demos," came the voice from the speaker. It was faint, as if Demos was only imagining it. "It's okay."

399

Demos slowly raised his head. He looked at the speaker, holding his breath to listen.

"It's okay," the voice repeated. Brian said something, cutting Ferris off. A moment later, the sound of water returned. He could hear Ferris struggling to keep quiet, only to give in and gasp in pain. Demos dropped his forehead against the black box; it was the closest thing to his friend that he could reach. He didn't notice how badly he was shaking, only able to concentrate on listening.

Demos ran his tongue between his teeth. When Ferris died, he would rather bleed to death than provide Peggy any more satisfaction. They would go together. This was it.

This was the end.

The sound of a gunshot almost made him bite down prematurely. Startled, Demos sat up. Had they shot Ferris? He strained to listen more carefully. Muffled shouts came through, followed by the sound of more bullets.

"The fuck was–"

Static.

"Where is–"

"Get him! Jesus Christ, you–" Static. "—The fuck over there!"

There was shouting and the echoes of more gunshots. Only chaos came through the speaker. Demos' heart threatened to pound itself out of his chest. There was a crash and the speaker went silent. Someone must have knocked it off of the table. It was dead.

"No…" Demos whispered. "Damn it!"

His eyes trailed up towards the ceiling. There were still gunshots, but they were muffled through layers of concrete. He would have given anything to see what was happening. Moments later, everything went quiet.

Demos waited on the floor for a noise, a sign, anything to let him know what had happened. Was Ferris alive? Did someone come into the warehouse? Minutes ticked by and he grasped the cloth over his knees, anxious in the silent room.

Footsteps – there were footsteps outside of the door, coming down the stairs. It was silent, then the doorknob rattled. When it wouldn't open, there was a gunshot. The knob clattered to the floor, rolling to a stop on the cement. The door opened, creaking on its hinges.

"Get up. Come with me."

Demos choked, unable to stand. All he could do was stare with disbelief at the man standing in the doorway.

"…Dad."

Demos couldn't move. He stared in disbelief at his father, who was standing only a few feet away. Killian Belmont, like his son, was a slender man. His sand colored hair was short and

400

neat, pushed back away from his forehead. On his nose rested a pair of round, wire glasses. In six years, he hadn't changed at all.

Trembling, Demos opened his mouth. He glared, running over a hundred angry sentences in his head. There was so much that he wanted to say. His mouth shut immediately, however, when he saw that Ferris wasn't with him. Wordlessly, he scrambled up, shoving past his father to run out the door and up the stairs. Killian turned his head slowly, watching Demos run as if a pack of wolves were chasing him.

Demos entered the warehouse breathless, his eyes darting from one space to the other. They locked on the table with Ferris' body. A kettle lay a few feet away on the floor, its contents spilled and still steaming. His feet nearly tripped over each other as he rushed up, getting a better look at the damage. The little color in his face immediately drained.

Ferris' eyes were shut. His body lay flat and still on the table. Red, burnt skin ran over his hip bone, peeling up the side of his stomach. It seemed that the burning continued beneath the seam of his pants along his thigh. Beads of sweat dotted his temples and bruises still covered his body from the day before. Demos quickly put his hands on the sides of his friend's face, leaning in to listen for breathing. After a moment, he felt a soft rush of air as Ferris inhaled.

Demos had nothing to say. His mind was blank, not even remotely close to prepared for this. Around them, a half-dozen bodies lay dead on the warehouse floor. Blood stained the ground and gave the air a sour, rusty scent. Demos didn't notice any of them until he heard a groan. Slowly, his eyes trailed towards the source of the sound. The body shifted, making another pained noise. Demos' eyes widened. It was Brian.

How was it that his father managed to hit every other man square in the forehead, but Brian was only suffering a blown-out knee? The answer came to Demos in the form of a gun. Killian, who'd come up unnoticed, placed the cold pistol in his son's hand with two words.

"He's yours."

Demos understood immediately. His thin fingers closed around the gun's handle, index running longingly over the trigger. His steps were slow as he approached. Demos' unnerving stare dropped down over Brian's body. His eyes were barren, somehow devoid of life or light. At the sight of him, Brian struggled to crawl away. His effort, though fierce, was useless. Demos crouched, grabbing a handful of brown hair before jerking Brian's head up to meet his face.

"Let... go!" Brian spit, letting blood dribble down his chin.

"Look at me, Brian."

"Get off! I'll fucking kill you."

"*Look at me,*" Demos repeated, forcing the end of the gun past Brian's teeth. The tip grazed over the man's tonsils. Demos' finger rolled over the trigger; he found it exceedingly difficult not to pull. Brian stopped talking; he didn't have much of a choice with a gun halfway down his throat.

There was nothing he could do to make Brian feel the same pain he had. There was no way to make this man suffer as much as Demos wanted him to. A thousand years burning in a thousand hells wouldn't even come close. He wanted to cut him, maim him, and burn him alive. He wanted to pour gasoline down his throat and let wild dogs tear him apart.

The warehouse was silent. Demos listened to Brian's short, ragged breaths. His eyes tightened at the sweet thought of making them stop forever. Another breath snapped Demos back to reality – it was Ferris. Ferris was dying. They had to get him out; Brian would have to go out quickly. So much for hours of torture.

"You really are lucky," Demos said under his breath before pulling the trigger.

The gun clicked against Brian's teeth as bits of skull and brain spattered across the cement floor. Small shards of white bone lay amongst pink fluid and soft matter. Brian's eyes were wide and still as Demos dropped him, letting the body slump to the floor. The spray of blood had drizzled over the floor and across Demos' shirt. He didn't take notice.

"Let's go. Now," Killian said, his tone stern. "Peggy escaped and the Marianis are on their way."

"But Ferris can't walk," Demos said, standing.

"Then leave him," his father demanded.

"No."

"We have to go, *now.*"

"You can go. I'm not leaving him here."

Killian's teeth held tightly together as he mulled over his options. His son was just as stubborn as he was. After a second, he turned, walking up to the table. He cut Ferris free, then hefted the boy up in his arms. He didn't look happy. Demos immediately followed after them, leaving the warehouse free of human life.

The car ride back to the city was stiff. It was a muggy, overcast day. Demos sat in the backseat with Ferris' head in his lap, gently pouring bottled water over the burns to keep them cool. Killian kept his eyes straight on the road as they drove in complete silence. After five minutes, Demos spoke up.

"Where are we going?"

"A flat I'm renting."

"He needs to go to the hospital."

"Then he'd be dead before nightfall," Killian said in a clear Manchester accent. "You honestly think a hospital would be safe from the Marianis?"

Demos hadn't thought of that and looked down in embarrassment. His father really hadn't changed at all.

"You can't take us home?" He asked quietly.

"Your entire family has a nasty vendetta against me. Have you forgotten?"

"No," Demos said bitterly.

Killian sighed.

"I have medical supplies. He'll be fine."

"His heel is–"

"I'm aware."

Demos quieted once more, looking out the window, then back at his father. After thinking for a moment, he made an attempt to say what was on his mind.

"Where have you been?"

"Working."

The answer killed the conversation and no further words were exchanged for the rest of the drive.

Killian's apartment was more modest than the man himself. Apparently, he was serious about keeping a low profile. It was a small walk-up rental on the second floor with a quiet kitchen and one bedroom. The curtains were always drawn; only thin slivers of light managed to peek their way in between the cracks of cloth. Ferris was put on the bed and Demos watched in silence as his father cleaned, sutured, and bandaged his friend. Every move Killian made was smooth and methodical.

"When I send you home tomorrow, don't leave the compound. Bring in an actual doctor. He may not be able to walk on that leg anymore."

Demos nodded. The thought was heartbreaking, but he was too grateful that Ferris was even alive to complain. Leaving his instructions in the air, Killian got up and left the room. Demos wanted nothing more than to stay by the bed; he didn't want Ferris to be alone when he woke up. He had, however, not seen his father for years. Demos had questions. If he didn't ask them now, he might never be able to.

Demos shut the door with care, making sure it clicked softly. When he turned around, he saw his father taking apart a gun at the kitchen table. He stood and watched for a moment, suddenly drawing the same mental image from his childhood – coming down the stairs in his pajamas, peeking through the railing to watch his father clean guns. 'Daddy is a salesman,' his mother would say. 'He has to go see a client.'

Even as a toddler, Demos knew better.

"Why did you save us?" Demos blurted.

"You," Killian corrected. "I only intended to save you."

"Why?"

"You needed me."

"Needed you? I've needed you for the last *six years*," Demos said, his voice strained.

"You turned out fine."

"Dad!" Demos said with clenched fists. "Stop being an asshole! You left! You left for no fucking reason!"

"Did I teach you to speak that way?"

"You didn't teach me anything!"

"I taught you how to help me clean these," Killian said, holding up a piece of a pistol. He drew out a chair, gesturing for his son to sit down. Demos frowned, fussed, then sat down. He sighed.

"Mom died after you left," Demos said, staring down at the table. He wasn't moving.

Killian didn't reply. The hand holding a pipe cleaner stilled.

"I'm aware," Killian finally replied. Slowly, he turned to look at the bedroom door. "Do you love him?"

Demos, caught off guard, glared at his father.

"Of course I do. He's my best friend."

"Don't."

"What?" Demos blurted.

"The more you love him, the more he will suffer."

"What am I supposed to do?" Demos asked. "Never speak to him again?"

Killian went back to his cleaning, answering the question with his silence.

"There is no room for love in a life like yours," he said, eyes still. "Like ours. Take a wife if you must, but do not love her."

"Is that how you felt about Mom?" Demos spat, his voice growing nastier.

"I loved your mother more than I could say in words."

"Then why did you leave?"

Killian only looked at his son. His expression was weary. Their eyes stayed on one another for a moment; Demos' mouth parted as if trying to find something to say. A noise from the bedroom broke their eye contact. Demos immediately turned, straining to hear Ferris moan once more. The chair scuffed the floor as he pushed it out, dropping the conversation to go into the room.

The bedroom was dark and cool. Ferris was still asleep, sweating at the brow and tightening his expression in discomfort. He shifted positions, inhaling sharply. He must have been having a bad dream. Demos sat next to him on the bed, putting a hand on Ferris' damp temple.

"Ferris, wake up."

404

As if obeying, Ferris' eyes snapped open. Startled, he tried to sit up, only to have Demos stop him by the chest.

"It's okay, lay down."

"You scared me," Ferris said, throat parched. The pain from his burns was muted. Earlier, Killian had injected him with a drug that Demos had suspected was morphine.

"Did you have a nightmare?" Demos asked gently, unable to keep in his smile. He thought he'd never hear that voice again.

"I always have nightmares."

"What was it about?"

Ferris didn't want to answer. It was the same thing he always dreamed about – the same source of all of his nightmares.

"You."

Demos' lips parted, but he said nothing. Somewhere in his chest, something was aching.

Ferris glanced from side to side. He was in an unfamiliar room, on a bed. Was it possible that it had all just been a dream? A quick look under the sheets told him otherwise. Bandages were wrapped around his left thigh and stomach and a deep, burning pain was making its way through his system as he woke up. With a sigh, he laid his head back down on the pillow.

"Where are we?" he whispered.

"Somewhere safe."

"What happened?"

Demos paused before answering. It was difficult to say, but it was the truth.

"My dad saved us," he finally said.

Ferris' eyes shut more tightly. The pain was growing stronger, searing from his ankle and burns. Demos' answer was strange, but Ferris didn't have the energy to question it.

"It hurts," he managed to say. His voice was barely audible. Demos reached for a glass of water and a few pills that were on the bedside table.

"Here, take these."

Sitting up as much as the burns would allow him to, Ferris propped himself on his elbows. Demos held the glass up to Ferris' lips, cupping his hand to catch any dripping water. A bit trailed down his chin and Ferris coughed. He groaned, swallowing with a bit of effort. As he weakened back into the mattress, Demos dabbed away the water from his chin and collar with a cloth.

"Just rest," Demos said, taking Ferris' hand. "We're going home tomorrow."

Ferris shut his eyes and barely nodded. It wasn't difficult for Ferris to follow the order; his body was still exhausted. In moments, his breathing slowed and his expression relaxed. All the while, Demos watched him. He hadn't let go of his hand.

He thought of why his father had left; he remembered how broken-hearted his mother had been. She had grown quiet and still, only a ghost of her former self. Bianca had once been a singer. When she died, she was ill, weak, and thin. Was it because of Killian? Could loneliness kill a person?

The door sneaked open. Killian's voice came through the crack, tired and stern.

"Go to sleep. We need to wake up early."

He shut the door without waiting for a response. Demos sighed. It looked like his father was going to sleep on the couch. Demos would have felt bad about it if he hadn't harbored a burning hatred for him for six years. Carefully, he pushed his shoes off with his toes, lying down next to Ferris on the large bed. It was lucky that Ferris fell asleep so easily. Demos knew he wouldn't have any such luck.

Ferris woke again at seven a.m. His head turned to the side, but the bed was empty. The strange situation and surroundings drew him to near-panic. Where was Demos? His frantic eyes stopped on the crack in the door. Through it, he could see the kitchen table. His vision was blurred without his glasses, but he could make out the form of a strange man, presumably Demos' father. The man was seated and doing something precisely with his hands. Squinting, Ferris saw that he was rolling cigarettes. Next to him sat Demos, head on his hands, quietly watching.

Ferris' lips drew into a faint smile before he shut his eyes to get more sleep.

58

A faint, steady beep hummed across the large room. Medical equipment sat neatly next to the large four poster bed and a humidifier sighed a breath of steam into the air. Demos stood next to the tall window, drawing back a curtain with the back of his hand. Warm, yellow light streamed in through the crack. He looked out onto the lawn of the Giorgetti compound, staring at nothing of particular importance. Every so often he would glance back to see if Ferris had woken up. A hopeful look over his shoulder told him 'no.'

Killian had dropped them off only yesterday and Ferris hadn't stirred since. Stress, trauma, and injury were more than enough to exhaust him. Ferris was getting a well-deserved rest.

Demos' father had driven his rental car up along a curb near the compound, handed his son a cell phone, and then left the car. He obviously couldn't be around when the Giorgettis arrived to fetch them. Before they parted ways, Demos asked one last thing.

"How did you find us, anyway?"

"They tried to hire me."

With that, Killian shut the car door, lit a cigarette, and walked away.

Behind closed eyes, Ferris saw darkness and phosphenes. When he opened them, his mind slowly pieced together a bedroom. The bed was soft and a quilt laid over him, comfortably heavy. A tube was being fed into his arm. His eyes wandered wearily over to the window, stopping on the back of Demos' drooping head.

"What are you looking at?" he asked, his voice scratchy as if it hadn't been used in years.

Instantly, Demos turned.

"Ferris..." He made his way over to the bed, sitting in the armchair next to it. He leaned forward eagerly. "How do you feel?"

"Kind of bad."

"You've been out since yesterday. A surgeon came in," Demos explained, adjusting the blanket over Ferris' chest. "It took a lot of work, but he said you might be able to walk normally when it heals."

"Really?" Ferris asked, though he didn't believe it. A gentle twist of his ankle revealed the sensation of stitches.

"Really," Demos said, smiling tiredly. A creak of door hinges caught their attention. Emily's face was the first to appear. Behind her were Victor, Ruth, and a few other Giorgettis.

"Demos? We heard voices," Emily said, her tone tired but hopeful. When she caught sight of Ferris with open eyes, a smile immediately spread over her lips. Ruth pushed in past them, leaning in next to the bed and holding his hand between her palms.

"Sweetheart!" Ruth cried out, instantly kissing the side of his face. Behind her large glasses, Ferris could tell she had been crying. "You had me worried to death."

She sat up, pushing back his hair in concern.

"How do you feel, are you hurting?"

He didn't answer immediately. Something didn't feel right. His eyes trailed from one person to the next, then to the door. His palms started to prickle and sweat. Lips parted slightly, he held his breath before asking a single desperate question.

"Where's Dad?"

The room was silent.

"Where's Dad?" he repeated, sitting up. His voice barely squeezed itself from his throat. The adults looked at one another in discomfort.

"Ferris," Victor finally said. "I'm sorry."

Ferris stared back at him, not understanding – not wanting to understand.

"The fire," Victor continued. "He didn't make it."

Ferris couldn't move. He stared at Victor, his eyes wide and glazed. His fingers trembled, then clenched against his palm.

"What?" his mouth pantomimed, but the word didn't come out. His chest was going numb.

"I'm sorry, Ferris," Demos said, his voice soft and sincere as he put his hand on Ferris' shoulder.

At first he tried to deny what he'd heard. They were mistaken – they were only guessing. It was impossible. Dad — *his* dad, couldn't be gone. Ferris' eyes began to well. His vision blurred; he could no longer see the people in the room. Their distorted images wavered in front of him, dimming as his eyes lost focus.

"No," he said. He shook his head once. The heat seemed to have been sucked from the room, leaving his skin cold. He shivered. This wasn't right — this couldn't be. He'd never once imagined being without his father. Going to college, graduating, finding a job – without his father. Never hearing another phone call start with, 'Hey, kiddo.'

His dad, who'd carry Ferris to bed when he'd fallen asleep over a book, who'd tried to sneak sweets when Ruth wasn't looking, and had been waiting in the restaurant to surprise Ferris for his birthday – he was gone.

As he stared forward, tears broke over the lids of his eyes and ran freely down his face. For the first time he could remember, Ferris curled forward and cried like a child.

59

All of the mirrors in the Levinstein house were covered with sheets. The rooms were silent and blue with morning light. Ferris was sitting on his bed, hands folded as he leaned forward on his knees. He was dressed for a funeral; his suit, tie, and shoes were a deep, slate black. Beneath the suit were layers of bandages and burn medication. A pair of long, wooden crutches were next to him, propped against the bed. He hadn't shaved in days.

Traditionally, a Jewish funeral took place no more than three days after death. They had waited for Ferris; Ruth couldn't have the ceremony without her son. They also needed to know if there would be only one funeral, or two. When the boys were found alive, she had wept, thanking God for not leaving her entirely alone. Ferris, however, had nothing to say to God.

"Ferris," Ruth said from the doorway. "It's time to go."

He nodded once, using the bed for support as he pulled himself up on the crutches. His mother put her hand on his back as they left the room.

"You should eat something," she said, though her voice lacked the vigor it usually held when she said such things. Ferris only shook his head. He hadn't been hungry in days.

The funeral service was slow and quiet, held entirely outdoors beside the grave. The rabbi had known Harold personally and spoke with a tired fondness in his voice. The Levinsteins from New York City and Long Island, the Giorgetti family, Harold's co-workers, and his clients were all present. Leading members of criminal families smaller than the Marianis had also appeared to show their respects. There were no flowers, only black clothing and grass. The rabbi offered Ferris a ribbon to be symbolically torn, which he refused. Nodding, the rabbi instead nicked the edge of Ferris' suit collar with a small knife. With a firm grasp, Ferris tore it the rest of the way. It was a sign of the rip in one's heart, but he felt as if he just couldn't tear it far enough.

Harold was buried under a tall tree in a plain, pine coffin. The Levinstein family had a plot reserved, marked by a large monument with an engraved cup underneath the family name. The graves themselves were marked with simple stone markers. His body was never shown, only wrapped in a white shroud inside of the closed coffin. When Ruth began to cry, Ferris reached over to hold her hand.

The rabbi began the Mourner's Kaddish, a prayer that Ferris knew, but had never used personally before.

"Yit'gadal v'yit'kadash sh'mei raba."

"Amen."

When the prayer was over, each family member dropped a handful of Israeli dirt over the coffin. Ferris' fingers parted slowly, letting the sand and dust trickle down over the coffin's lid. Wind kicked up pieces of it, scattering the dirt over the long length of pine. A moment later, his hand was empty. Ferris looked up, catching Demos' eyes from across the grave. His friend gave him a gentle look, one of apology and understanding. Demos had lost his mother once; he knew exactly how it felt. They looked at each other for a moment, neither of them noticing the call of birds in the trees above.

Back in the Levinstein home, Ferris watched as his mother lit a tall, white candle in a glass. It would burn for seven days. The curtains were drawn, leaving the room dark despite the small, flickering flame. She set down the book of matches, turning to watch her son.

"Sweetheart," she said, her voice tired and low. "Come sit."

Ferris leaned his crutches against the wall, carefully lowering himself to sit next to her on the Victorian sofa. Ruth's hands rose, holding the sides of his face. She kissed his forehead.

"Ferris, I need you to promise me something," she said. There were already tears in her eyes.

"What is it?" he asked, searching her face for a hint.

"That first day," she said, her voice breaking, "I thought I'd lost you both."

She ran her hand over the top of his head, pushing back his hair. He could feel the hard bump of her wedding ring slide against his head.

"Don't make me go through that again," she continued.

"I'll be careful," Ferris assured her.

"No, that's not enough. It's not enough to be careful."

"I don't understand," Ferris said slowly. "What do you want me to do?"

Ruth hadn't let go of him. Her eyes tightened, flickering from one part of his face to another. She knew it would be difficult for him to hear; she knew that he would try to refuse.

"You can't see him anymore," she finally said. "You can't see Demos."

"Mom," he breathed, knitting his brow after a moment of shock. "You know I can't–"

"Ferris," his mother said, not moving to wipe the tears that were now freely running down her face. "Listen to me."

"Mom…"

"If I lost you, if I had to hear someone tell me that you were dead... what would I do?" she wept. "What would I do without you?"

Guilt overcame the anger in his heart and he moved to hold his mother, gently pulling the woman into his arms. She cried into his shoulder, shaking as if she'd already lost him.

"Mom, don't cry," he said, rubbing her back. "Please don't cry."

"Promise me," she said, her eyes red and throat dry.

Ferris shut his eyes tightly. He knew there was no way he could drop Demos from his life. He didn't blame his friend for the things they had gone through; he didn't blame him for his father's death. They had already gone through so much — survived so much. How could he abandon him now, at the birth of a war, at a time like this? He couldn't, however, ignore his mother's crying.

He'd never thought of what she must have gone through. Pain, torture, and death, he could handle. He would do anything for Demos. But his mother, how could he forget what it must be like for her? How would she feel if she lost her husband and her son, growing to be an old woman who was completely alone, a woman who had lost everything?

"But we live here," Ferris said quietly, leaning back from their embrace. "How could I avoid him?"

"After you graduate, after school," Ruth replied, having already thought of this, "you go to New York City, with your uncle. Find a job there — live there."

Ferris' eyes dropped, trailing down to the floor.

"You can visit me during school, just for a week at a time. You can stay home, with me," Ruth added. Ferris sighed. Her plan actually sounded feasible. He rubbed his arm as if he were cold.

"Please promise me," Ruth repeated, lifting her glasses to dab at her eyes with a handkerchief.

"I'll talk to him, Mom."

The answer was more than Ruth had hoped for, and she pulled her son into a strong hug.

"Okay. You talk to him tonight."

Ferris only nodded.

The evening came faster than he would have liked. Demos agreed to come by for a talk and they met outside, on the sidewalk. It was a warm night. Fireflies faded in and out over the small patches of grass along the trees. They didn't speak at first, simply watching one another from the stoop to the curb.

"Do you want to go for a walk?" Demos finally asked, his tone subdued. Ferris adjusted his crutches and stepped down to join him. They began down the street in a slow, deliberate place. They didn't have anywhere to be.

For a few minutes, they didn't say anything. Ferris could have sworn that Demos knew what was coming and was trying to avoid it. Finally, the Italian spoke.

"How is your ankle?"

"A little better," Ferris said, forcing the words out. His ankle was the last thing on his mind.

"You said that... you wanted to ask me something?"

"Yeah."

"What is it?" Demos asked gently.

"Well, I need your opinion on something," Ferris said, stalling. He didn't want to actually say it.

"All right."

"Mom thinks... it would be better if I didn't see you anymore. She's worried."

"She's right."

Ferris stopped walking. He stared at Demos, stunned.

"What?"

"She's right," Demos said, his voice growing weaker by the moment. "You shouldn't see me anymore."

"But... Demos."

Demos only looked at him. His dark eyes were tired; they belonged to a man much older than himself.

"We've gone through so much," Ferris whispered.

"Too much."

"Demos," Ferris repeated. His voice was starting to plead.

"I almost watched you die," Demos said, his expression blank. "I wasn't ready for that."

Slowly, Demos turned to look at his friend. He locked eyes with him, showing that he was absolutely sure of his words.

"I'll *never* be ready for that," Demos finished. His voice was firm; Ferris could feel it under his skin.

"But..."

"Something big is going to happen soon," Demos said. "I don't want you to be here for it."

"I can't let you run into a war without me," Ferris said, his voice rising.

"You're not going to die because of me," Demos snapped. "Forget it."

They stopped walking; they'd already circled back in front of his house.

"So... this is it?" Ferris asked weakly. "We'll never see each other again?"

Demos broke their eye contact and nodded.

"I'll tell Emily to come see you tomorrow," Demos said, struggling to keep any emotion out of his voice.

"Okay."

412

They both looked down at the sidewalk. Ferris was still in shock. He couldn't believe that this was it.

"All right," he said slowly. "So... goodbye."

"Goodbye, Ferris," Demos said with a nod. He listened, not watching as Ferris headed up the stairs to the entrance. The moment he heard the door open, Demos lost his composure.

Demos rushed up to the stoop, throwing his arms around his friend's neck for a tight hug. One of the crutches clattered to the ground. Ferris didn't stop to think, putting his free arm around Demos' back. They held each other for a minute and Demos blinked back a few tears.

"I..." Demos whispered, then changed his line of thought. "Take care, Fish."

"You too, Ghost."

When Ferris let go, Demos handed him the crutch. He watched the door shut, keeping his eyes on the crack until Ferris' face was out of sight. For a moment, Demos simply stared at the door. He rubbed a sleeve over his eye, turned around, and walked away.

60

Ferris was waiting at the Sparrow. A small bag sat on the table in front of him, as well as an untouched cup of coffee. He was staring out the window, trying not to think about never meeting Demos there again. His mother had laid out her request very specifically: no contact with any Giorgetti or their associates, no phone calls, no letters, and no e-mails. Demos would be cut entirely from his life — and so would Emily.

His staring was interrupted by Emily as she slid into the seat across from him; he hadn't noticed her approach. When his eyes rose to meet hers, he saw that she was worried.

"How are you doing?" she asked, reaching across the table to put her hands over his. He tried not to think about how soft her hands were, or that he'd never feel them on his skin again. Her question went ignored. He knew she wouldn't want to hear the honest answer. Instead, he only looked down at the bag in front of him.

"Demos said you wanted to talk to me," she said gently, pulling a slip of paper from her pocket. "And he wanted me to give you this."

She passed the folded paper over to him and he accepted it, avoiding the temptation to read it immediately.

"Actually, I need you to give him something, too," Ferris said slowly, pushing the bag over to her. Her brow furrowed as she took it.

"Why, did you two get in a fight or something?"

"No."

Unable to contain her curiosity, she dug into the bag. Ferris wasn't giving her any answers, but she might find some in there. She pulled out the first thing her hand touched – a small photo book. Ferris averted his eyes at the sight of it.

"What's going on?" Emily demanded. "Why are you giving this stuff back? He made this for you."

"I know," Ferris said, his voice still dull. He buried his forehead in his hand, hiding part of his face from her. His mother had decided that no such photos could be kept in his possession, or anything else tying the two together. He couldn't just throw it away. She reached into the bag again, feeling over the wooden case that held his gun. Her hand withdrew quickly.

"What did you want to tell me?" Emily said, though her tone hinted that she already knew the answer.

"I'm leaving," Ferris said, "and I'm not coming back."

Emily was quiet for a while, clenching her hands on top of the table.

"Never?" she asked.

"Never," he repeated.

"Why?"

"It's hard to explain."

"Well, *try*," she said, angrier than he expected her to be.

"We think it would be best," Ferris said, "if I weren't involved anymore."

"Involved with what? Our family? Who's 'we,' anyway?"

Ferris took in a short breath. She was making this harder than he'd been prepared for.

"Yeah. Your family. And 'we' is…"

She lowered her head, keeping her eyes on him expectantly.

"Demos and I… and my mother."

"You're ditching us because your *mom* is making you?" she snapped.

Ferris stared at her. He rarely ever saw Emily angry, but he couldn't blame her. He was breaking her heart.

"I'm not… *ditching* you," he said unconvincingly. "Please try to understand."

"We waited so long to be together, and went through so much, and… and I love you so much. You're leaving forever? Just like that? It's that easy for you?" she said, starting to ramble in her frustration.

"It's not easy for me," he insisted. "It's the hardest thing I've ever had to do. I have to, Emily. I can't put my mom through that again."

"Fine," she said, blinking back tears. "Fine. Leave forever."

Ferris opened his mouth but didn't have a chance to speak before she got out of her seat. She grabbed the bag, turning to leave. He stared at her back as she left the diner, letting the glass door glide shut behind her. When she passed the window, out of view, Ferris took in a sharp breath. He wiped the back of his hand over his eyes, burying his face in his palms.

"Damn it," he mumbled. "God damn it."

A few minutes later, he paid for the coffee he never drank and left the restaurant.

Ferris went for a walk, going wherever his feet would take him. He found himself walking towards the restaurant, or what remained of it. When he turned the corner to look up at where the building normally was, all that greeted him was yellow caution tape and rubble.

No one was around. Hesitantly, he approached the burnt foundation. Black ash stained the sidewalk and concrete and the air still smelled burnt. Ducking, he slipped underneath a line of tape to walk through the remains. His hand trailed along what used to be a wall. Only small patches of wallpaper remained, though its color had been seared away. A glance to his left revealed the pieces of what used to be the black grand piano. A

415

few ivory keys littered the floor, half buried in soot. He pictured Demos playing, easily remembering the sound in his head. It was then that he remembered the paper Emily had given him.

He felt through his pocket, pulling the slip out and unfolding it curiously.

> *It's going to happen tonight. They didn't want to wait until you were out of town. Stay home.*
> *P.S. Sit on the left side.*

Ferris closed the paper, feeling an ache of disappointment. He had hoped the last message Demos wrote him would have been more affectionate. Instead, his friend's familiar, elegant handwriting was cold and brief. He could only guess that 'it' was the start of a gang war, and 'they' were Gino & Co. It wouldn't be difficult to stay home that night; he had nowhere to go. The last part was puzzling. Ferris wasn't sure what Demos meant by 'the left side,' running over various possibilities in his head. Nothing made sense and he slid the paper back into his pocket. He would figure it out later.

Ferris gave the restaurant's ashes one last look, then turned to walk home.

That night, he found himself in his father's office. Nothing had been touched since Harold last used it. A date book had been left open on top of the desk, filled with appointments that would never be kept. A pen lay on top, slightly askew. Ferris was seated in the leather swivel chair, head down on his arms. His glasses lay folded to the side, removed so he could bury his eyes. This wasn't how things were supposed to end.

His fingers curled over the glass that covered the wooden desk. He stared at the pen cup in the corner, wishing that this was just another one of his bad dreams, that a phone call would wake him up and the voice on the line would tell him he was late for his birthday party. He closed his eyes, weary with regret. It wasn't until he heard sirens that he opened them again. A glance out the window revealed flashing lights as a fire truck roared by. It was followed by three police cars.

When Ferris stepped into the living room, he saw that the television was on. Ruth was glued to the set, wringing a dish towel unconsciously. She was watching the news.

"The explosions have been reported in more than one location, suggesting that tonight's fires are no accident," came the voice of an anchorman from Channel Five. "It appears that the city's fire department and emergency crews will not be enough to address every location. We will now take you to our on-scene correspondent."

416

The screen changed to reveal a woman with a microphone, standing amidst a sea of police cars. Meters away, glowing embers drifted down like snow.

"Though at first these events may seem like a terrorist attack, many have reasons to believe that this is the start of a mob war involving the Giorgetti family. Most of the targeted warehouses have been found to belong to Angelo Mariani, who has gone missing," she said, offering the microphone to the man standing next to her. "Tell us, Detective Lee, do these rumors have any bearing?"

The detective adjusted the jacket over his shoulders, barely giving the reporter any mind as he snapped orders to passing policemen.

"Tabloid fodder," he said, though his face was nowhere near the microphone. "We're very busy, thank you."

With that, the detective cleared his throat and stepped out of the frame. Ruth looked over her shoulder, but Ferris had already left the room.

Miles away, at the Woodrow Wilson airport, a middle-aged Englishman was reading the *New York Times*. With a nonchalant look over the top of his newspaper, he saw a crowd of people gathering around one of the large television sets mounted on a column. Their chatter was overpowered by a loud, tense voice from the overhead speakers.

"Ladies and gentlemen, we would like to confirm that your flight to Rome is still scheduled for take-off. The reported fires are not close enough to cause any delays on our runways. Thank you."

There was more chatter, though relieved.

"Hm," Killian smirked, then lowered his eyes to finish the article he'd been reading.

Back in the heart of the city, Ferris had found his way to the roof of the house. Far away, on the north side of Southport, he could see an orange glow. The sky, though dark, was black with smoke. He stepped up to the ledge, craning his head to see over the distant, taller buildings. His eyes widened, catching sight of the far-off, raging flames. They reflected in the lenses of his glasses and the sound of sirens still filled the night air.

As Killian waited in line for economy boarding, he gave the television one last glimpse. The man in the suit looked rigid and his voice did nothing to hide it.

"—Are simply too much for the force to handle. Tonight we can only watch," the man said hesitantly, "as Southport burns."

61

When the fires finally died down, newspapers nationwide pumped out dramatic stories, photos, and casualty numbers. Ferris was leaning over the kitchen table, eyes half-lidded as he read the newest issue of the *Southport Daily*. The damage done totaled a value of 2.8 billion dollars. Eight warehouses, nine homes, a mile of docks, one casino, and a strip club had all been reduced to black rubble. Among those who lost their lives were infamous criminal leader Angelo Mariani, his consigliere Enrico Carducci, and numerous men of all ranks. Though most of the men died in flame, Angelo's body was found in six pieces in his wife's car. As Ferris read, one name in particular stood out to him as his eyes stopped on the text.

Tito Russo.

Tito, the one who'd threatened to attack Sergio – the reason Emily was dating Chris and the source of years of frustration. He was gone.

So, she was free. The thought of Emily made his stomach wrench and he looked away to take a sip of coffee. He tried not to think of what she would do now. Ferris skimmed the rest of the article, surprised to see several Irish names as well. So they'd gotten to Peggy. Bound, burned alive, and shot in the mouth – sounded like Demos' work.

Ferris couldn't find it in himself to feel any pleasure in her suffering. Rather than fill him with joy or remorse, the words on the paper left nothing but numbness in his chest.

Tilting back his head, he finished his coffee and folded the newspaper. He had to finish packing.

His bedroom was quiet as he put the last shirt into his luggage. His other possessions would be shipped to New Haven later. Outside the window, it was starting to rain. He zipped the suitcase shut, about to pick it up, when the doorbell rang. He looked towards the door, palm freezing on the suitcase handle. Who could that be?

A peek down the hall revealed his mother still putting on makeup. He went down the stairs, squinting as he looked through the door's peephole. His lips drew up into a faint smile and he unlocked the door.

"Oi, you were gonna leave without saying goodbye?" Seamus snapped, mussing droplets from his damp hair as he walked inside.

"I left you a message," Ferris said, too pleased to see his friend to mention the wet shoes on the clean floor.

"Some friend you are. I'm lucky I caught you."

"Yeah, we're leaving in a few minutes."

"Ah, let me help you load the car."

"It's fine, it's not—" Ferris protested as Seamus stomped up the stairs, "—not that heavy."

Ferris rubbed the back of his neck as he looked at the bits of mud in his friend's wake. He did want to see Seamus but knew that he would be too miserable to be pleasant company. Secretly, he was quite grateful that the Brit stopped by. A moment later, Seamus was downstairs with the suitcase in one hand and a messenger bag slung over his shoulder.

"Thanks," Ferris said under his breath, reaching to take the suitcase. Seamus only pushed past him, refusing to hand anything over.

They ignored the drizzle as they loaded the car, quiet for a minute as they thought about what to say to one another.

"Demos told me. About, you know," Seamus said, uncharacteristically subdued.

"Yeah."

"That doesn't include me, does it?"

"No. You're too boring to be dangerous."

"Brilliant," Seamus said, grinning as he slammed the trunk shut. After a second, his expression fell. "Though… it won't be the same, without the three of us."

"You think I don't know that?" Ferris said, unable to help the bitter tone of his voice.

"Sorry."

"Mh."

"Oh, thought I should tell you," Seamus said. "Dad got me into Cornell."

"Really?" Ferris asked, trying not to sound insultingly surprised.

"Yeah, I'm starting in the fall. Don't know what he expects me to do there."

"Get an education, I'm guessing."

"Eh, who needs one of them?" Seamus grinned, ruffling the top of Ferris' head. Ferris smirked, though his eyes flickered down to the driveway. For a moment neither of them spoke, then Seamus took a step forward. Before Ferris could protest, he was pulled into a strong hug.

"You know I'll miss you," Seamus mumbled into his shoulder.

"Yeah," Ferris said, finally putting his arms around the other. "Me too."

Seamus' hold on him was tight, as if he had no plans to let go. When Ferris stood back, he was surprised to see a strange look on Seamus' face. His eyes were tight and glassy, creasing at the corners.

"You're really never going to see him again?" Seamus said, so softly that it seemed like someone else's voice.

Ferris fought the urge to sigh; he'd been doing a lot of that lately. Instead, he kept his eyes down and gently nodded.

"So that's the end of us?"

"You can still visit me," Ferris murmured. Seamus seemed to be struggling with himself. After a moment, he looked up and smiled.

"You best not be bluffing, because I really will."

"I'm serious," Ferris said, matching the smile. "And I look forward to it."

When the front door opened, they both turned towards the sound. Ruth stepped outside, holding a flower print umbrella. She held Stanley with one arm, approaching them to greet Seamus. He smiled at her politely before Ruth's attention turned to her son.

"Bubele, get in the car. Let's not be late."

Ferris nodded, giving the house one last look, then Seamus.

"Take care, mate," Seamus grinned.

"You, too," Ferris said, getting into the passenger seat and pulling the door shut. Seamus stood in the driveway as the car pulled out, raising his arm to give a wave. Ferris returned the gesture. Seamus waited there until the car had gone down the block, turned, and disappeared from sight. When he was alone, his smile dropped. He rubbed some of the rain from his face, then turned to walk home.

The car parked in front of the large building downtown that served as a bus terminal and train station. Ruth couldn't drive him to New Haven; there was still a lot of paperwork to go over regarding Harold's will. Ferris had briefly spoken to their lawyer. Because he was already eighteen, he had inherited a large sum of money. He didn't recall the exact number, nor did he want to think about it. His father's estate was the last thing on his mind.

Ruth waited with him at the terminal, stopping what she was doing every so often to wipe her eyes. She had never lived alone before. There would be no one to bake for, talk to, or nag. Ferris assured her that she could still nag him over the phone. His mother managed a smile.

The teleprompter flashed in yellow digital letters, letting them know it was time to board the train. He scratched Stanley behind the ears and kissed his mother on the cheek. Fishing in his pocket, he handed her a handkerchief.

"I promise I'll call," he said with a smile.

With some effort, he hefted up his suitcase, waved goodbye, and boarded the train. As he walked down the aisle, he eyed the ticket in his hand. There were no assigned seats. He looked from one row to another, wondering if he could manage to sit alone. Suddenly, he straightened as a thought rushed through his head.

Sit on the left side.

Ferris' eyes narrowed. Did Demos mean the train? What else could he have been referring to? Nothing else seemed to make sense, though he couldn't understand why sitting on the left side would make a difference. Was the right side going to break off and tumble over a bridge?

He stared at an empty seat on the left side of the aisle. Well, it couldn't hurt.

Stretching to reach, he pushed his suitcase onto the rack above the seat. He sat down, settling into a slouch and resting his forehead against the glass. He'd brought a book but didn't feel much like reading. A few minutes later, the train began to tug forward. The inside of the terminal slid by as the rails clacked rhythmically below. The dark tunnel peeled away to reveal the gray, misty day outside as the train pulled out of the station. Along the tracks were parking lots and patches of parched grass. A few trucks rolled past his vision and he looked ahead to see an entirely empty lot – empty but for one car.

A black Lincoln Town Car.

Ferris sat upright. Victor's car? No, thousands of people drove Lincoln Town Cars, most of them cab drivers. But the door was open; someone was standing with an umbrella. Ferris' heart began to pound hopefully. The figure was still and slender in the foggy air. Was it really him?

As the train pulled closer to the car, Ferris' mouth parted. Standing in the rain, with a white shirt and black umbrella, was Demos. He was there, on the left side. Ferris moved closer to the window, flattening one hand on the glass. His fingers curled as he stared at the figure past the droplets. The train whipped past, giving him only a quick glimpse of his friend's face. His head craned to look behind just in time to see Demos raise his hand to wave goodbye. By the time Ferris swallowed, the car had disappeared from sight.

Ferris' body slouched, his hand still on the glass. He couldn't bring himself to turn his head away. The train pulled into full speed, assuring a timely arrival at its next destination. The passengers on the 10:07 to Connecticut were all looking forward, whether it be at the passing scenery or at their newspapers. Only Ferris, who hadn't moved from the window, could do nothing but look back.

62

The Timothy Dwight dining hall had soaring ceilings, spotted with circled chandeliers above rich, wooden walls. It was part of one of the twelve residential colleges at Yale and the one that Ferris had been assigned to. More accurately, the one that he had chosen.

"You should ask to be put in TD," his father had said nearly a year ago. "I had such a great time there."

Ferris did not regret his decision. The students were brilliant and friendly. It was more of a small community than a dormitory. His room had a view of a tree that was now a beautiful shade of yellow and even the food in the dining hall was pretty good. Even so, he was absolutely miserable. He was pushing a cherry tomato around on his plate, staring at it, past it, through the tray and into the table. Around him, his peers were eating and chatting, talking about politics, classes, and beer pong. Next to him were his roommate Hiro, a chemical engineering major, and a few of their mutual friends. They were arguing over which *Star Wars* film was the best while chipping away at their sandwiches.

"Ferris?" came a voice next to him. He blinked once, then looked over.

"Huh?"

"Are you even listening?" his roommate asked, a little impatient.

"Oh, yeah," Ferris said, his voice hollow. "*Empire.*"

"See, I told you," Hiro said with a self-satisfied grin. "It's the subtext."

"Hiro, I really don't–" one of their friends protested.

"If you say *Attack of the Clones* one more time, I will kill you in your sleep," Hiro hissed.

"*Empire* was boring, it was all dialogue."

"Yeah, I guess if all you want is explosions…"

Ferris stood, picking up his tray.

"You done?" Hiro asked.

"Yeah, I have a paper tomorrow that I haven't even started yet," Ferris lied, nodding a goodbye before heading up to their room. It was simply furnished with a futon, a flat screen TV, an *Enter the Dragon* poster, and a framed cross stitch with morning glories and the words 'Fuck Harvard.'

He slumped down at his desk, hitting the spacebar to wake up his computer. He'd gotten a new one for college, another PowerBook. The old one was back at his mother's house, shut away in a closet with all of his old documents and photos. This one had started almost completely fresh, begging for its hard drive to be filled with new memories. It was nearly empty.

He had no reason to be so lackluster. His school was perfect, his roommate was great, and his grades were nearly flawless. Every once in a while he'd overhear someone talking about him in the dining hall.

"Why's he so depressed? He seems nice."

"I think his dad passed away in the summer."

"Oh, that's sad," they'd say. "Poor guy."

Ferris leaned forward on his desk, putting his face in one hand. He considered studying. He did a lot of it, to take his mind off of the things that were haunting him. It certainly didn't hurt his grades, but his classmates were beginning to think he was a bit of a bore. College was a special, life-changing time; he felt as if he was wasting it.

His thoughts were once again giving him a headache. He reached over to the clock radio at the end of his desk, turning it on to fill the room with low classical music. It was a piece by Mozart. The song was soothing and he picked up his head to begin an email to his mother. She'd finally figured out the computer and, once it had been conquered, demanded he email her every five minutes. He was in the middle of writing a reply to assure her he'd been eating enough when the song on the radio changed. His fingers froze over the keys.

As he listened to the slow piano song, his head lowered. His hands rested on top of the keyboard, clenching very slightly.

It was Erik Satie's *Gymnopédie No. 1*.

"Fuck," Ferris mumbled, firmly switching the radio off. He sat in silence for a minute, looking down at the desk and trying not to think. The only thing he could hear was the wind outside; it was rustling the yellow tree. He looked out the window, then at the radio. Slowly, and carefully, he reached to turn it back on. The song was halfway through. Each note from the piano was calm and sweet, forgiving him for his sudden interruption. Ferris let his eyes shut, fighting a smile as he listened all the way to the end.

An hour later, Hiro popped his head into their common room.

"Hey, you coming to Movie Night?"

"Sorry, I still need to finish this paper," Ferris replied, not turning around from his typing.

"You never come out," Hiro complained.

"I will next time."

"Yeah, right. See you."

The door shut and Ferris turned to look, making sure he was alone. He closed his computer, checked the time, and went to bed. It was early, but he didn't want to do anything but dream. Unfortunately, his dreams had been scarce the last few months.

423

Where once lived nightmare after nightmare, there was nothing. There were no fires, no corpses, and no blood. He would fall asleep and wake up with a blank spot in between.

He missed his nightmares.

A harsh knocking woke him up. He sat up slowly, rubbing over his eye while catching a glimpse of the time. It was only 11:30. Maybe Hiro forgot his key.

The door cracked open, letting a stream of hallway light into their common room.

"Ferris," said the girl who was standing there. Her voice was firm. "There's a huge spider in my room."

He squinted at her for a few seconds.

"Congrats," Ferris replied before moving to shut the door.

"I don't think you heard me. It's *huge*."

"How huge?" he asked skeptically. She held up her fingers to show the approximate size of an Oreo cookie.

"You can handle it."

She grabbed his wrist, tugging him down the hallway towards her room.

"Hey, wait, let me put a shirt on," he protested, pulling back with tired effort.

"You're the only guy who isn't at Movie Night and you're killing this spider *now*."

"Amy," he whined.

She dragged him into the room, pushing at his back as if he was a barrier between her and the arthropod.

"Where is it?" he asked with very little interest.

"There." She was pointing over his shoulder to the far corner. Lowering his glasses, he crouched down to take a look under the chair.

"It's just a wolf spider. She has an egg sac."

Amy shuddered audibly. Ferris started looking around for a sheet of paper.

"What are you doing? I have a shoe."

"I'm going to let it outside."

"Fine, sure, whatever. Just get it out of here."

Ferris actually smiled, just a little bit. Her dialogue was reminiscent of the time Demos had been collecting protection payment from a deli owner and had seen an enormous cockroach skittering across the tile floor. In half a second his demeanor had gone from stone-cold mobster to scared little girl. 'Argh, get it away. Get it the hell away from me. Oh, God. It's near my shoe!'

He coaxed the spider onto the sheet, opened the window, and shook it onto the grass.

"Out the window?" she asked. 'What if it comes back in?"

"You'll be fine."

She didn't respond immediately; he could feel her eyes on him.

"So," she started carefully, "do you mind if I ask… what happened to your…?"

When he looked over, she was staring at the large burn scar on his side.

"Oh, that," he said, suddenly embarrassed. He turned away from her. "Kitchen accident — hot water. It was kind of stupid, really."

"Yeesh, that sucks."

"Yeah."

"Well, thanks. Though if some kid sitting on the lawn gets killed by that thing, it's your fault."

"Sure," he said with a shrug. "Night, Amy."

"Night," she said, closing the door after him. He rolled his eyes, then went back to bed. He'd sleep with a T-shirt from then on.

Later that week, Ferris was studying again. Originally, his required language class would have been in Italian. The first week of class, however, he'd unexplainably switched to French. He was about to turn a page in his textbook when a small, decorative pillow hit the side of his head.

"Cut it out, Hiro."

"Only if you come out with us tonight," Hiro said, already holding up another pillow to throw.

"What are we doing?"

"Smoking up at Pete's apartment. He always does the day before *The Game*."

The next day was the annual football game between Harvard and Yale, hosted in Cambridge. To some students, it seemed more important than studying.

"Or are you afraid of doing anything illegal," Hiro teased. Ferris stared at him, deadpanned.

"You have no idea."

"What's that supposed to mean?"

Ferris thought about it. He thought of the last time he'd smoked with Demos and Seamus in Victor's basement. He didn't remember what movie they were watching, but it was both hilarious and frightening at the same time. He'd forgotten where he was and what he was supposed to be doing that day. For just a few hours, he'd forgotten everything.

"I'll go."

"About fucking time."

That night, in a dimly lit New Haven apartment, Ferris stared up at the ceiling to watch the smoke gather. He could still feel it tickling his throat. His body felt heavy and he slouched further down on the sofa.

"Is exorcising... exercising? It probably burns a lot of calories. Evil calories. You'd burn so many," Hiro said, perching on his chair in forced dignity.

"Oh my God," said one of their friends. "Hiro, shut up."

"You're not listening," Hiro complained, eating a handful of Doritos. He paused, then lit up. "Hey, you know... deaf people can have faster conversations."

"What?"

"They can see and talk at the same time!" Hiro exclaimed while sucking orange Dorito powder off of his thumb.

"Wait, whoa. You're right."

"Cause we like, we can't talk and listen at the same time."

For the next hour, they watched an infomercial. Ferris inhaled through his nose. The air smelled earthy and the chatter of his friends was becoming undecipherable. He smiled as he watched the walls and, for the rest of the night, forgot about absolutely everything.

The next day, Yale lost 30 to 13.

63

What was once an expanse of dead grass was now snow and hard ice. Ferris had just left his music class, violin case in one hand and a bag slung over his shoulder. On either side of the path lay inches of snow, peppered with footprints from the students who just couldn't help themselves. Before he'd left the music hall, his professor had once again suggested he switch his major to music. As usual, Ferris had politely declined, then left. There weren't many students outside. The cold weather was excellent at holing everyone up next to cozy fireplaces and brown wainscoting. Fixated on the snow, his mind had just started to wander when a vibration in his pocket stole his attention. Digging with his free hand, he pulled out his cell phone and flipped it open.

"Hello?"

"Hey, which of those residential… dormy things did you say you were in, again?"

"Seamus?" Ferris asked, raising an eyebrow.

"That's me. Answer my question."

"It's a residential *college*."

"Yeah, that's what I said. Which one?"

"TD. Timothy Dwight. Why?"

"TD? Sounds like titty."

"You're hilarious, Seamus."

"All right, then. See you," Seamus said cheerfully, then hung up.

The line died and Ferris made a face at his phone. He and Seamus had been exchanging correspondence since school had started and it was one of the only things keeping Ferris happy. These bizarre random phone calls, however, he could do without.

Dusting bits of snow off of his jacket, Ferris entered the building and made his way up to his room. He slipped inside, unwinding his scarf and setting his violin case down on a chair. A sound from the left caught his attention. Next to the window was a black futon, on top of which sat Hiro, on top of whom was a brunette who visited quite often. Hiro's hands had ventured into the far reaches of her shirt and she was very intensely fixated on his lips. Ferris cringed, then backed out of the room.

"Great," he mumbled, shutting the door silently behind him. Ferris was irritated. Hiro had his own bedroom, but he just *had* to extend the territory of his escapades into their common area. In addition, it was an unwelcome reminder of just how single he was, and probably would remain, for quite some time. He pushed up his glasses to pinch the bridge of his nose, holding in a groan.

Once outside, his cell phone vibrated again.

"What now, Seamus?" Ferris snapped, kicking a small pile of snow so that it scattered across the sidewalk.

"You shouldn't make a mess in the snow," came Seamus' snide reply. Ferris could hear the grin in his voice. Instantly, he looked over his shoulder, then left and right. His eyes caught the source of the voice and, just for a moment, he froze.

About ten yards down the side of the building stood Seamus, one hand stuffed into the pocket of his brown coat, the other holding a cell phone. He wore a smile that could kill.

"Seamus!"

Like a child, Seamus ran over, immediately pulling Ferris into a hug that twirled 360 degrees. Ferris didn't protest, at least not until he could feel his feet leaving the ground.

"Organs," Ferris choked. "Seamus, organs."

"Sorry," the Brit replied, breathless as he released his friend. He stood back, as if admiring his work. "Look how much you've grown!"

"I'm the same height," Ferris breathed, still bent up over the bear hug. Even though his insides were hurting, it was good to see Seamus – really good. Though they'd kept in contact, they hadn't physically seen one another since the day Ferris had left Southport.

"You lost weight…" Seamus said, knitting his brow with concern as his voice trailed off. "You look like a cholera victim."

"Don't you have class today?" Ferris mumbled, changing the subject without much grace.

"No," Seamus said as innocently as he could. "Just took the train over. Thought I'd surprise you."

"Well, it worked. I think you took five years off of my life."

"Want to grab a coffee?" Seamus asked, gesturing in a random direction with his thumb. Ferris looked at him, then up where his room was on the second floor.

"Yeah, let's get out of here. There's a vegetarian restaurant called Claire's—"

"Vegetarian," Seamus whined dramatically as they began to walk. "Really?"

"It's kosher. Deal with it."

Seamus dealt with it, albeit with much effort and noise.

The restaurant was small and warm. White winter light streamed in through the windows and there was an ambiance of chatter, silverware, and locals typing on their laptops. Seamus was dumping another packet of sugar into his coffee while Ferris took a sip of his own.

"I can't believe you randomly got on a train to New Haven."

"Wasn't random. I've been planning it for a week," Seamus said as his spoon clinked around in the ceramic cup.

"What would you have done if I had a class right now?"

"Convince you to skip," Seamus said, clearly quite sure of himself.

"Of course. Well..."

"Well what?"

"I'm glad you're here," Ferris said, his voice quieter than normal.

"Me *too*," Seamus said in his sweetest voice, teasingly reaching across the table to hold Ferris' hands. Ferris rolled his eyes.

"Did you choose a major, yet?" Ferris asked, swatting Seamus off.

"Well, not... exactly."

Ferris' eyes dropped, half-lidded as they stared across the table. They were both silent.

"You dropped out."

"No! I couldn't drop out, Dad would kill me."

"You were expelled."

"Well," Seamus said, rubbing the back of his neck. The rest of his response was barely a mumble. "Guess you could say that..."

"What did you do, Seamus?

"Came to class pissed."

Ferris waited.

"Few times."

Ferris continued to wait.

"Daily, all right? Are you happy?"

"Of course I'm not happy, you're back to being a drunken failure again."

"I never *stopped* being a drunken failure," he replied matter-of-factly.

"Does your Dad know?"

"Not yet," Seamus said, twirling his finger around. "I've been back in Southport for a bit. Mum doesn't talk to him, so it's not like she would tattle."

"Oh."

Ferris was thinking. Just the offhanded mention of Southport made him ache with nostalgia. Seamus must have been seeing Demos again, living their old life, hanging around their old places.

"So..." Ferris started. "How is everyone doing?"

"Everyone?"

"Everyone," Ferris confirmed.

"Do you want me to tell you what Demos told me to tell you, or do you want me to tell you the truth?"

Something inside of Ferris lit up, excited that he might actually hear news about Demos and Emily. He'd been putting them in the back of his head for half a year, but it was only a weak effort to mask the pain their memories brought.

"Both."

"Well," Seamus said, poking at his Lithuanian coffee cake with a fork. "He wanted me to say that they gave him more territory, he's dating a new guy, and that he's basically doing well."

"Well, is he?"

"He's a wreck, Ferris."

Ferris' expression dropped.

"What do you mean?" he asked.

"He's no fun, now. Never wants to come out, and when he does, he just stares into space for three hours. All he cares about is work and church. Yeah, you heard me. He goes to church now. Oh, and…" Seamus said, leaning in to whisper. "His new boyfriend wears glasses."

"What?" Ferris squinted. "So?"

"Never mind."

"Why is he going to church?"

"Don't know," Seamus muttered. "I told him God doesn't listen to queers, but he doesn't care."

"Oh…"

They both filled the strange pause with a drink of their coffee.

"Well, what about Emily?" Ferris asked, stirring his coffee to give his hands something to do.

"She got accepted to Southport Arts."

"Really? That's great," Ferris said, smiling despite himself.

"But she's not going."

"What?" Ferris asked, sitting up straight. "Why not?"

"She's just going to get a degree in law or something."

Ferris didn't answer, only looking down into his drink. The last time he'd spoken to her, they'd parted on bad terms. He wondered if she ever thought of him and if she still hated him for leaving.

"Is she dating anyone?"

"Yeah. Some Chinese guy."

"Oh."

Ferris' hands fiddled with each other as he tried to ignore the way his chest was hurting. He had no right to be upset. It was his fault – he was the one who left.

"There's nothing in your nails, you know."

"What?"

"Stop picking at them."

Ferris' hands went flat on the table. He felt ill.

"Sorry, mate," Seamus said, genuinely sympathetic for once.

430

"It's fine. *I* made this decision," Ferris said, though it didn't come out as firmly as he wanted it to. He shut his eyes for a second.

"I miss them," Ferris finally admitted. Seamus didn't answer, simply listening.

"It sounds like they've moved on," Ferris added, not looking up. "*I* should do that."

"They miss you, too," Seamus said. Ferris glanced at him. He wasn't sure if it was true, or if Seamus was only trying to make him feel better. He was at least pretty sure that Emily didn't miss him.

"Yeah…"

"Chin up, Ferret. You've still got me and your mum."

"The only two people who really understand me," Ferris said snidely.

"Take what you can get," he replied, putting a piece of cake into his mouth before offering Ferris some of it.

"No, thanks," Ferris said, declining the forkful of pastry.

"Have you been eating at all? Honestly, you look terrible."

"You sound like my mother."

From that point on, Seamus switched the conversation away from their old friends, not wanting the mood to grow any more somber.

"Why don't you try dating again?"

"I don't really feel like it," Ferris replied, now distracted by something outside the window.

"You're an idiot. I saw some nice arse on the way to your dorm."

"Running away from you, I'm guessing," Ferris said, changing the subject yet again. "How long do you have tonight? Maybe we could catch a movie."

"Oh, about that… you're allowed to have guests overnight, right? I was just going to leave in the morning."

Ferris glared at him.

"If you don't mind sleeping on the floor," he said, his voice hard.

"The floor? I thought we could spoon."

"You know, I actually don't think I *can* have guests."

"Okay, okay. The floor is fine," Seamus insisted, waving his hands apologetically.

Once outside, Seamus lit a cigarette. The smell was both terrible and wonderful to Ferris and he knew that by morning, his bedroom and clothes would probably smell the same way. Though he was being his usual annoyed self, he was quite grateful to see a familiar face and to finally feel at ease with someone.

"So, which film do you want to see?"

"Doesn't matter," Ferris shrugged. "Oh, and Seamus…"

"Yeah?" the Brit asked, flicking some ash onto the street.

Ferris smiled, keeping his hands in his pockets.

"You can stay as long as you want."

64

It was spring and the weather outside was appropriately gray and rainy. Drops trailed down the windows of the Metro North train as it traveled south to New York. Ferris was listening to music with a pair of large headphones, watching the trees go by with little interest. He made this trip several times every year, traveling from New Haven to Southport in a little over an hour. It had been over three years since Ferris had first come to Yale and he'd taken the train eighteen times.

Each time he had visited his mother, he'd spent most of his days pent up inside of the house. He couldn't risk going to any of his old places: the Sparrow, St. Basil's, Foley Park, or Ristorante Giorgetti. The restaurant had finished being rebuilt two years ago. It was as busy as ever, or so he'd heard. It supposedly had a brand new design with shining glass and aged wood, festooned with deep, red fabric, antique frames, and white candles. The candles, as assumed, were very carefully watched. He'd also heard there was a new grand piano. Ferris longed to see it for himself but knew he would never be able to dine within its walls. The train pulled into the station, slow and heavy. Ferris grabbed his suitcase.

On the platform, Ruth pulled him into a hug. Every year these hugs only grew in strength and severity. She still had not become accustomed to losing her son; each time he went back to school, she wept fresh, new tears.

On the car ride home, Ferris was about to fall asleep against the window when his mother's voice tugged him back into consciousness.

"So, what do you think?"

"Think?" he repeated, his voice groggy.

"About Long Island."

"Long Island?"

"Have you been listening to a word I've said this entire ride?" she said, her voice becoming shrill.

"What about Long Island?" he asked, ignoring her accusation.

"I'm thinking of moving there, where your aunt Esther lives."

"Why?"

"Well, it's such a shame that you can't go out much when you visit me. There isn't anything for us here now. And that way I could be closer to you when you move to New York City."

"Oh... I guess."

"You guess? That's all you have to say? You should write an advice column!" she said. "You *guess*."

"I don't know, Mom. I grew up in this house."

"I know, Sweetheart," she replied, putting her hand on his shoulder. Her eyes left the road momentarily to glance at him. "I grew up here, too. But I think it's time to move on, don't you?"

"…I guess."

Ruth heaved a sigh, then put her attention back to her driving.

Once they were home, Ferris did the same thing he always did when he first walked in the front door: fight off the advances of a fat, excited pug. Stanley was hopping around his heels, furiously wagging his tail, which in turned wagged his entire back half. Paws scraped at Ferris' shins and the sound of dog nails clicked on the wood floor.

"Hey, pal," Ferris said, kneeling low enough that the dog could lick his face.

"Come in the kitchen and wash up," Ruth called. "I've got dinner in the Crock Pot."

That night, Ruth came into the living room with two cups of hot tea, only to find that her son had fallen asleep on the sofa. There was an open book splayed across his lap, as well as a snoring dog. She took the book, marking the spot and setting it aside. Her hands reached forward to slide off his glasses; they were set on top of the book and a flannel throw was draped over his chest.

"Goodnight, bubele."

The light clicked off and the house was quiet. Four hours later, Ferris was gone.

At night, when everyone was asleep, was the only time he could wander. He walked past the school and the park, heading east at a slow gait. The spring air was warm and the city lights were more than enough to illuminate his way. Cars would drive past and he would walk by the occasional pedestrian at a crosswalk, but otherwise, he was alone. When his watch read two a.m., he started to wonder if his friends were asleep or just starting their nights out. He stopped and looked up at a street sign, starting to feel a knot in his stomach. His feet had taken him to Little Italy. Unable to help himself, he walked deeper into the neighborhood.

Victor Giorgetti's house looked just as it always had — tall and elegant with a stone exterior and finely manicured rose bushes. Victor's Lincoln Town Car was parked out front. The lights were off. Ferris felt relieved; everyone must have been asleep. If one of them came outside and saw him standing there, he had no idea what he would do.

For a while, he simply looked. He remembered the time he'd stopped by after school and Demos was sitting on the curb, heartbroken from his break-up. Victor would often be outside drying his car down with a shammy, tenderly wiping off smudges while a Canary Island cigar hung from the corner of his mouth. Ferris shut his eyes, angry with himself. It was over. He had to stop this. He had to tell his mother that yes, she should move to Long Island — then he'd never have to walk past this house again.

His attention was caught by a porch light snapping on. The side door opened and Ferris quickly turned to walk away. Someone stepped outside, lighting a cigarette. By the time the figure looked up, the street was empty.

The next morning, they visited the cemetery. Ruth tightened her coat against the wind as they got out of the car. Her collar was lined with vintage fur that fluttered against her cheek. They walked up the hill together, passing rows of gravestones. The grass was neat and freshly budding trees towered over their path, creaking against the gale. Ferris' fingers ran over the flat stone in his pocket; he could still feel a thin layer of dust across the surface. When they found the white monument that read 'Levinstein,' they stopped and stood quietly for a minute. Ferris knelt near the marker in the ground that bore his father's name.

Harold Levinstein
Beloved Husband, Devoted Father

"Mom," Ferris said. "Could I have a minute with Dad?"

"Sure," she said, letting a sniffle betray her. She left a stone on the grave, paused for a moment, then turned to disappear behind some trees.

Ferris waited for a while, listening to the wind in the grass. He pulled the cool, smooth stone from his coat pocket, turning it over in his hand before setting it down on top of the gravestone. It lay flat with a soft click.

"Hi, Dad," he said, straightening himself to a standing position once more. "I'm sorry it's been so long. You know... school."

He removed his glasses to rub the inner corners of his eyes. His hand withdrew, but he didn't replace the frames on his face.

"I'm sure you know how it is, since you went there, too. I've been meaning to talk to you, though."

Ferris had gone through this line of thought before, but it was still difficult to put into words.

"I'm doing well. Getting A's. I'm graduating next year. I think... I know you'd be proud. I wish you could be there to see it. My graduation, I mean. I guess... in a way, that's all I ever wanted. I don't really know what I want anymore. I used to know exactly what I'd do for the rest of my life. I always thought

I'd stand by him until we grew old and died. I wanted to take care of him… repay him for everything he ever did for me. I have new friends, but… we're not close. I don't want to be close. I don't want to fill that hole in my life with something else. I… I guess it'll always just be there.

"I've tried, Dad. I tried to forget everything I had, to take advantage of all of the opportunities I have now. The chance for a new life, a safe one? I can't do it. It's been three years and nothing has changed. Everything I do feels so empty, so pointless. Why am I getting this degree? Am I just going to work in an office for the rest of my life? That's it, that's my life?

"I used to wake up for a reason. I don't know why anymore. I can't forget him — I can't forget *them*. I walked past his house last night. It would have been so easy to just go up… and knock on the door. I don't care what happens to me. I just don't want Mom to cry again. I don't know what I'm doing, anymore. Dad, I… I wish you were here. I wish you could tell me what to do.

"Dad," Ferris said, his voice growing weaker. He rubbed a hand over his eyes. "Tell me what to do."

The wind was his only reply and Ferris slowly put his glasses back on. When he turned to walk back towards the car, he was startled by the sight of his mother standing next to a tree. It was obvious she'd been listening – her expression was hurt and disappointed. Softly, she spoke to him.

"Let's go."

Feeling a wash of guilt, Ferris followed obediently. The car doors closed, shutting out the cool, spring air. They began to drive.

It was a painfully silent trip. Ferris lifted both hands to run down his face. He felt a headache coming on. His fingers stopped over his nose and he inhaled; they smelled like rocks and grass. For once, he wished his mother would say something. After a moment, his hands dropped to his lap. She wasn't talking.

"I'm sorry," he finally said, lying his head back against the seat and looking up at the car's ceiling. Ruth didn't answer. Too weary to be frustrated, he closed his eyes in the hopes that his headache wouldn't blossom into a migraine.

Quite some time had passed before he noticed that their drive was taking too long. Ruth probably had some errands to run. When the car stopped, he leaned forward and rubbed his wrist over his eyes. He looked out the window, expecting to see a kosher deli or perhaps the dry cleaners. This establishment didn't appear to be either. He tried to remember the building, scrutinizing the dark, wooden façade. His eyes trailed up to see letters painted on the glass above the door and a long, red awning that stretched to the curb. His breath was only halfway down his throat when it stopped. A sudden prickling washed over his arms and hands.

'Ristorante Giorgetti,' read the golden letters on the building, new and fresh and lined with burgundy. When he finally tore his eyes away, his attention snapped over towards his mother. She was simply gazing at the steering wheel; she looked tired and old. When she looked up to see her son's expression, she found that it was silent and pleading — pleading for this to be real, for it to be okay. His eyes creased at the corners and he watched her, silent but for the pounding in his chest. Her face told him everything.

"Go ahead," she said, trying to keep her eyes from watering. Ferris' mouth trickled into a smile.

"Thanks, Mom," he said, leaning forward to kiss her cheek. The door shut with a hasty slam and he was gone.

The new restaurant was beautiful. Small chandeliers hung in a row down the ceiling, bathing the dining area in a warm, dim light. Red curtains rested along the sides of the windows, tied back with silk rope. Ferris tried to think over his bothersome heartbeat; it was echoing in the back of his head. His eyes darted towards the piano, then the bar. He scanned the customers, swallowing his anxiety. They didn't look familiar. Impatient, he touched the back of the hostess' shoulder.

"Excuse me, is–"

When she turned around, his hand drew back. The hostess, she was—

"Emily?" he stammered. Her hair was longer and she looked older — well, three years older. There was something narrower about her face, and from behind, he'd thought she was a grown woman. In a way, he supposed she was. Her eyes were wide, yet tight. She was holding a leather folio to her chest, lips silently parted.

Ferris couldn't find anything to say to her. He'd had years to think about it, but had wasted them lamenting. He could see her finally glance out the window to see Ruth sitting in her parked car. Something clicked, a realization, but she couldn't seem to put together a single thing to say.

Finally, after ages of staring, Emily spoke.

"Excuse me," was all she said, then turned to leave. Hastily, she weaved past the tables to the back room. The knot in his stomach tightened. She couldn't stand to look at him.

The back doors swung in and a man in a suit stepped out.

"Fish?" Victor asked incredulously, lifting his glasses as if they were fogged. "Jesus Christ, it really is you."

There was only one thing Ferris wanted to ask, but he couldn't bring himself to blurt it out.

"So your old lady got over it," Victor continued, eyeing her car past the window.

Ferris' mouth opened, but he swallowed his words.

"You got taller," the Italian added. Ferris managed a slight nod and Victor smirked.

"You want to know where Demos is?"

Ferris immediately nodded.

"Fifty bucks," Victor said as he reached out an open hand. Not missing a beat, Ferris smiled.

"Get out of here," Ferris said, ignoring the hand. Victor's grin spread into a short laugh and he slapped a hand on Ferris' shoulder.

"Just giving you shit. He's at church, St. Anthony of Padua. It's four blocks west."

"Thanks," Ferris said, already turning to leave.

"Hey, Fish."

"Yeah?" he replied, stopping in mid-step.

"Good to see you around," Victor said. Ferris smiled, then pushed the door open.

The moment he was outside, he began to run.

From the car, Ruth called to him, asking if he needed a ride somewhere. Ferris didn't stop running, shouting that it was okay before turning the corner and out of her sight. The soles of his shoes slapped against the sidewalk and the wind threatened to take anything on him that wasn't tied down. He panted against the chilly air, breathing, rushing. The lines of the sidewalk blurred under his feet. At the crosswalk, he briefly glanced to the side before running across traffic. A car honked as it gunned past him. Ferris kept running; these were the longest four blocks of his life. He couldn't breathe. The thought of seeing his friend's face, hearing his voice – just a glimpse of him, was something he could barely fathom. He kept running.

The church was one block away. He could see the gray, stone steps leading to the entrance and he pushed past a few people who were milling about on the sidewalk. At the top of the stairs, he leaned hard on the iron handle, using his weight to heave the heavy door open. It creaked and the noise echoed across the massive, arching ceilings.

It was quiet. From somewhere in the church, footsteps echoed across a stone wall. Outside, past the stained glass and wood, the wind howled in vengeance. Rows of candles flickered below paintings and tapestries of Jesus, Mary, and various saints. Throughout the rows of seats, several heads were scattered, each of them low in prayer. Slowly, he walked down the center aisle. His eyes combed for that particular haircut, one fine and absolutely black. Then, twelve rows in, he saw him.

Sitting in a long, wooden pew to the right was a well-dressed young man. He was kneeling, arms resting on the wooden rail and fingers intertwined. His head was cast down in silence, forehead touching his knuckles. Ferris stopped walking.

For a while, he watched him. He was afraid to move — afraid to speak. The slightest sound might wake him from this dream, one that seemed so real and close. Demos hadn't changed very much. His stature had remained slight, his eyes heavy with the weight of his world. Slender hands sat motionless, clasped and white. Ferris imagined that if he reached out, the image he was seeing might ripple away. Instead, he knelt next to the pew, drawing his voice close behind Demos' ear.

"What are you praying for?" Ferris asked. His voice was hushed against the vast space of the cathedral.

The Italian's eyes snapped open. He didn't turn around immediately, only staring straight ahead. His hands parted and went rigid. Slowly, he turned to look over his shoulder. His mouth opened and Ferris could hear him inhale.

Demos was still, pupils quivering and chest rigid. The lids of his eyes were strained, struggling to keep dry. They widened in acceptance and, suddenly, Demos was moving. He nearly knocked the padding from the kneeler as he stumbled to his feet, clutching his friend over his shoulders. They held each other, arms rumpling the fabric that covered their backs. Ferris could feel Demos' fingers tightening on his sweater as he buried his face against it. He was real and warm; Ferris could feel him shaking and he knew he was awake.

"Hi, Ghost," he said, whispering his words against dark strands of hair. Demos smiled, eyes closed and voice muffled.

"Hey, Fishbones."